Disney DESCENDANTS

Dizzy's NEW FORTUNE

BASED ON CHARACTERS CREATED BY JOSANN MCGIBBON AND SARA PARRIOTT

WRITTEN BY: JASON MUELL

ART BY: NATSUKI MINAMI

TOKYOPOP®

TABLE OF CONTENTS

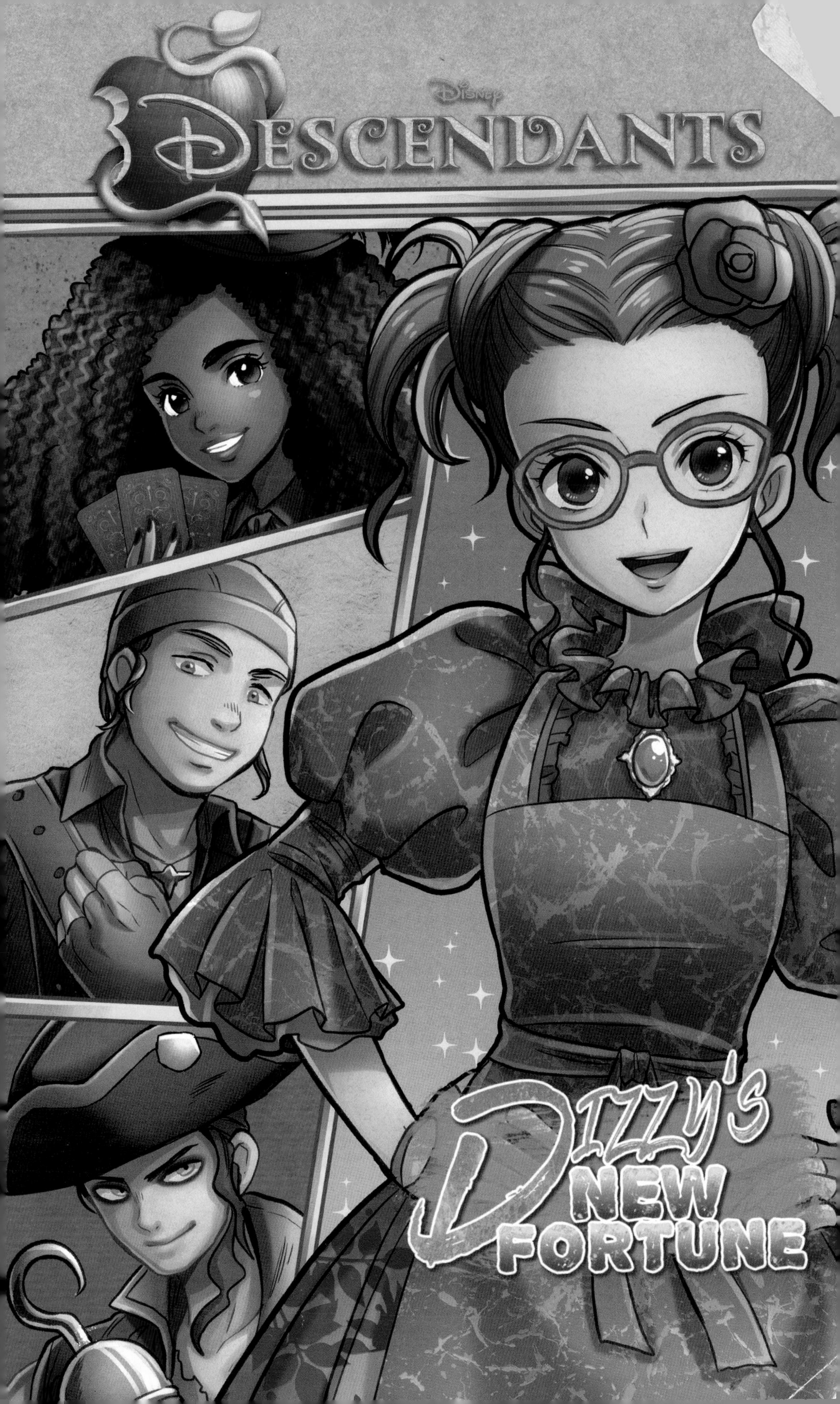
Disney
DESCENDANTS
Dizzy's
NEW
FORTUNE

CHAPTER 1

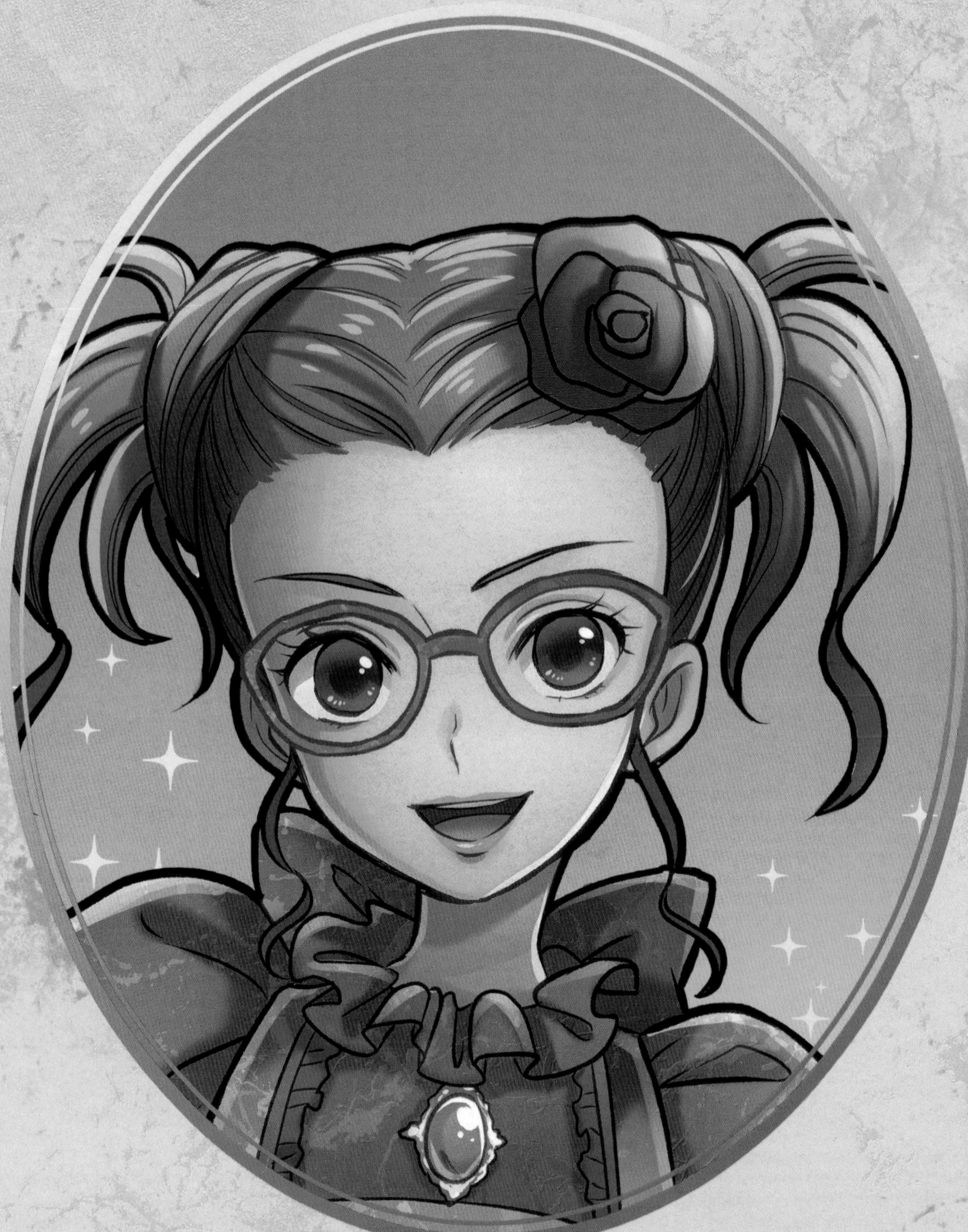

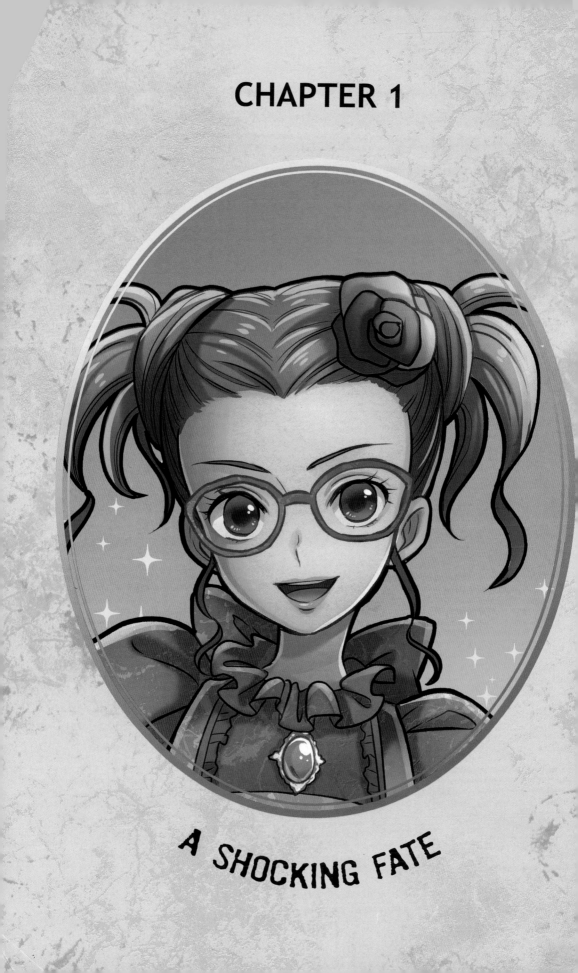

A SHOCKING FATE

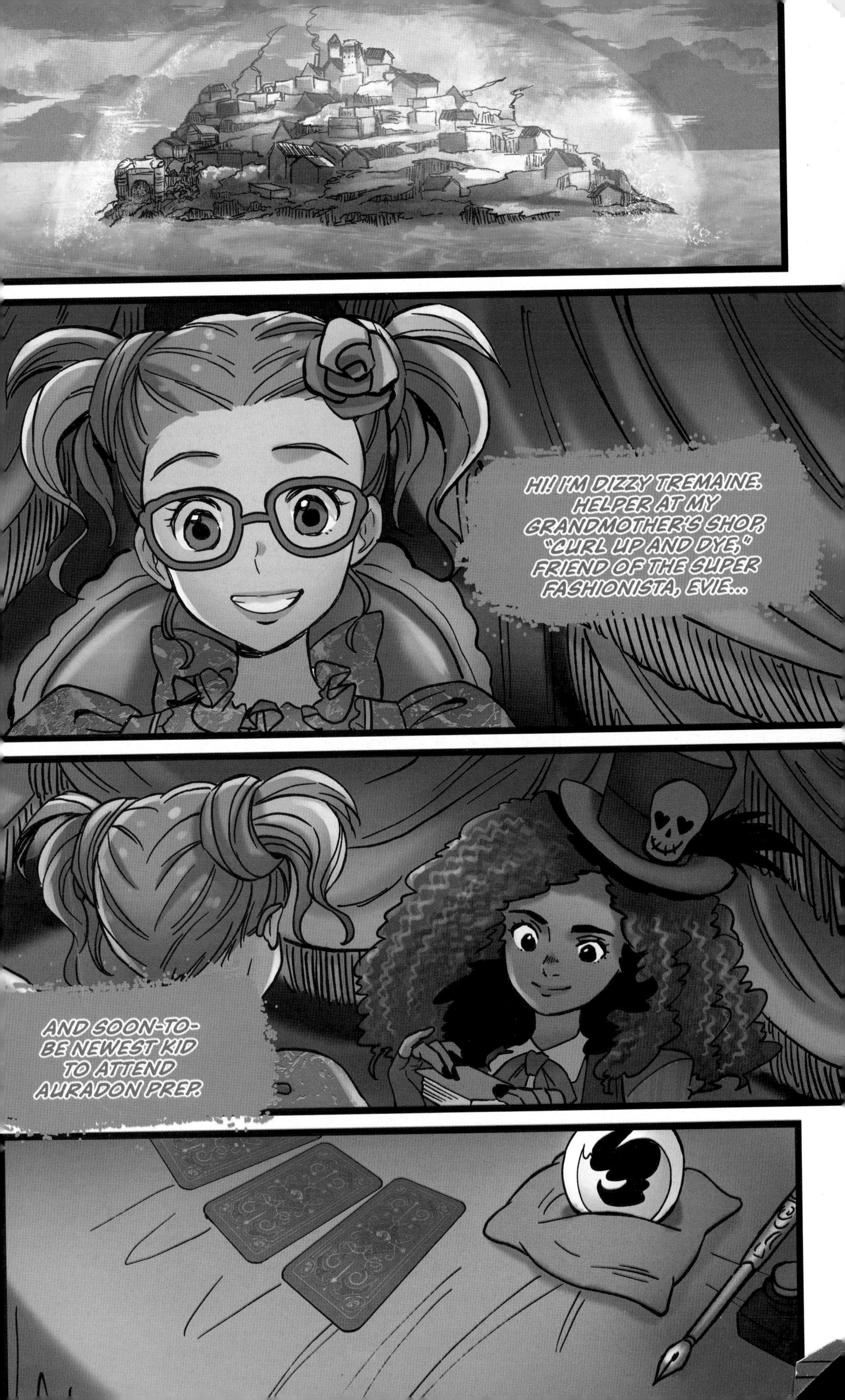
HI! I'M DIZZY TREMAINE. HELPER AT MY GRANDMOTHER'S SHOP, "CURL UP AND DYE," FRIEND OF THE SUPER FASHIONISTA, EVIE...
AND SOON-TO-BE NEWEST KID TO ATTEND AURADON PREP.

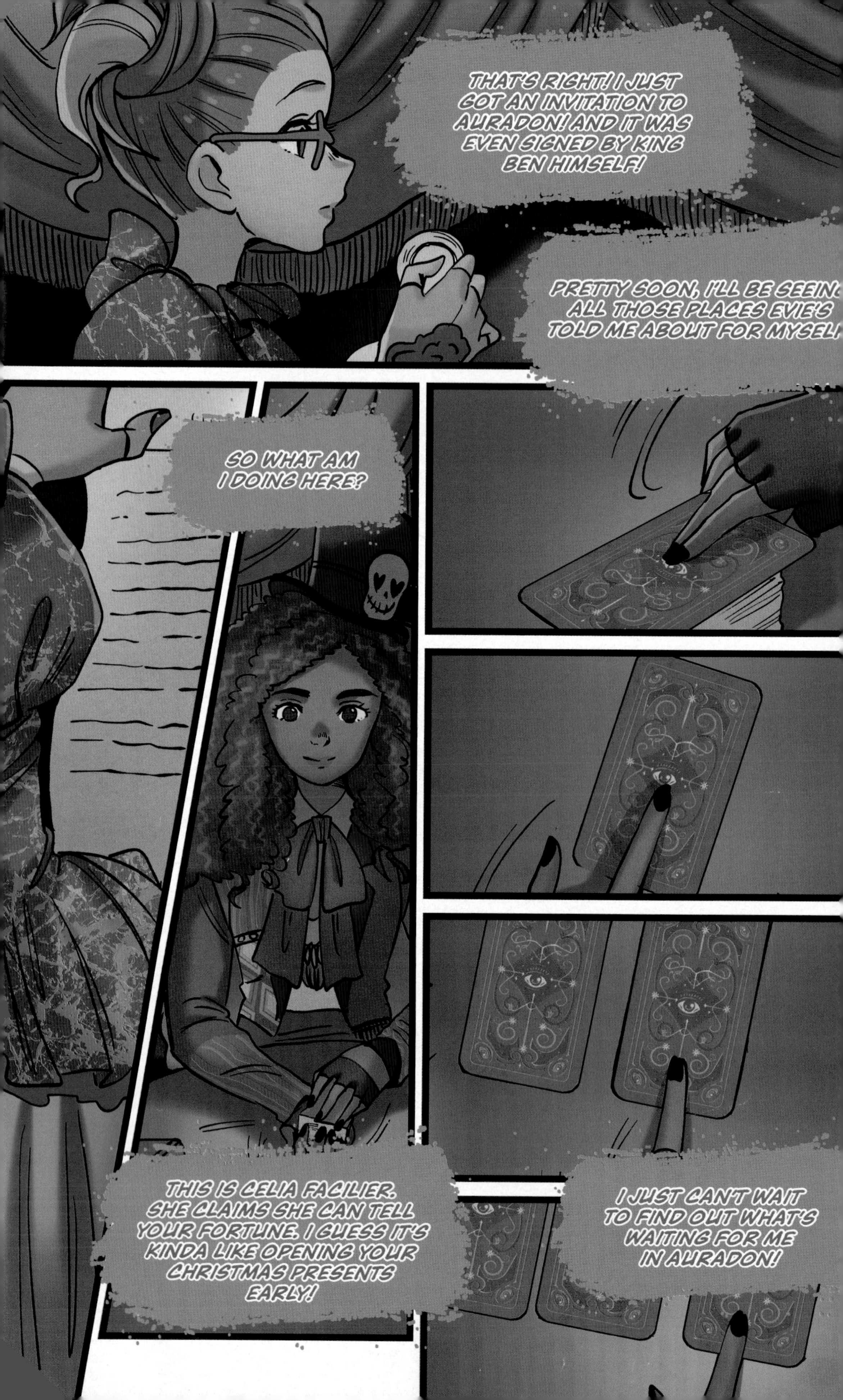
THAT'S RIGHT! I JUST GOT AN INVITATION TO AURADON! AND IT WAS EVEN SIGNED BY KING BEN HIMSELF!
PRETTY SOON, I'LL BE SEEIN ALL THOSE PLACES EVIE'S TOLD ME ABOUT FOR MYSEL
SO WHAT AM I DOING HERE?
THIS IS CELIA FACILIER. SHE CLAIMS SHE CAN TELL YOUR FORTUNE. I GUESS IT'S KINDA LIKE OPENING YOUR CHRISTMAS PRESENTS EARLY!
I JUST CAN'T WAIT TO FIND OUT WHAT'S WAITING FOR ME IN AURADON!

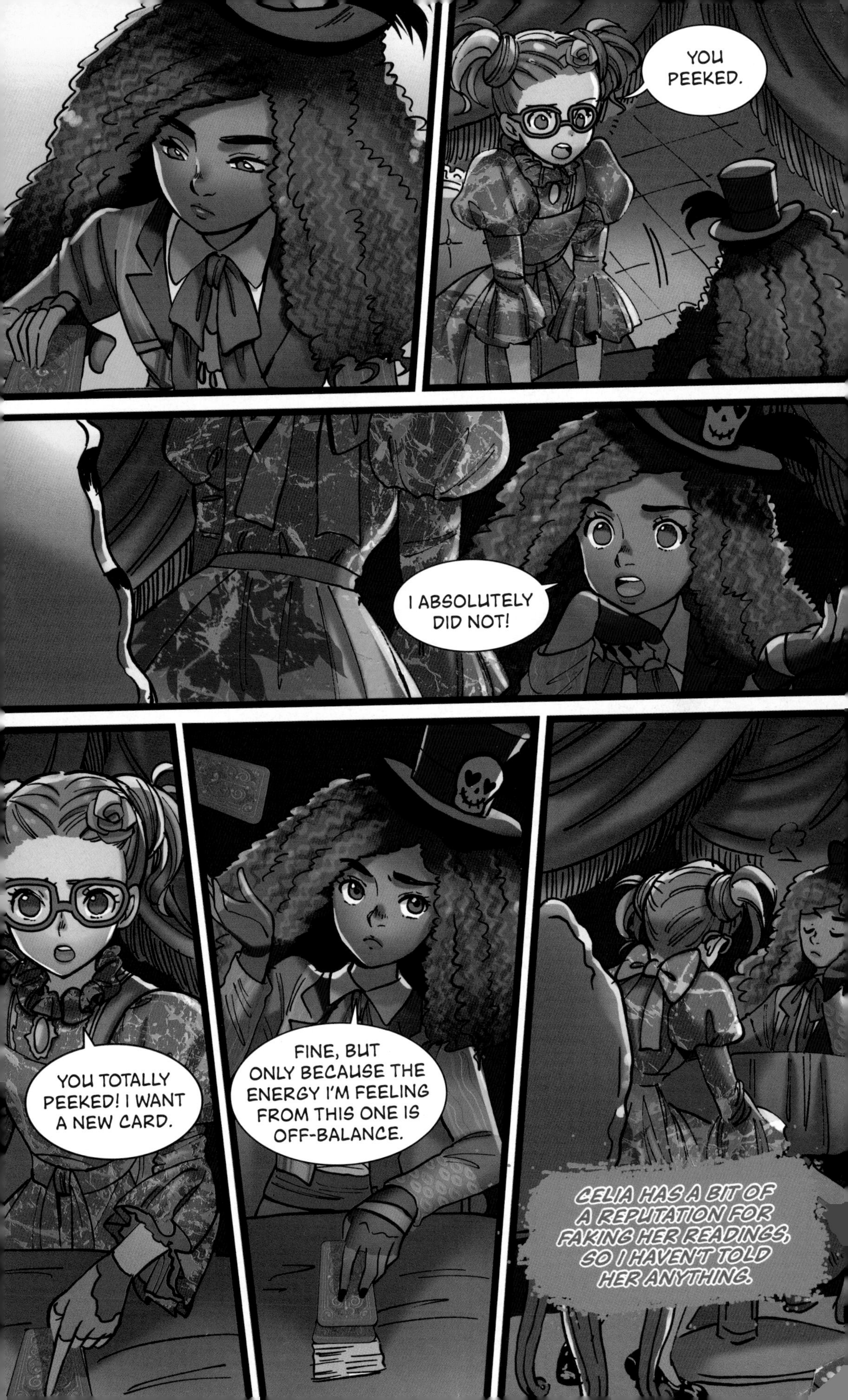
YOU PEEKED.
I ABSOLUTELY DID NOT!
YOU TOTALLY PEEKED! I WANT A NEW CARD.
FINE, BUT ONLY BECAUSE THE ENERGY I'M FEELING FROM THIS ONE IS OFF-BALANCE.
CELIA HAS A BIT OF A REPUTATION FOR FAKING HER READINGS, SO I HAVEN'T TOLD HER ANYTHING.

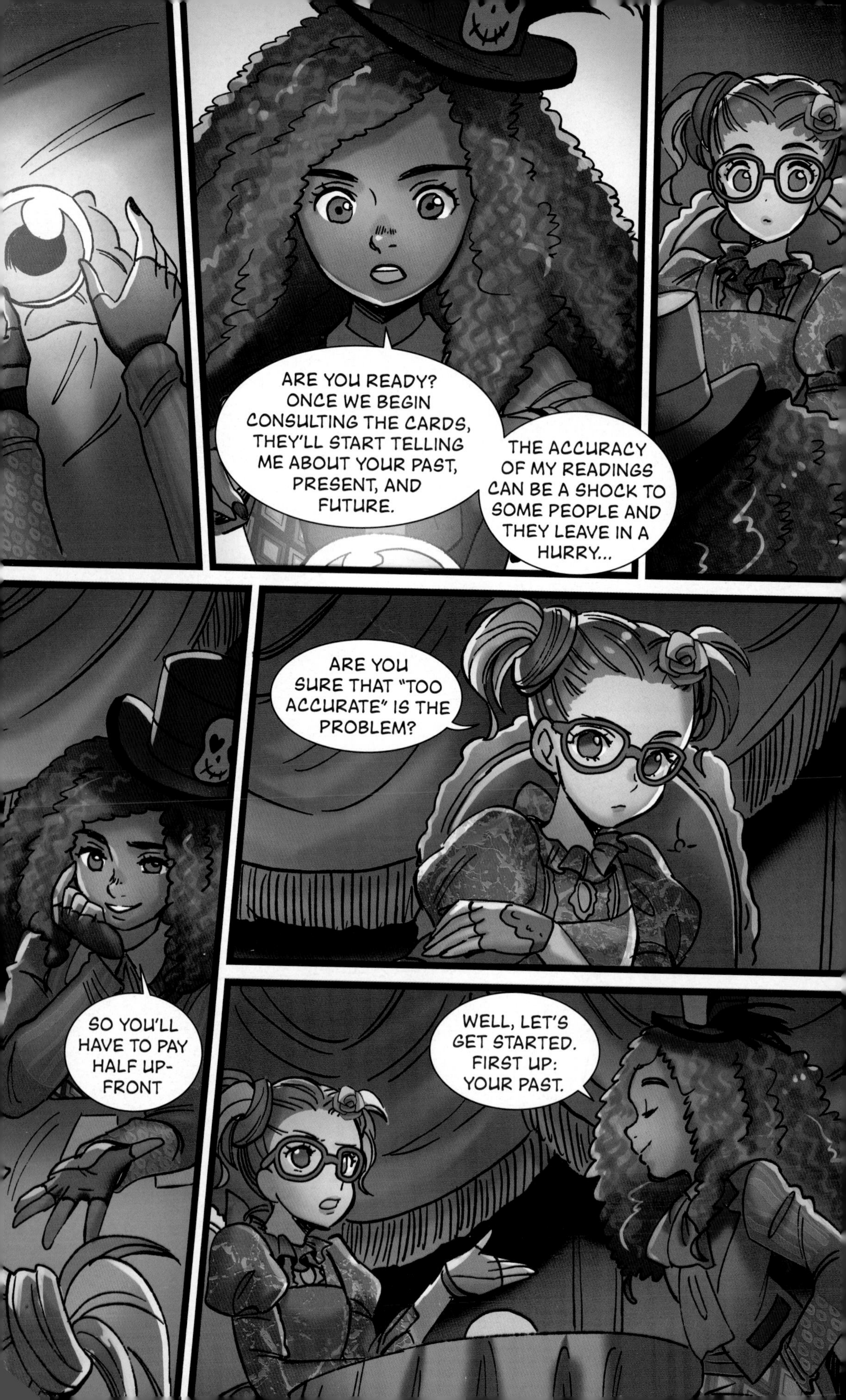
ARE YOU READY? ONCE WE BEGIN CONSULTING THE CARDS, THEY'LL START TELLING ME ABOUT YOUR PAST, PRESENT, AND FUTURE.
THE ACCURACY OF MY READINGS CAN BE A SHOCK TO SOME PEOPLE AND THEY LEAVE IN A HURRY...
SO YOU'LL HAVE TO PAY HALF UP-FRONT
ARE YOU SURE THAT "TOO ACCURATE" IS THE PROBLEM?
WELL, LET'S GET STARTED. FIRST UP: YOUR PAST.

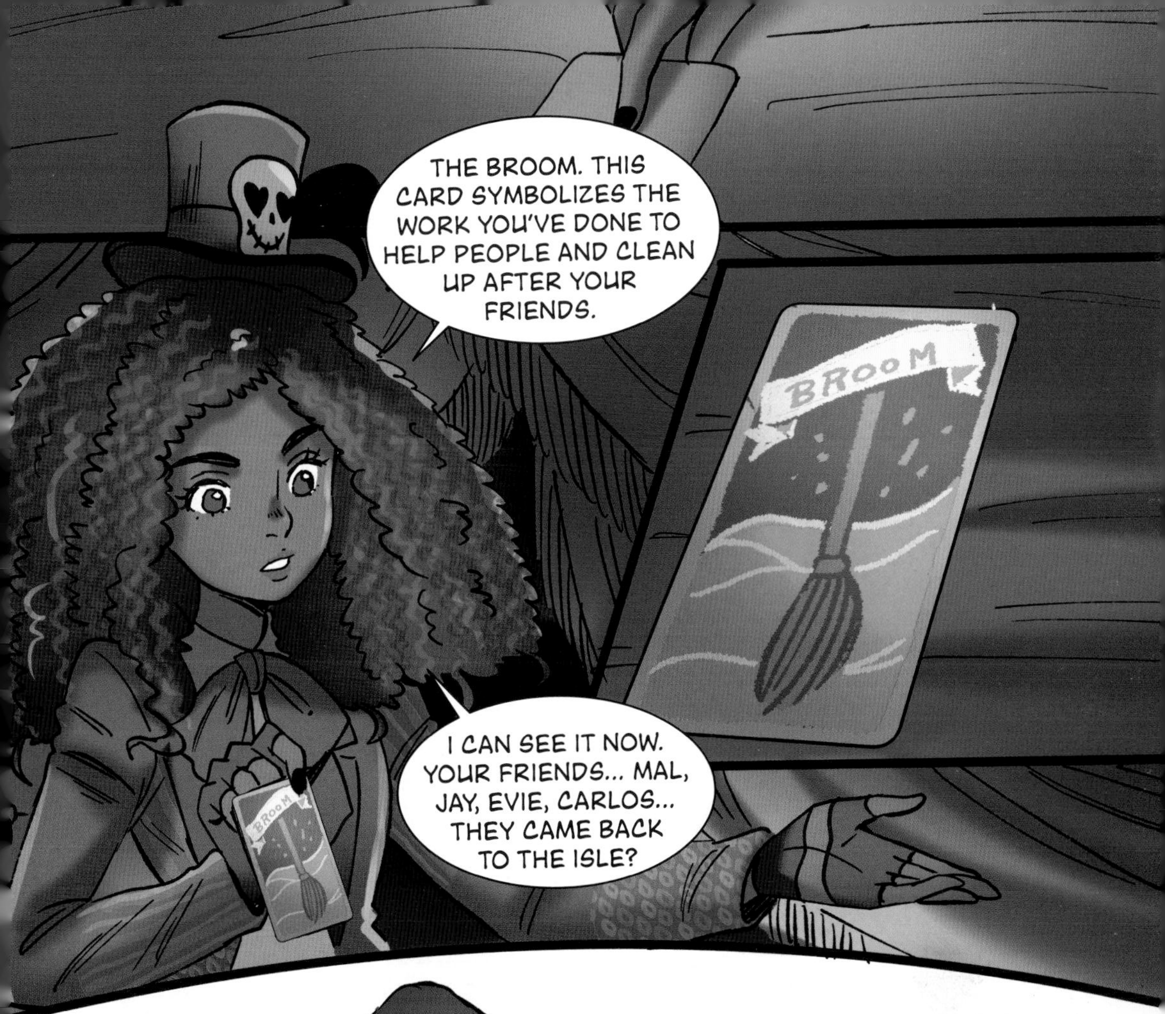
THE BROOM. THIS CARD SYMBOLIZES THE WORK YOU'VE DONE TO HELP PEOPLE AND CLEAN UP AFTER YOUR FRIENDS.
BROOM
I CAN SEE IT NOW. YOUR FRIENDS... MAL, JAY, EVIE, CARLOS... THEY CAME BACK TO THE ISLE?
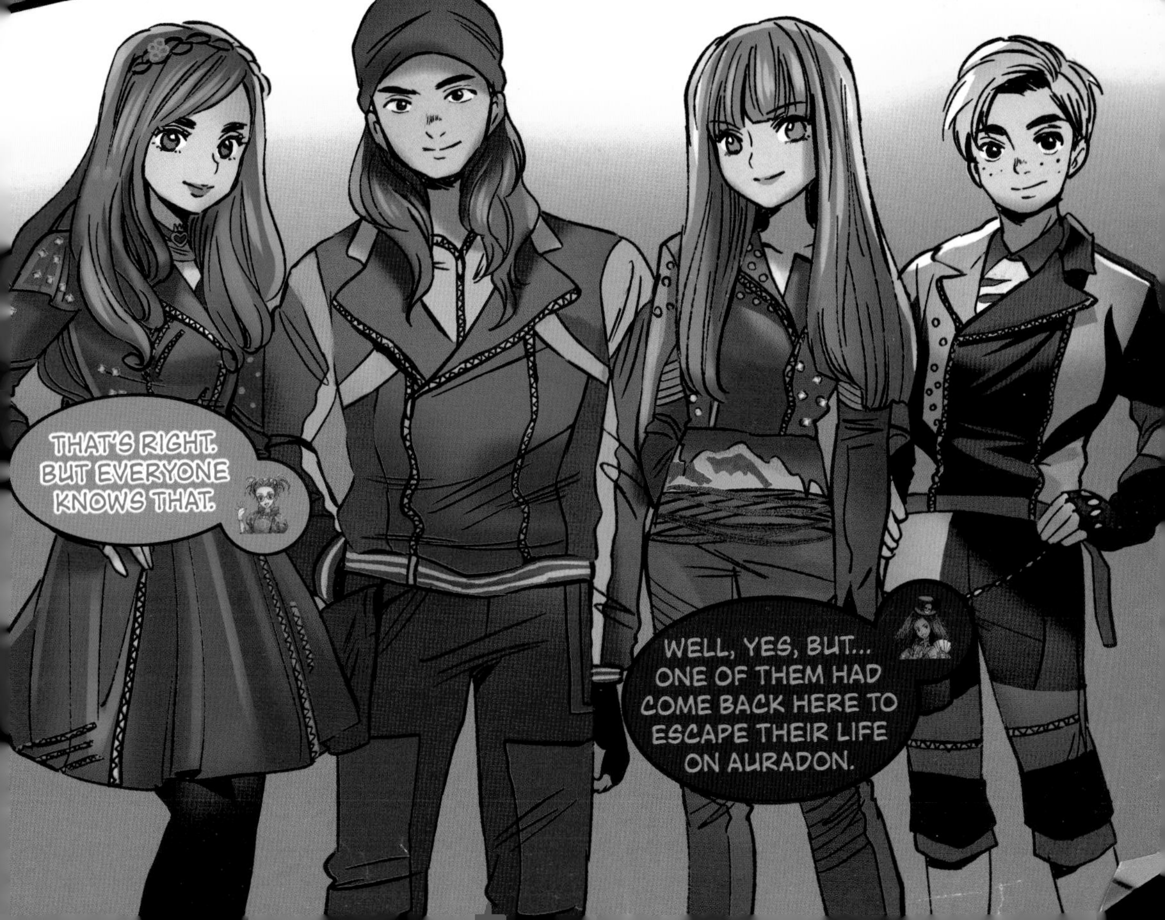
THAT'S RIGHT. BUT EVERYONE KNOWS THAT.
WELL, YES, BUT... ONE OF THEM HAD COME BACK HERE TO ESCAPE THEIR LIFE ON AURADON.

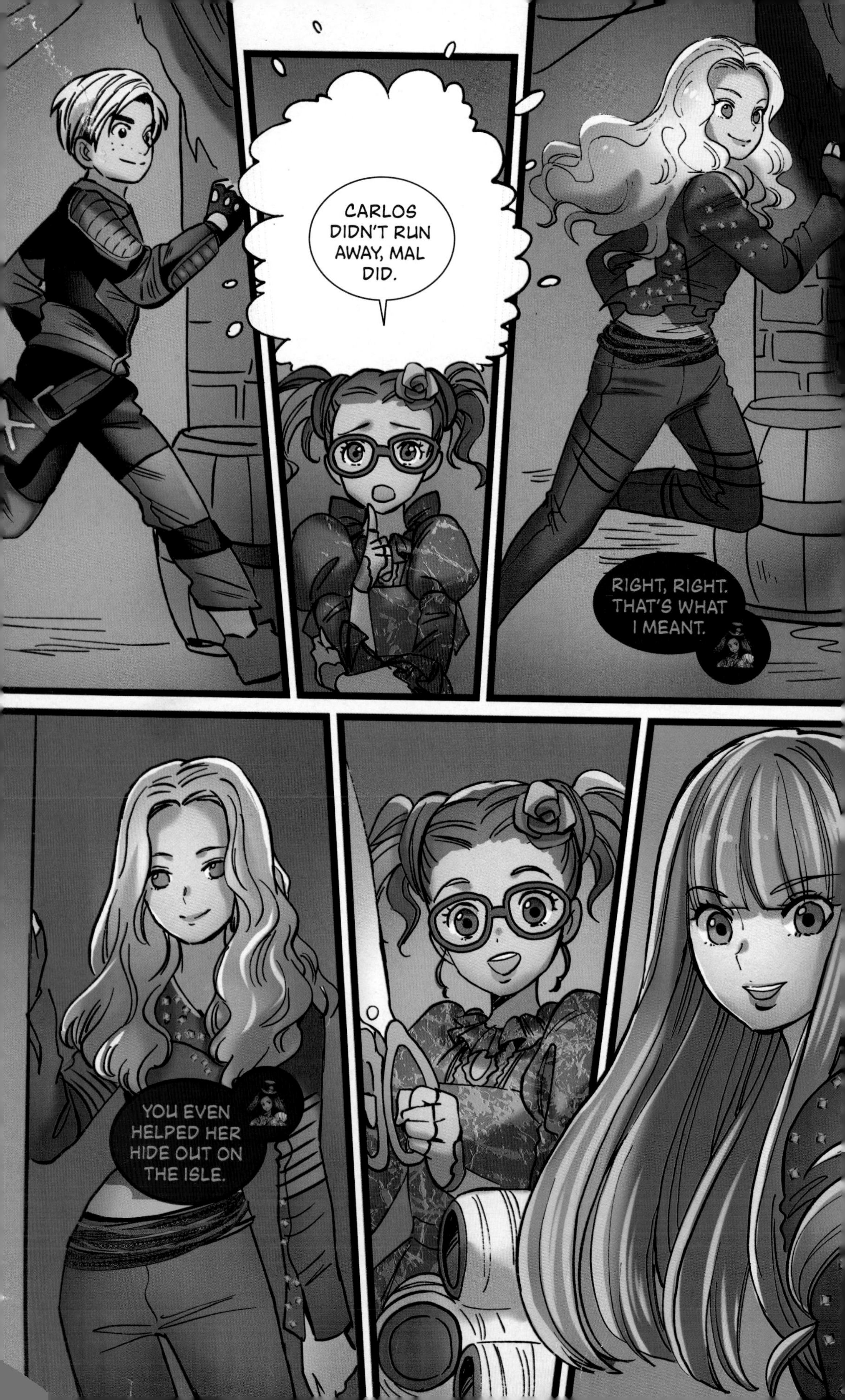
CARLOS DIDN'T RUN AWAY, MAL DID.
RIGHT, RIGHT. THAT'S WHAT I MEANT.
YOU EVEN HELPED HER HIDE OUT ON THE ISLE.

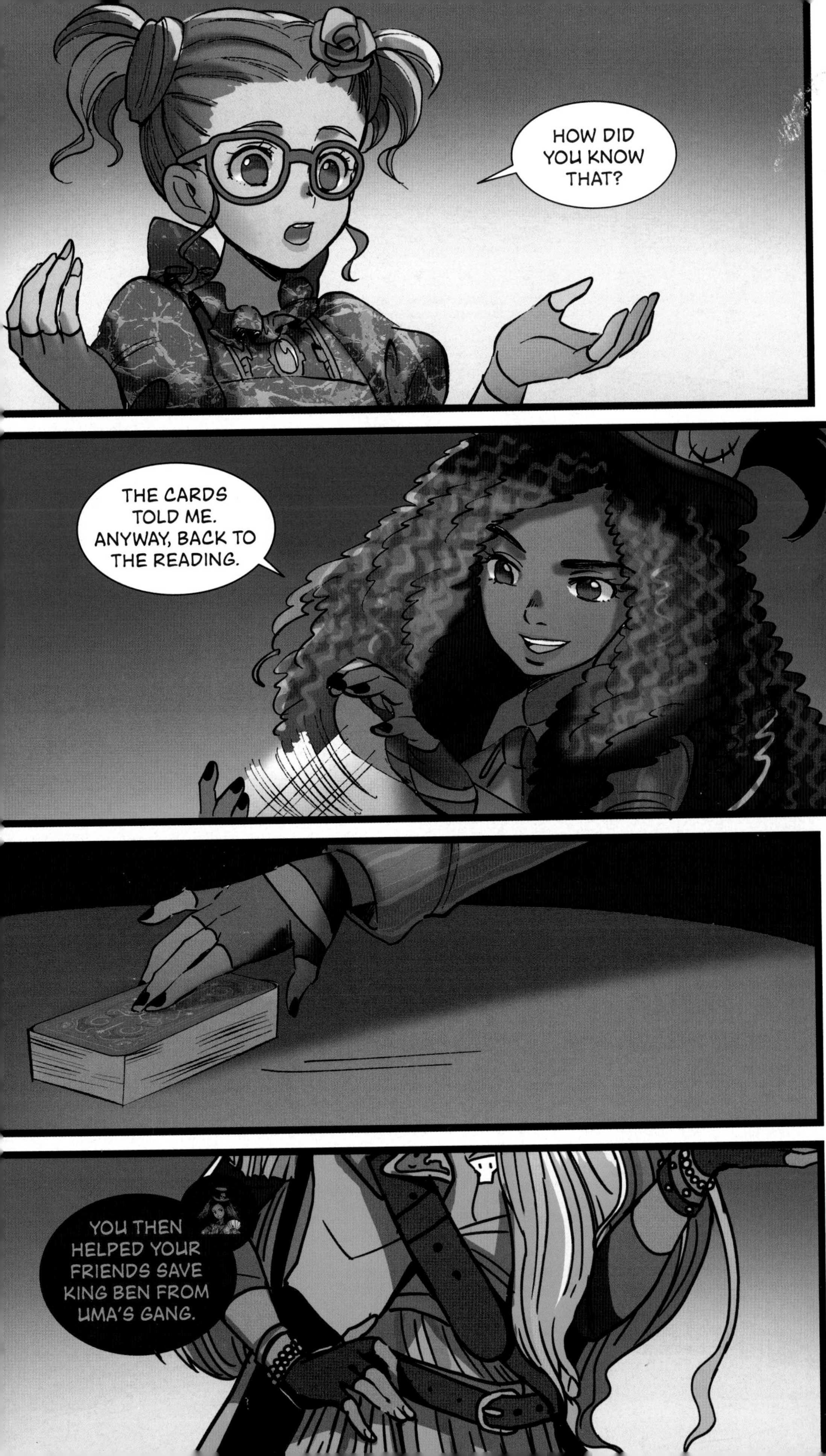
HOW DID YOU KNOW THAT?
THE CARDS TOLD ME. ANYWAY, BACK TO THE READING.
YOU THEN HELPED YOUR FRIENDS SAVE KING BEN FROM UMA'S GANG.

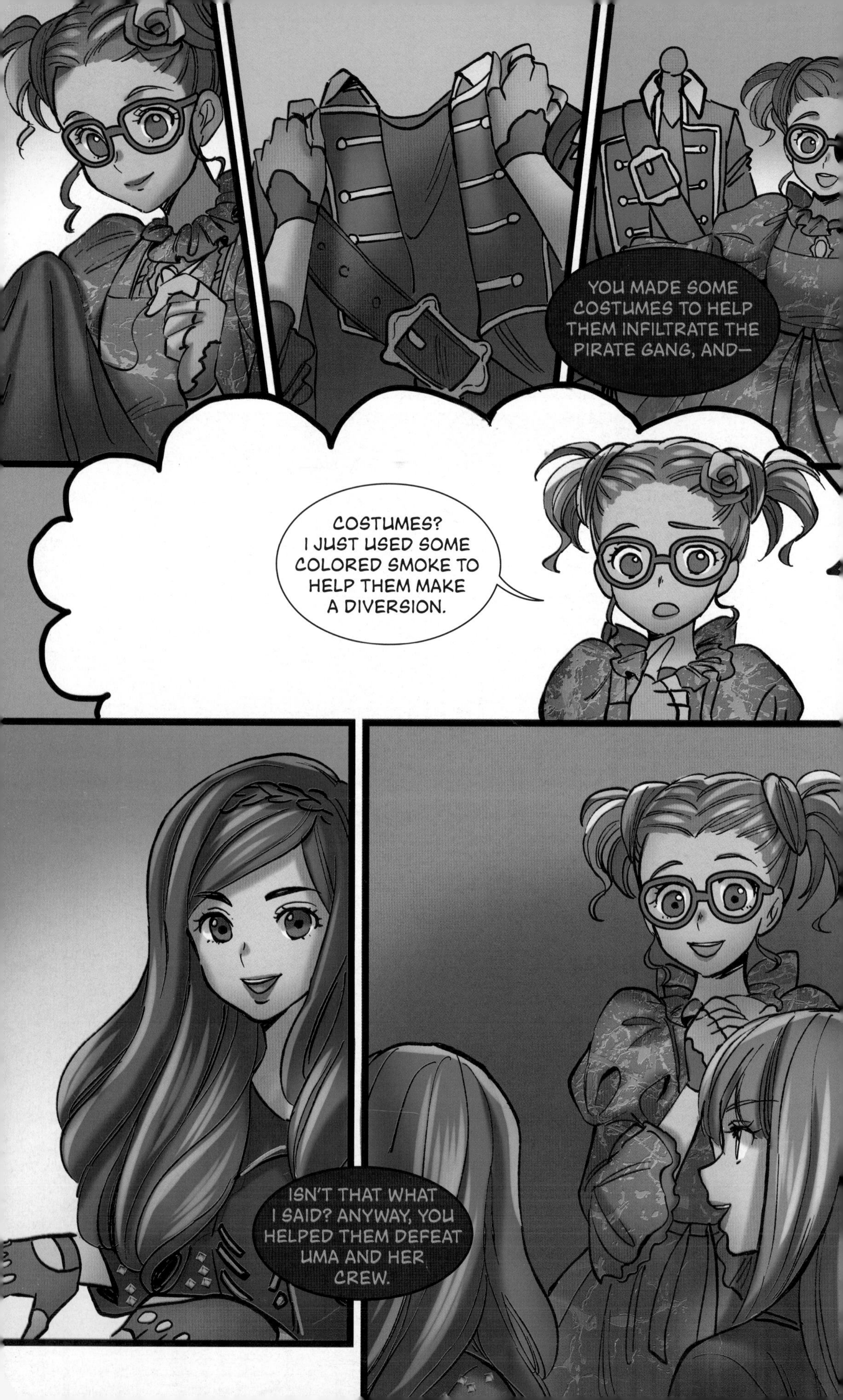
YOU MADE SOME COSTUMES TO HELP THEM INFILTRATE THE PIRATE GANG, AND—
COSTUMES? I JUST USED SOME COLORED SMOKE TO HELP THEM MAKE A DIVERSION.
ISN'T THAT WHAT I SAID? ANYWAY, YOU HELPED THEM DEFEAT UMA AND HER CREW.

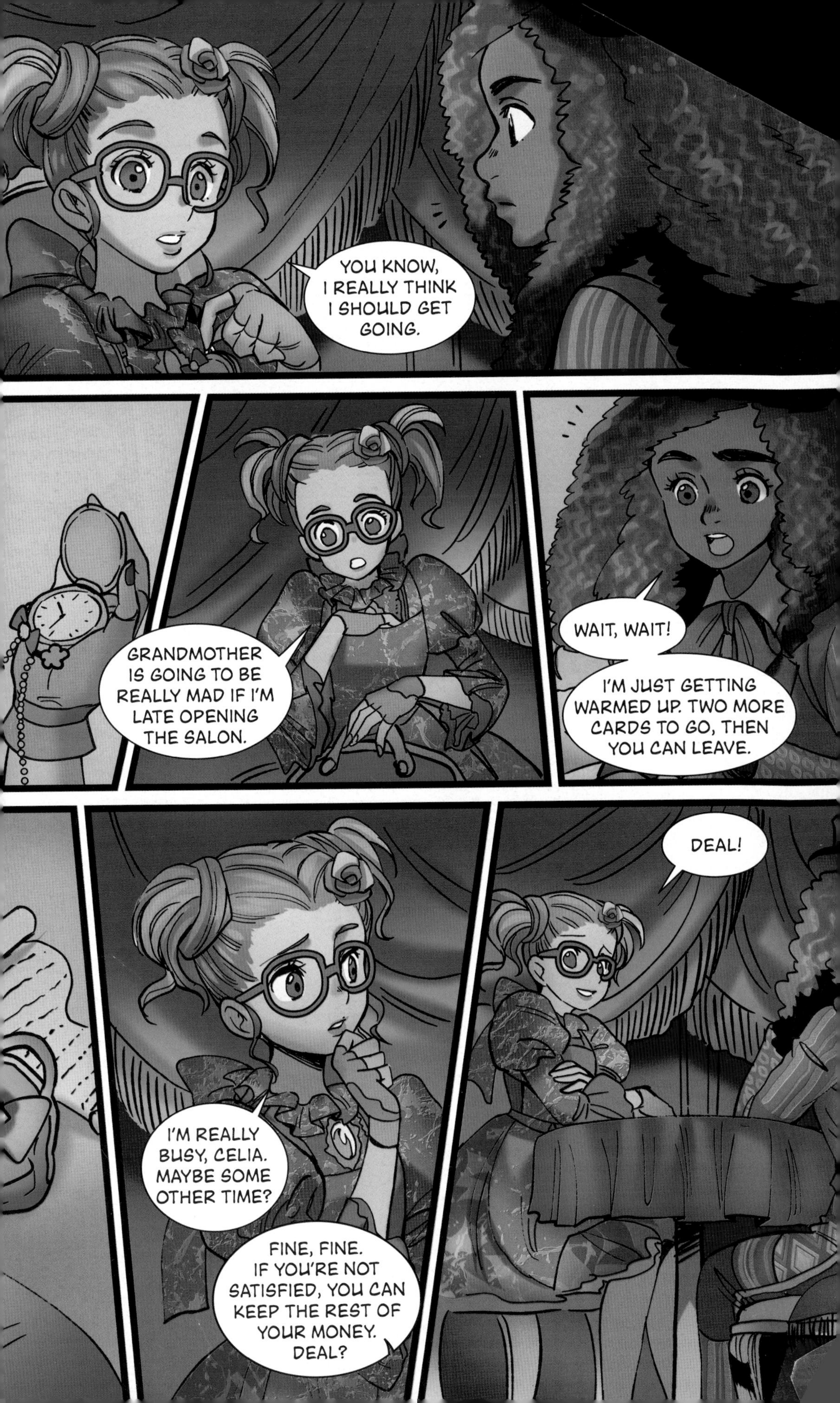
YOU KNOW, I REALLY THINK I SHOULD GET GOING.
GRANDMOTHER IS GOING TO BE REALLY MAD IF I'M LATE OPENING THE SALON.
WAIT, WAIT!
I'M JUST GETTING WARMED UP. TWO MORE CARDS TO GO, THEN YOU CAN LEAVE.
I'M REALLY BUSY, CELIA. MAYBE SOME OTHER TIME?
FINE, FINE. IF YOU'RE NOT SATISFIED, YOU CAN KEEP THE REST OF YOUR MONEY. DEAL?
DEAL!

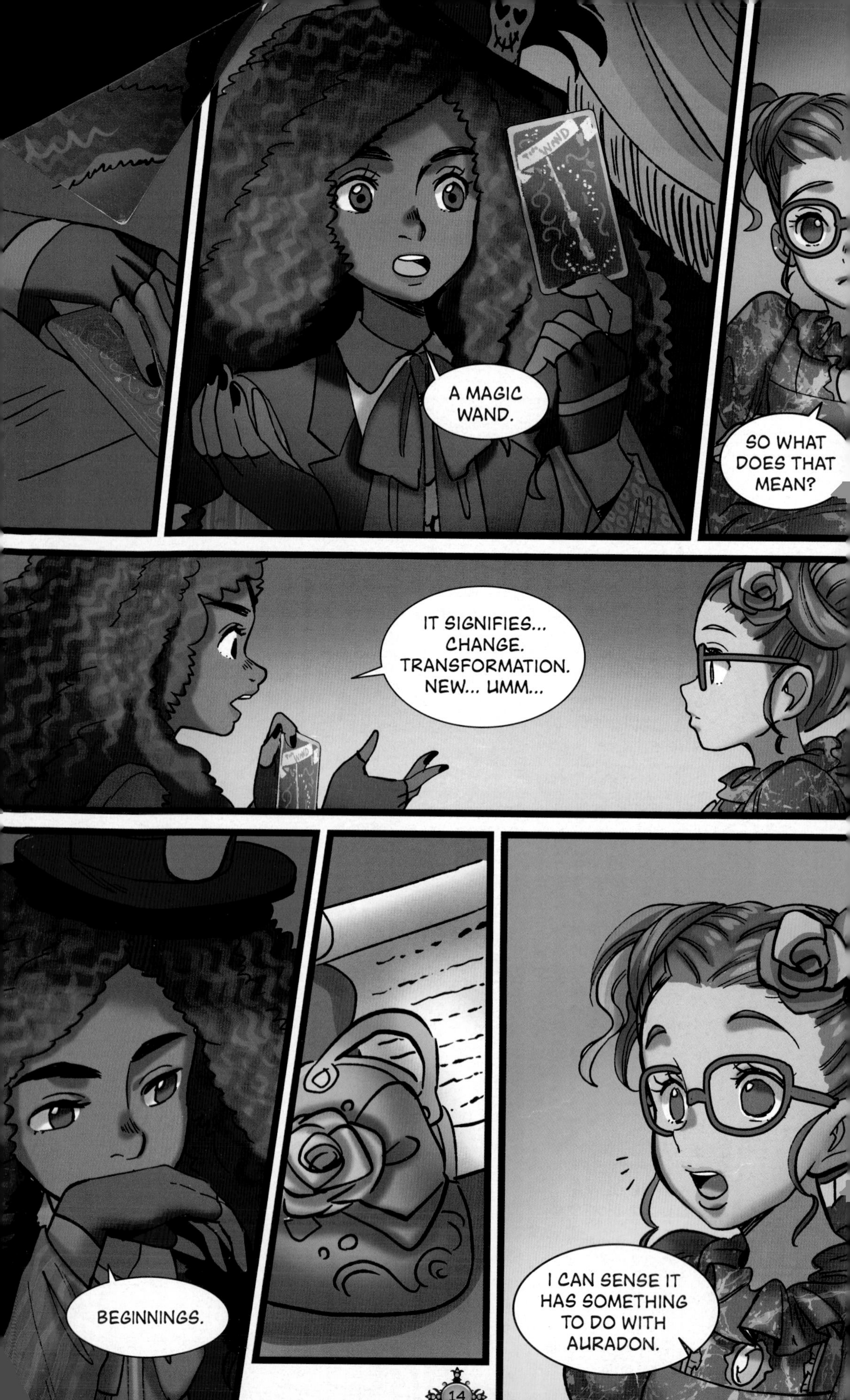
A MAGIC WAND.
SO WHAT DOES THAT MEAN?
IT SIGNIFIES... CHANGE. TRANSFORMATION. NEW... UMM...
BEGINNINGS.
I CAN SENSE IT HAS SOMETHING TO DO WITH AURADON.

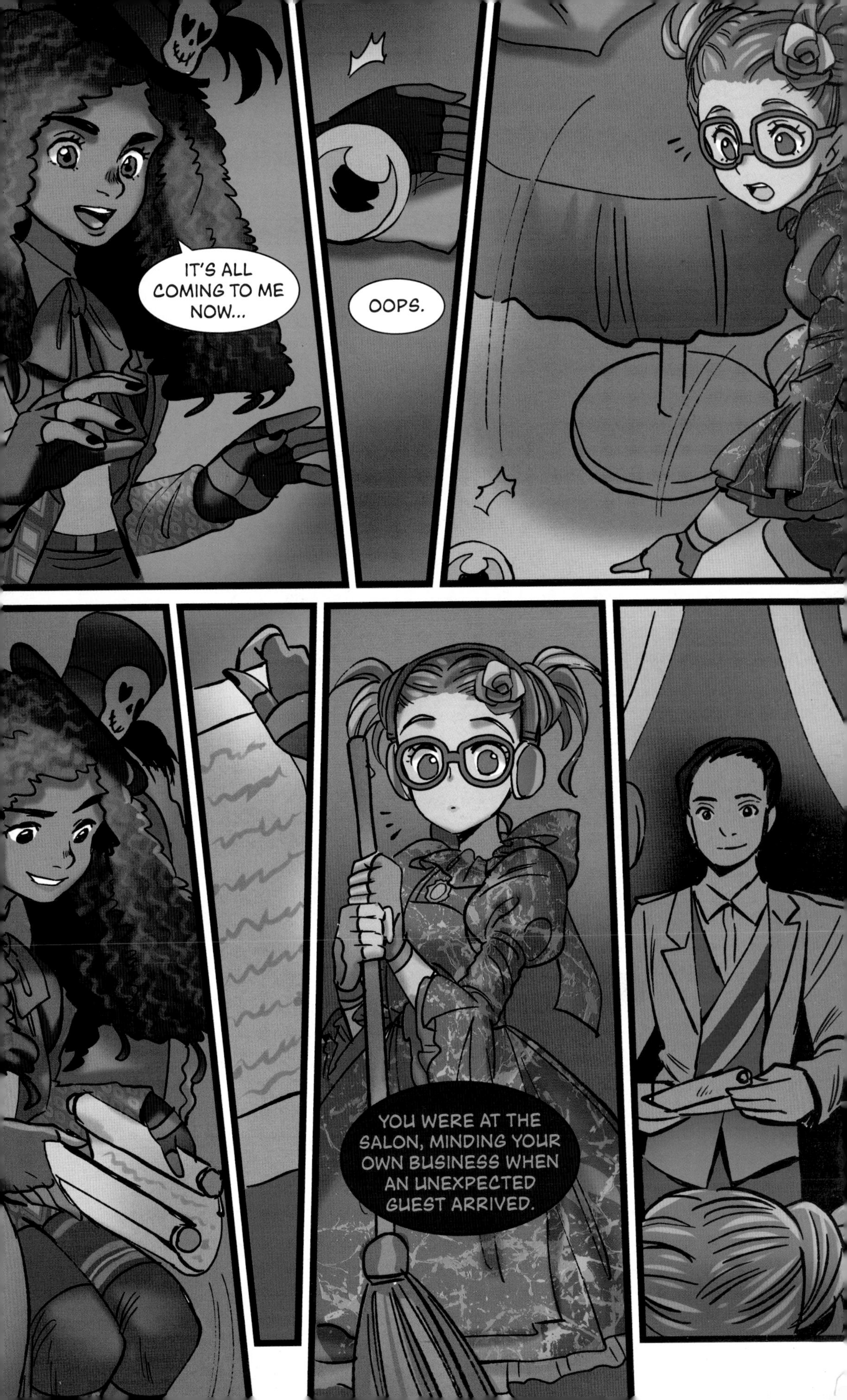
IT'S ALL COMING TO ME NOW...
OOPS.
YOU WERE AT THE SALON, MINDING YOUR OWN BUSINESS WHEN AN UNEXPECTED GUEST ARRIVED.

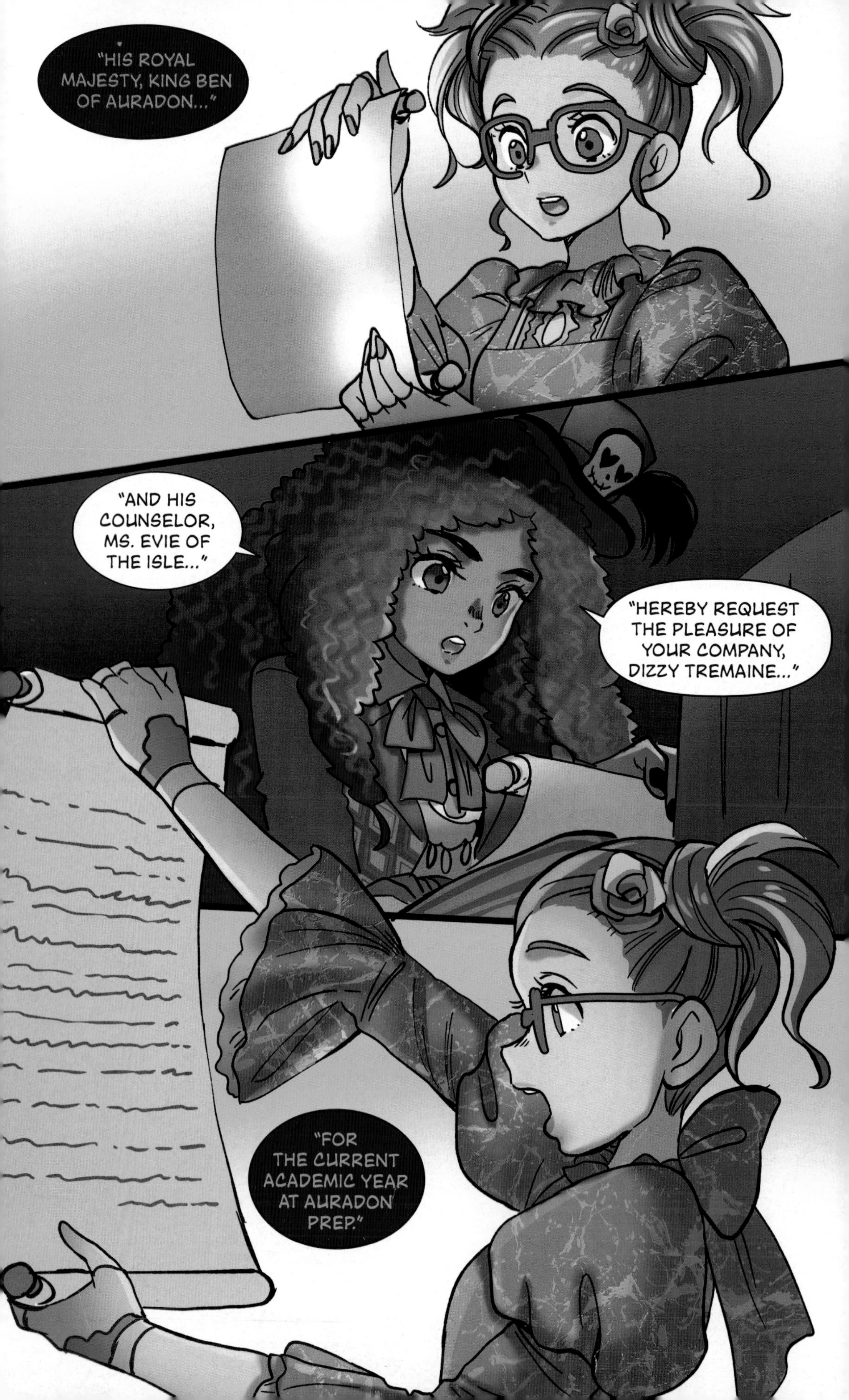
"HIS ROYAL MAJESTY, KING BEN OF AURADON..."
"AND HIS COUNSELOR, MS. EVIE OF THE ISLE..."
"HEREBY REQUEST THE PLEASURE OF YOUR COMPANY, DIZZY TREMAINE..."
"FOR THE CURRENT ACADEMIC YEAR AT AURADON PREP."

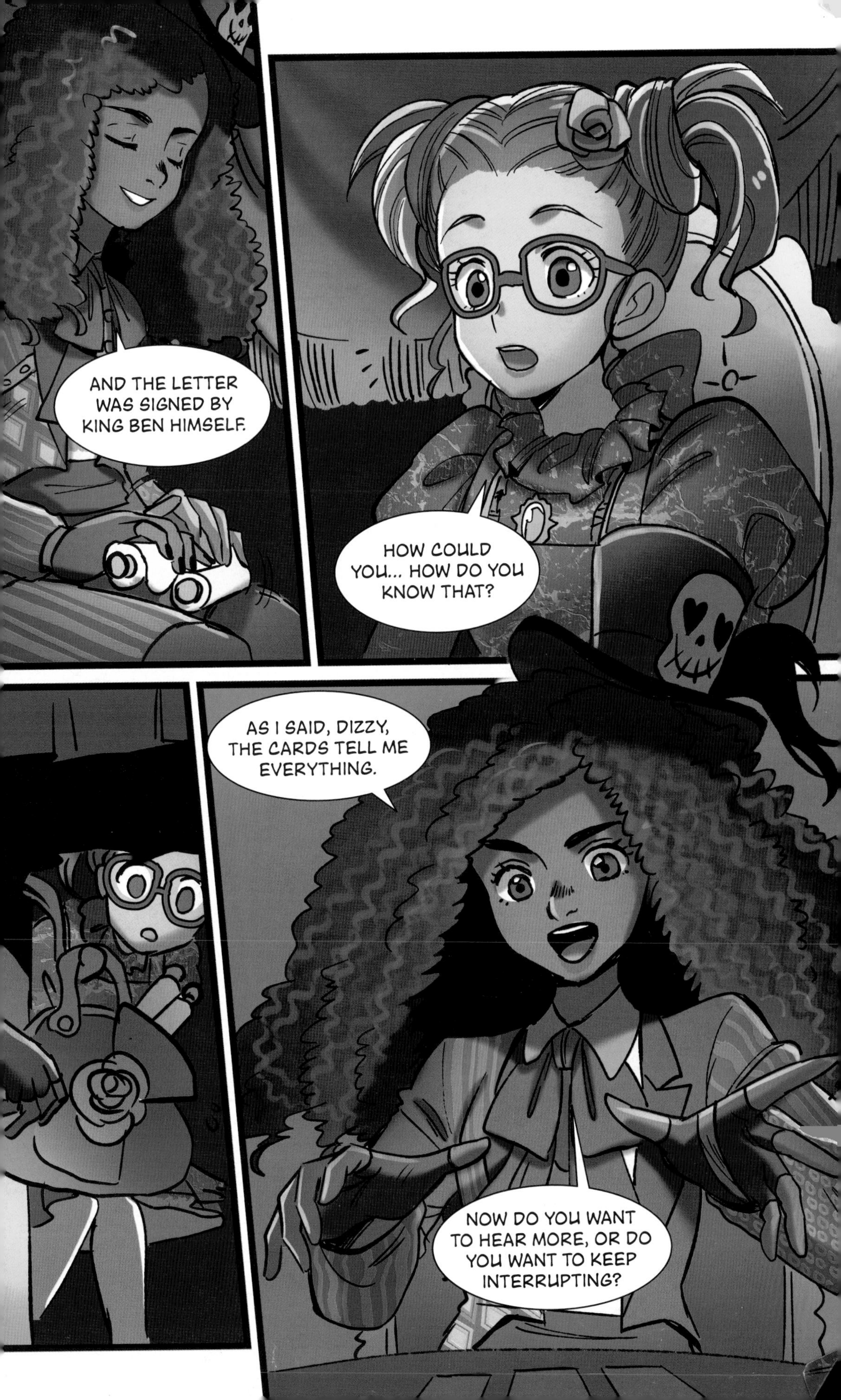
AND THE LETTER WAS SIGNED BY KING BEN HIMSELF.
HOW COULD YOU... HOW DO YOU KNOW THAT?
AS I SAID, DIZZY, THE CARDS TELL ME EVERYTHING.
NOW DO YOU WANT TO HEAR MORE, OR DO YOU WANT TO KEEP INTERRUPTING?

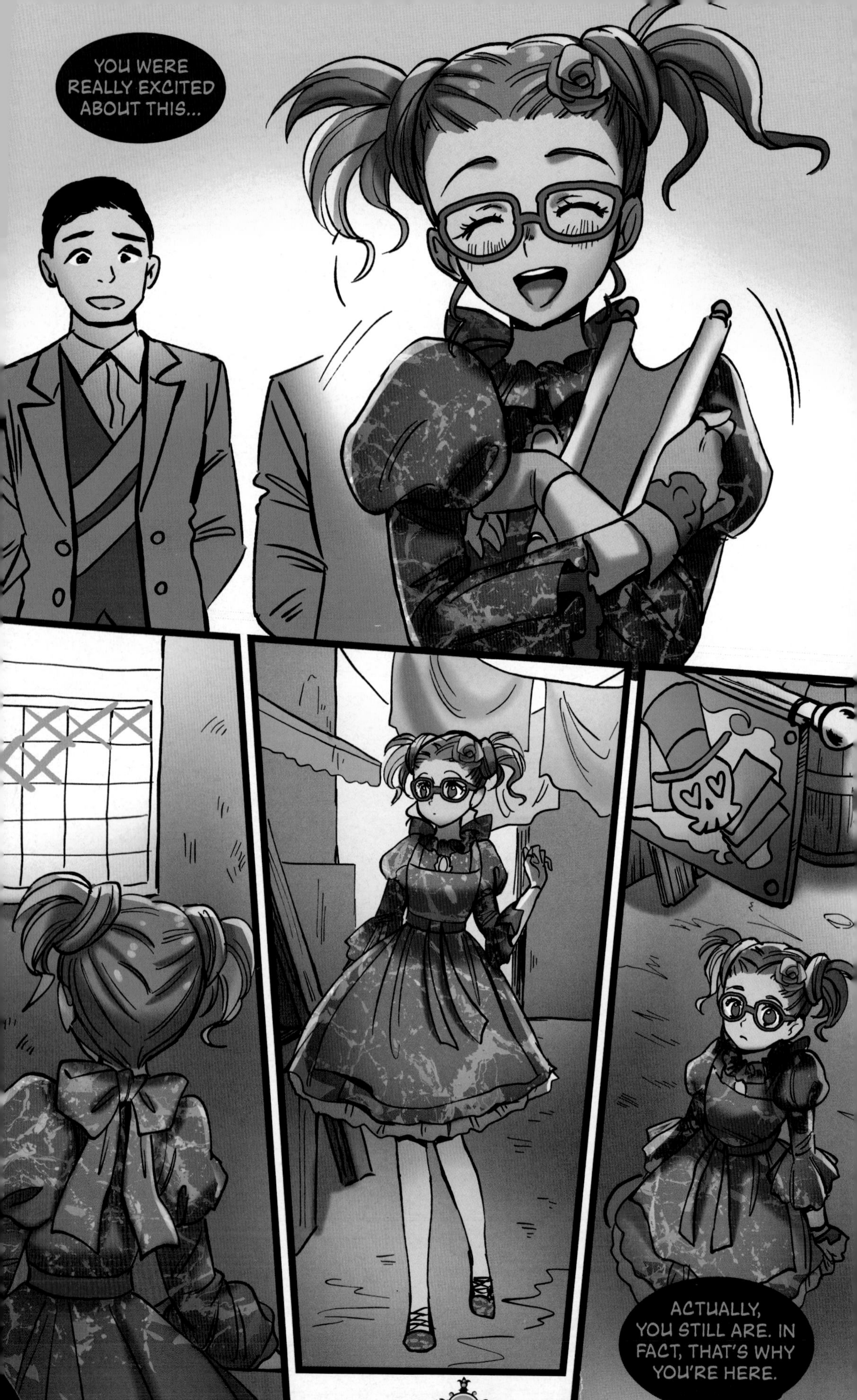
YOU WERE REALLY EXCITED ABOUT THIS...
ACTUALLY, YOU STILL ARE. IN FACT, THAT'S WHY YOU'RE HERE.

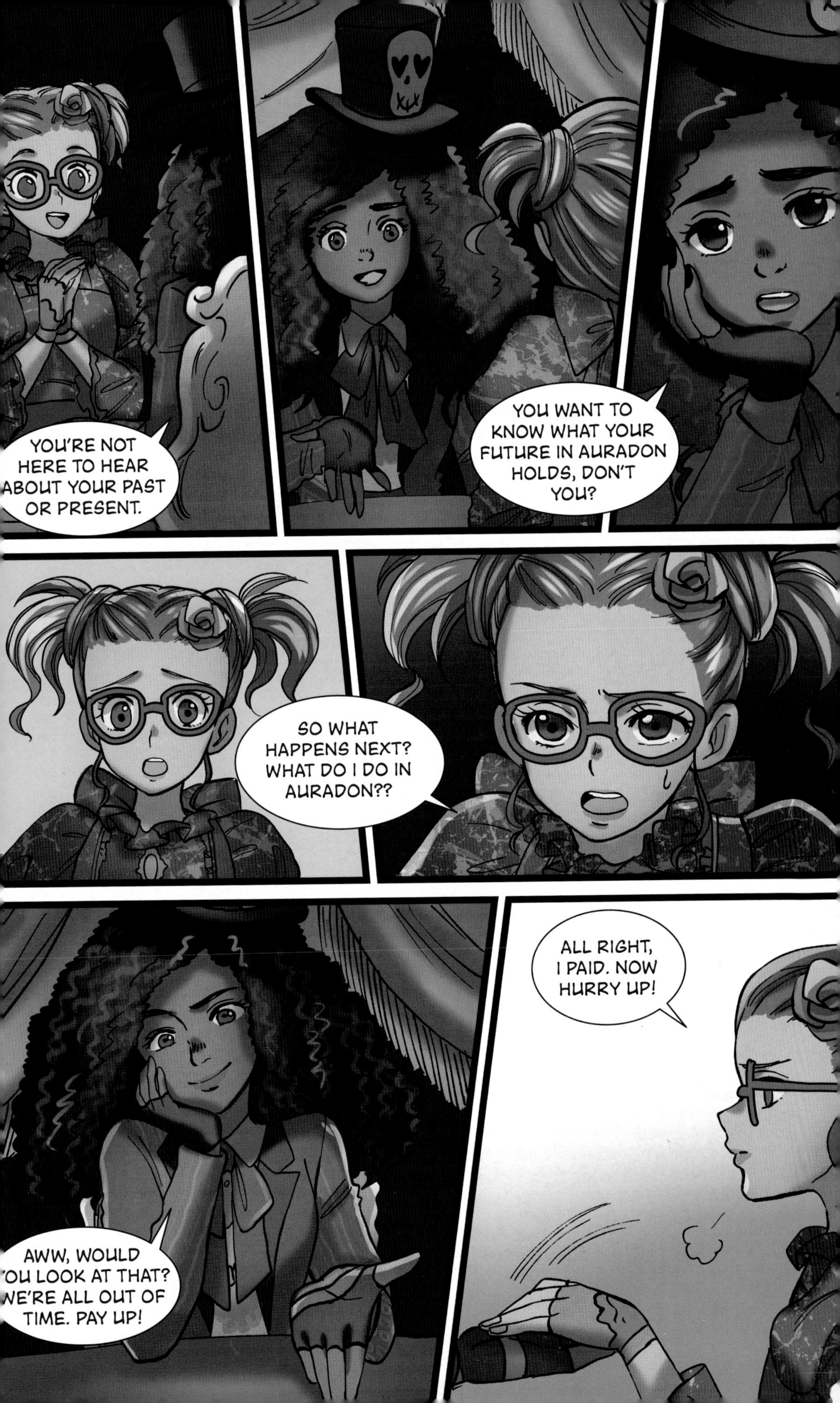
YOU'RE NOT HERE TO HEAR ABOUT YOUR PAST OR PRESENT.
YOU WANT TO KNOW WHAT YOUR FUTURE IN AURADON HOLDS, DON'T YOU?
SO WHAT HAPPENS NEXT? WHAT DO I DO IN AURADON??
AWW, WOULD YOU LOOK AT THAT? WE'RE ALL OUT OF TIME. PAY UP!
ALL RIGHT, I PAID. NOW HURRY UP!

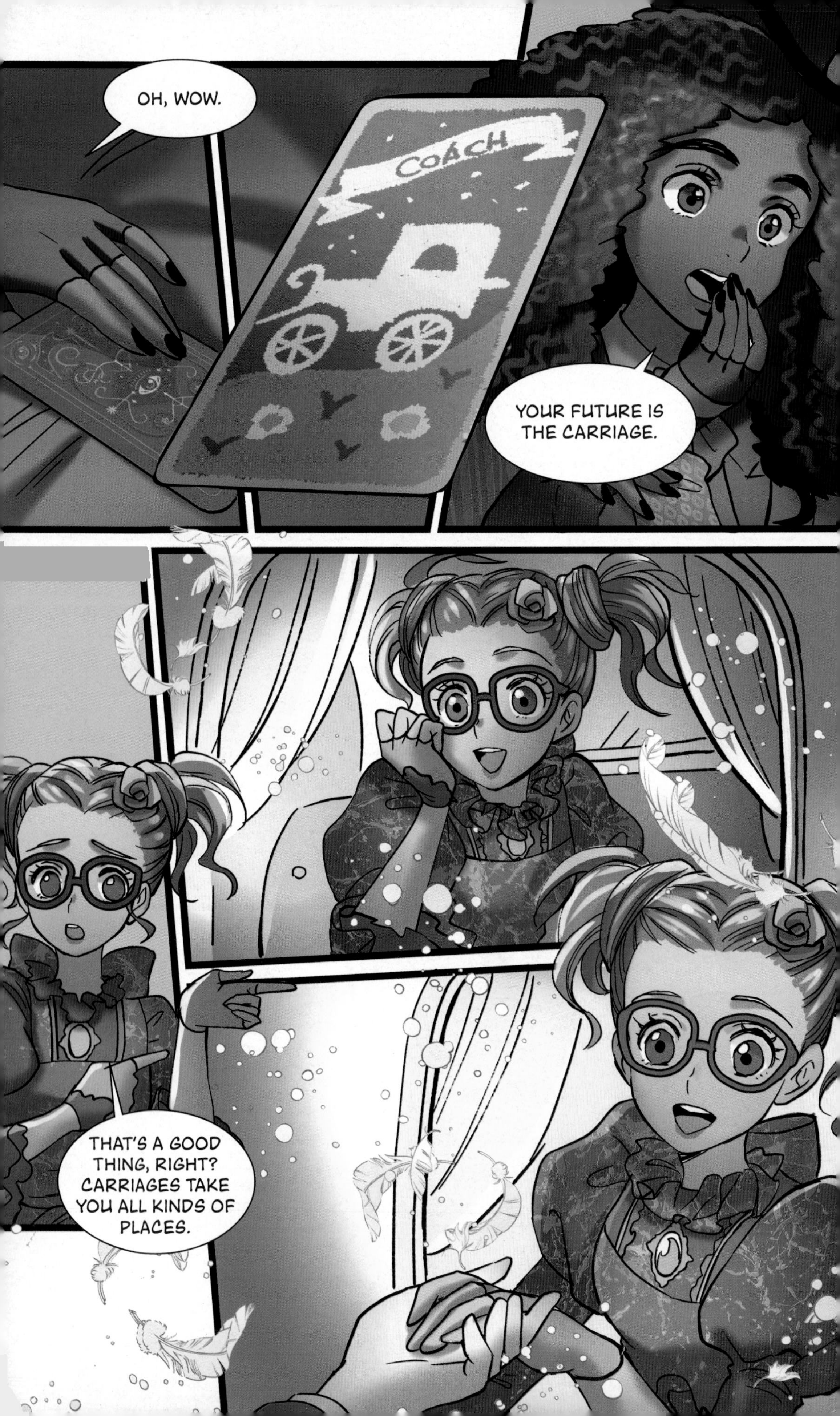
OH, WOW.
COACH
YOUR FUTURE IS THE CARRIAGE.
THAT'S A GOOD THING, RIGHT? CARRIAGES TAKE YOU ALL KINDS OF PLACES.

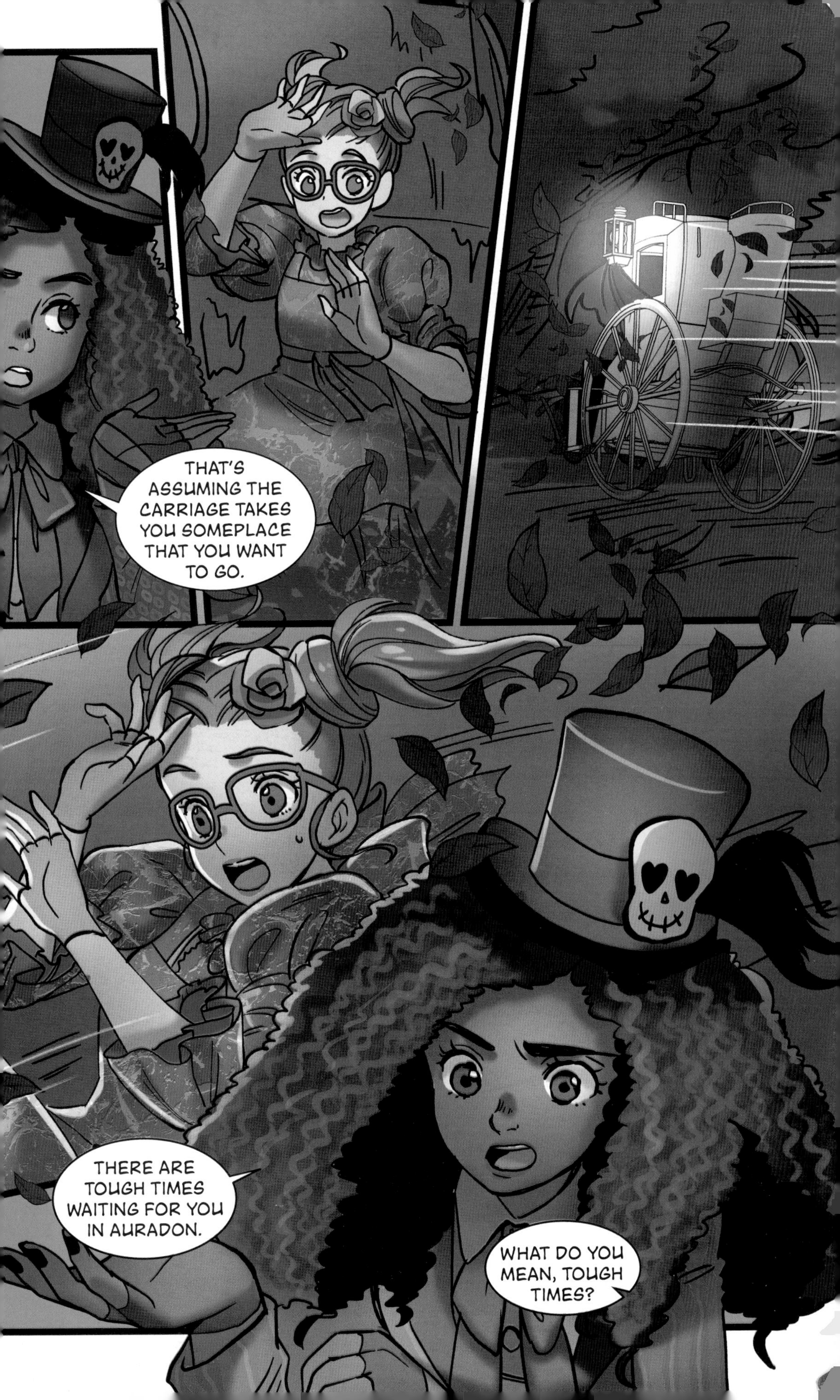
THAT'S ASSUMING THE CARRIAGE TAKES YOU SOMEPLACE THAT YOU WANT TO GO.
THERE ARE TOUGH TIMES WAITING FOR YOU IN AURADON.
WHAT DO YOU MEAN, TOUGH TIMES?

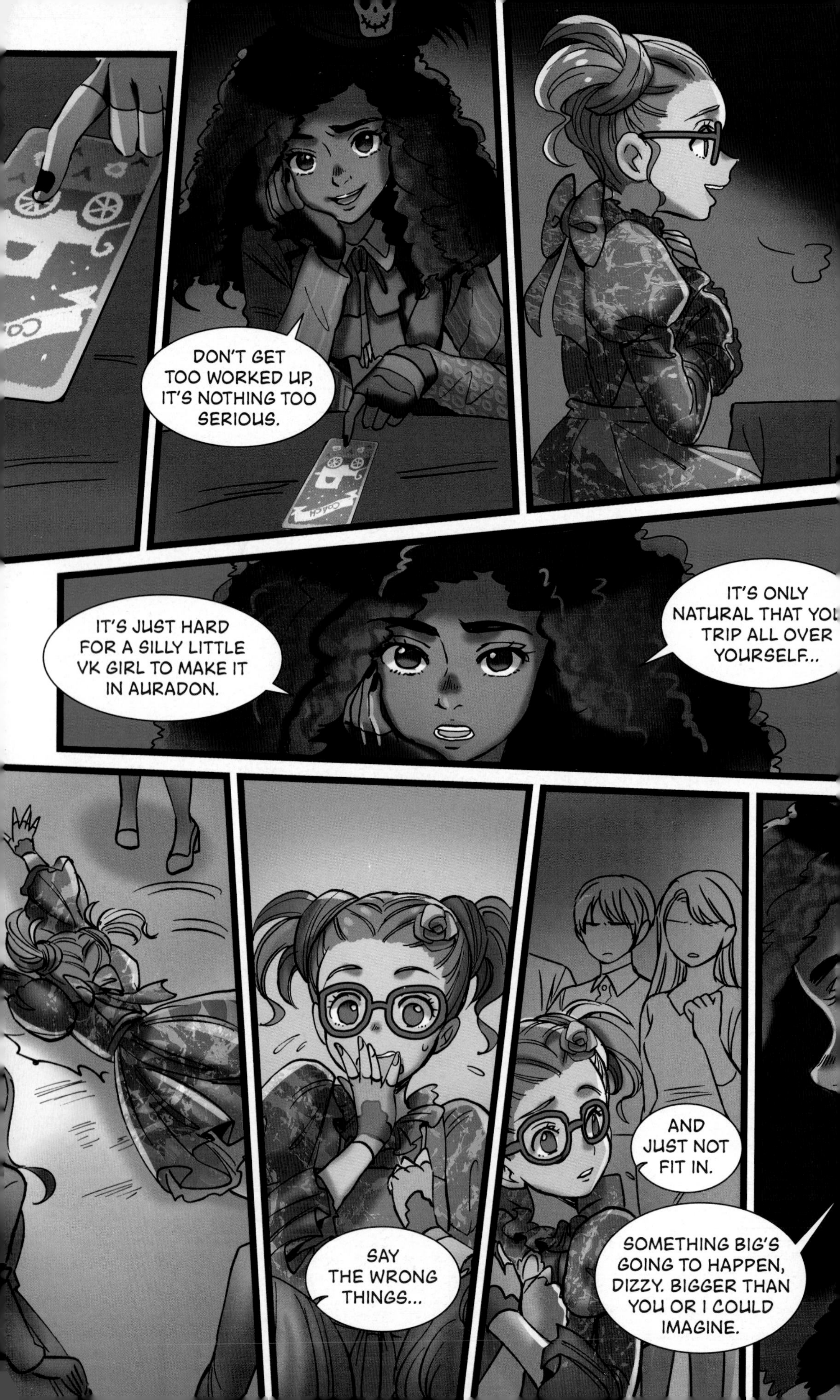
DON'T GET TOO WORKED UP, IT'S NOTHING TOO SERIOUS.
IT'S JUST HARD FOR A SILLY LITTLE VK GIRL TO MAKE IT IN AURADON.
IT'S ONLY NATURAL THAT YO TRIP ALL OVER YOURSELF...
SAY THE WRONG THINGS...
AND JUST NOT FIT IN.
SOMETHING BIG'S GOING TO HAPPEN, DIZZY. BIGGER THAN YOU OR I COULD IMAGINE.

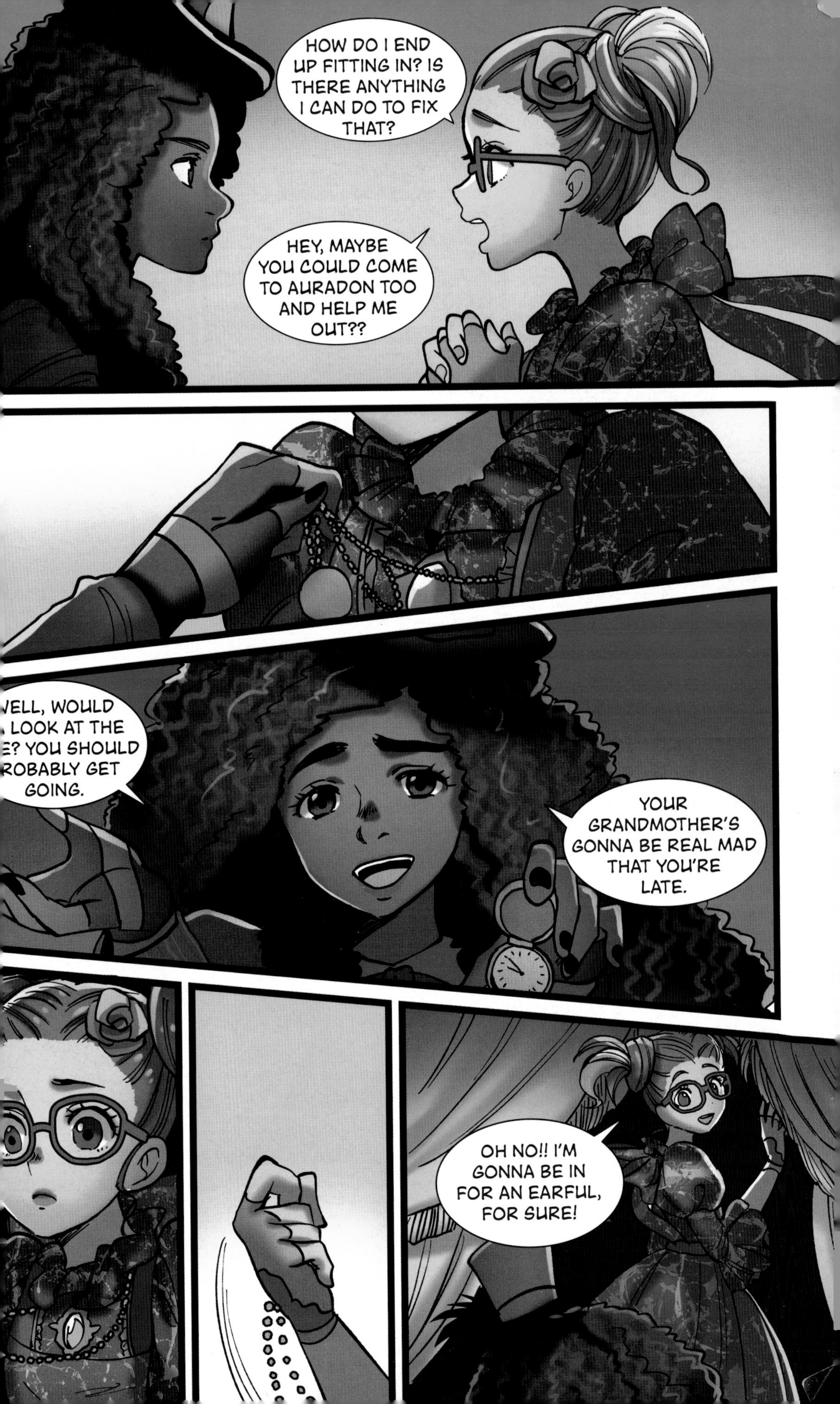
HOW DO I END UP FITTING IN? IS THERE ANYTHING I CAN DO TO FIX THAT?
HEY, MAYBE YOU COULD COME TO AURADON TOO AND HELP ME OUT??
WELL, WOULD LOOK AT THE ? YOU SHOULD ROBABLY GET GOING.
YOUR GRANDMOTHER'S GONNA BE REAL MAD THAT YOU'RE LATE.
OH NO!! I'M GONNA BE IN FOR AN EARFUL, FOR SURE!

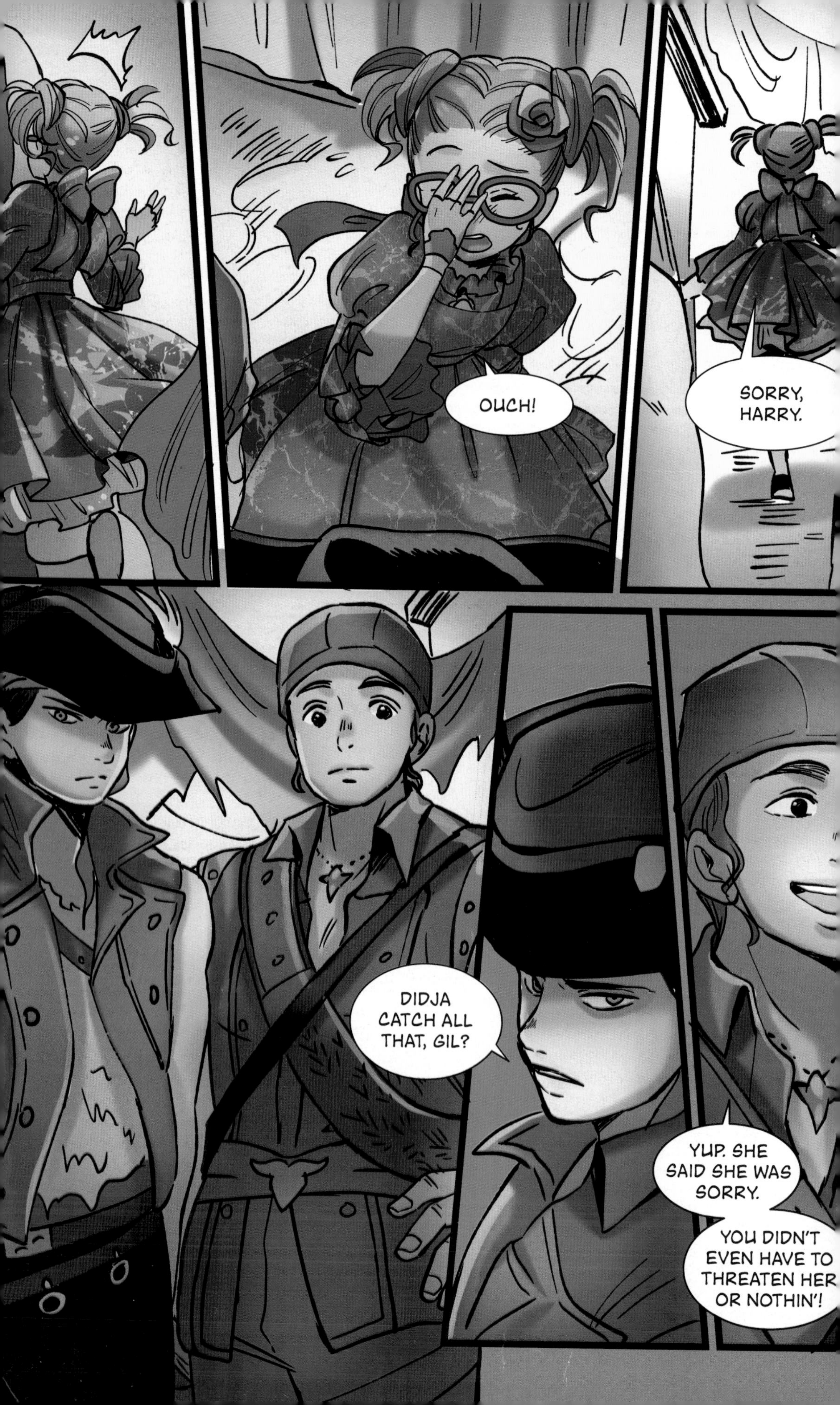
OUCH!
SORRY, HARRY.
DIDJA CATCH ALL THAT, GIL?
YUP. SHE SAID SHE WAS SORRY.
YOU DIDN'T EVEN HAVE TO THREATEN HER OR NOTHIN'!

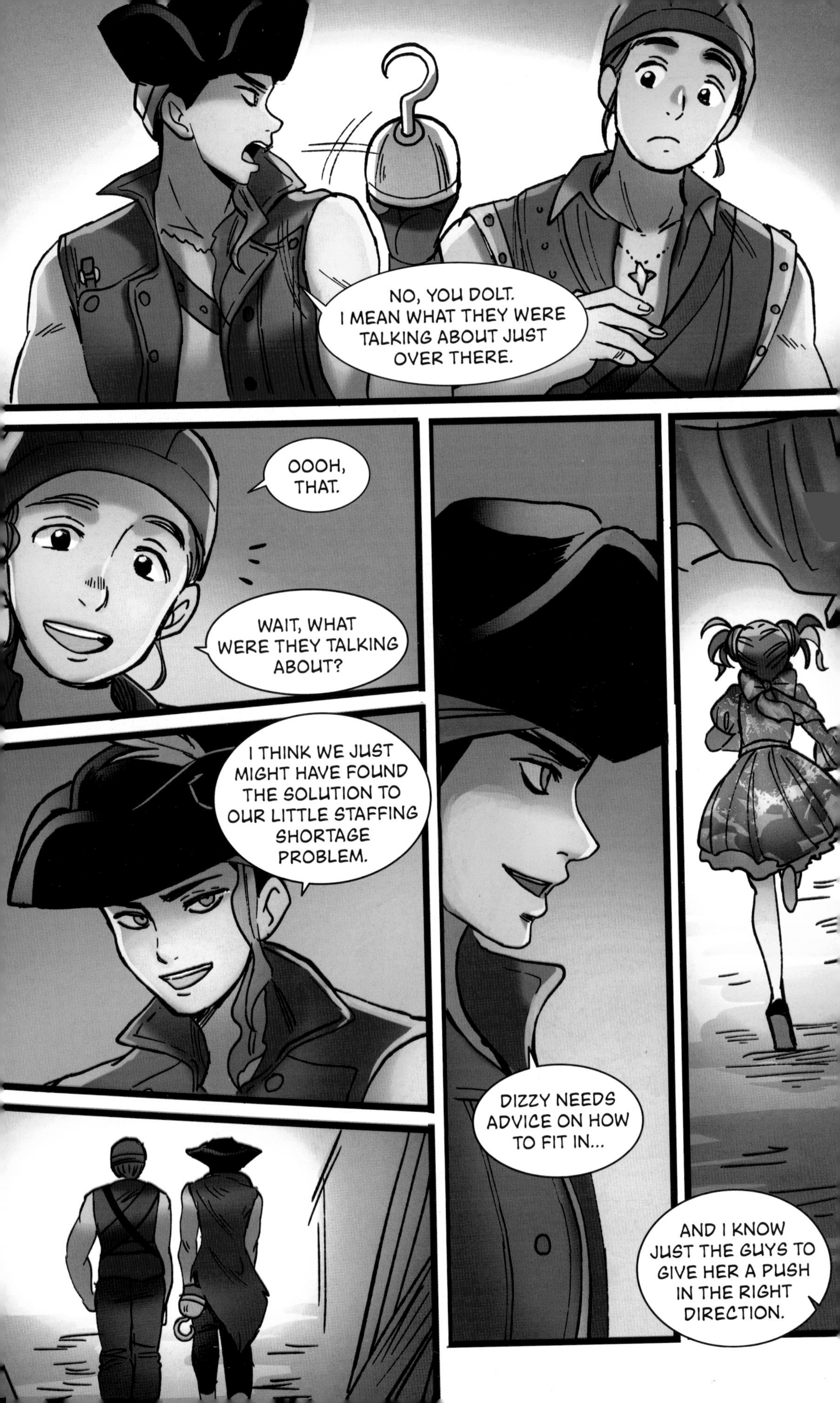
NO, YOU DOLT. I MEAN WHAT THEY WERE TALKING ABOUT JUST OVER THERE.
OOOH, THAT.
WAIT, WHAT WERE THEY TALKING ABOUT?
I THINK WE JUST MIGHT HAVE FOUND THE SOLUTION TO OUR LITTLE STAFFING SHORTAGE PROBLEM.
DIZZY NEEDS ADVICE ON HOW TO FIT IN...
AND I KNOW JUST THE GUYS TO GIVE HER A PUSH IN THE RIGHT DIRECTION.

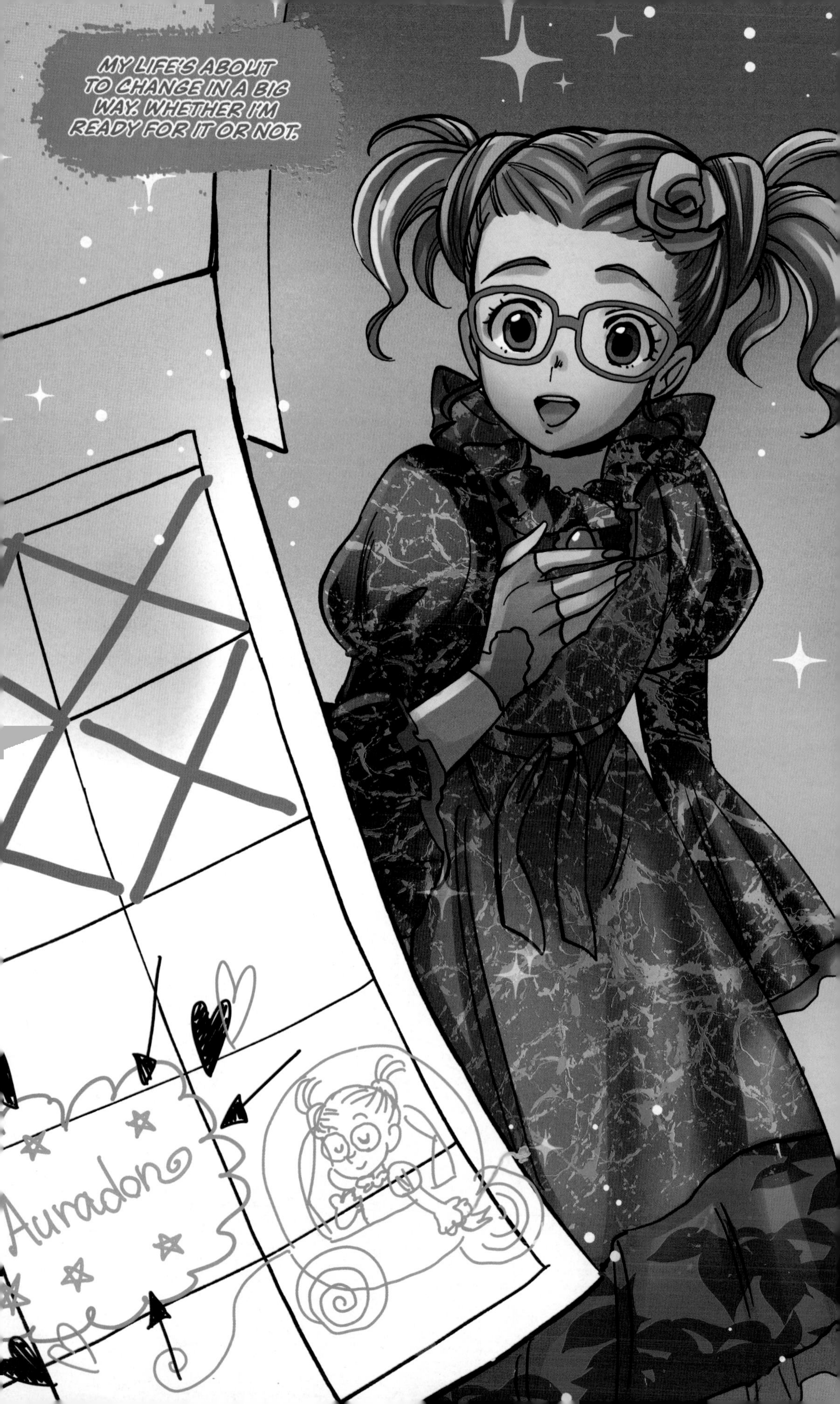
MY LIFE'S ABOUT TO CHANGE IN A BIG WAY. WHETHER I'M READY FOR IT OR NOT.
Auradon

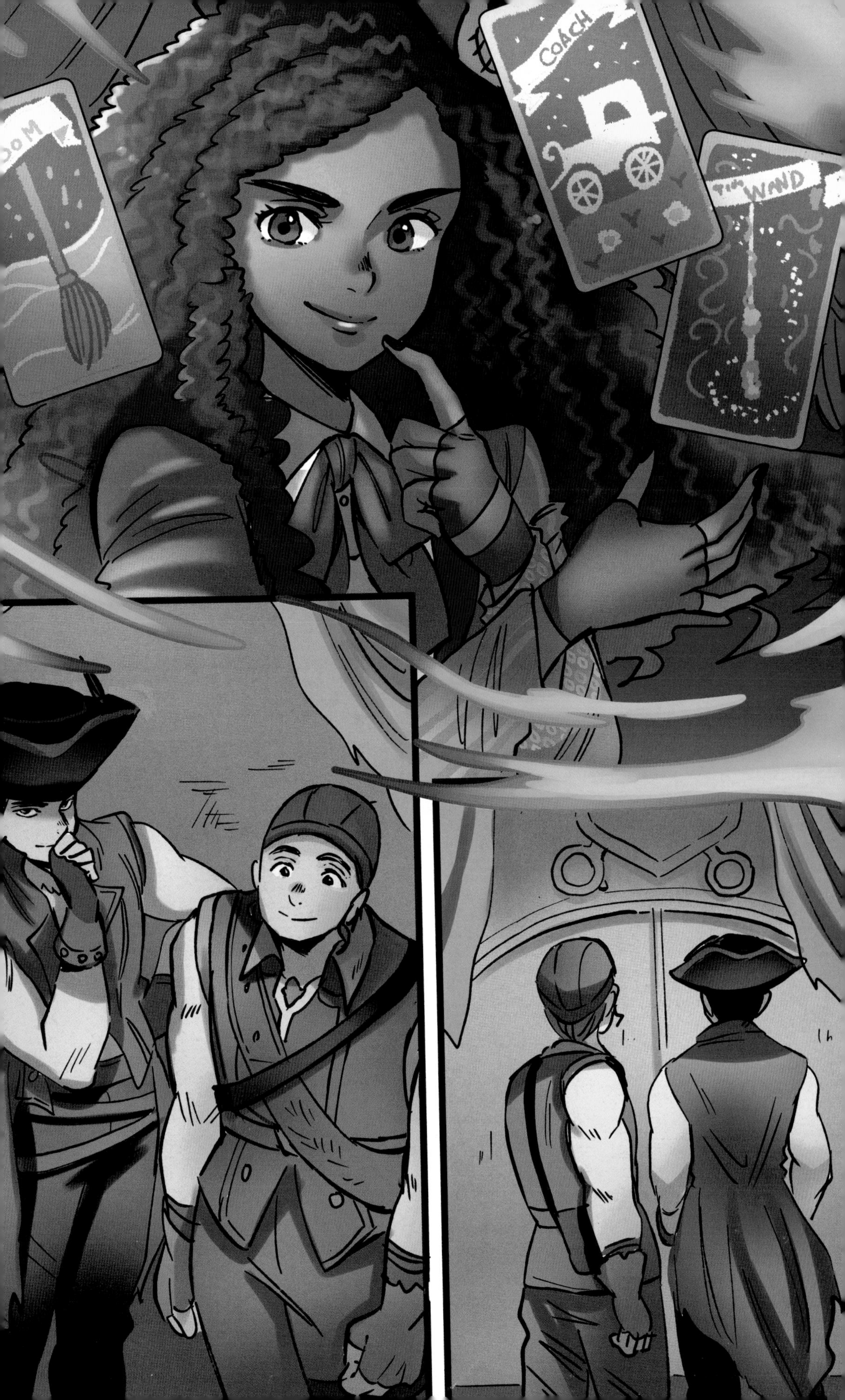
COACH
WAND

Dizzy's
NEW
FORTUNE

CHAPTER 2

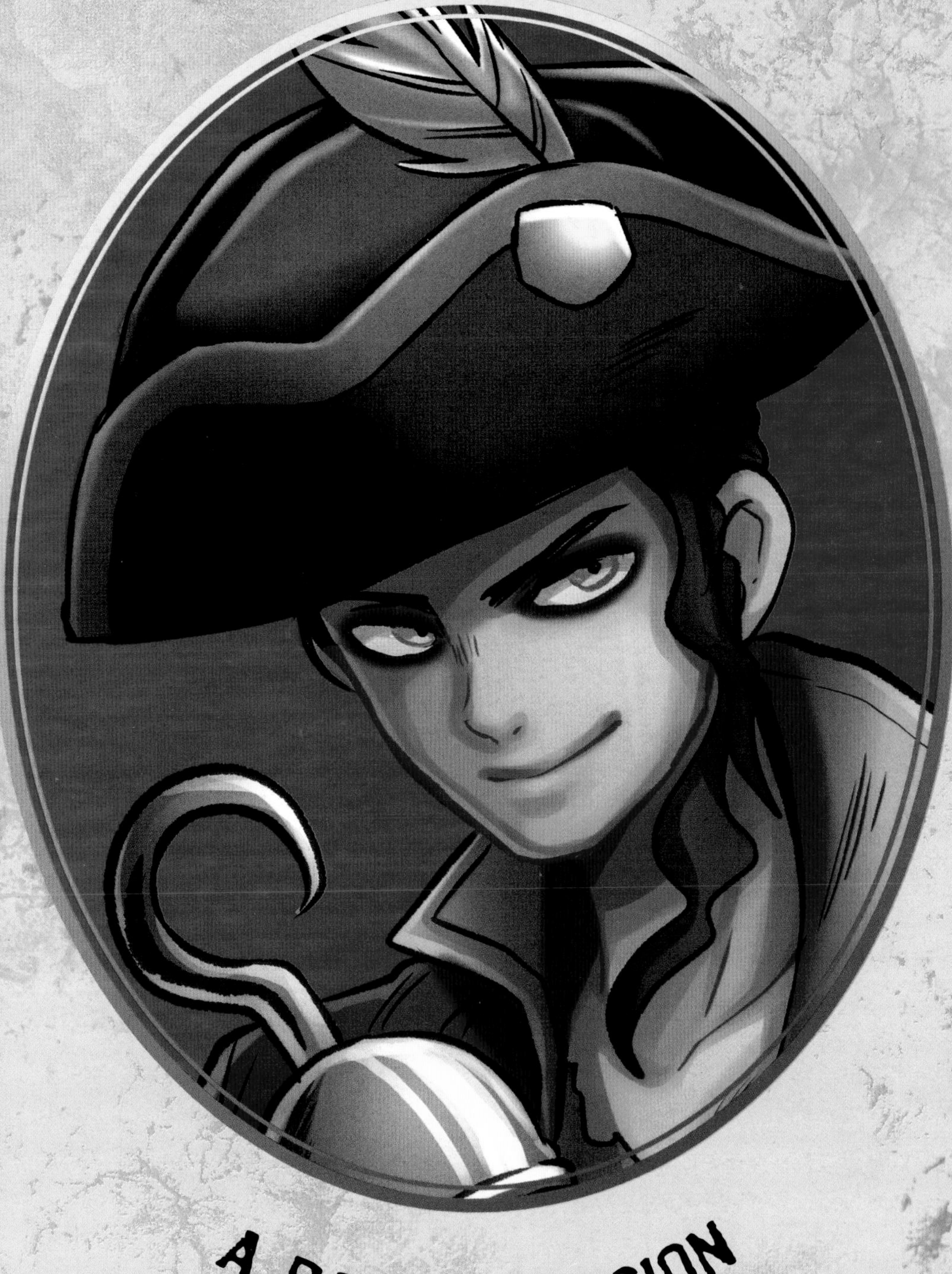

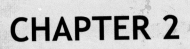

A DARING MISSION

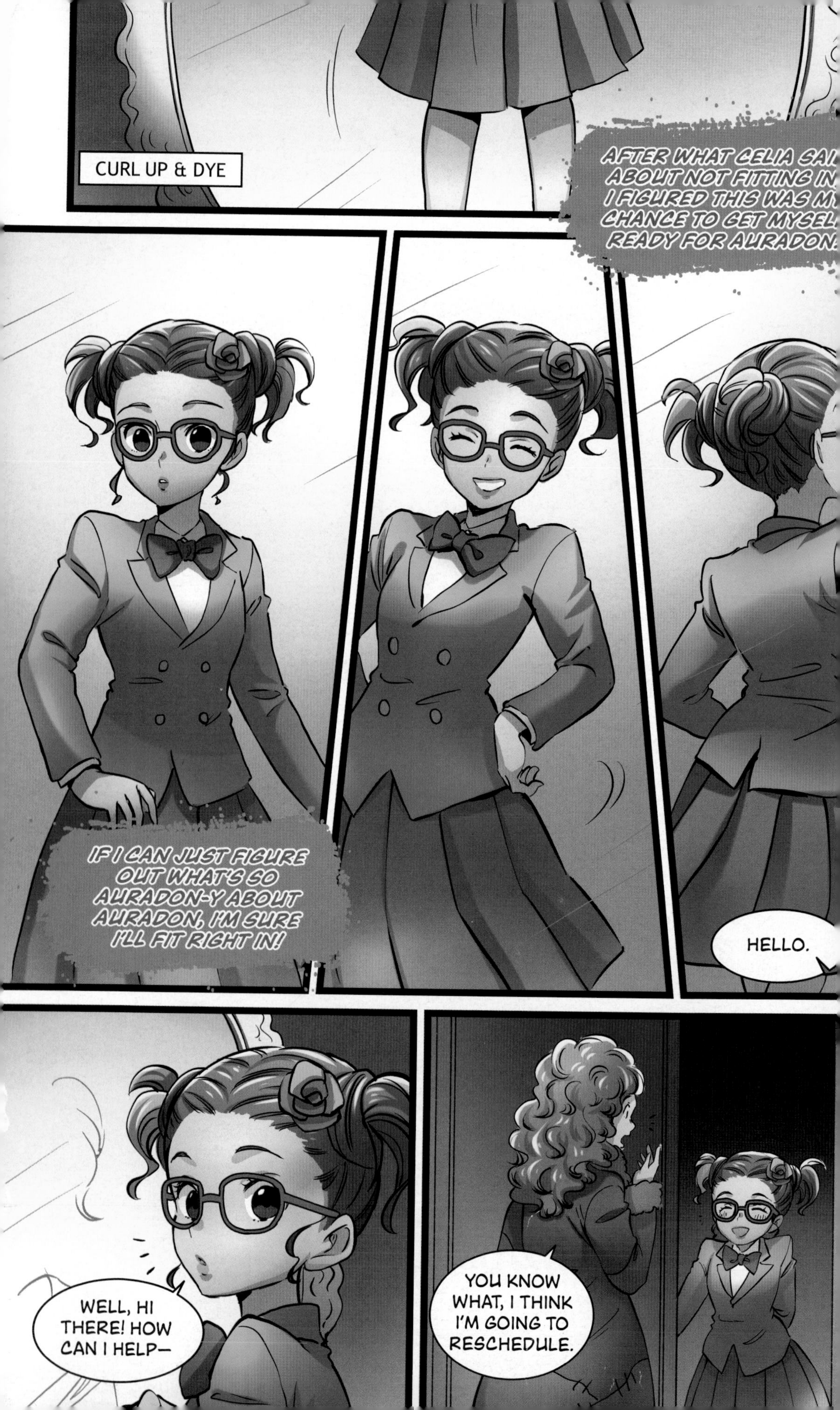

CURL UP & DYE
AFTER WHAT CELIA SAI ABOUT NOT FITTING IN I FIGURED THIS WAS M CHANCE TO GET MYSEL READY FOR AURADON.
IF I CAN JUST FIGURE OUT WHAT'S SO AURADON-Y ABOUT AURADON, I'M SURE I'LL FIT RIGHT IN!
HELLO.
WELL, HI THERE! HOW CAN I HELP—
YOU KNOW WHAT, I THINK I'M GOING TO RESCHEDULE.

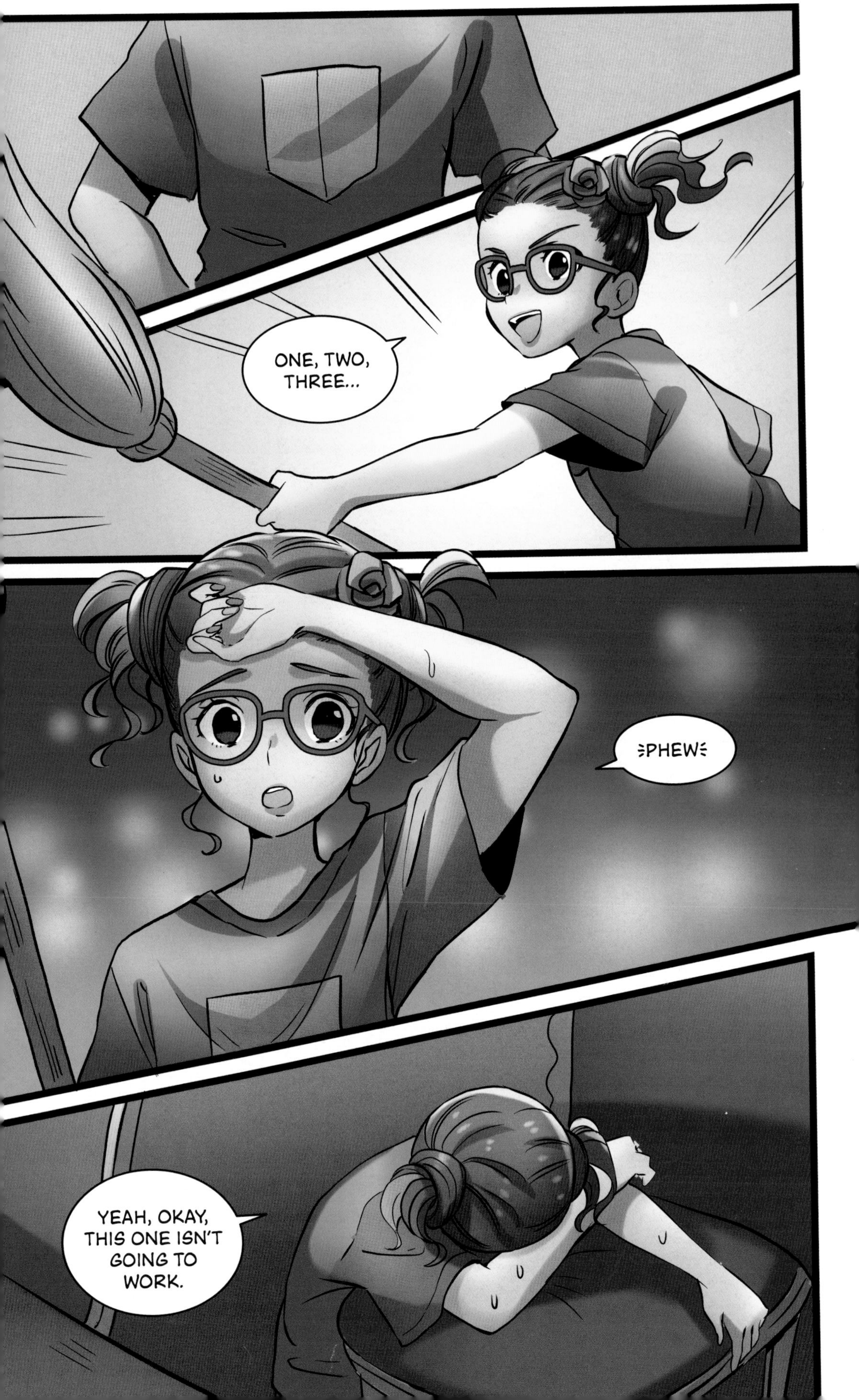
ONE, TWO, THREE...
PHEW
YEAH, OKAY, THIS ONE ISN'T GOING TO WORK.

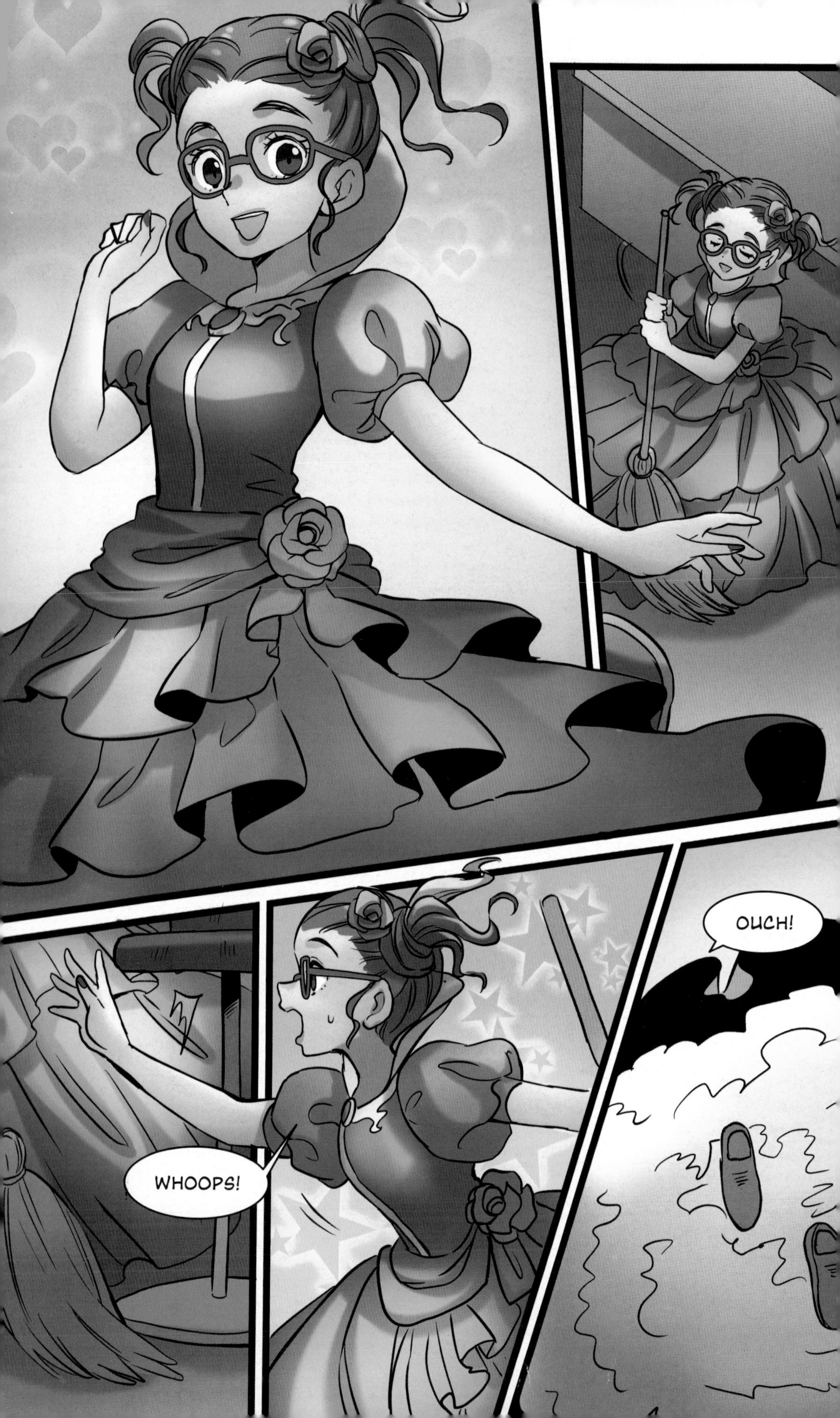
WHOOPS!
OUCH!

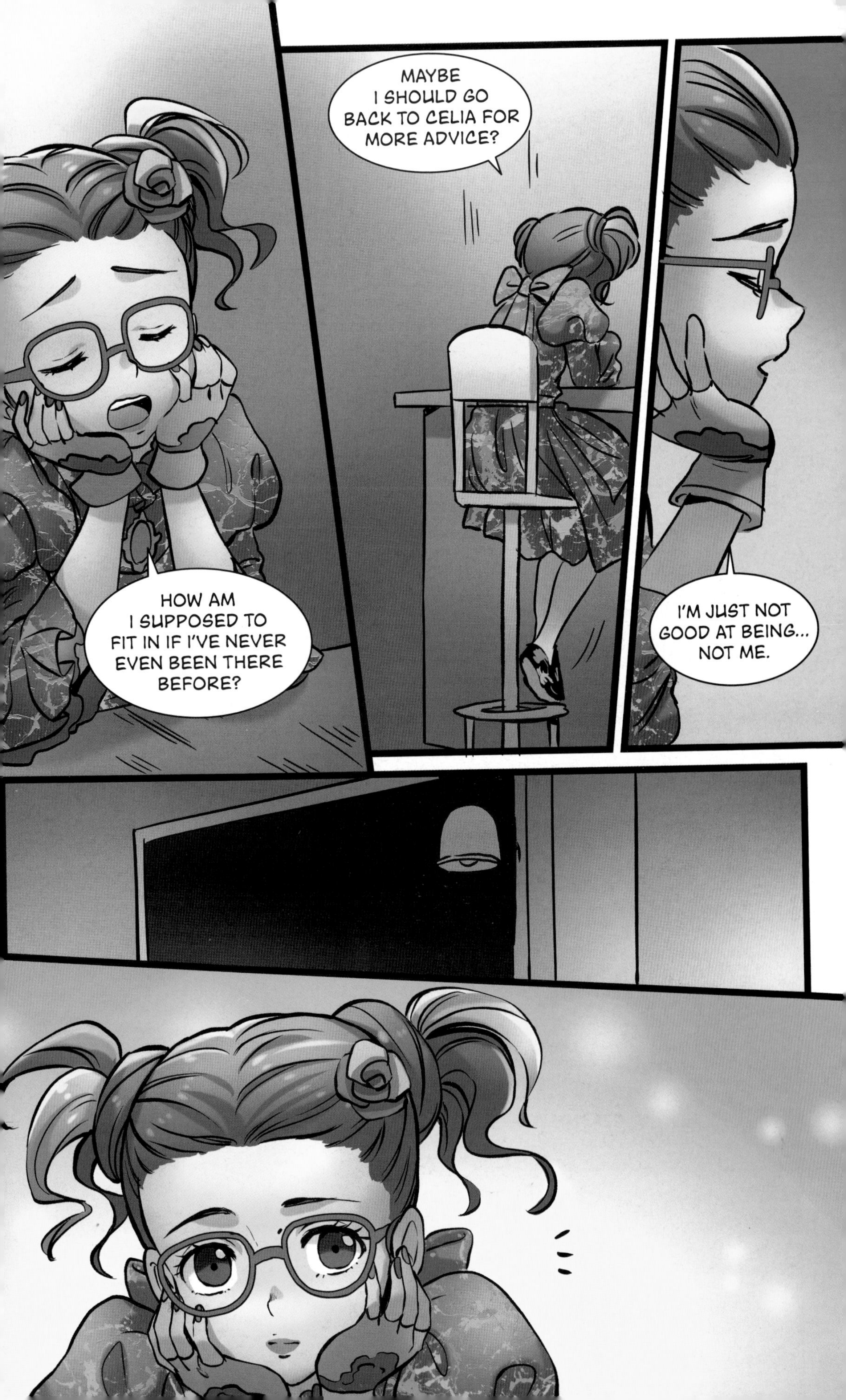
HOW AM I SUPPOSED TO FIT IN IF I'VE NEVER EVEN BEEN THERE BEFORE?
MAYBE I SHOULD GO BACK TO CELIA FOR MORE ADVICE?
I'M JUST NOT GOOD AT BEING... NOT ME.

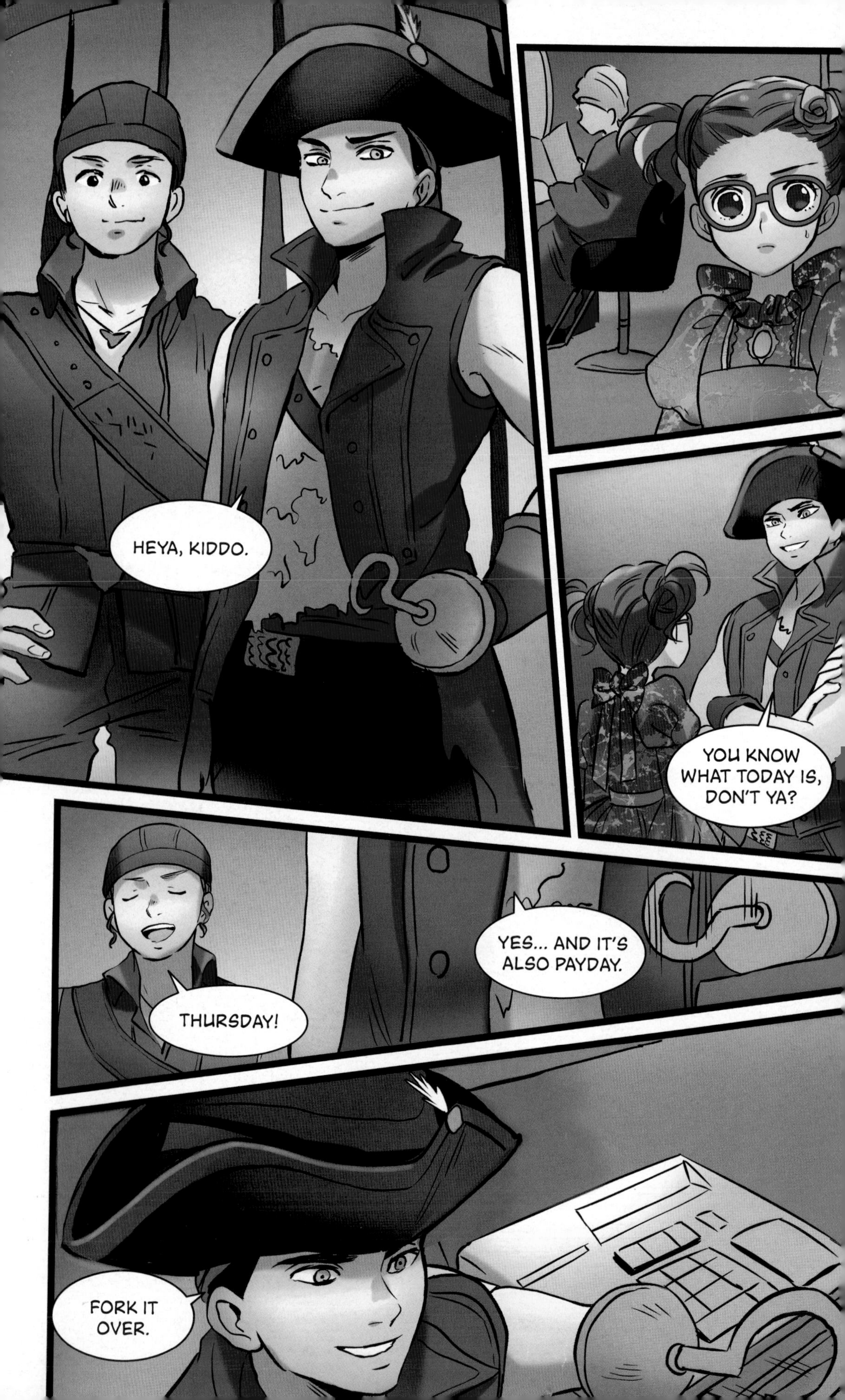
HEYA, KIDDO.
YOU KNOW WHAT TODAY IS, DON'T YA?
THURSDAY!
YES... AND IT'S ALSO PAYDAY.
FORK IT OVER.

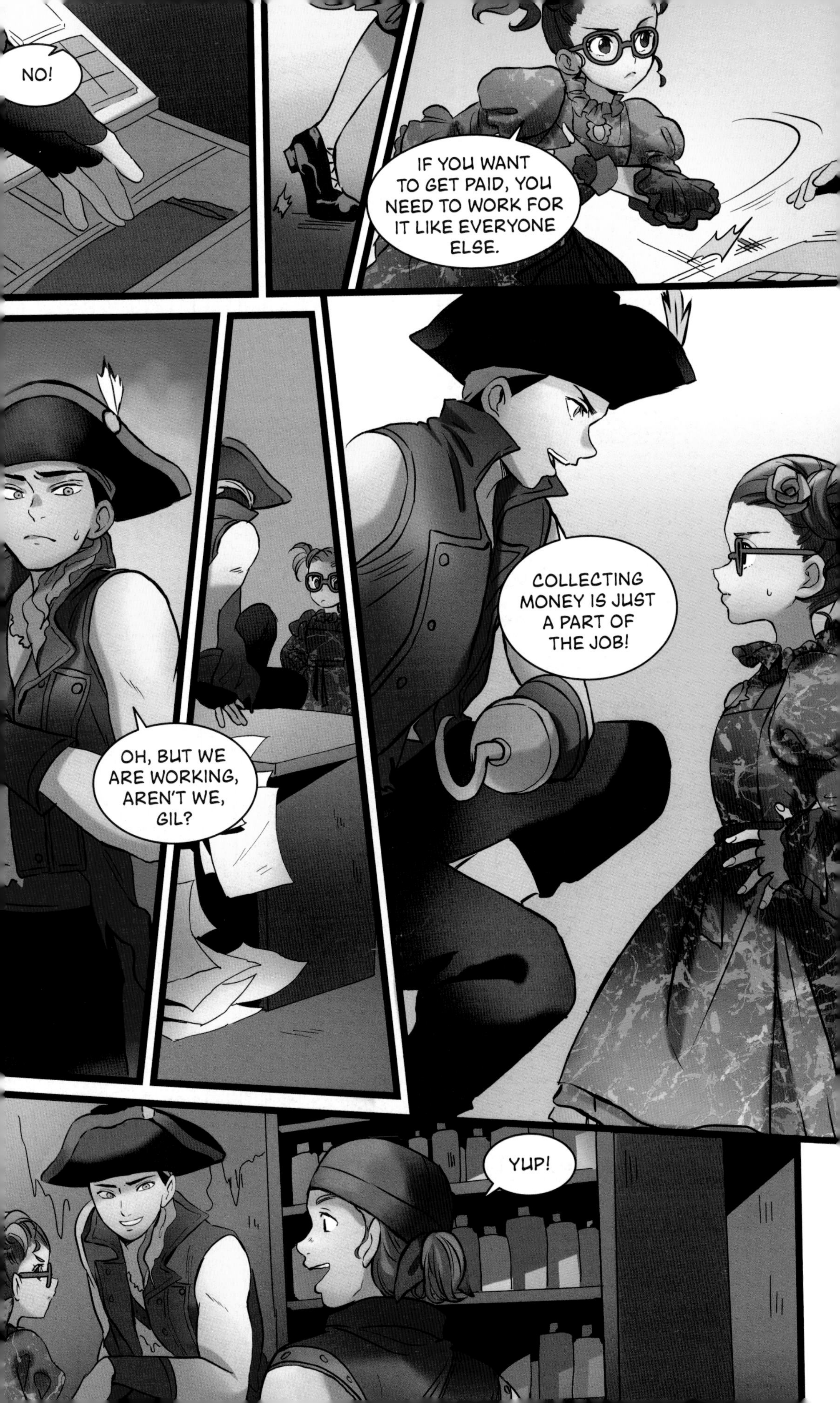
NO!
IF YOU WANT TO GET PAID, YOU NEED TO WORK FOR IT LIKE EVERYONE ELSE.
OH, BUT WE ARE WORKING, AREN'T WE, GIL?
COLLECTING MONEY IS JUST A PART OF THE JOB!
YUP!

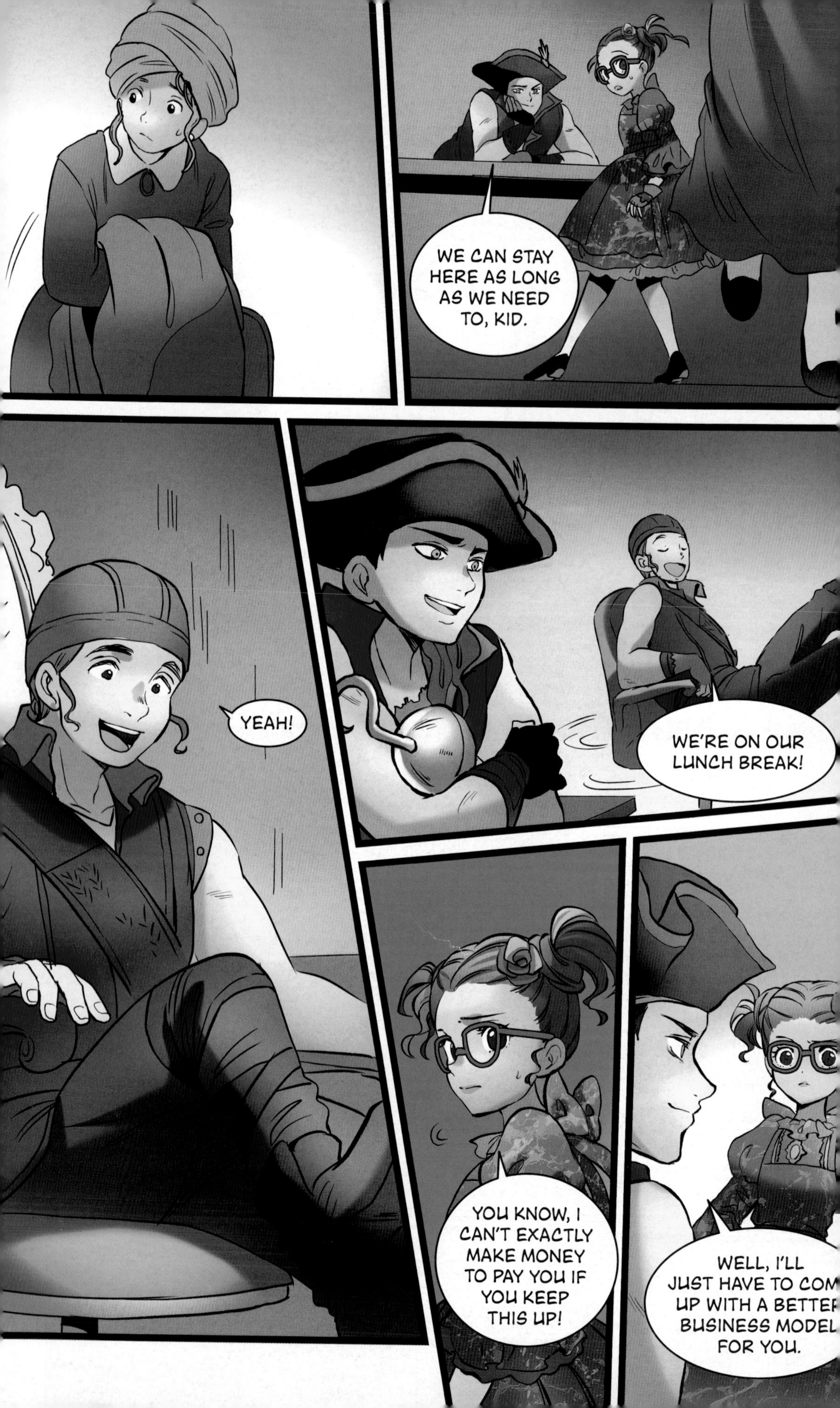

WE CAN STAY HERE AS LONG AS WE NEED TO, KID.
YEAH!
WE'RE ON OUR LUNCH BREAK!
YOU KNOW, I CAN'T EXACTLY MAKE MONEY TO PAY YOU IF YOU KEEP THIS UP!
WELL, I'LL JUST HAVE TO COM UP WITH A BETTEF BUSINESS MODEL FOR YOU.

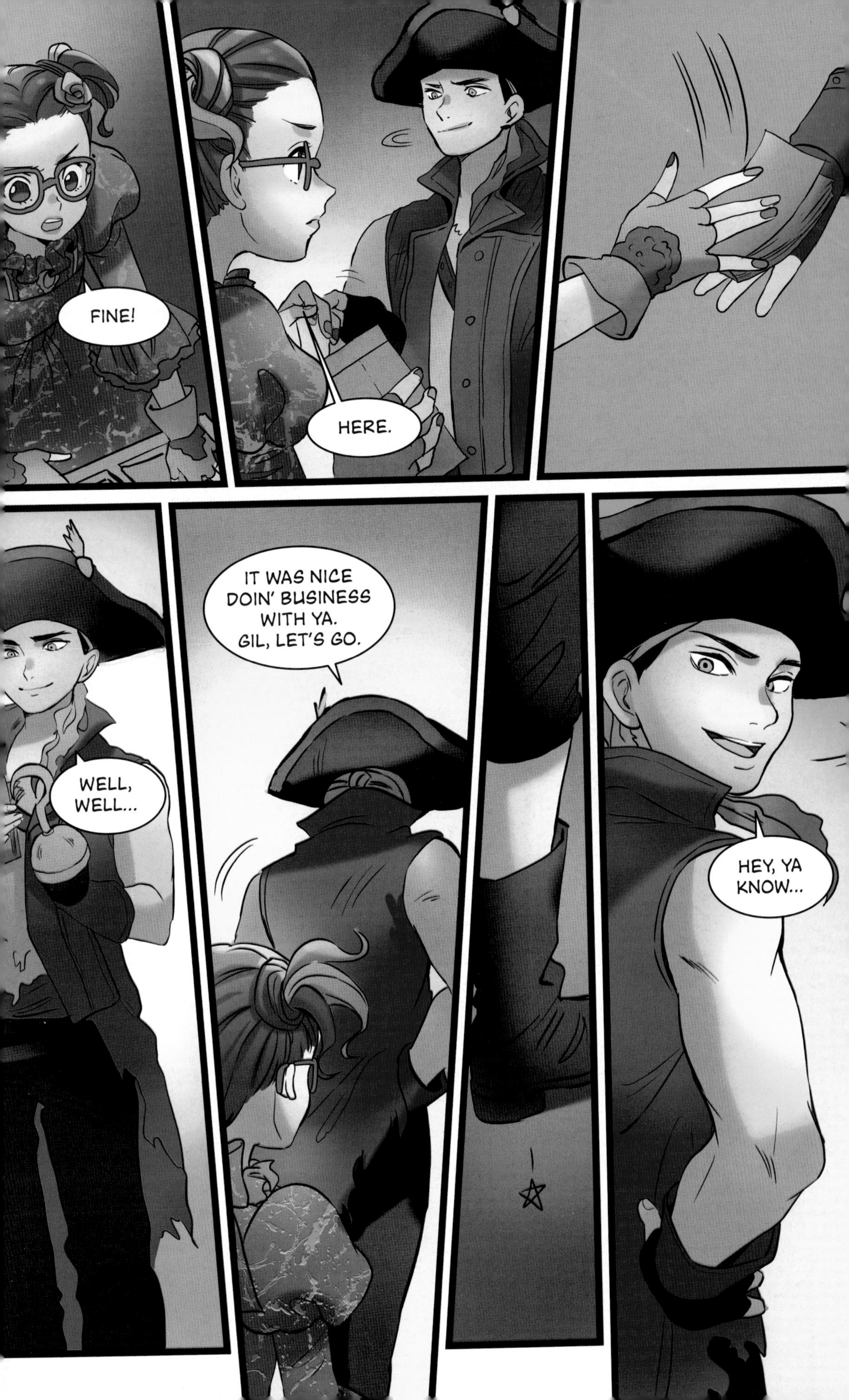
FINE!
HERE.
WELL, WELL...
IT WAS NICE DOIN' BUSINESS WITH YA. GIL, LET'S GO.
!
HEY, YA KNOW...

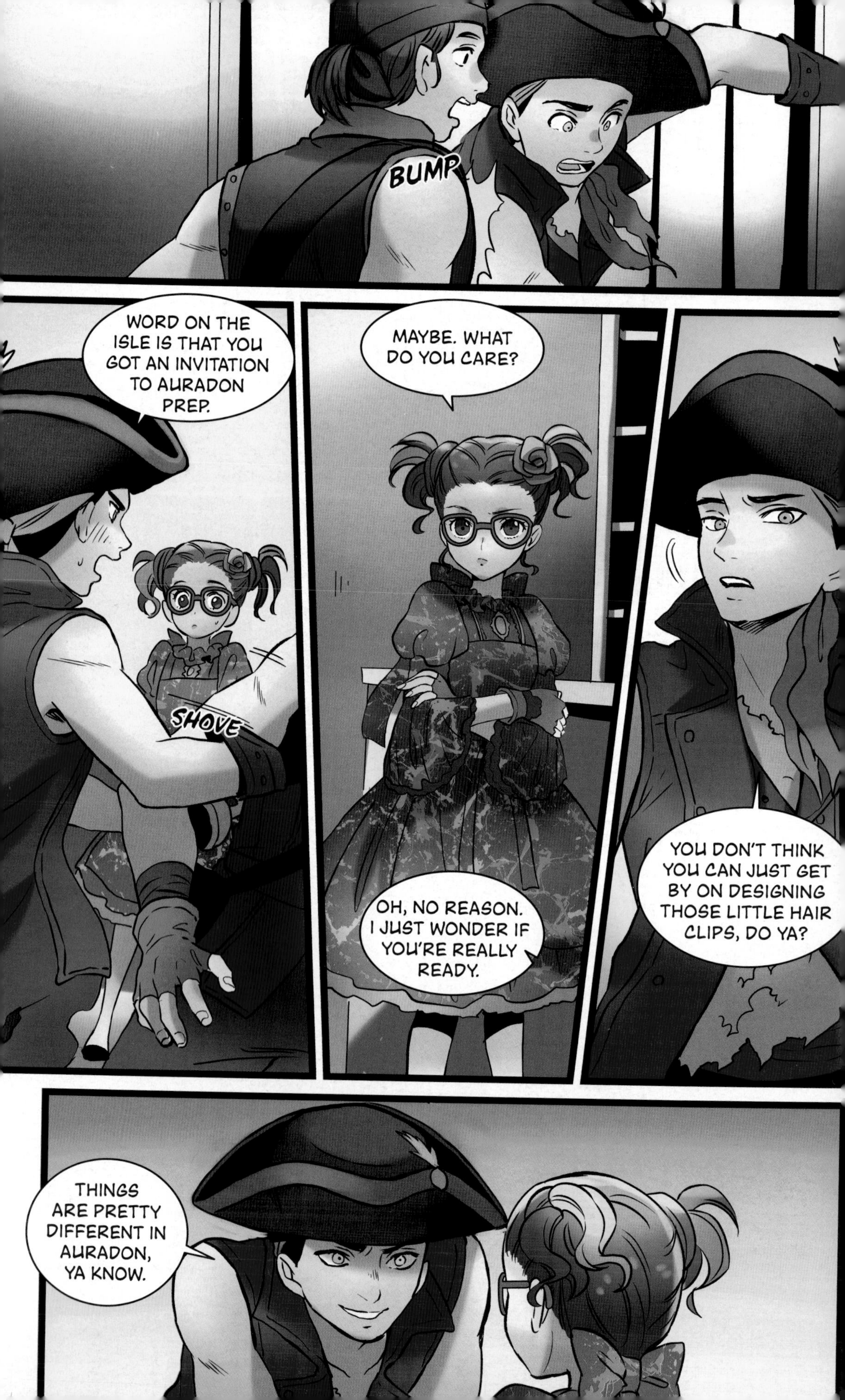
BUMP
WORD ON THE ISLE IS THAT YOU GOT AN INVITATION TO AURADON PREP.
SHOVE
MAYBE. WHAT DO YOU CARE?
OH, NO REASON. I JUST WONDER IF YOU'RE REALLY READY.
YOU DON'T THINK YOU CAN JUST GET BY ON DESIGNING THOSE LITTLE HAIR CLIPS, DO YA?
THINGS ARE PRETTY DIFFERENT IN AURADON, YA KNOW.

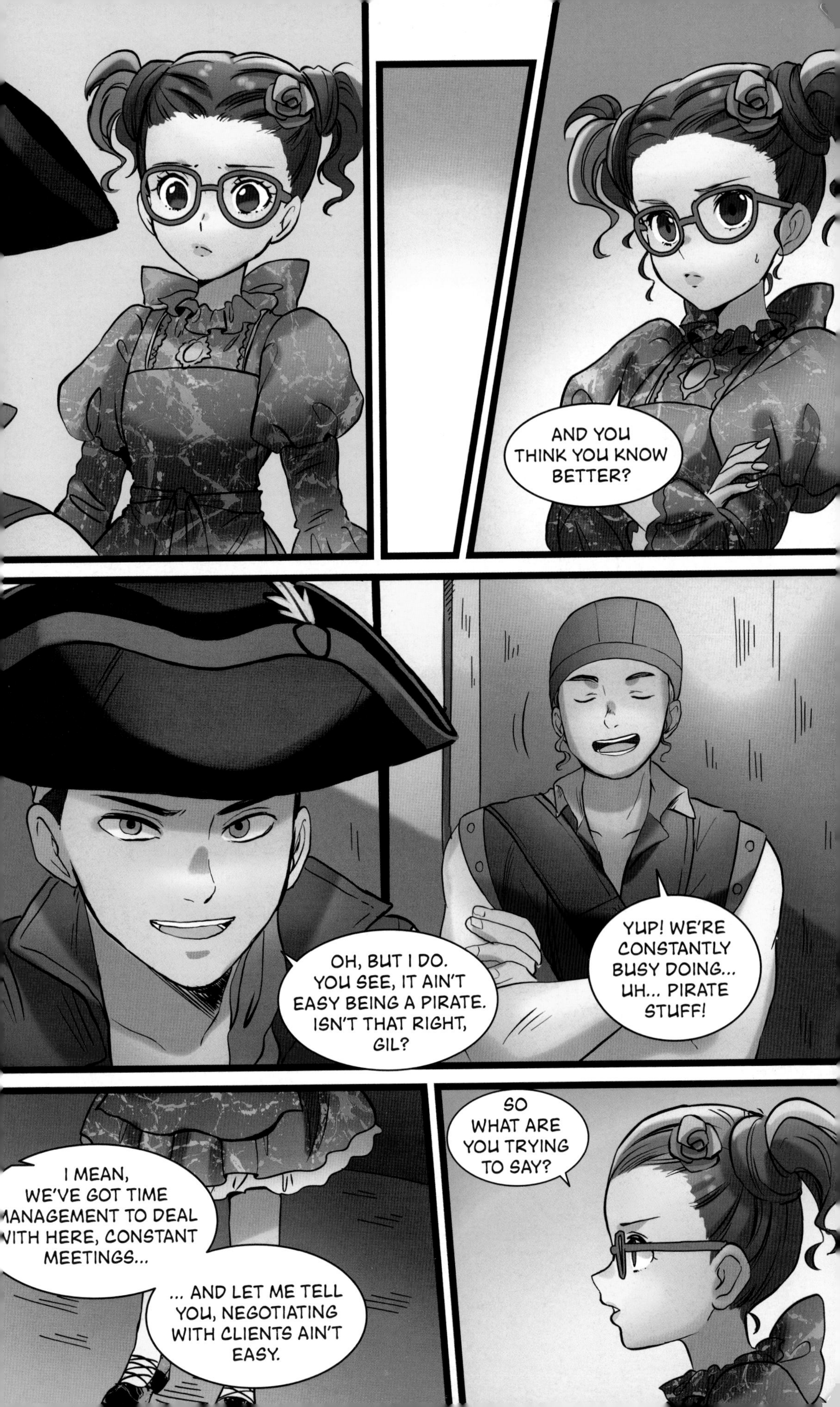
AND YOU THINK YOU KNOW BETTER?
OH, BUT I DO. YOU SEE, IT AIN'T EASY BEING A PIRATE. ISN'T THAT RIGHT, GIL?
YUP! WE'RE CONSTANTLY BUSY DOING... UH... PIRATE STUFF!
I MEAN, WE'VE GOT TIME ANAGEMENT TO DEAL ITH HERE, CONSTANT MEETINGS...
... AND LET ME TELL YOU, NEGOTIATING WITH CLIENTS AIN'T EASY.
SO WHAT ARE YOU TRYING TO SAY?

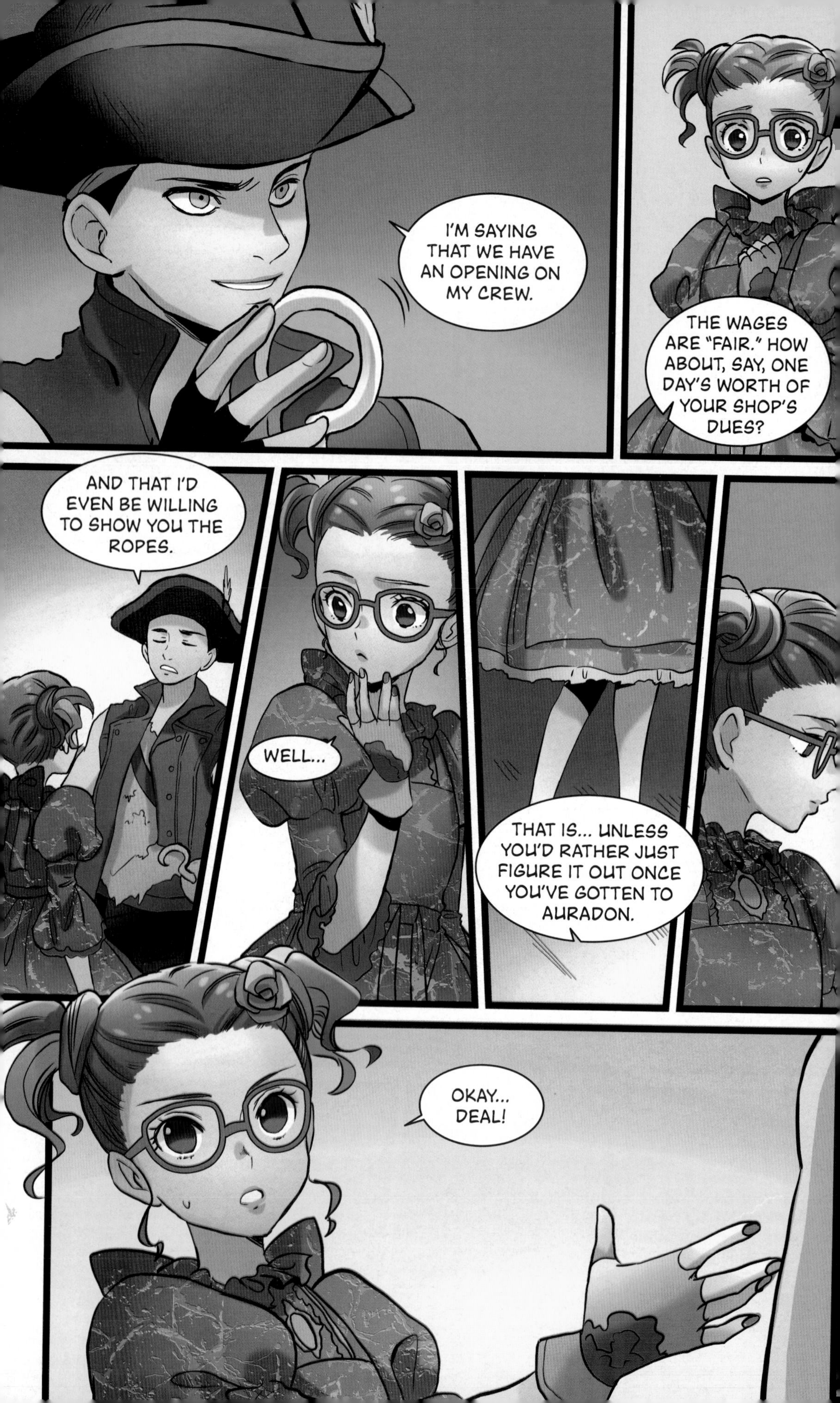
I'M SAYING THAT WE HAVE AN OPENING ON MY CREW.
THE WAGES ARE "FAIR." HOW ABOUT, SAY, ONE DAY'S WORTH OF YOUR SHOP'S DUES?
AND THAT I'D EVEN BE WILLING TO SHOW YOU THE ROPES.
WELL...
THAT IS... UNLESS YOU'D RATHER JUST FIGURE IT OUT ONCE YOU'VE GOTTEN TO AURADON.
OKAY... DEAL!

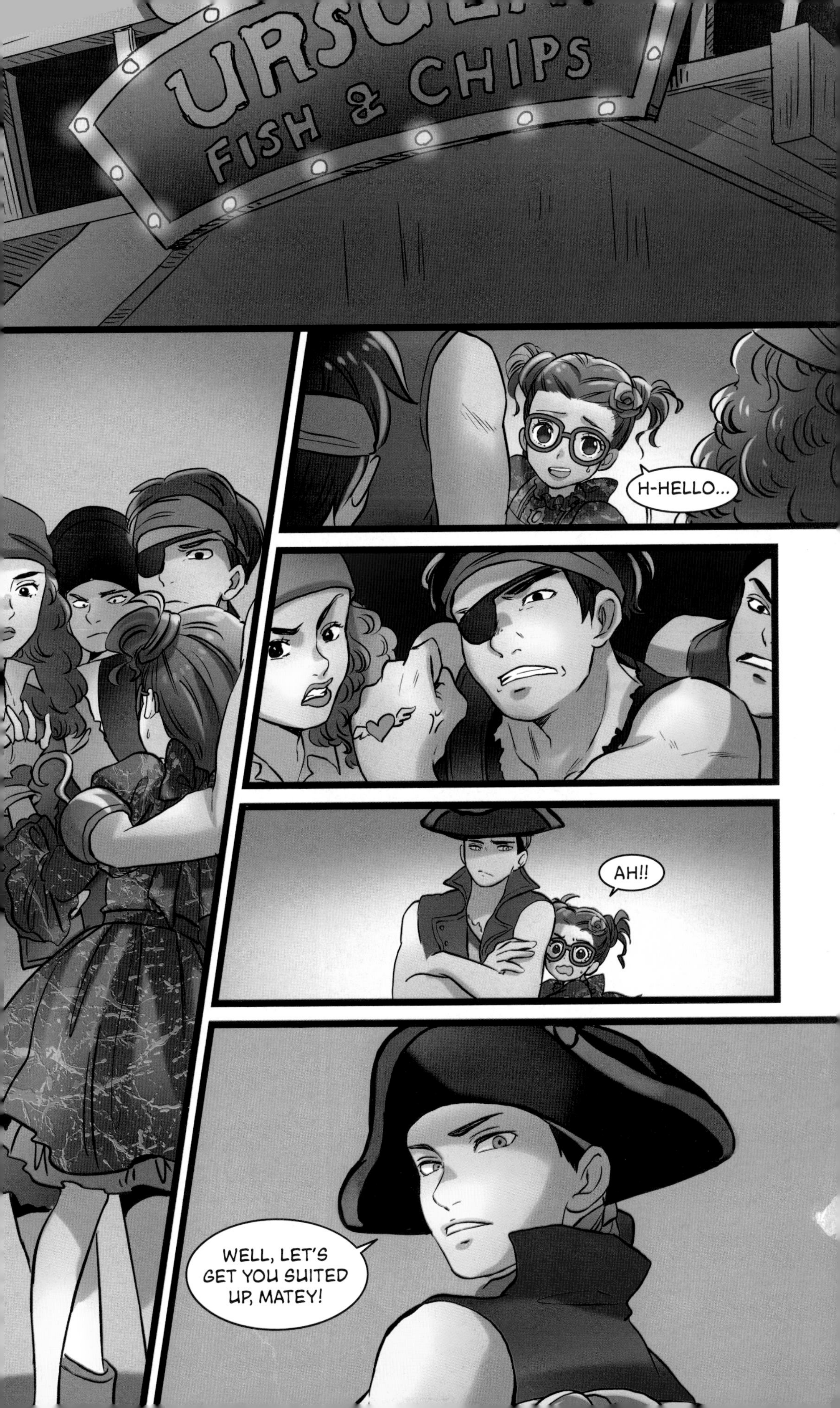
FISH & CHIPS
H-HELLO...
AH!!
WELL, LET'S GET YOU SUITED UP, MATEY!

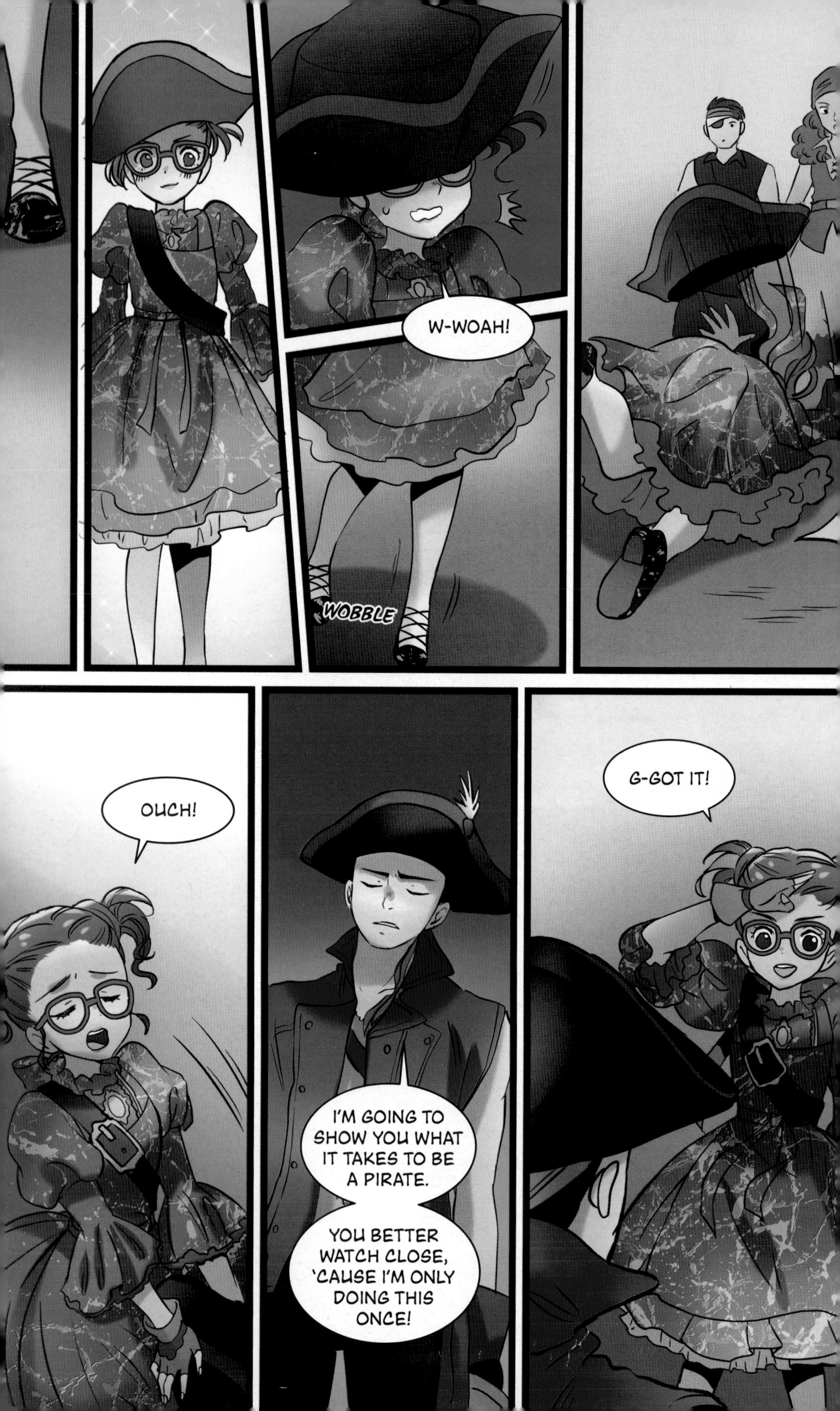
W-WOAH!
WOBBLE
OUCH!
I'M GOING TO SHOW YOU WHAT IT TAKES TO BE A PIRATE.
YOU BETTER WATCH CLOSE, 'CAUSE I'M ONLY DOING THIS ONCE!
G-GOT IT!

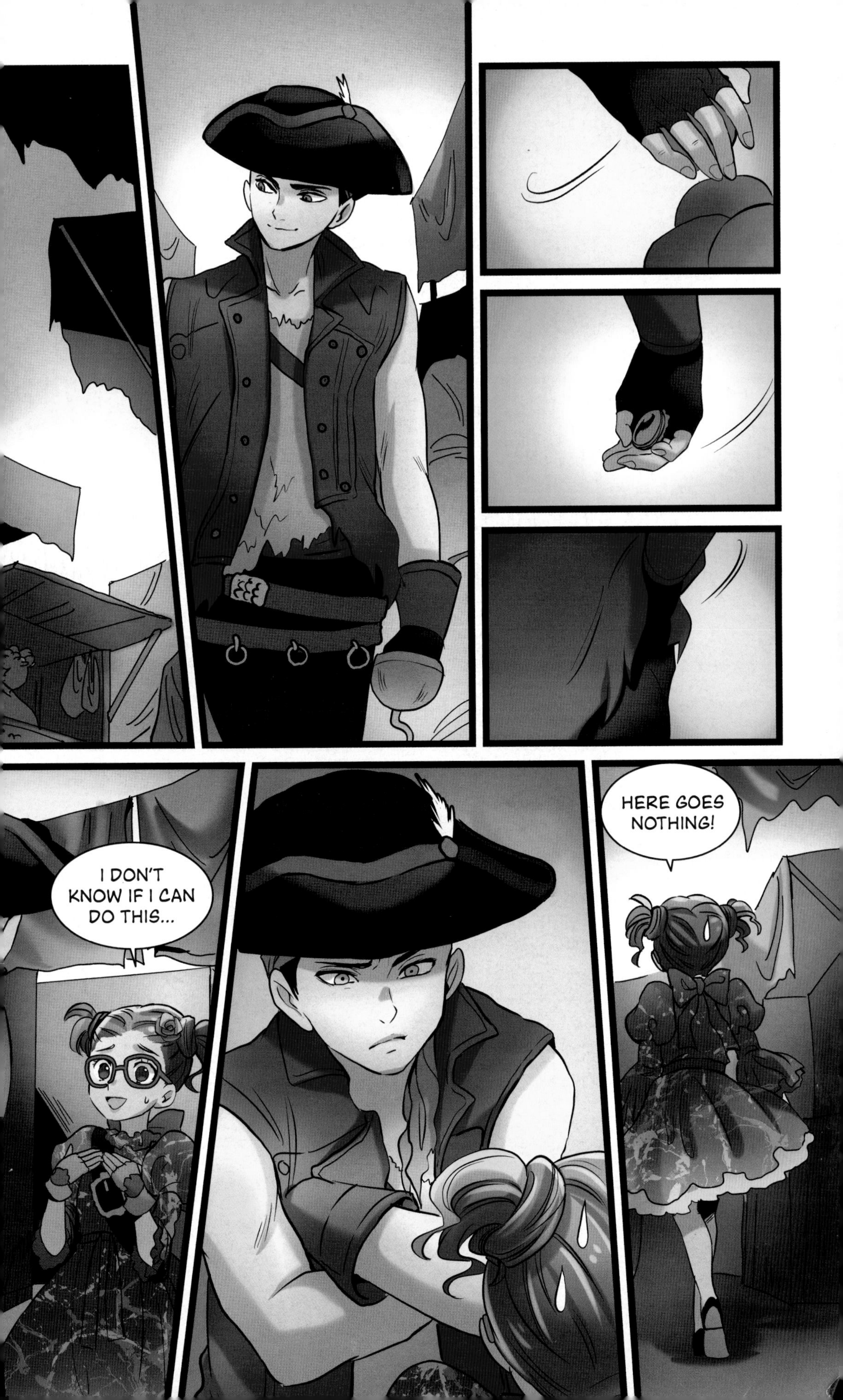
I DON'T KNOW IF I CAN DO THIS...
HERE GOES NOTHING!

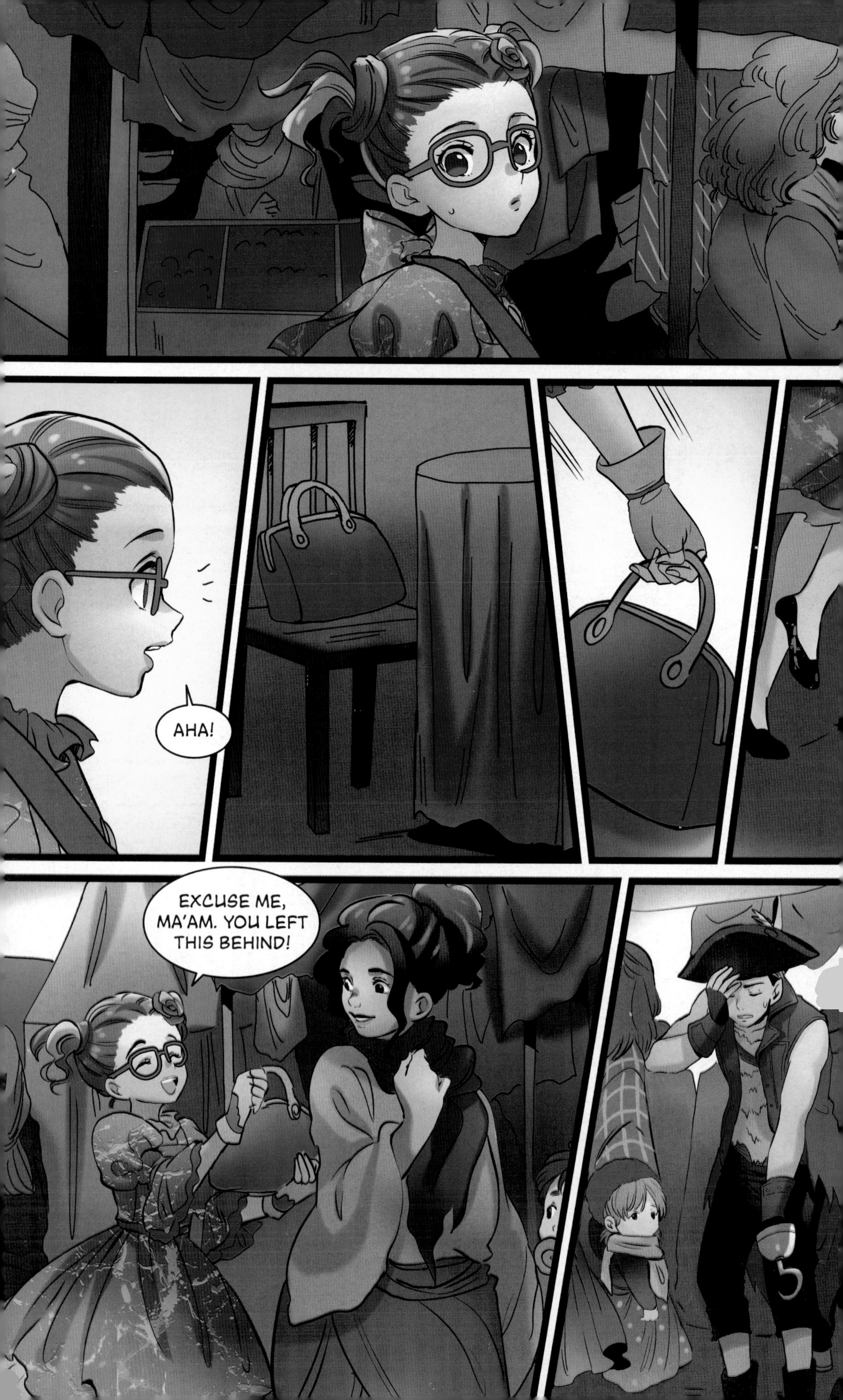
AHA!
EXCUSE ME, MA'AM. YOU LEFT THIS BEHIND!

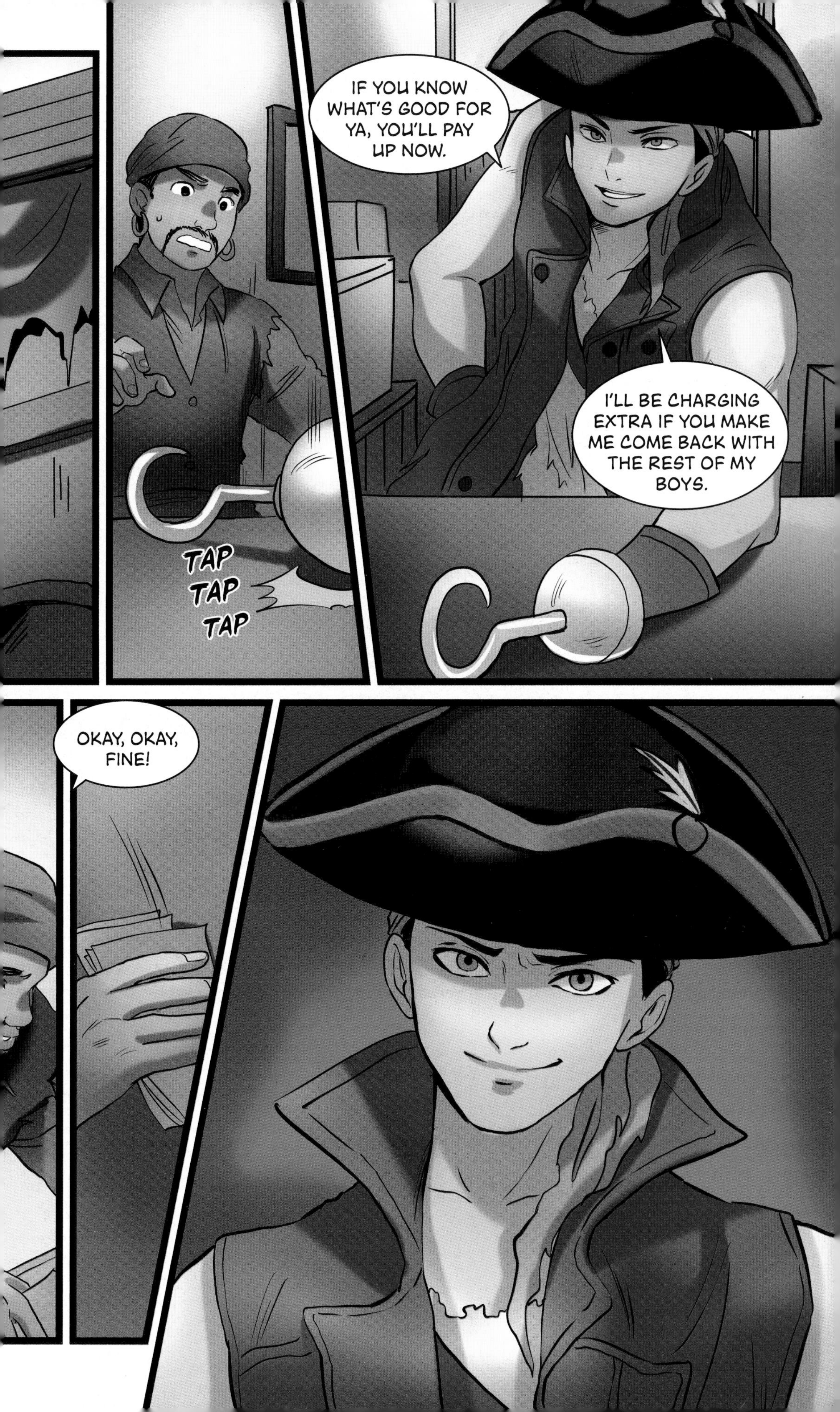

TAP
TAP
TAP
IF YOU KNOW WHAT'S GOOD FOR YA, YOU'LL PAY UP NOW.
I'LL BE CHARGING EXTRA IF YOU MAKE ME COME BACK WITH THE REST OF MY BOYS.
OKAY, OKAY, FINE!

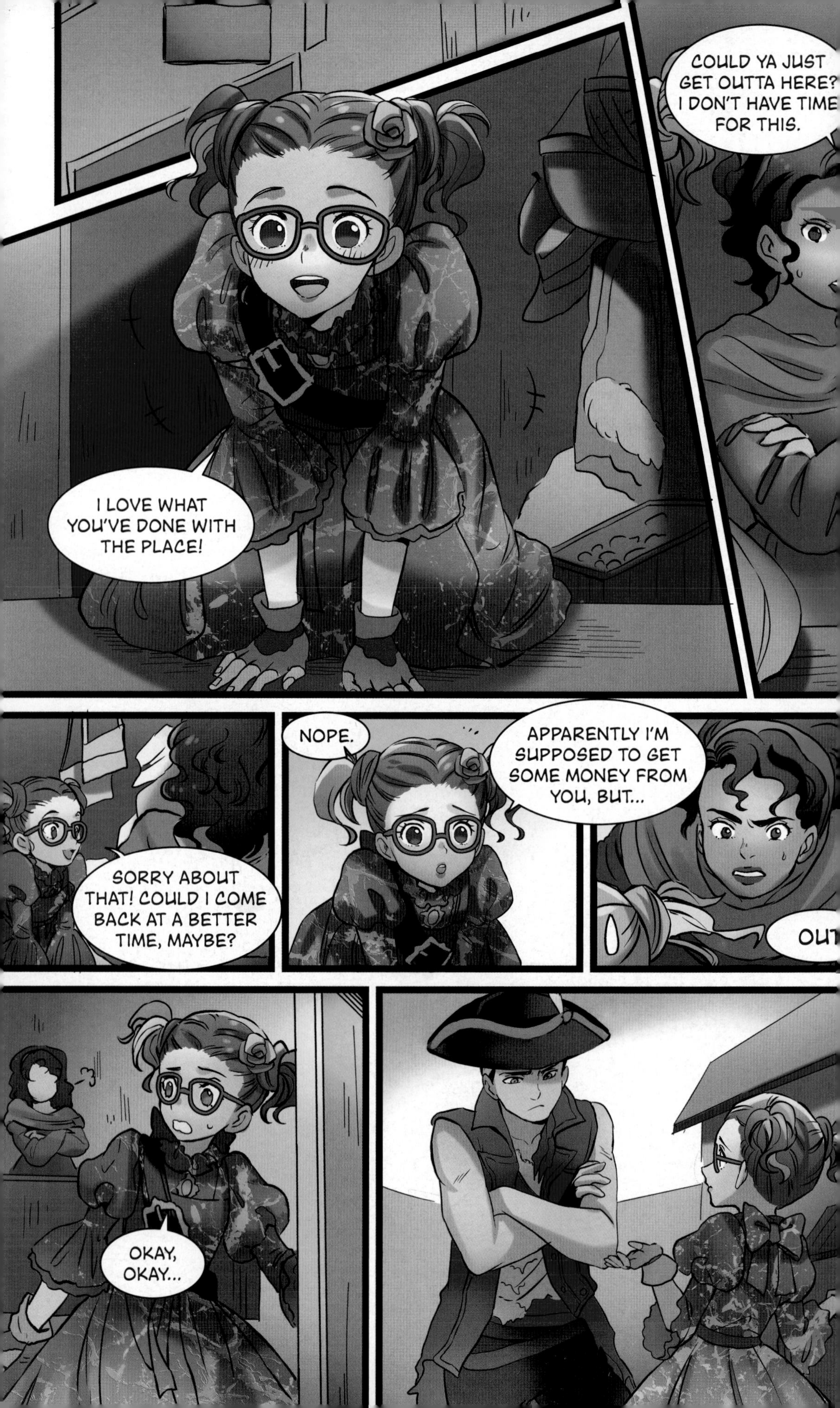
I LOVE WHAT YOU'VE DONE WITH THE PLACE!
COULD YA JUST GET OUTTA HERE? I DON'T HAVE TIME FOR THIS.
SORRY ABOUT THAT! COULD I COME BACK AT A BETTER TIME, MAYBE?
NOPE.
APPARENTLY I'M SUPPOSED TO GET SOME MONEY FROM YOU, BUT...
OUT
OKAY, OKAY...

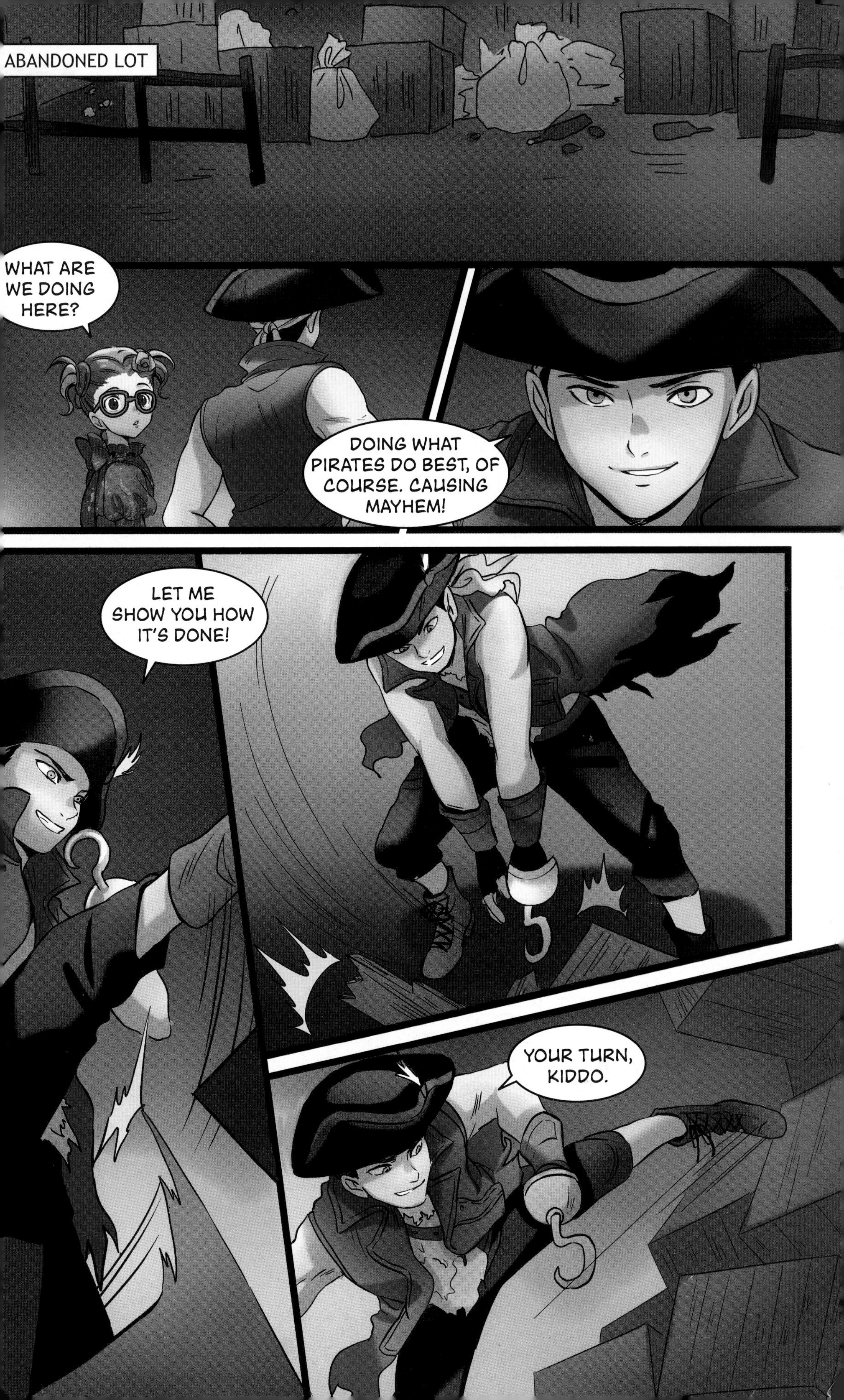
ABANDONED LOT
WHAT ARE WE DOING HERE?
DOING WHAT PIRATES DO BEST, OF COURSE. CAUSING MAYHEM!
LET ME SHOW YOU HOW IT'S DONE!
YOUR TURN, KIDDO.

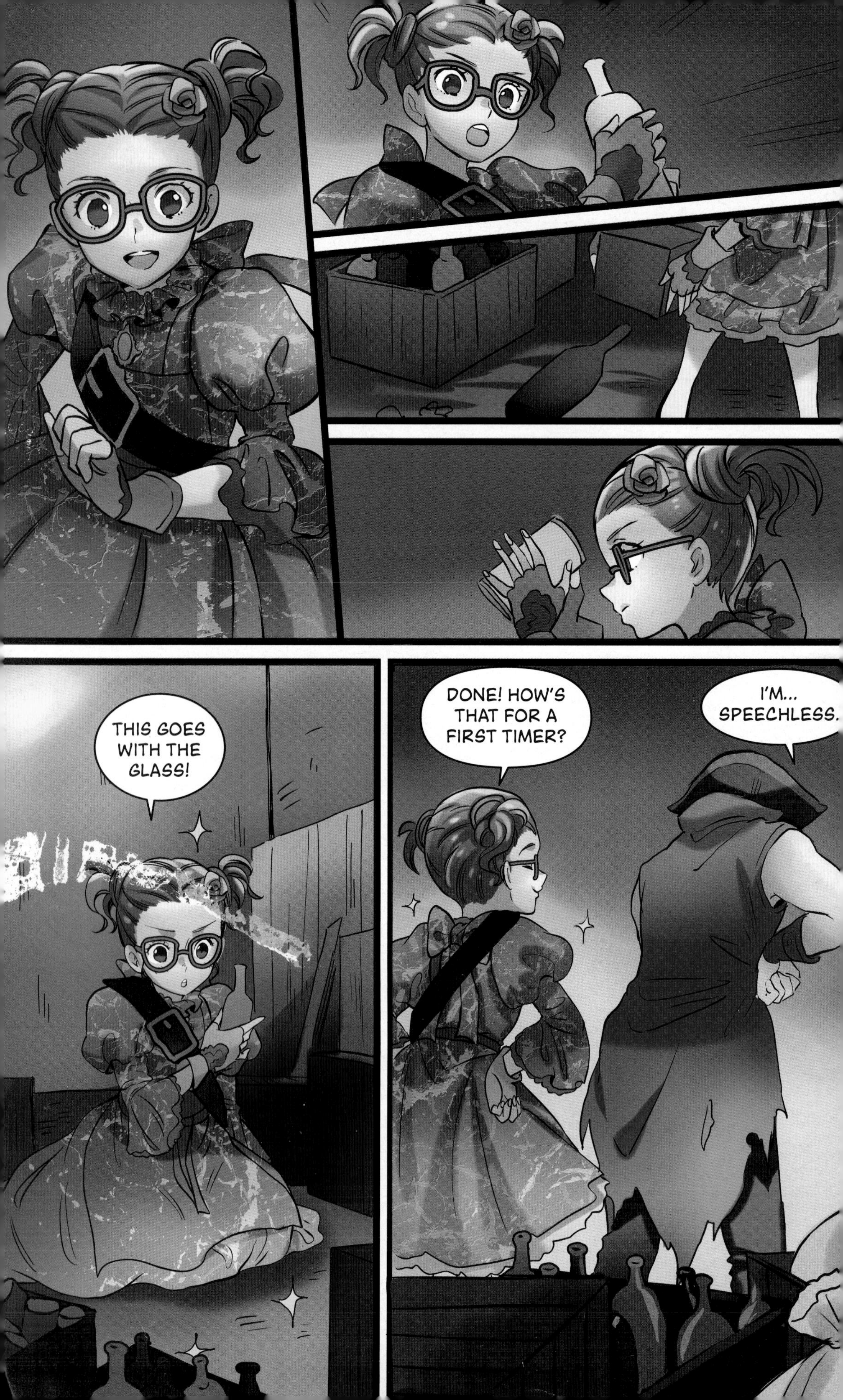
THIS GOES WITH THE GLASS!
DONE! HOW'S THAT FOR A FIRST TIMER?
I'M... SPEECHLESS.

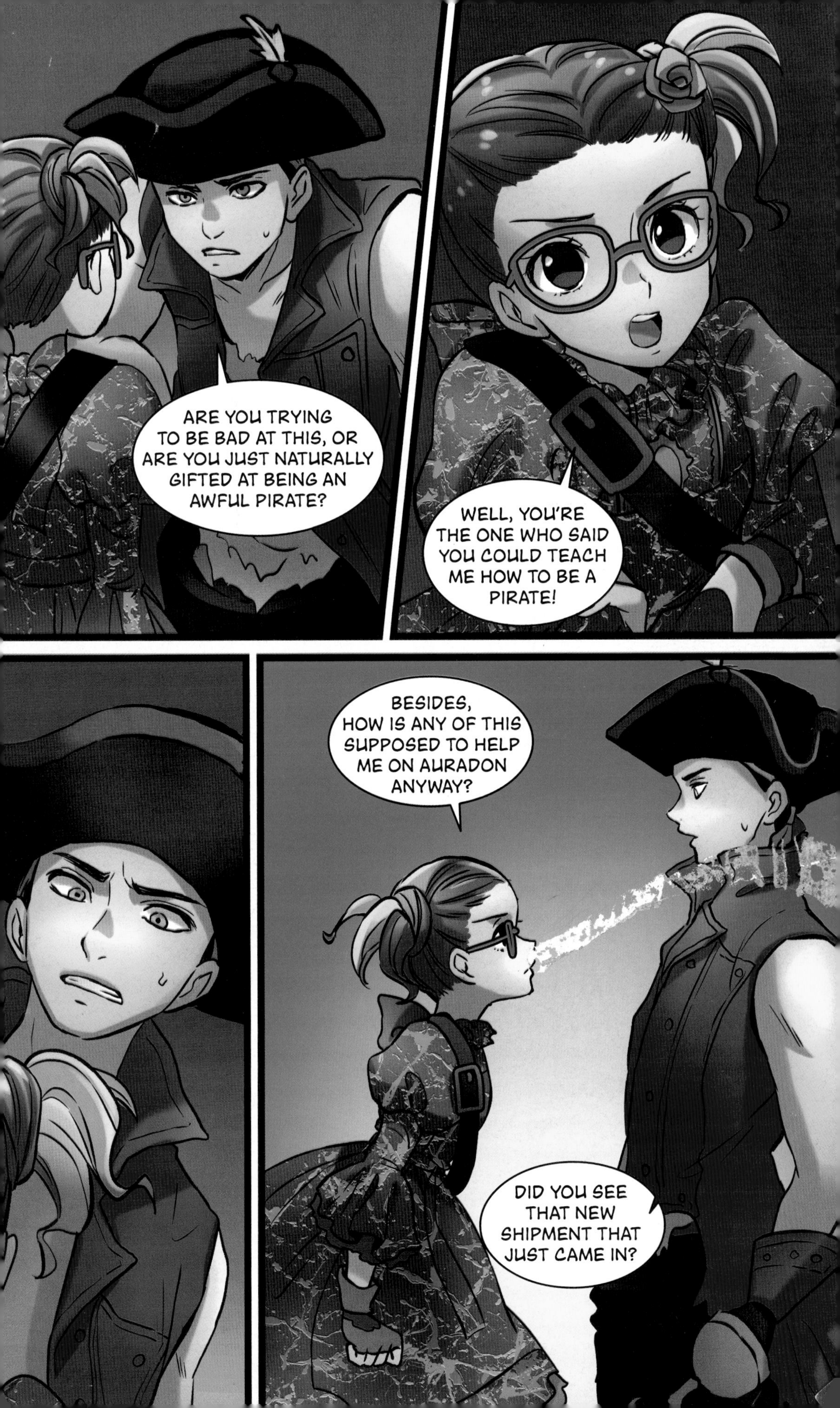
ARE YOU TRYING TO BE BAD AT THIS, OR ARE YOU JUST NATURALLY GIFTED AT BEING AN AWFUL PIRATE?
WELL, YOU'RE THE ONE WHO SAID YOU COULD TEACH ME HOW TO BE A PIRATE!
BESIDES, HOW IS ANY OF THIS SUPPOSED TO HELP ME ON AURADON ANYWAY?
DID YOU SEE THAT NEW SHIPMENT THAT JUST CAME IN?

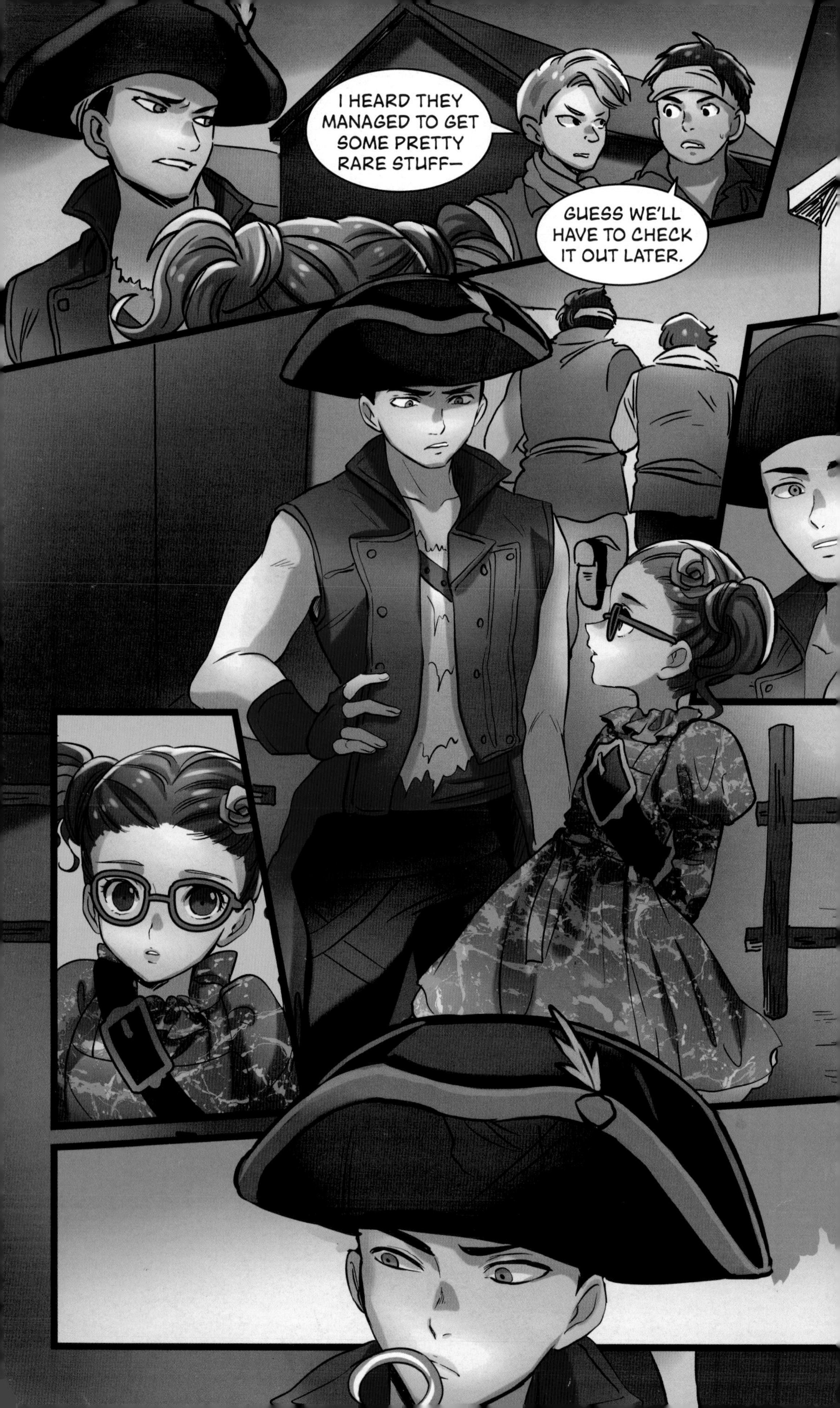
I HEARD THEY MANAGED TO GET SOME PRETTY RARE STUFF—
GUESS WE'LL HAVE TO CHECK IT OUT LATER.

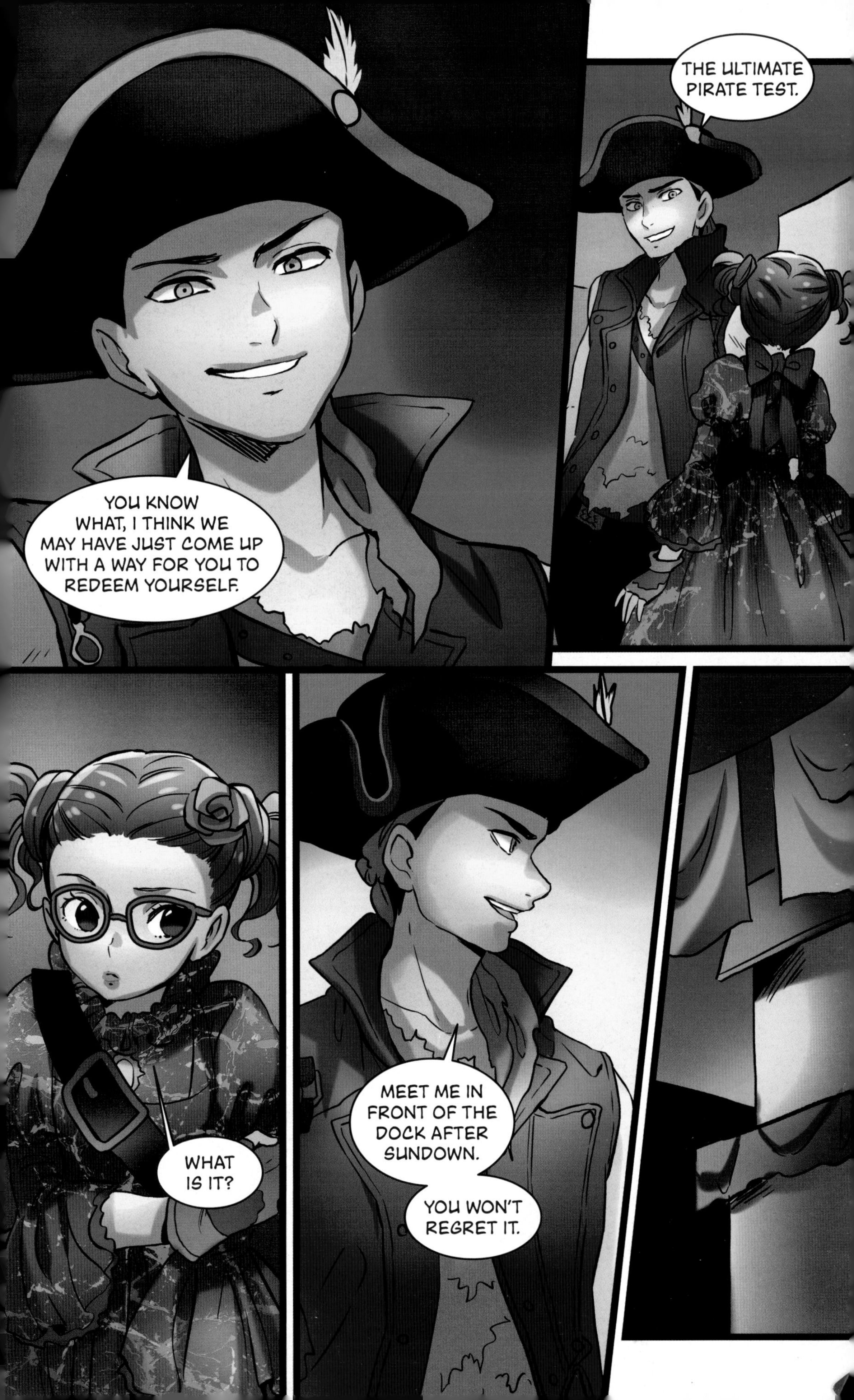
YOU KNOW WHAT, I THINK WE MAY HAVE JUST COME UP WITH A WAY FOR YOU TO REDEEM YOURSELF.
THE ULTIMATE PIRATE TEST.
WHAT IS IT?
MEET ME IN FRONT OF THE DOCK AFTER SUNDOWN.
YOU WON'T REGRET IT.

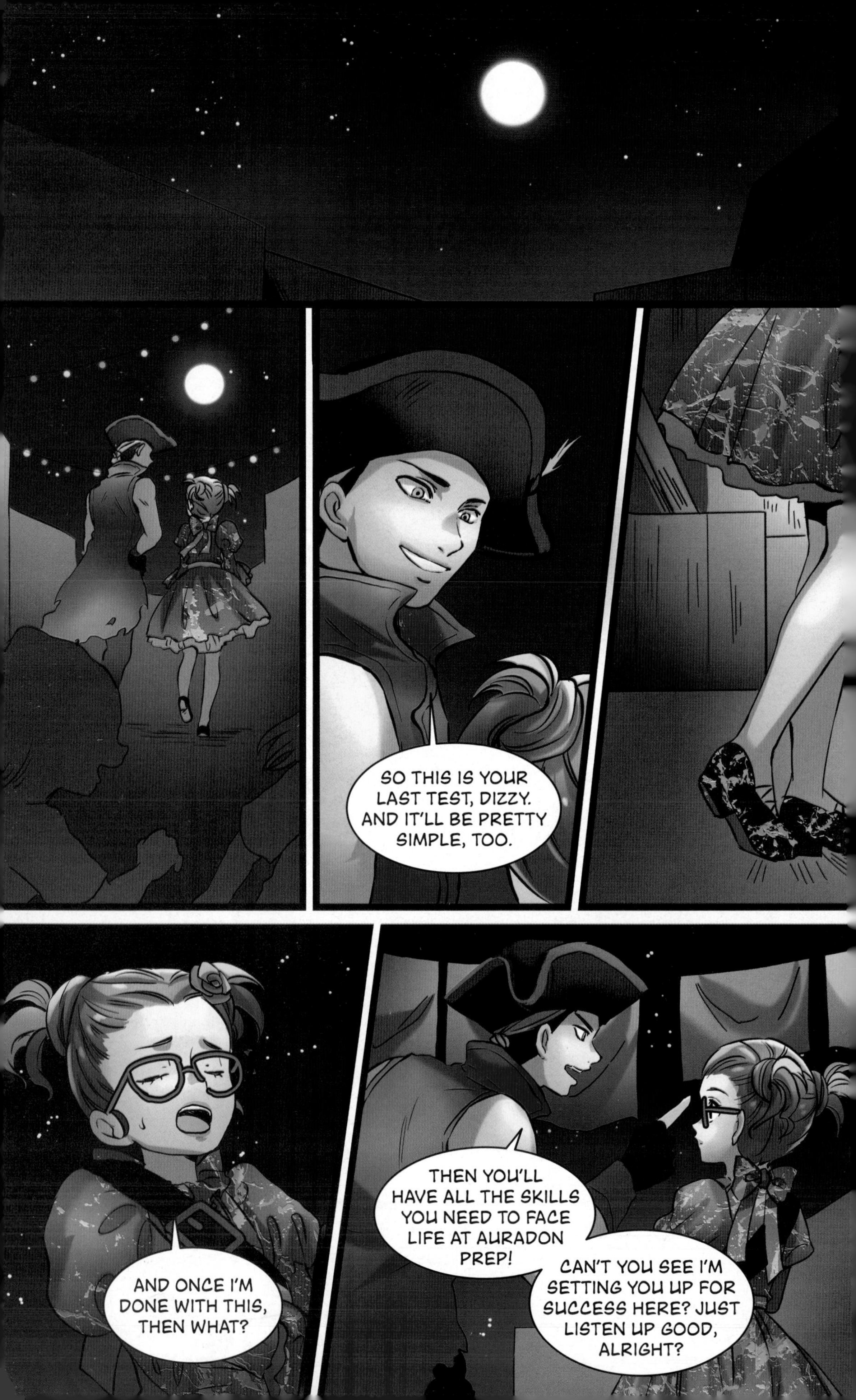
SO THIS IS YOUR LAST TEST, DIZZY. AND IT'LL BE PRETTY SIMPLE, TOO.
AND ONCE I'M DONE WITH THIS, THEN WHAT?
THEN YOU'LL HAVE ALL THE SKILLS YOU NEED TO FACE LIFE AT AURADON PREP!
CAN'T YOU SEE I'M SETTING YOU UP FOR SUCCESS HERE? JUST LISTEN UP GOOD, ALRIGHT?

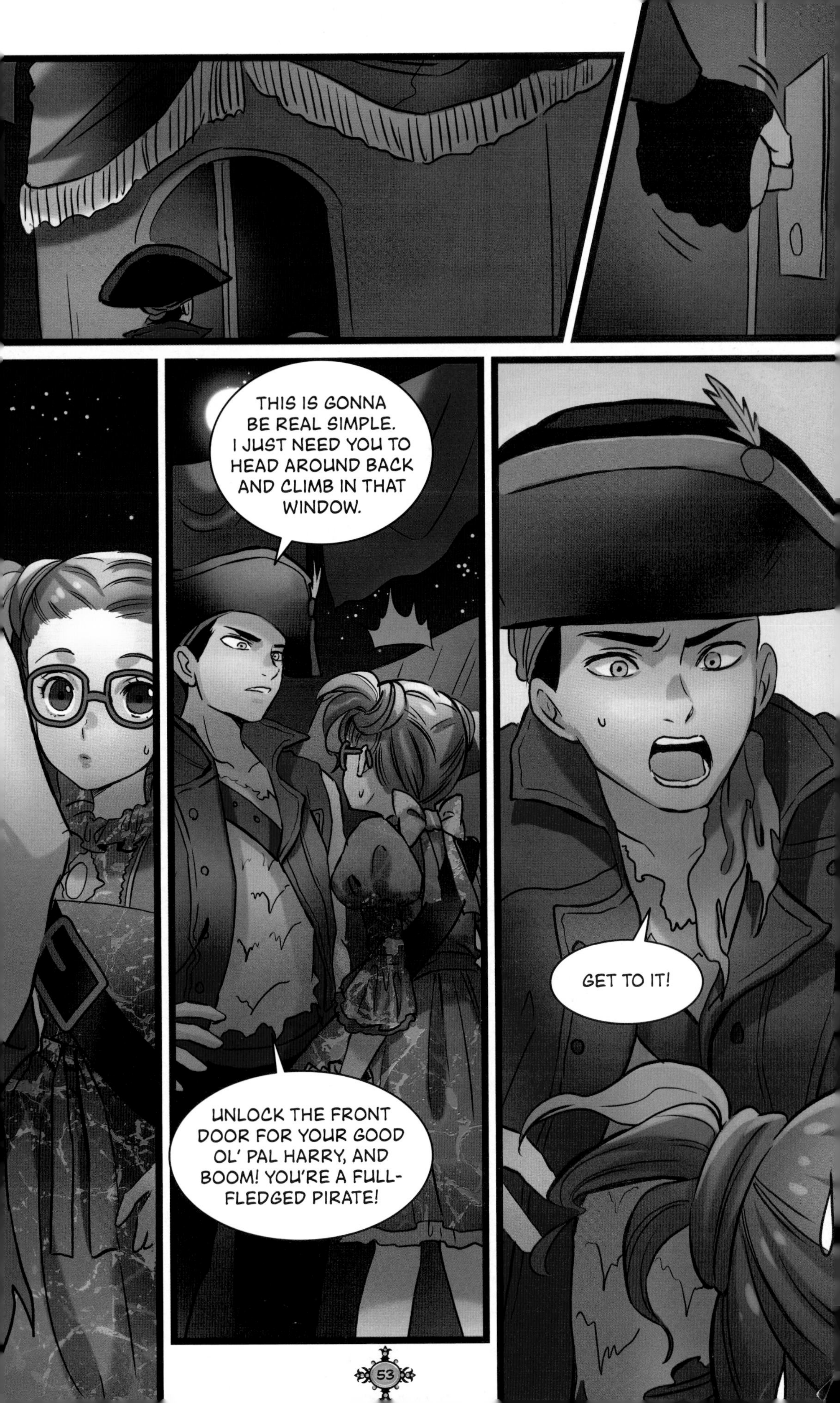
THIS IS GONNA BE REAL SIMPLE. I JUST NEED YOU TO HEAD AROUND BACK AND CLIMB IN THAT WINDOW.
UNLOCK THE FRONT DOOR FOR YOUR GOOD OL' PAL HARRY, AND BOOM! YOU'RE A FULL-FLEDGED PIRATE!
GET TO IT!

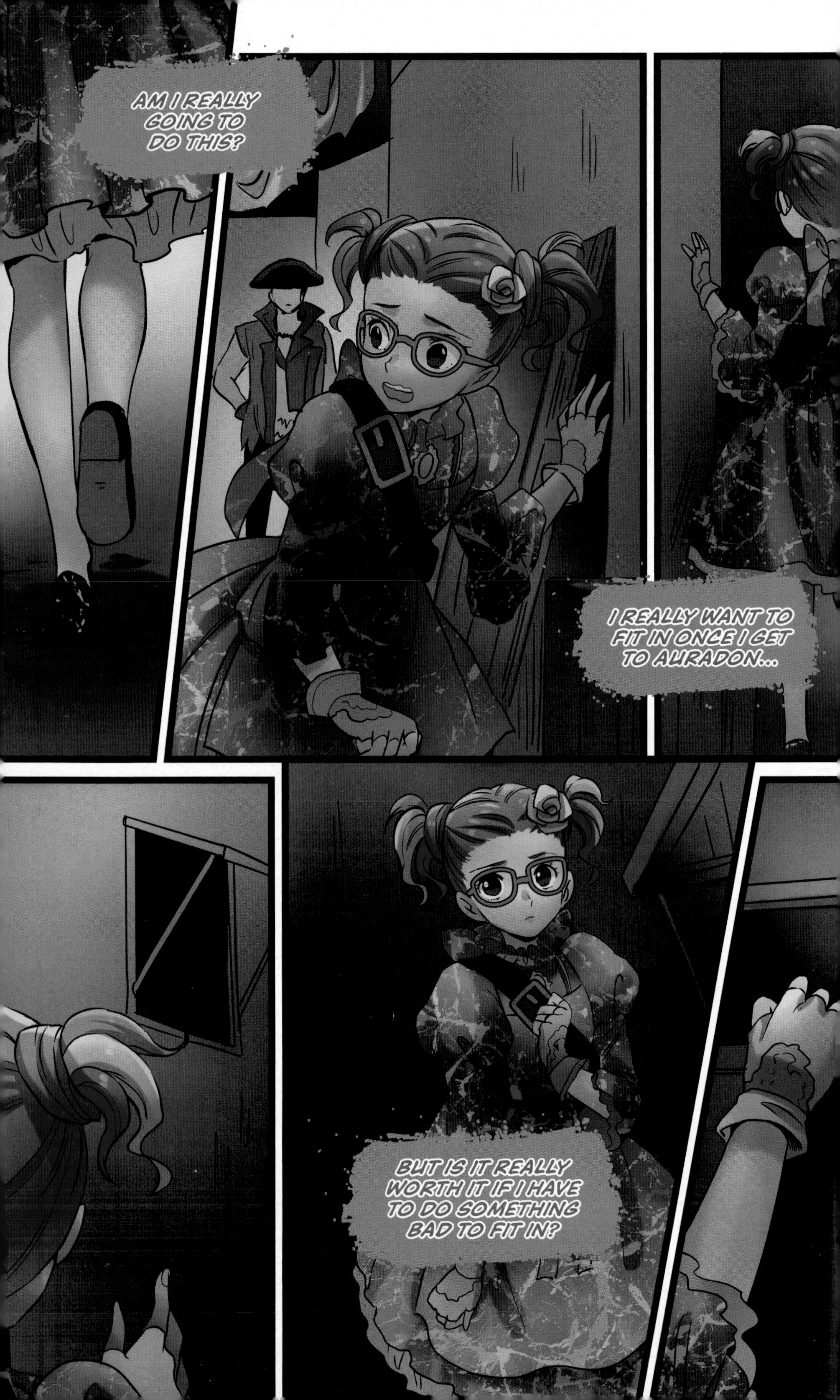
AM I REALLY GOING TO DO THIS?
I REALLY WANT TO FIT IN ONCE I GET TO AURADON...
BUT IS IT REALLY WORTH IT IF I HAVE TO DO SOMETHING BAD TO FIT IN?

CHAPTER 3

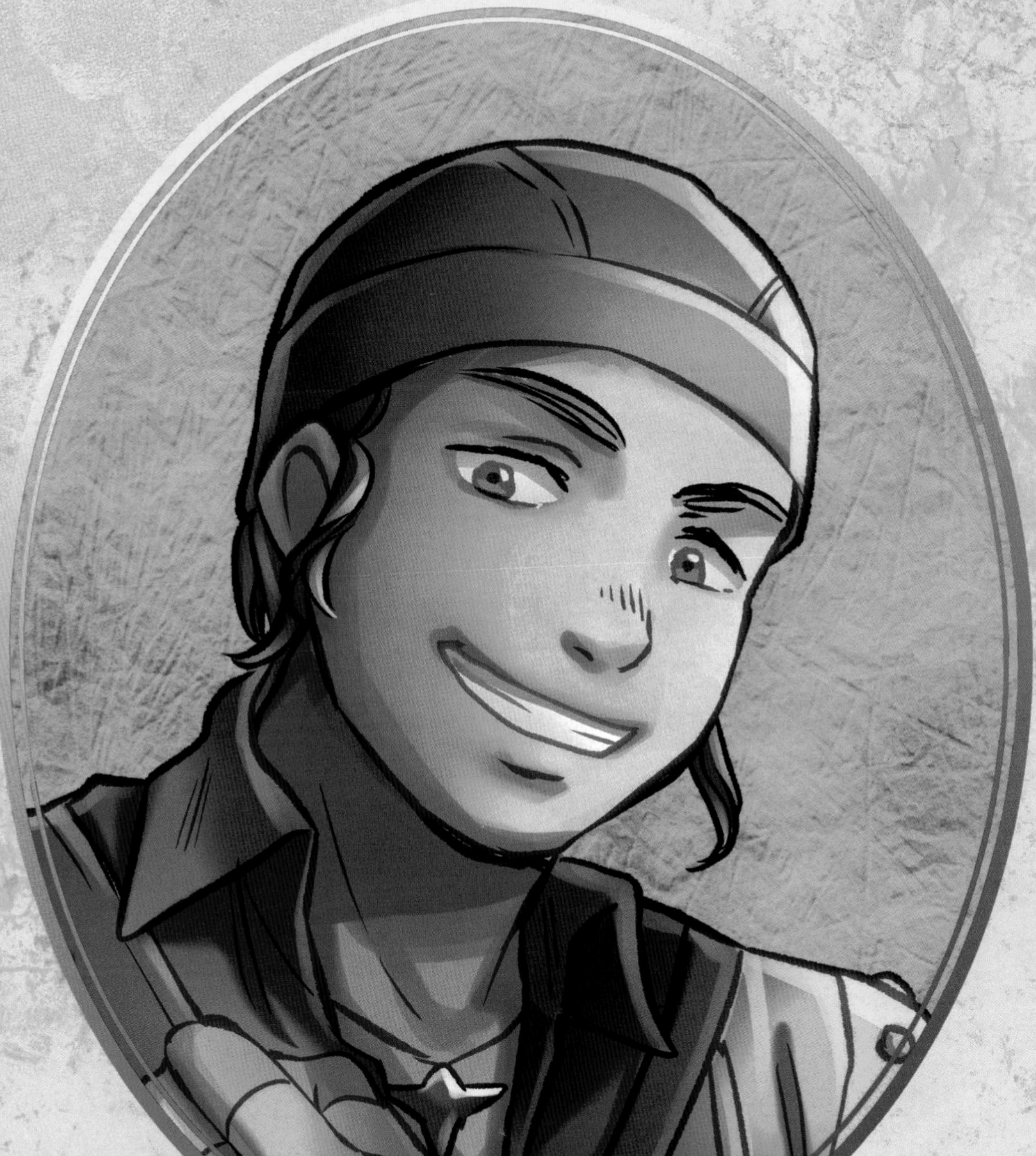

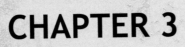

A COMPLETE FIASCO

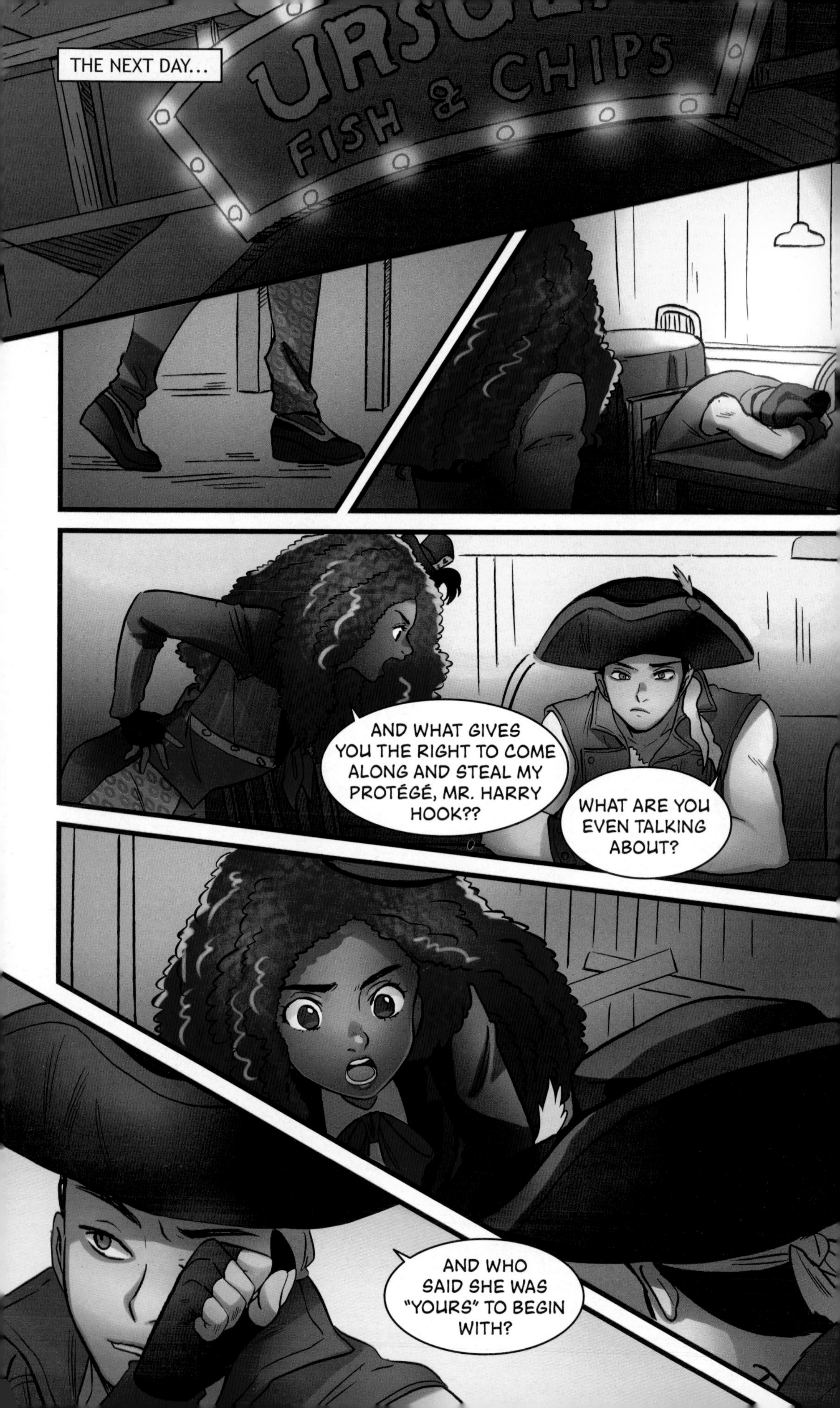
THE NEXT DAY...
URSULA'S FISH & CHIPS
AND WHAT GIVES YOU THE RIGHT TO COME ALONG AND STEAL MY PROTÉGÉ, MR. HARRY HOOK??
WHAT ARE YOU EVEN TALKING ABOUT?
AND WHO SAID SHE WAS "YOURS" TO BEGIN WITH?

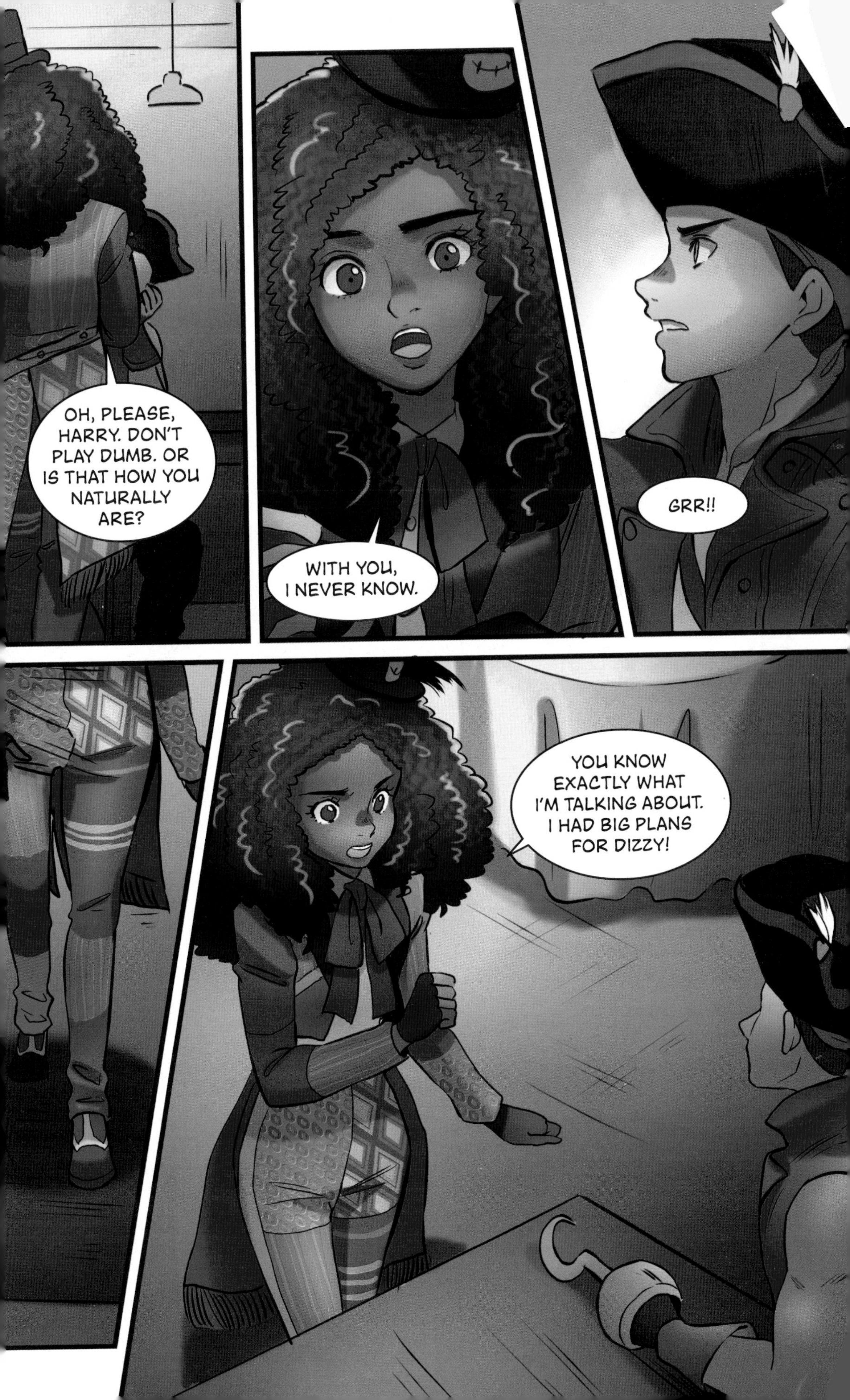
OH, PLEASE, HARRY. DON'T PLAY DUMB. OR IS THAT HOW YOU NATURALLY ARE?
WITH YOU, I NEVER KNOW.
GRR!!
YOU KNOW EXACTLY WHAT I'M TALKING ABOUT. I HAD BIG PLANS FOR DIZZY!

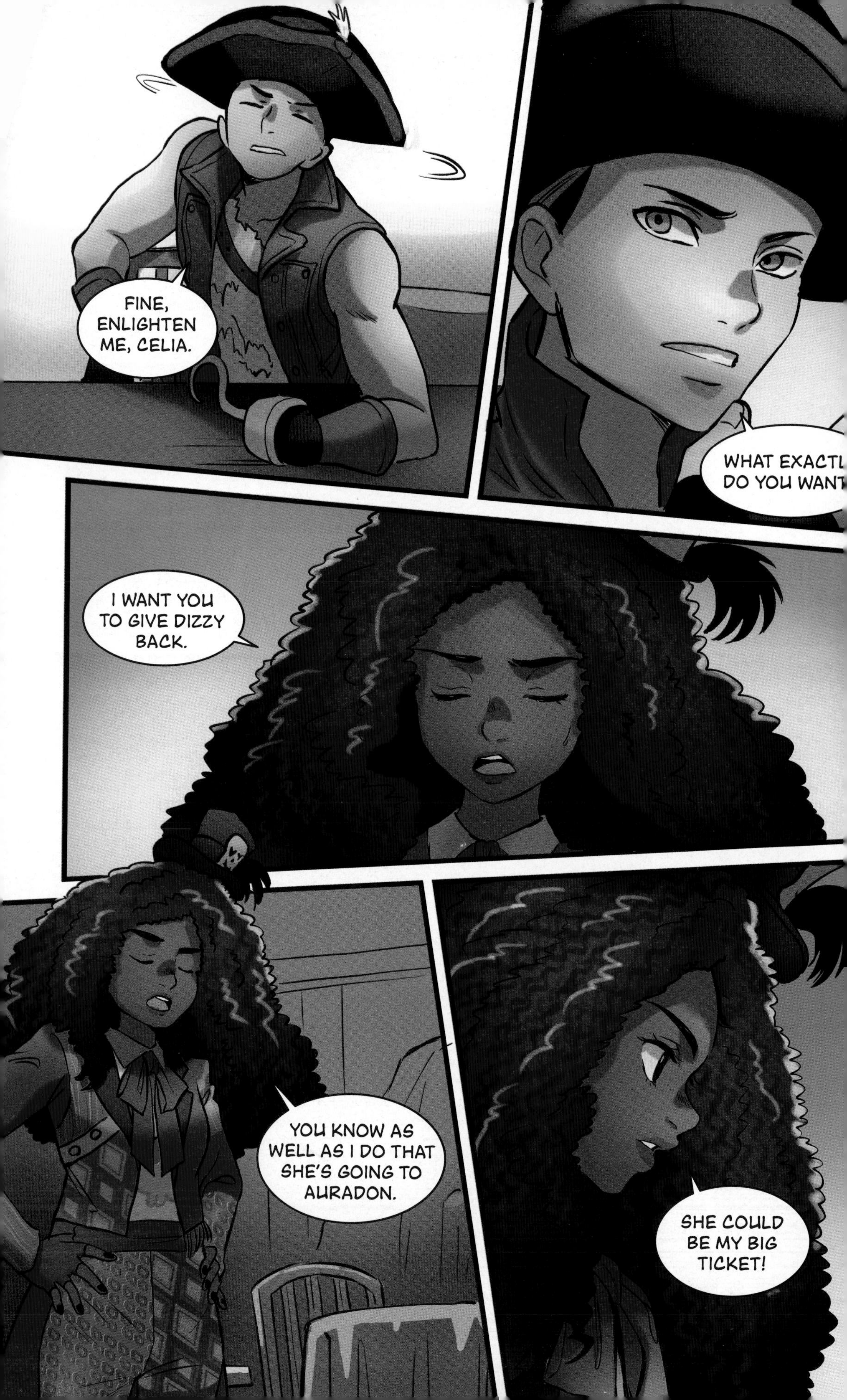
FINE, ENLIGHTEN ME, CELIA.
WHAT EXACTL DO YOU WANT
I WANT YOU TO GIVE DIZZY BACK.
YOU KNOW AS WELL AS I DO THAT SHE'S GOING TO AURADON.
SHE COULD BE MY BIG TICKET!

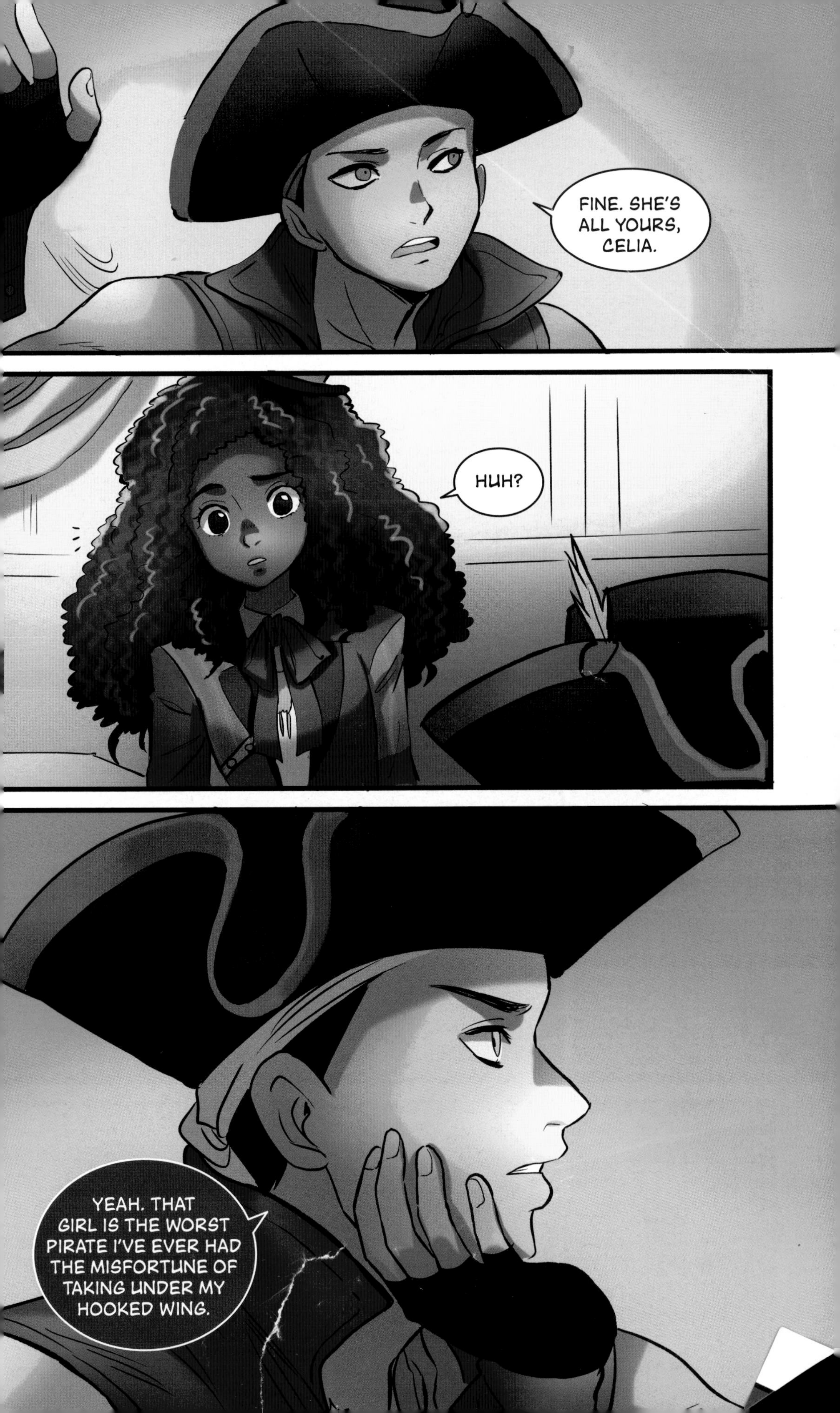
FINE. SHE'S ALL YOURS, CELIA.
HUH?
YEAH. THAT GIRL IS THE WORST PIRATE I'VE EVER HAD THE MISFORTUNE OF TAKING UNDER MY HOOKED WING.

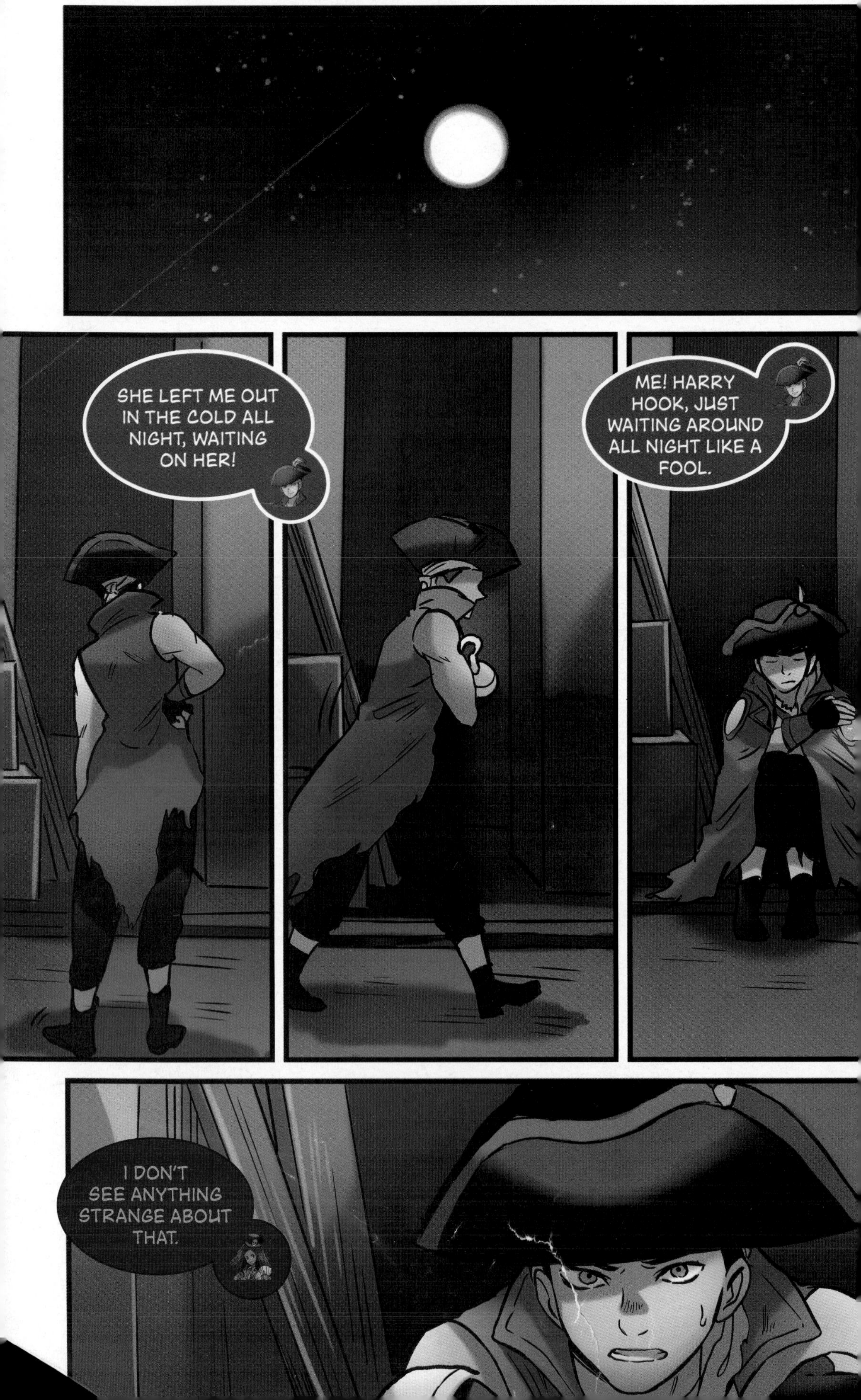
SHE LEFT ME OUT IN THE COLD ALL NIGHT, WAITING ON HER!
ME! HARRY HOOK, JUST WAITING AROUND ALL NIGHT LIKE A FOOL.
I DON'T SEE ANYTHING STRANGE ABOUT THAT.

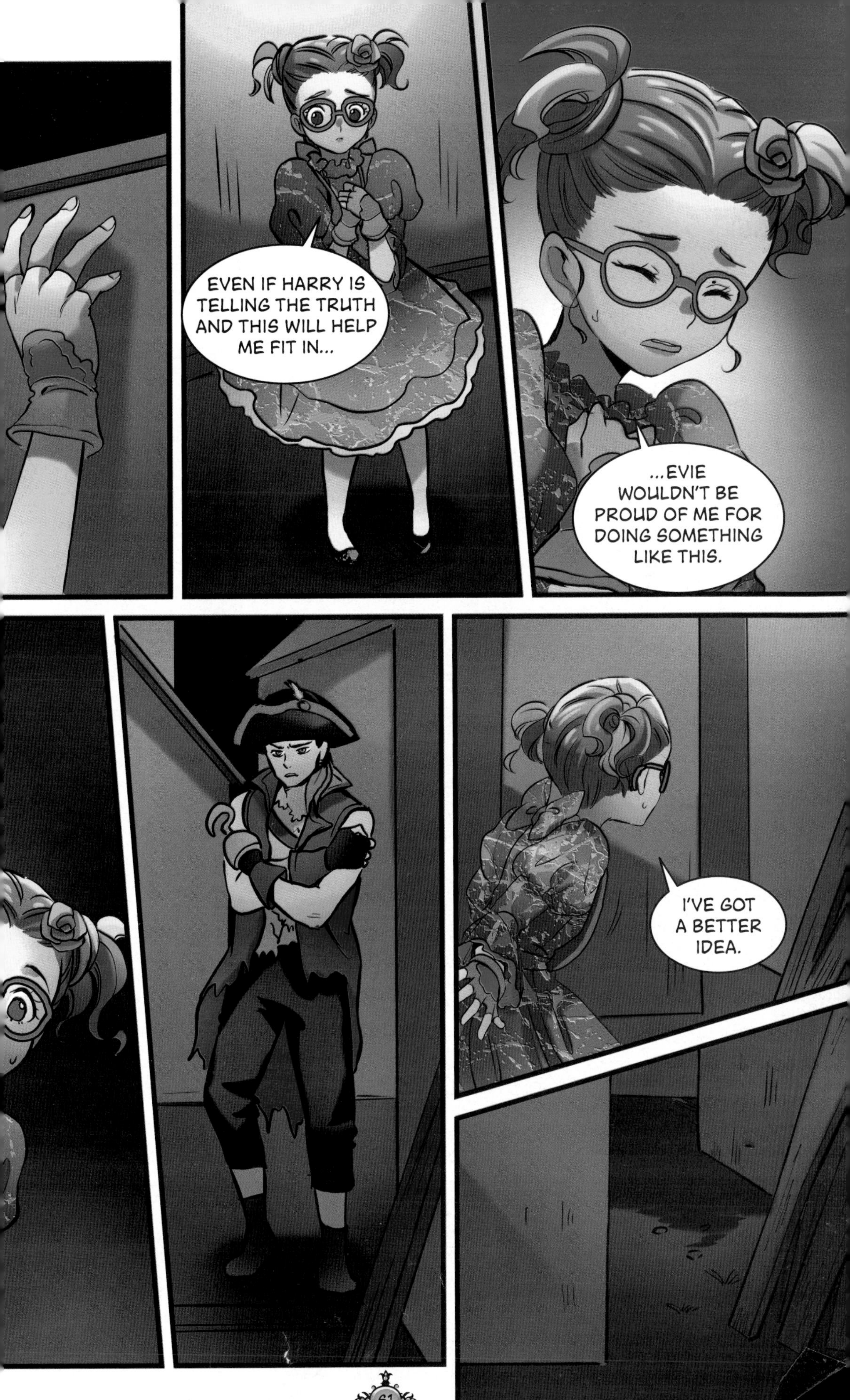

EVEN IF HARRY IS TELLING THE TRUTH AND THIS WILL HELP ME FIT IN...
...EVIE WOULDN'T BE PROUD OF ME FOR DOING SOMETHING LIKE THIS.
I'VE GOT A BETTER IDEA.

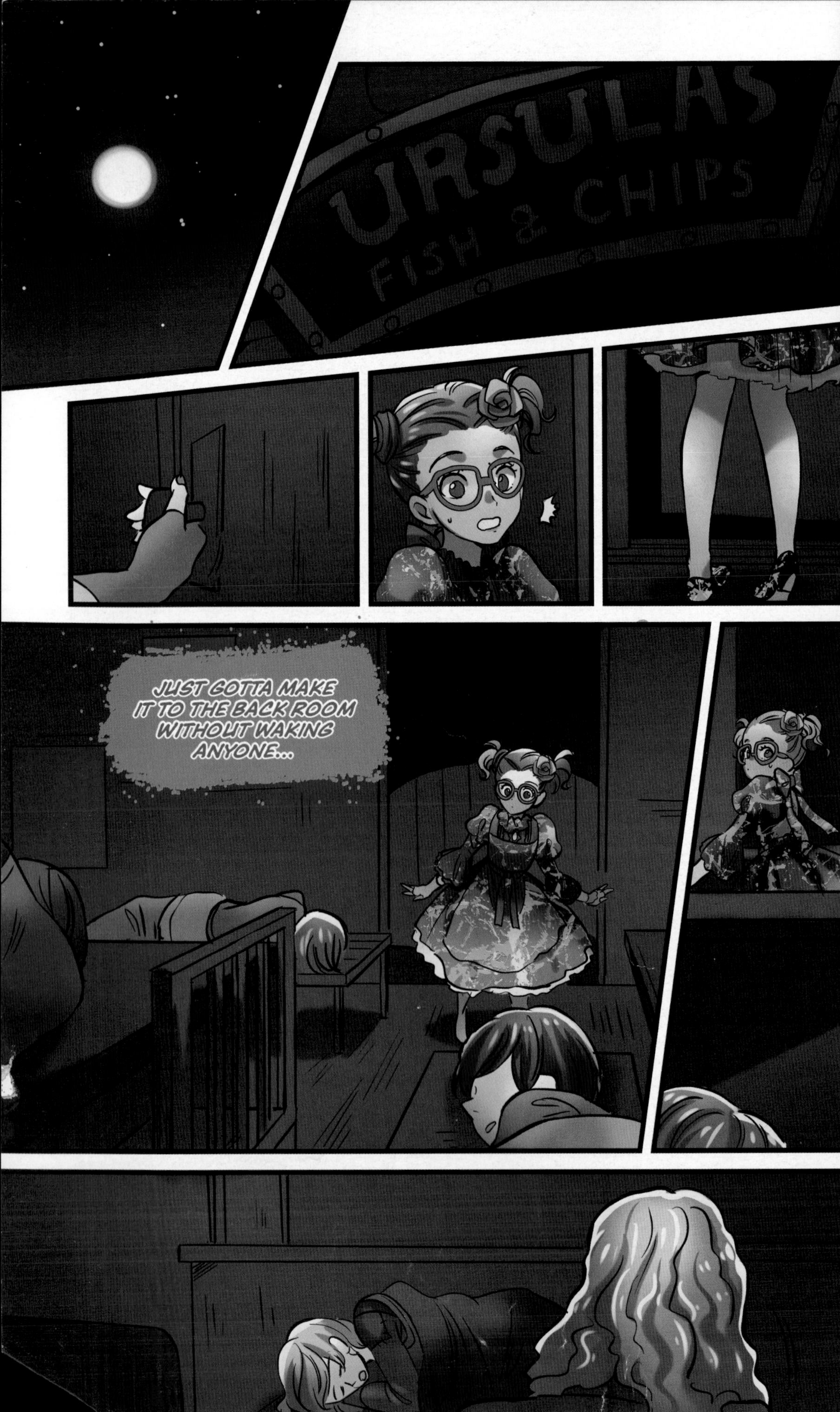
URSULA'S
FISH & CHIPS
JUST GOTTA MAKE IT TO THE BACK ROOM WITHOUT WAKING ANYONE...

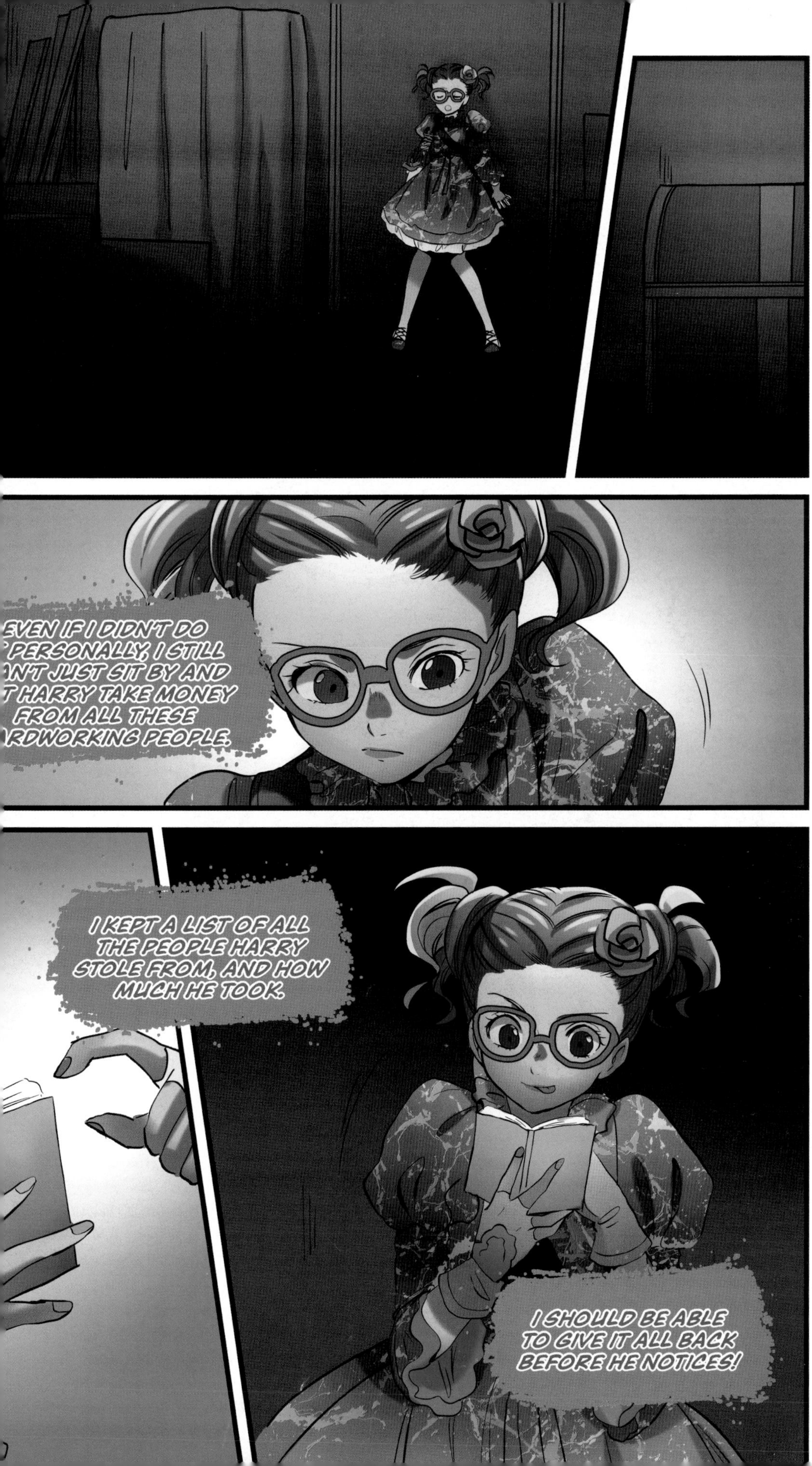
EVEN IF I DIDN'T DO
T PERSONALLY, I STILL
AN'T JUST SIT BY AND
T HARRY TAKE MONEY
FROM ALL THESE
RDWORKING PEOPLE.
I KEPT A LIST OF ALL THE PEOPLE HARRY STOLE FROM, AND HOW MUCH HE TOOK.
I SHOULD BE ABLE TO GIVE IT ALL BACK BEFORE HE NOTICES!

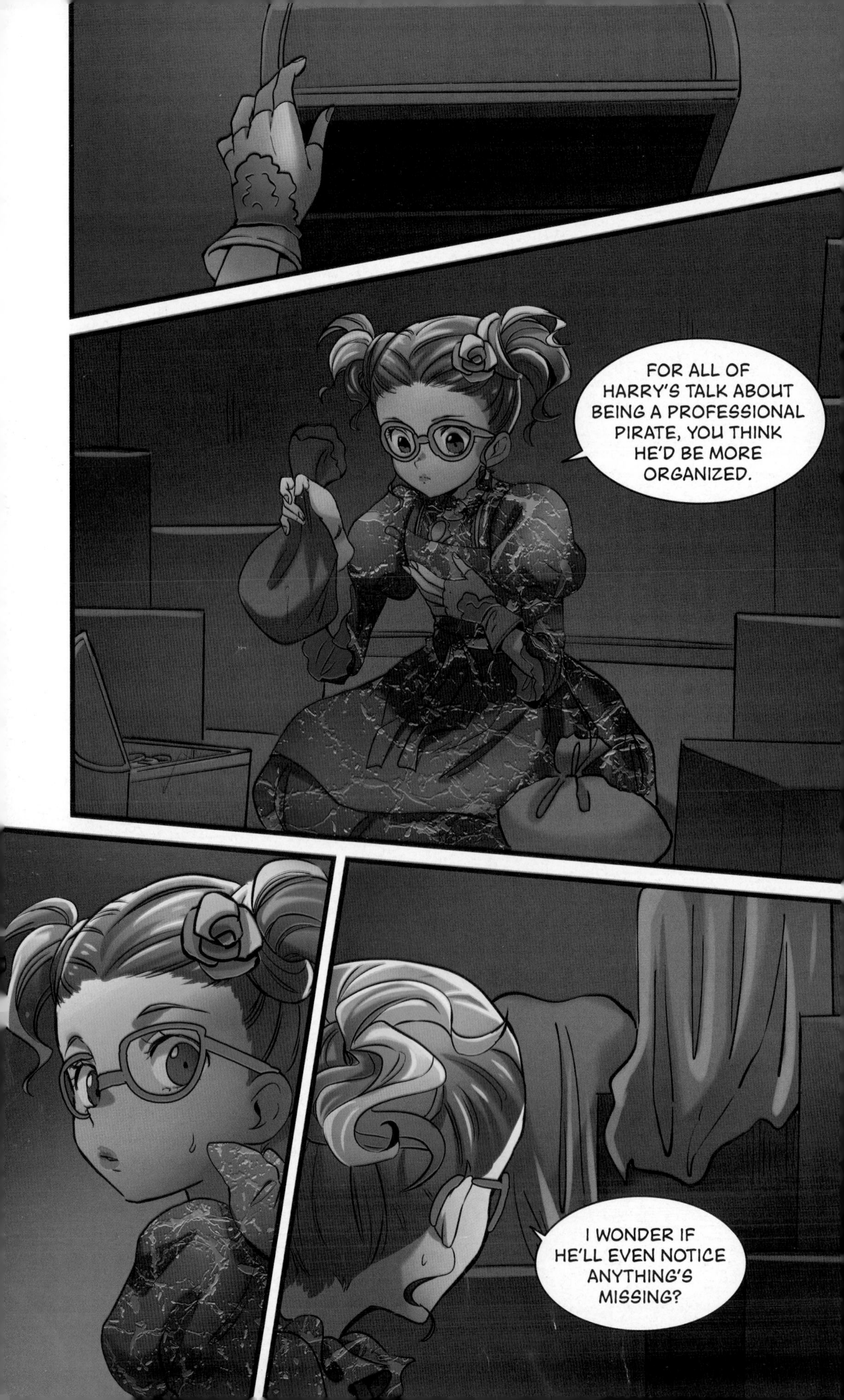
FOR ALL OF HARRY'S TALK ABOUT BEING A PROFESSIONAL PIRATE, YOU THINK HE'D BE MORE ORGANIZED.
I WONDER IF HE'LL EVEN NOTICE ANYTHING'S MISSING?

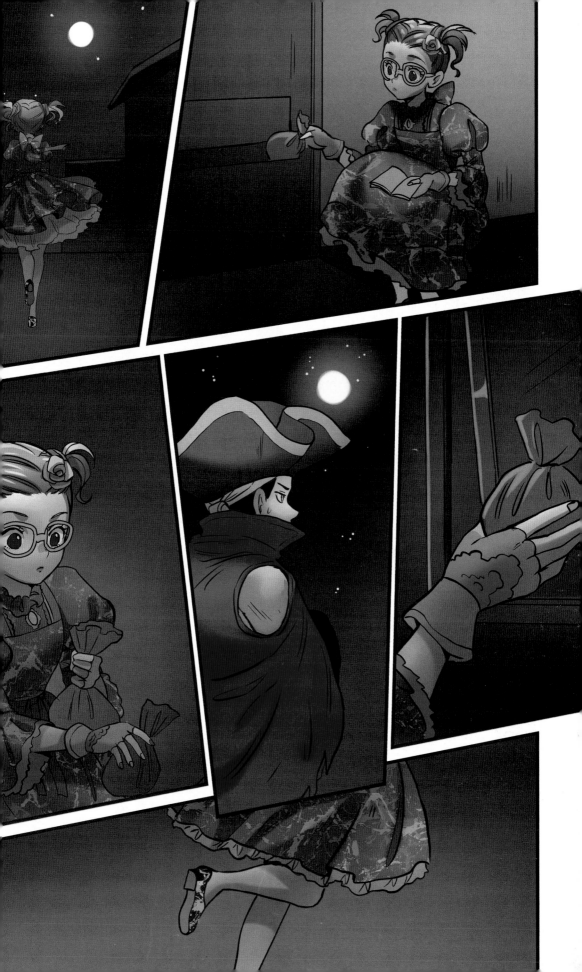

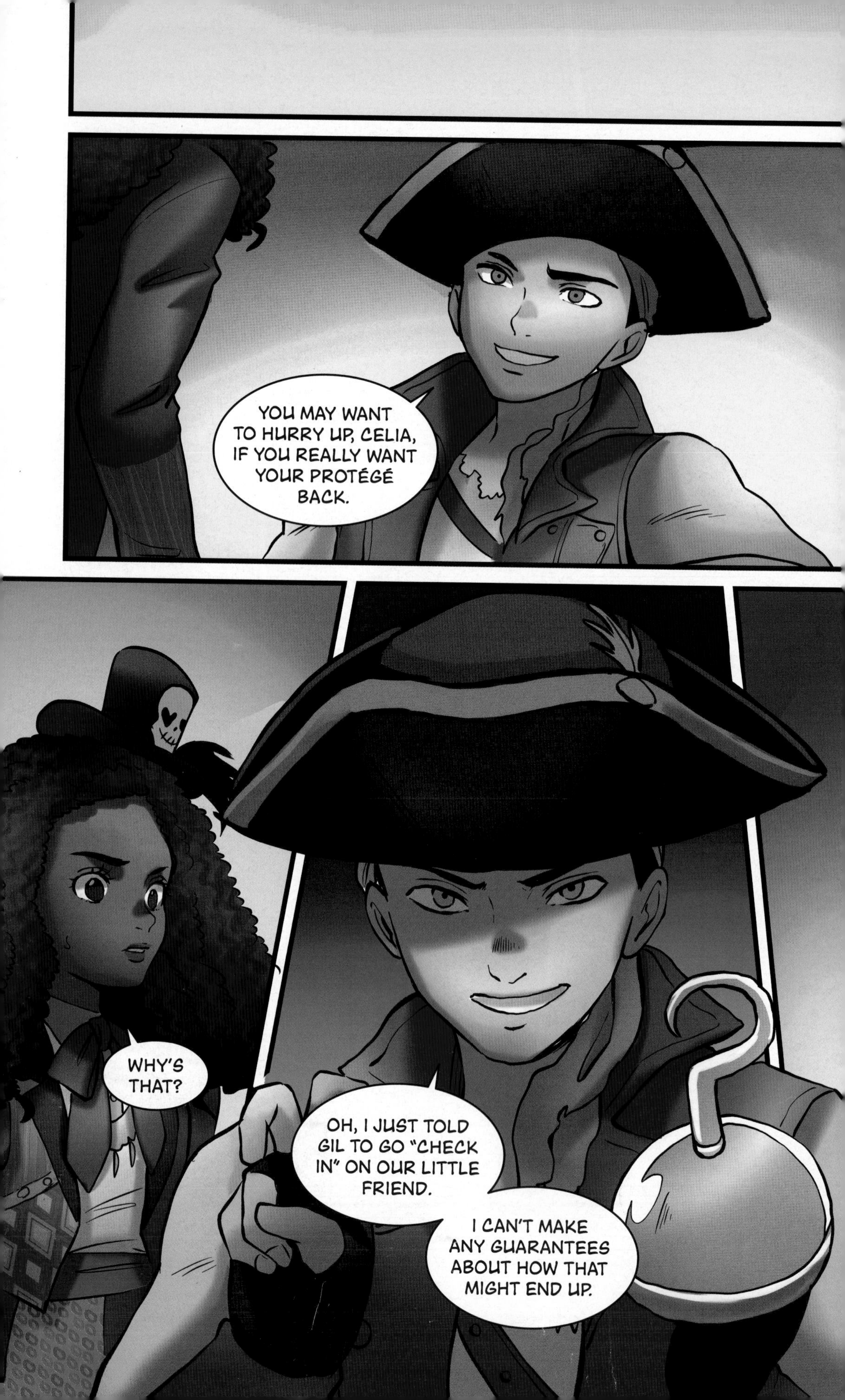
YOU MAY WANT TO HURRY UP, CELIA, IF YOU REALLY WANT YOUR PROTÉGÉ BACK.
WHY'S THAT?
OH, I JUST TOLD GIL TO GO "CHECK IN" ON OUR LITTLE FRIEND.
I CAN'T MAKE ANY GUARANTEES ABOUT HOW THAT MIGHT END UP.

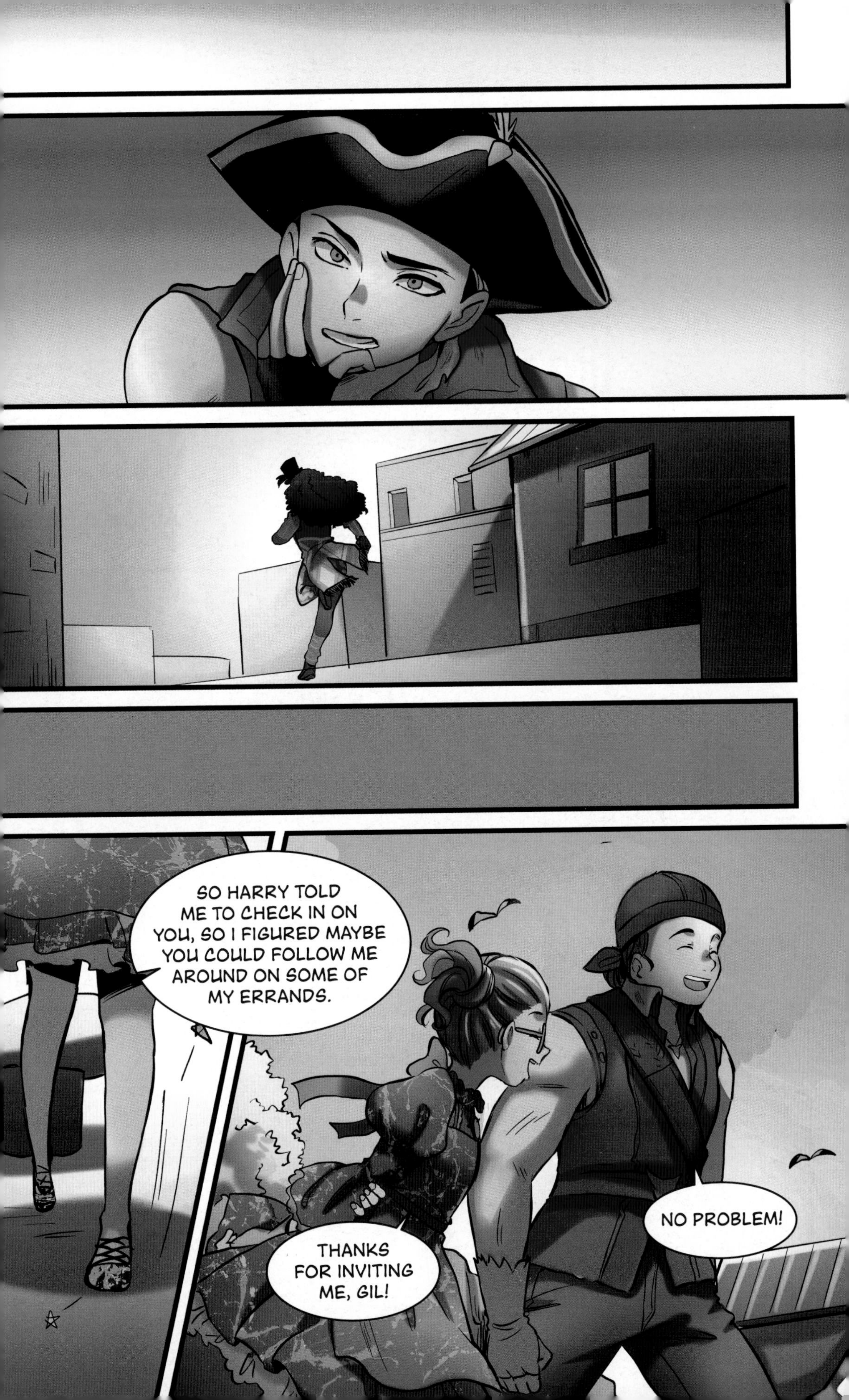
SO HARRY TOLD ME TO CHECK IN ON YOU, SO I FIGURED MAYBE YOU COULD FOLLOW ME AROUND ON SOME OF MY ERRANDS.
THANKS FOR INVITING ME, GIL!
NO PROBLEM!

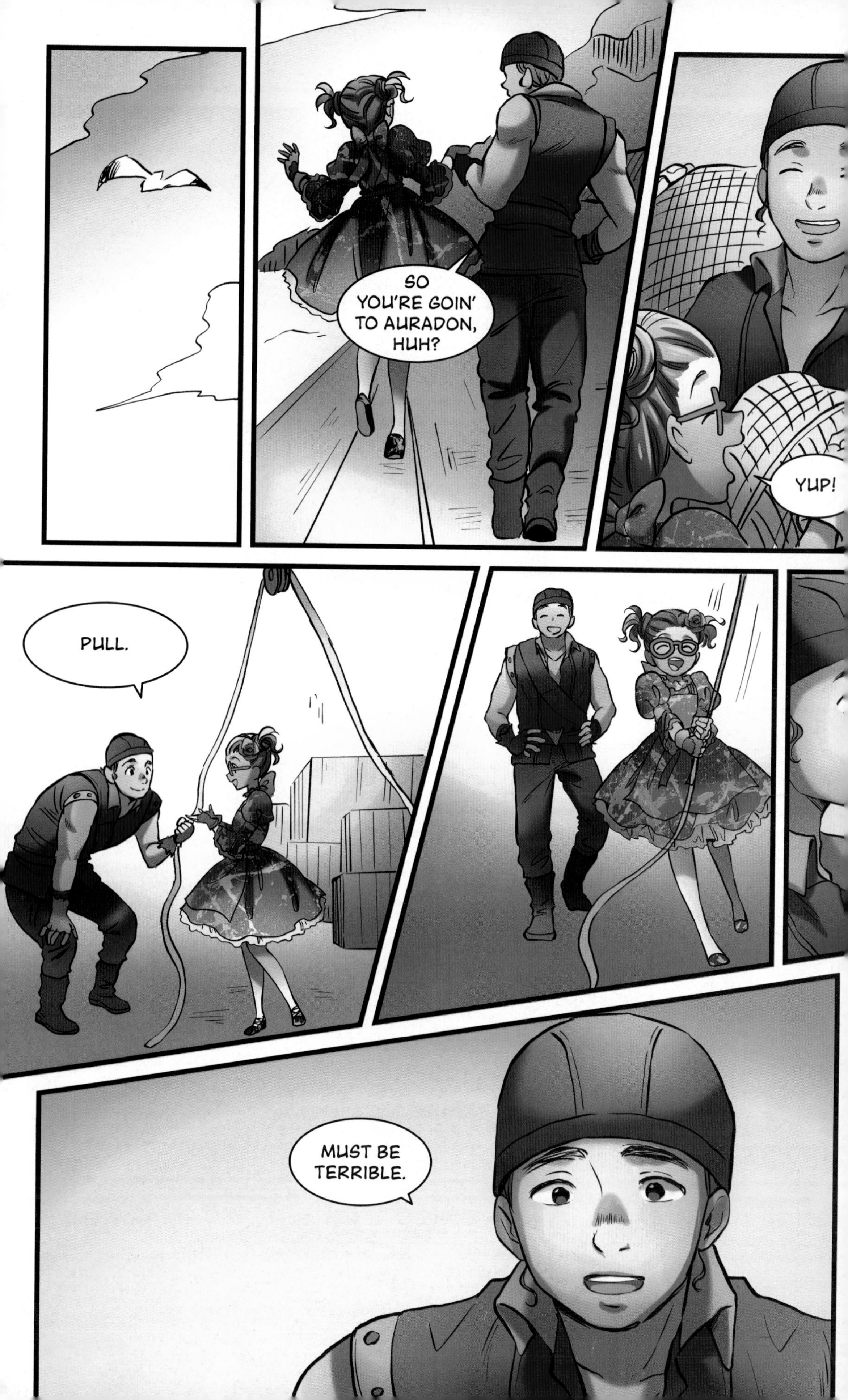
SO YOU'RE GOIN' TO AURADON, HUH?
YUP!
PULL.
MUST BE TERRIBLE.

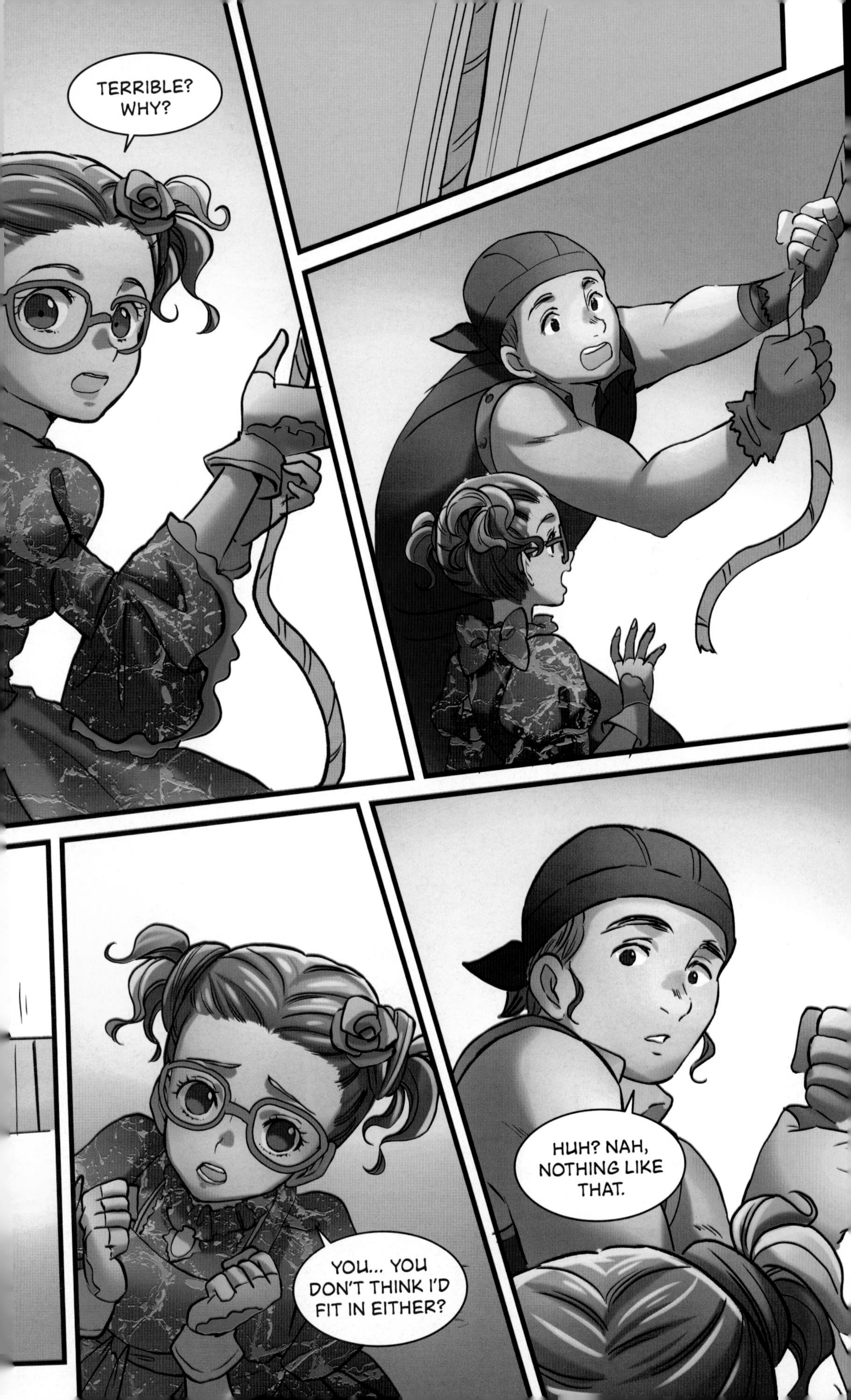
TERRIBLE? WHY?
YOU... YOU DON'T THINK I'D FIT IN EITHER?
HUH? NAH, NOTHING LIKE THAT.

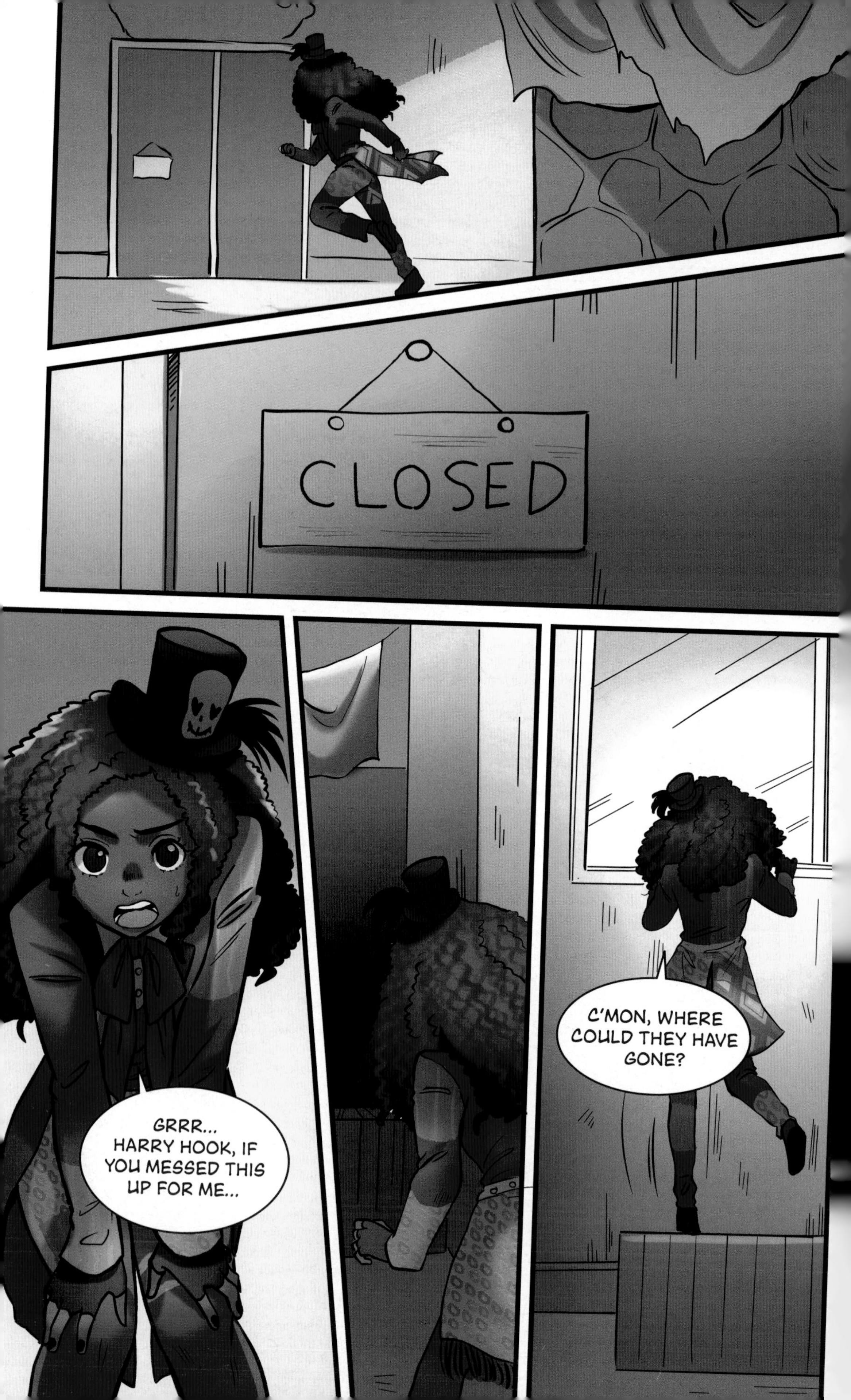
CLOSED
GRRR... HARRY HOOK, IF YOU MESSED THIS UP FOR ME...
C'MON, WHERE COULD THEY HAVE GONE?

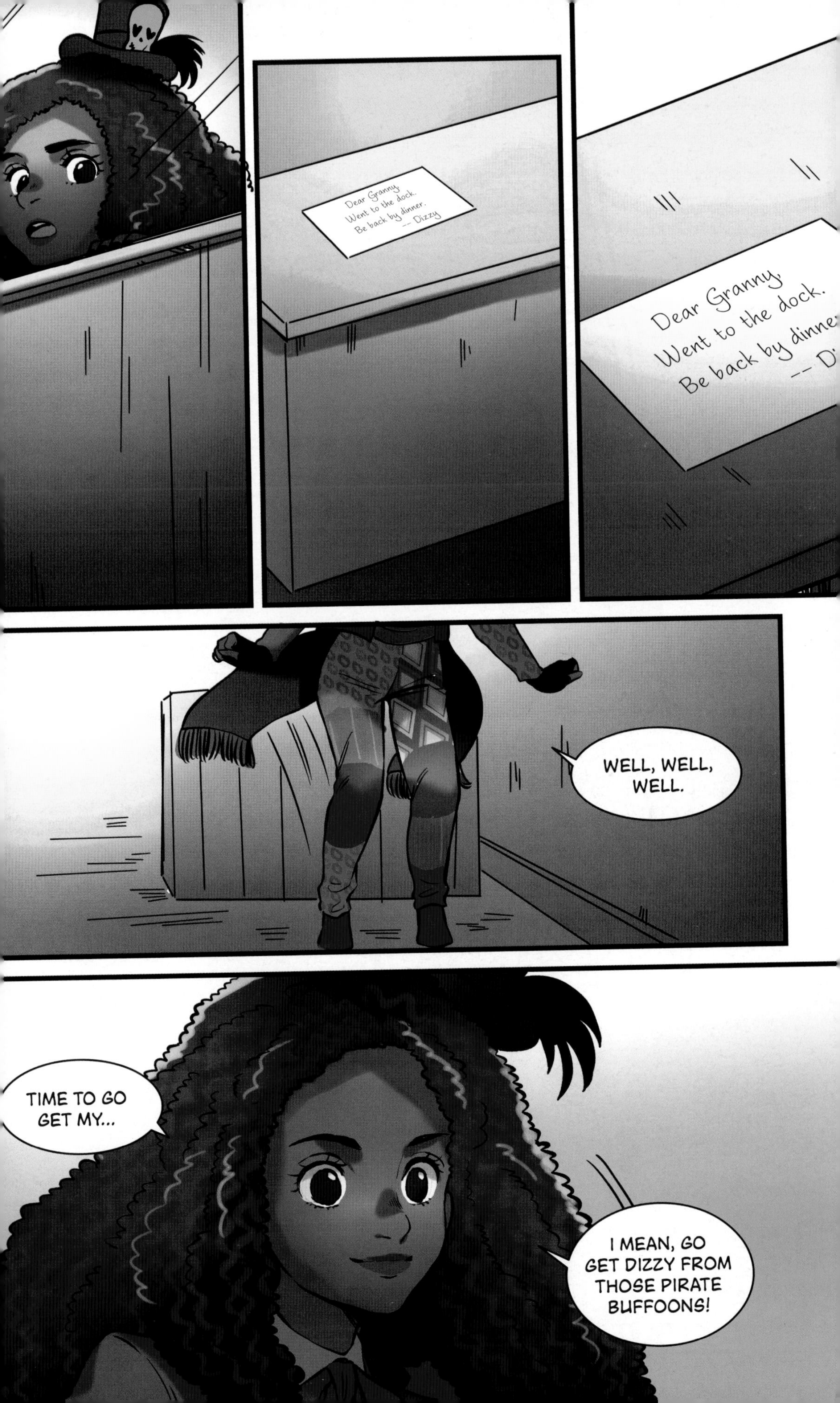
Dear Granny,
Went to the dock.
Be back by dinner.
-- Dizzy
Dear Granny,
Went to the dock.
Be back by dinne
--
WELL, WELL, WELL.
TIME TO GO GET MY...
I MEAN, GO GET DIZZY FROM THOSE PIRATE BUFFOONS!

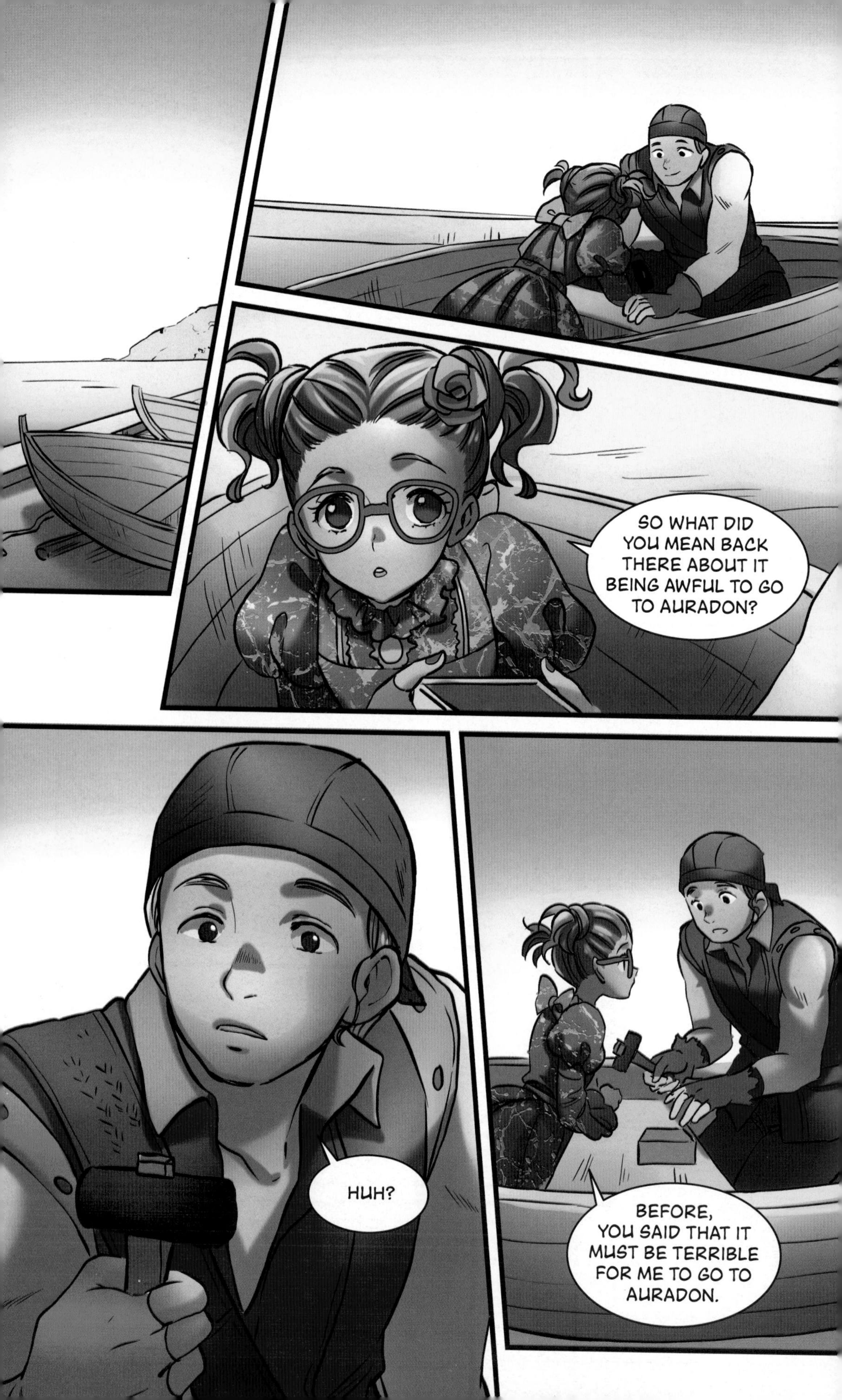
SO WHAT DID YOU MEAN BACK THERE ABOUT IT BEING AWFUL TO GO TO AURADON?
HUH?
BEFORE, YOU SAID THAT IT MUST BE TERRIBLE FOR ME TO GO TO AURADON.

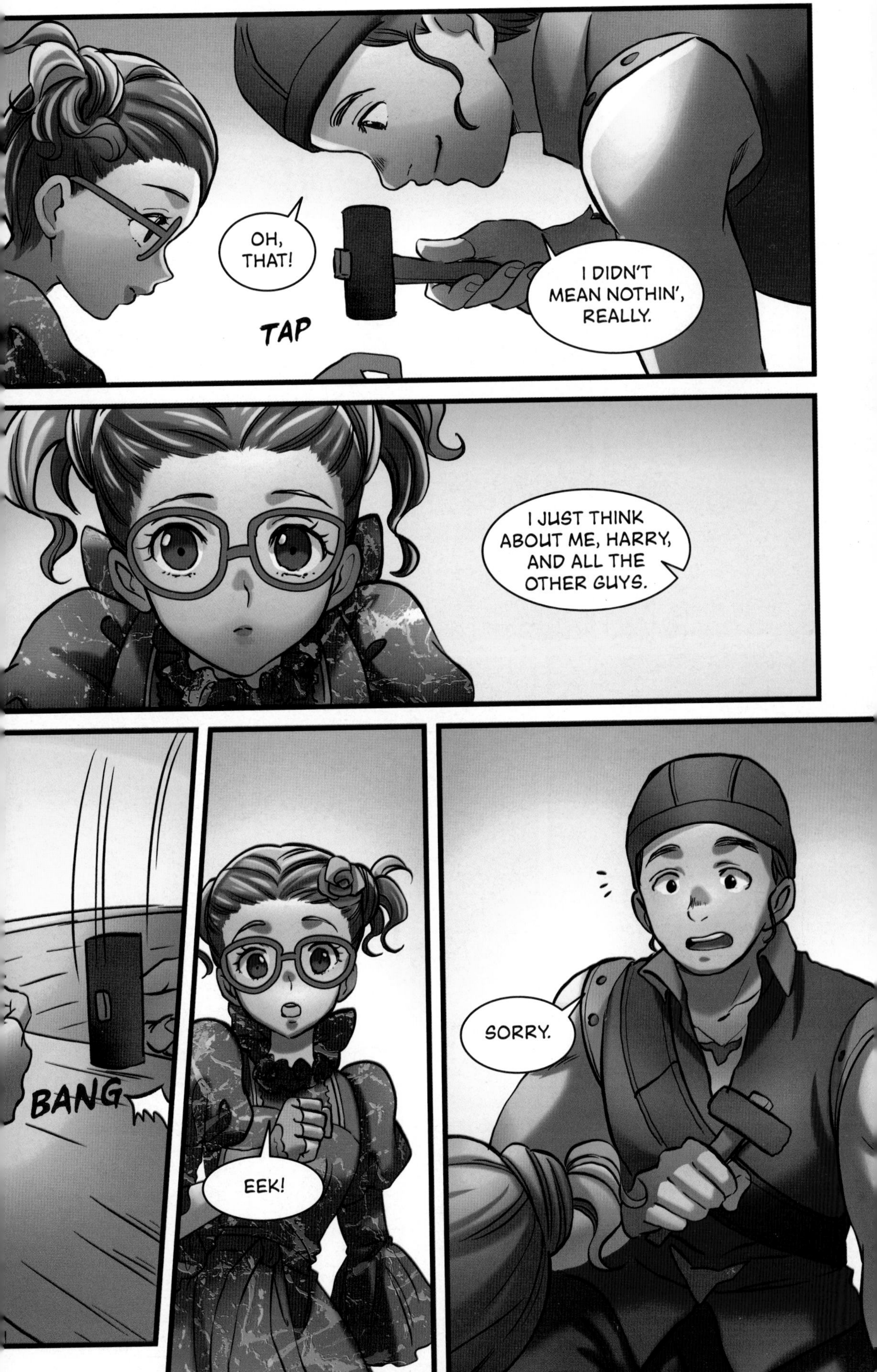
OH, THAT!
TAP
I DIDN'T MEAN NOTHIN', REALLY.
I JUST THINK ABOUT ME, HARRY, AND ALL THE OTHER GUYS.
BANG
EEK!
SORRY.

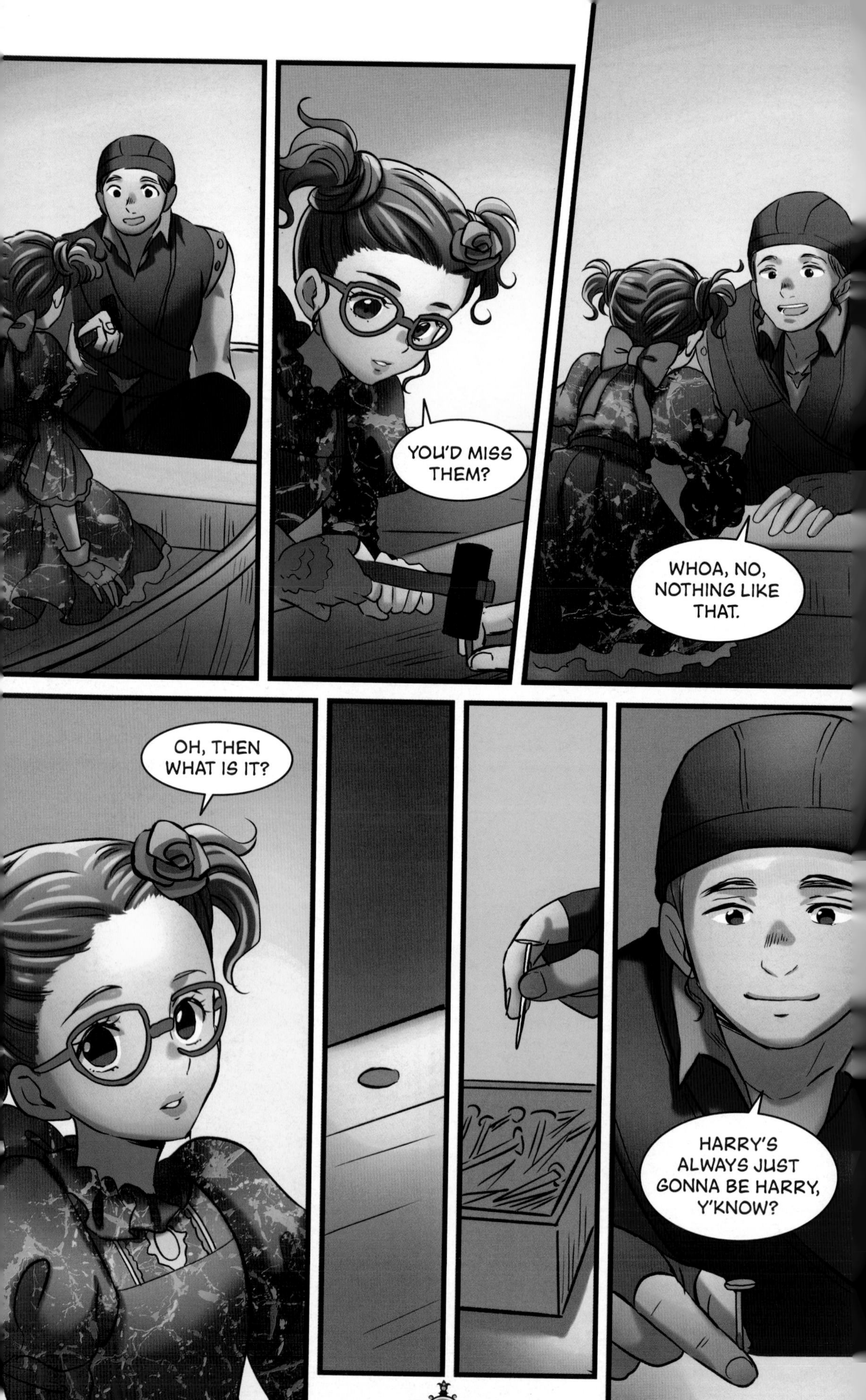
YOU'D MISS THEM?
WHOA, NO, NOTHING LIKE THAT.
OH, THEN WHAT IS IT?
HARRY'S ALWAYS JUST GONNA BE HARRY, Y'KNOW?

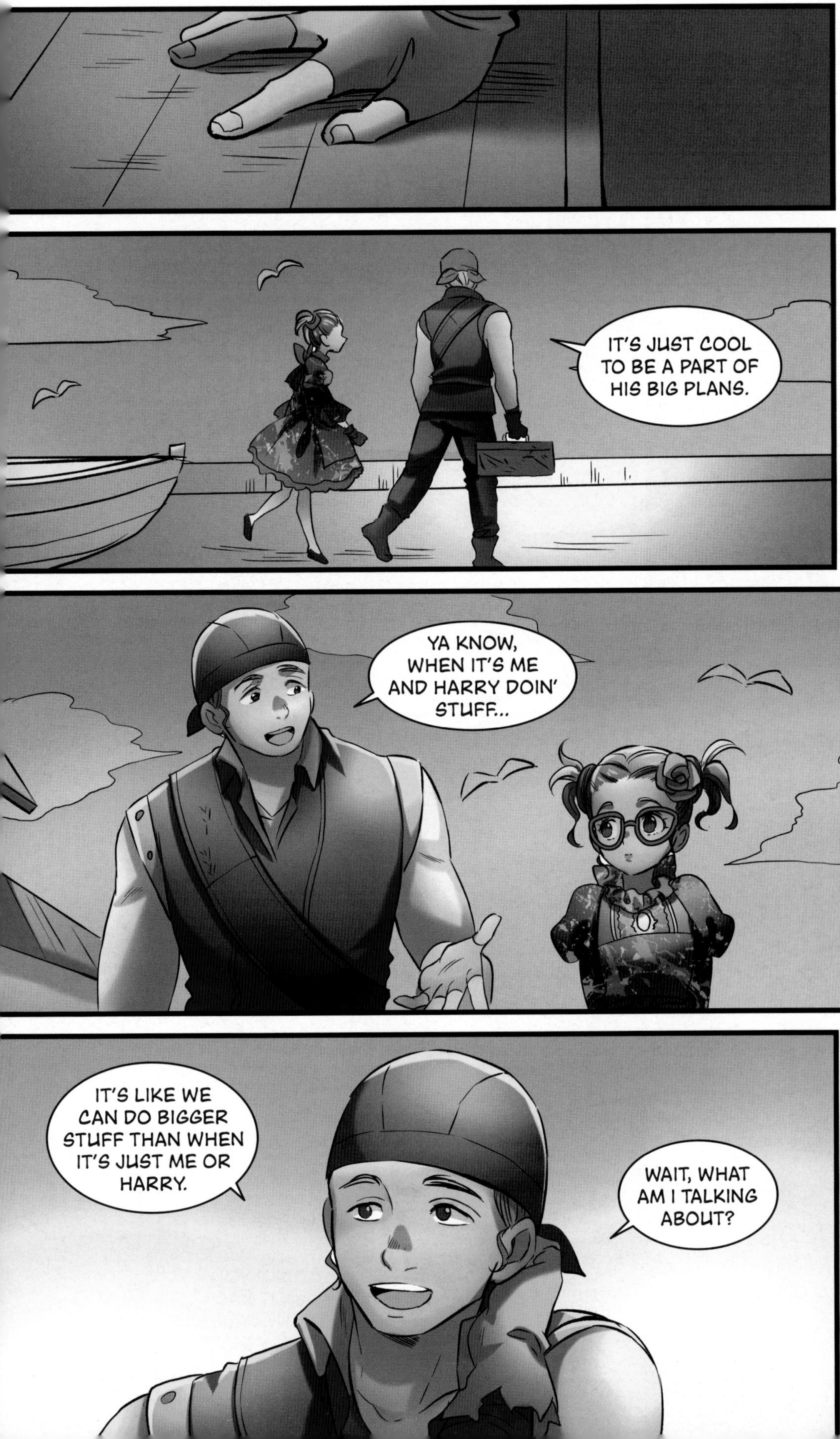
IT'S JUST COOL TO BE A PART OF HIS BIG PLANS.
YA KNOW, WHEN IT'S ME AND HARRY DOIN' STUFF...
IT'S LIKE WE CAN DO BIGGER STUFF THAN WHEN IT'S JUST ME OR HARRY.
WAIT, WHAT AM I TALKING ABOUT?

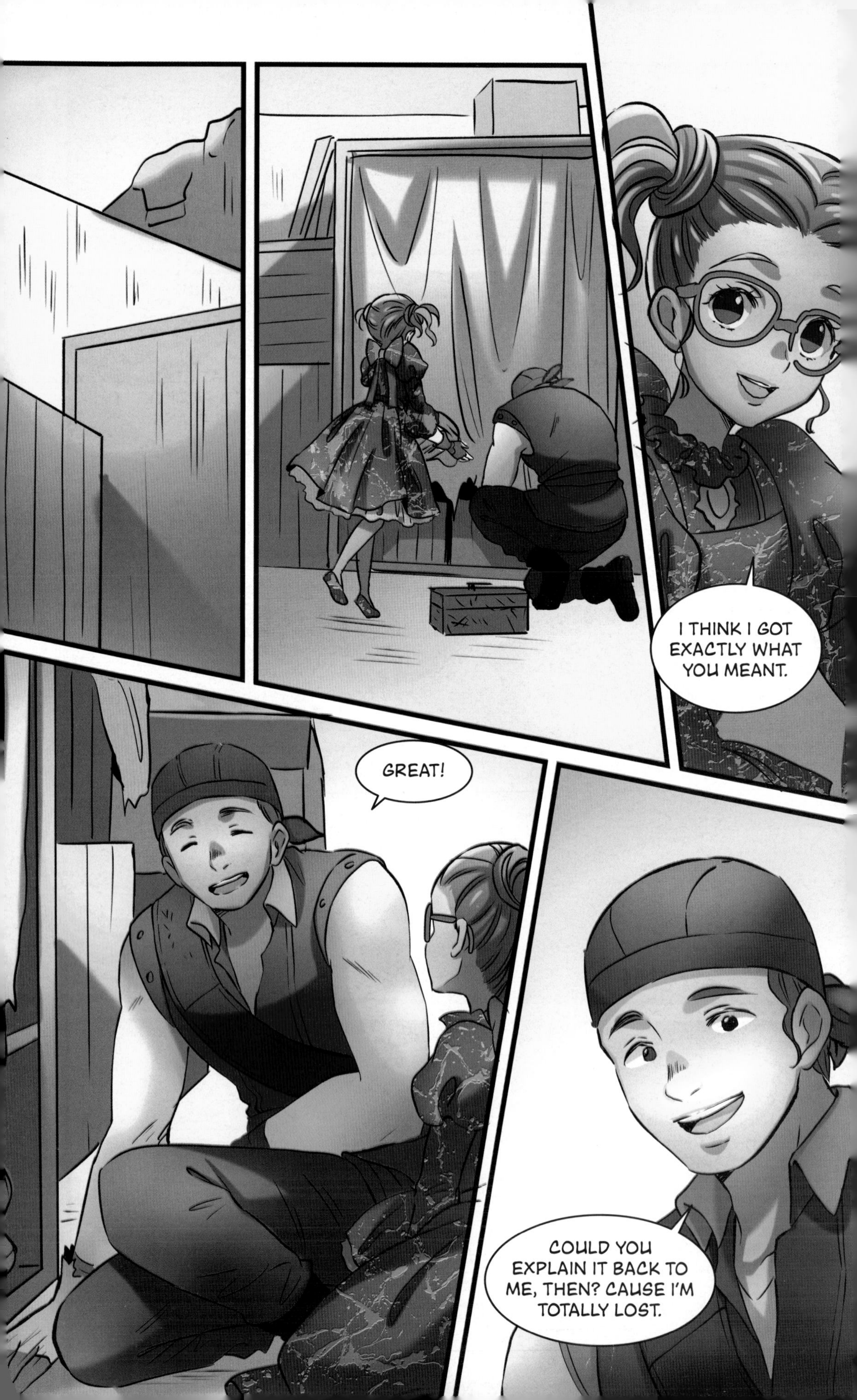
I THINK I GOT EXACTLY WHAT YOU MEANT.
GREAT!
COULD YOU EXPLAIN IT BACK TO ME, THEN? CAUSE I'M TOTALLY LOST.

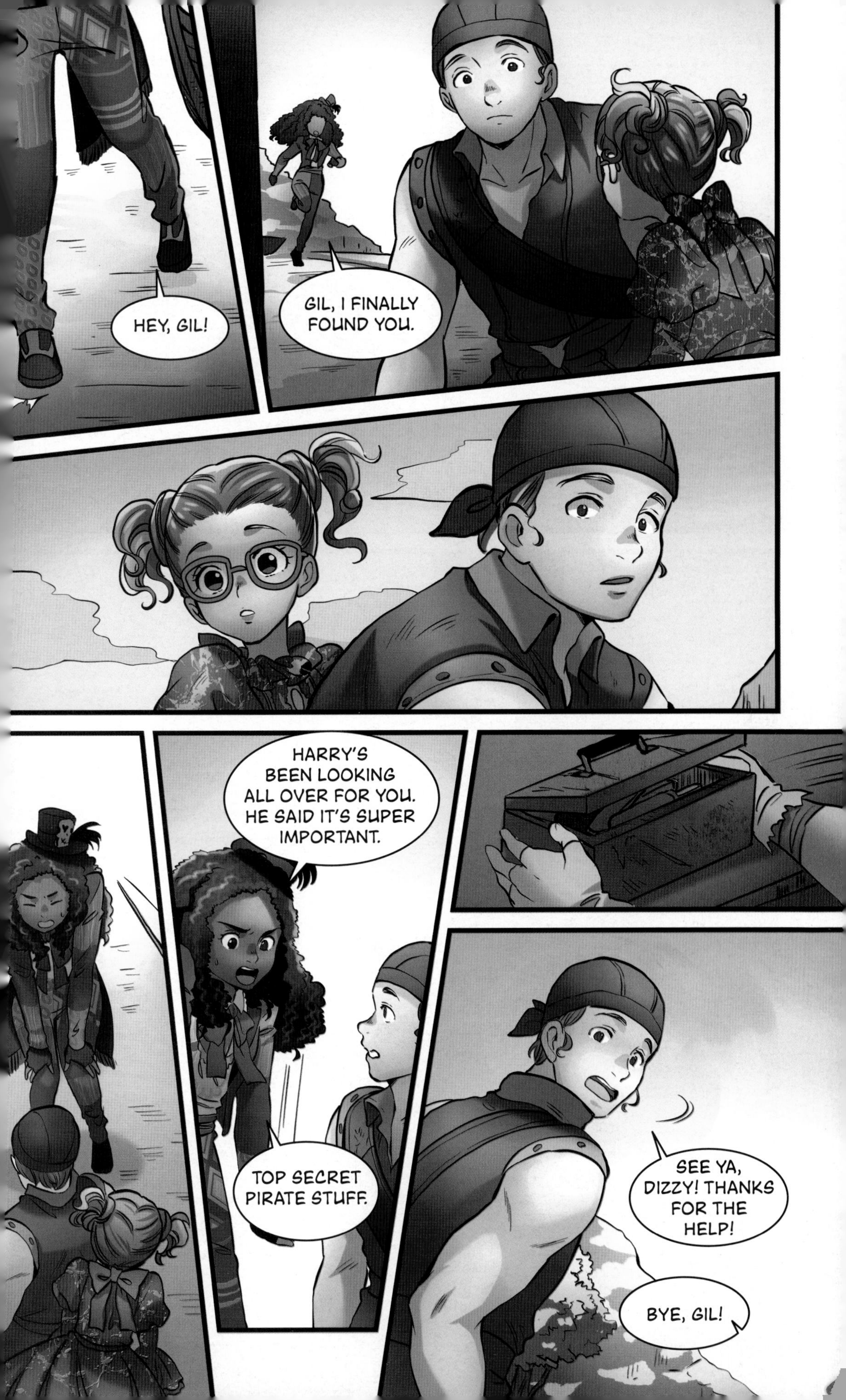
HEY, GIL!
GIL, I FINALLY FOUND YOU.
HARRY'S BEEN LOOKING ALL OVER FOR YOU. HE SAID IT'S SUPER IMPORTANT.
TOP SECRET PIRATE STUFF.
SEE YA, DIZZY! THANKS FOR THE HELP!
BYE, GIL!

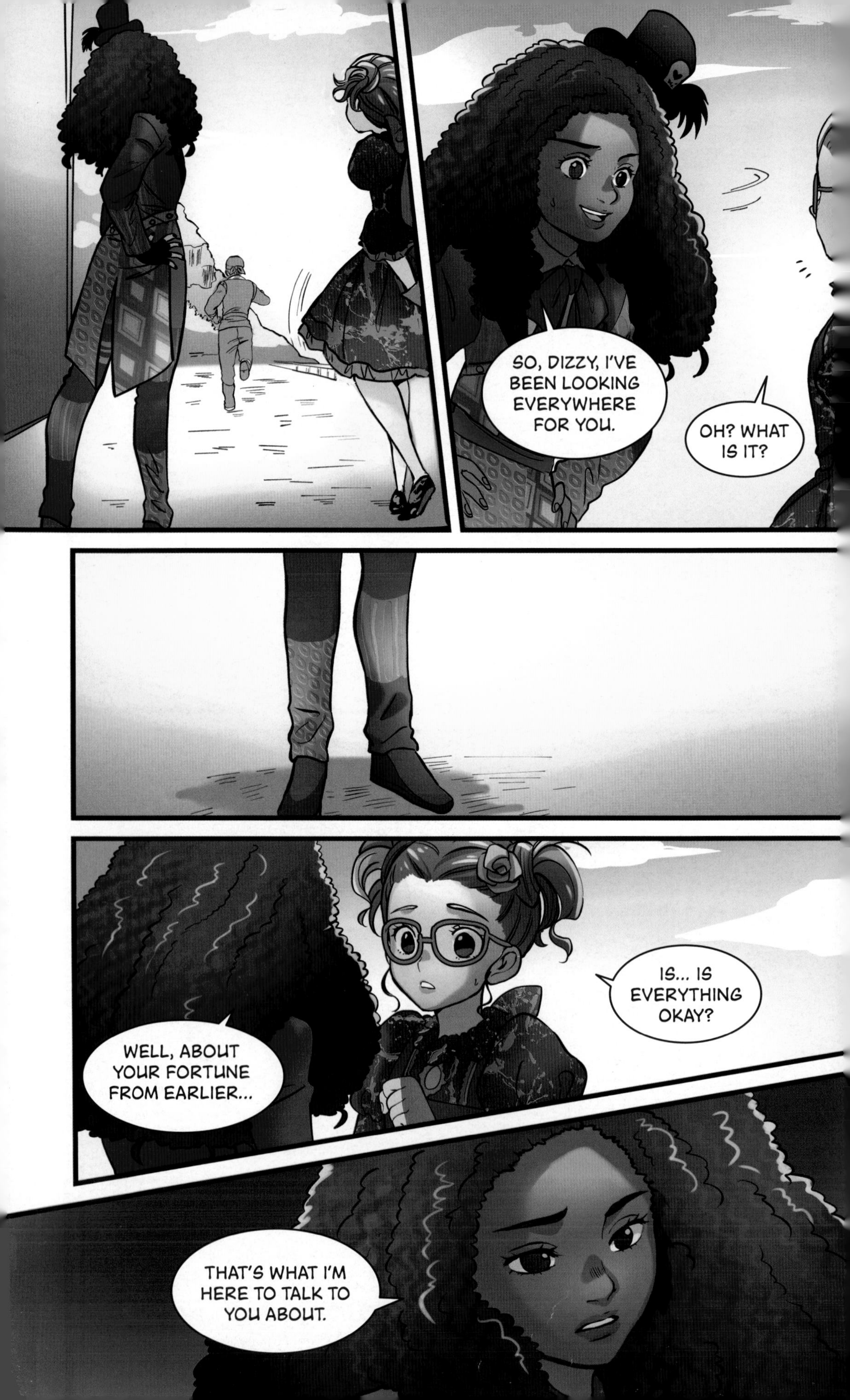
SO, DIZZY, I'VE BEEN LOOKING EVERYWHERE FOR YOU.
OH? WHAT IS IT?
IS... IS EVERYTHING OKAY?
WELL, ABOUT YOUR FORTUNE FROM EARLIER...
THAT'S WHAT I'M HERE TO TALK TO YOU ABOUT.

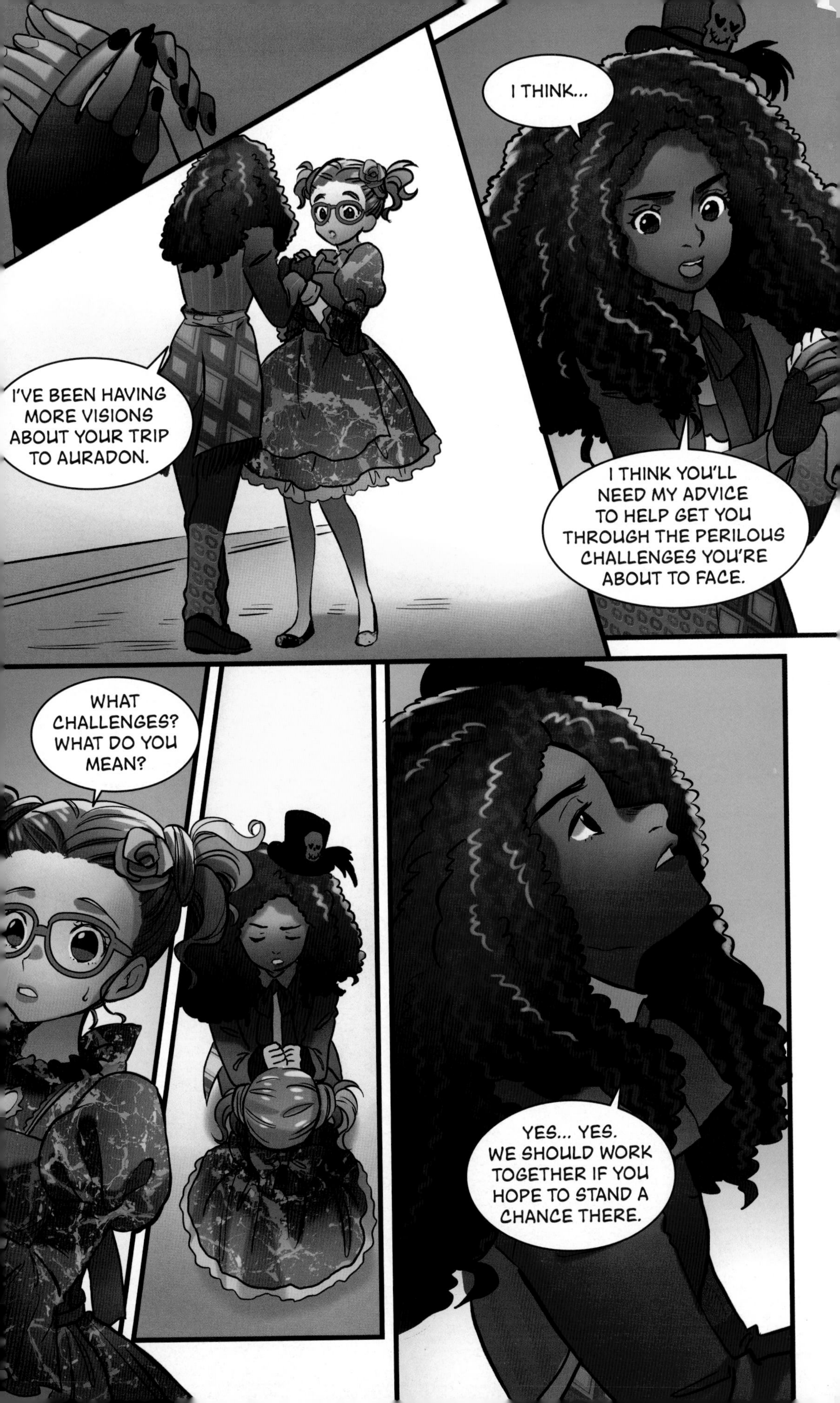
I'VE BEEN HAVING MORE VISIONS ABOUT YOUR TRIP TO AURADON.
I THINK...
I THINK YOU'LL NEED MY ADVICE TO HELP GET YOU THROUGH THE PERILOUS CHALLENGES YOU'RE ABOUT TO FACE.
WHAT CHALLENGES? WHAT DO YOU MEAN?
YES... YES. WE SHOULD WORK TOGETHER IF YOU HOPE TO STAND A CHANCE THERE.

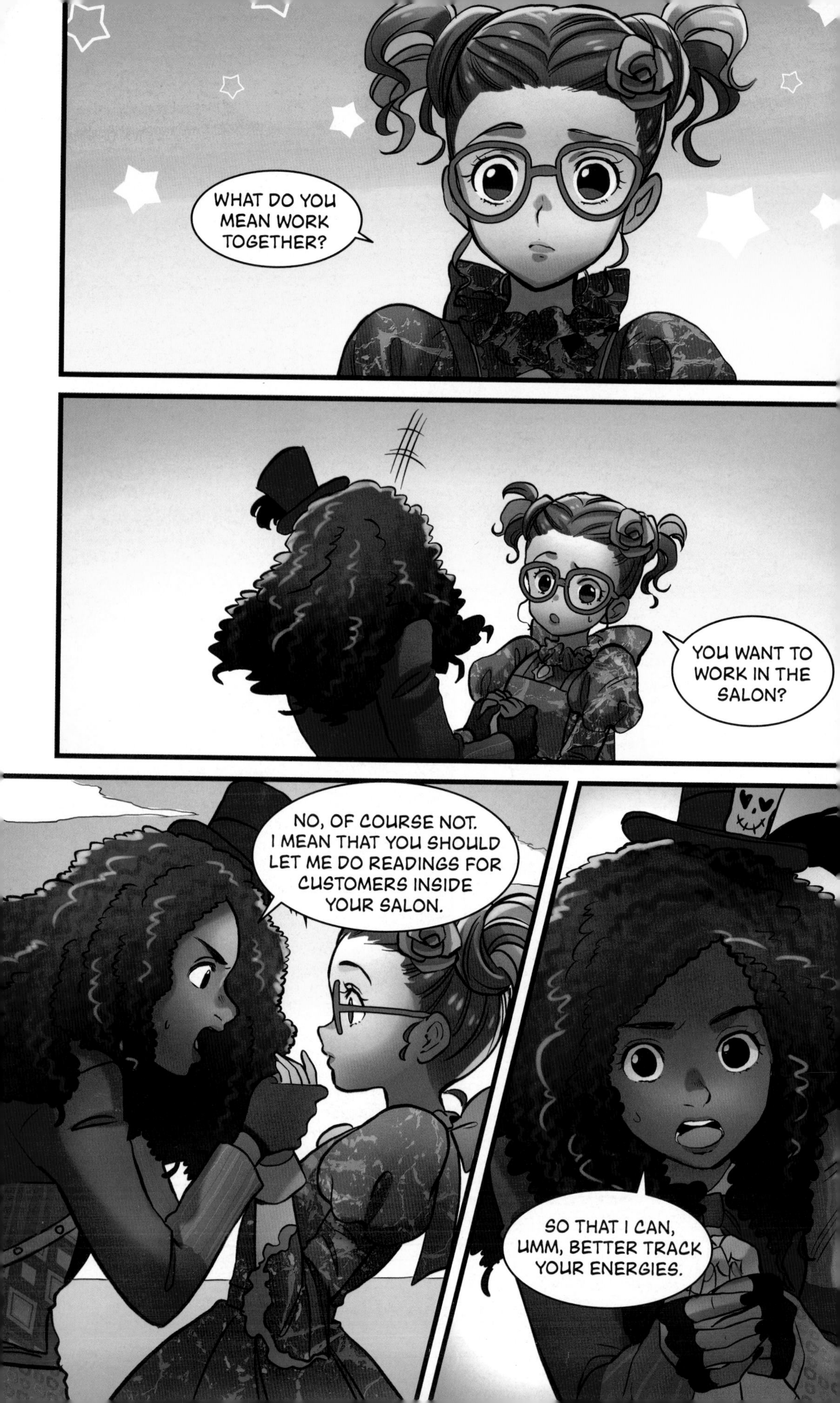
WHAT DO YOU MEAN WORK TOGETHER?
YOU WANT TO WORK IN THE SALON?
NO, OF COURSE NOT. I MEAN THAT YOU SHOULD LET ME DO READINGS FOR CUSTOMERS INSIDE YOUR SALON.
SO THAT I CAN, UMM, BETTER TRACK YOUR ENERGIES.

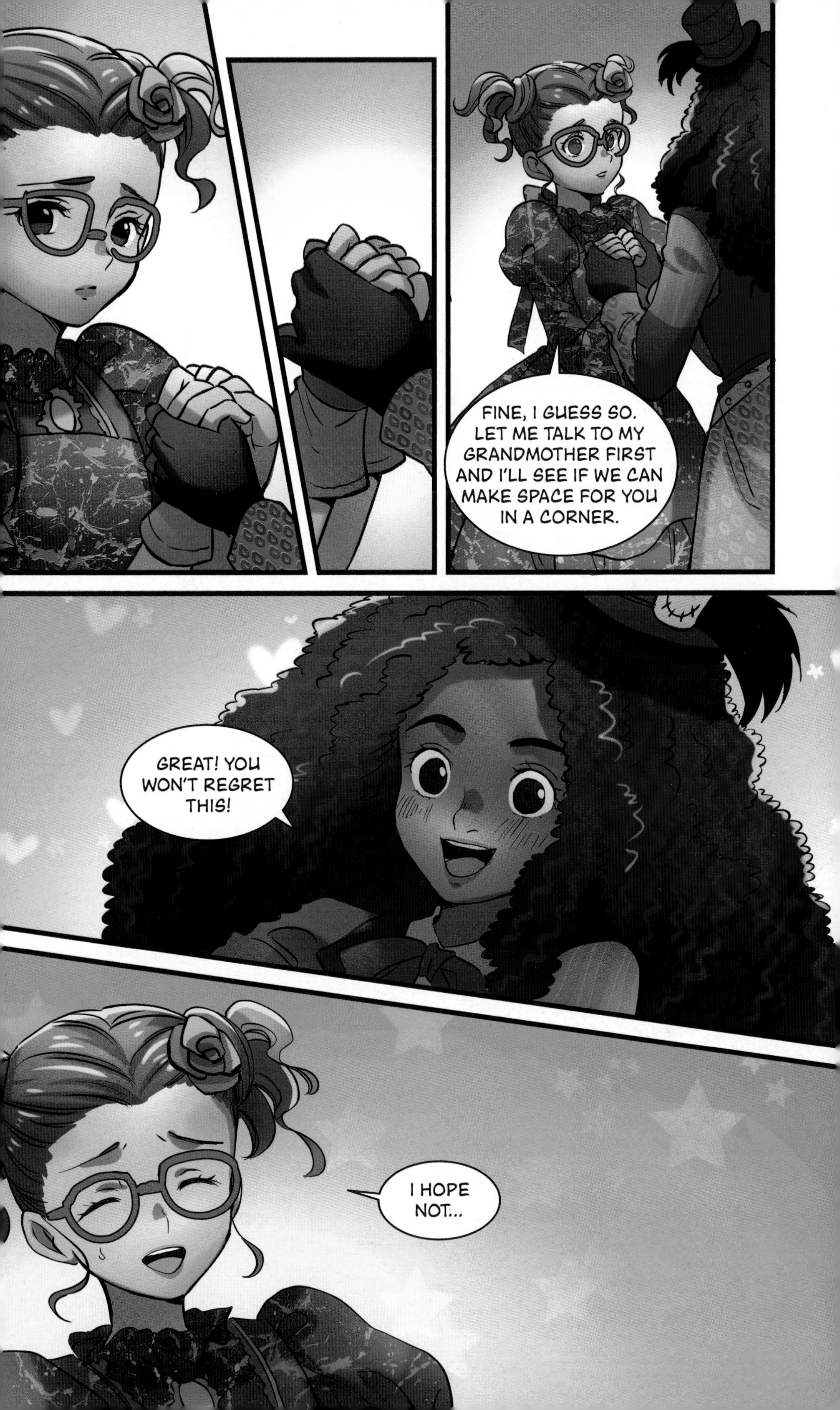
FINE, I GUESS SO. LET ME TALK TO MY GRANDMOTHER FIRST AND I'LL SEE IF WE CAN MAKE SPACE FOR YOU IN A CORNER.
GREAT! YOU WON'T REGRET THIS!
I HOPE NOT...

Dizzy's NEW FORTUNE

CHAPTER 4

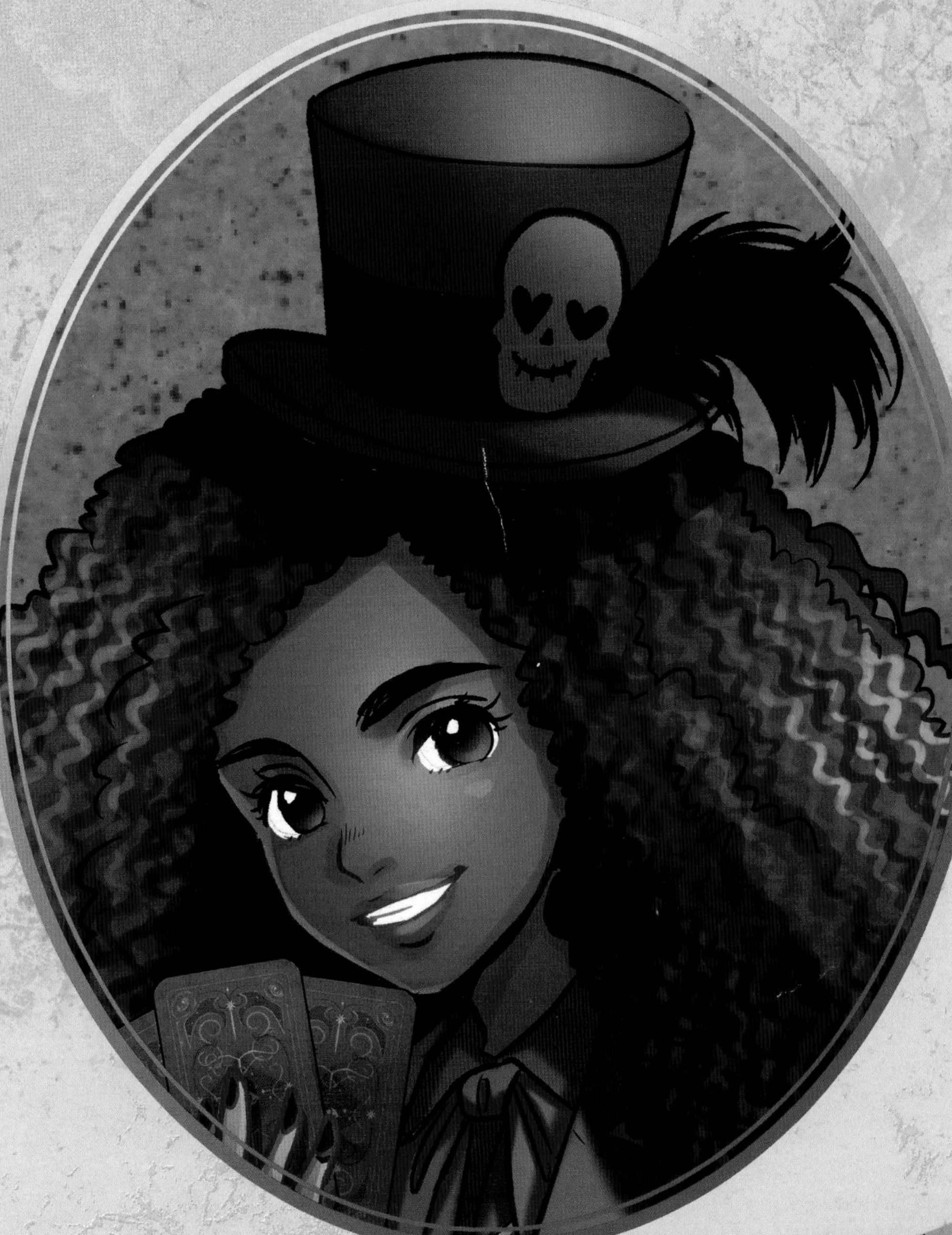

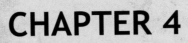

A BRIGHT FUTURE

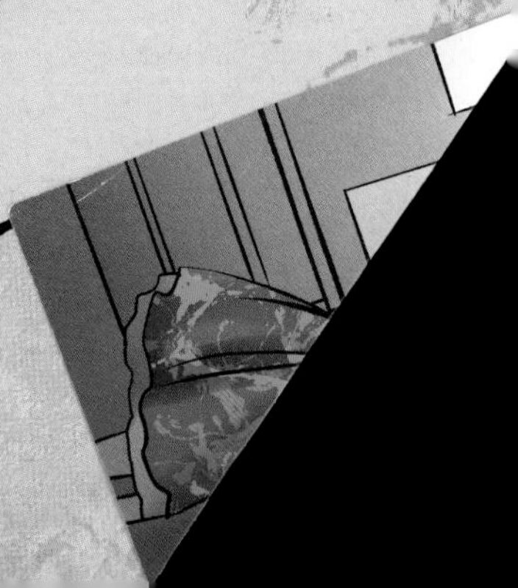

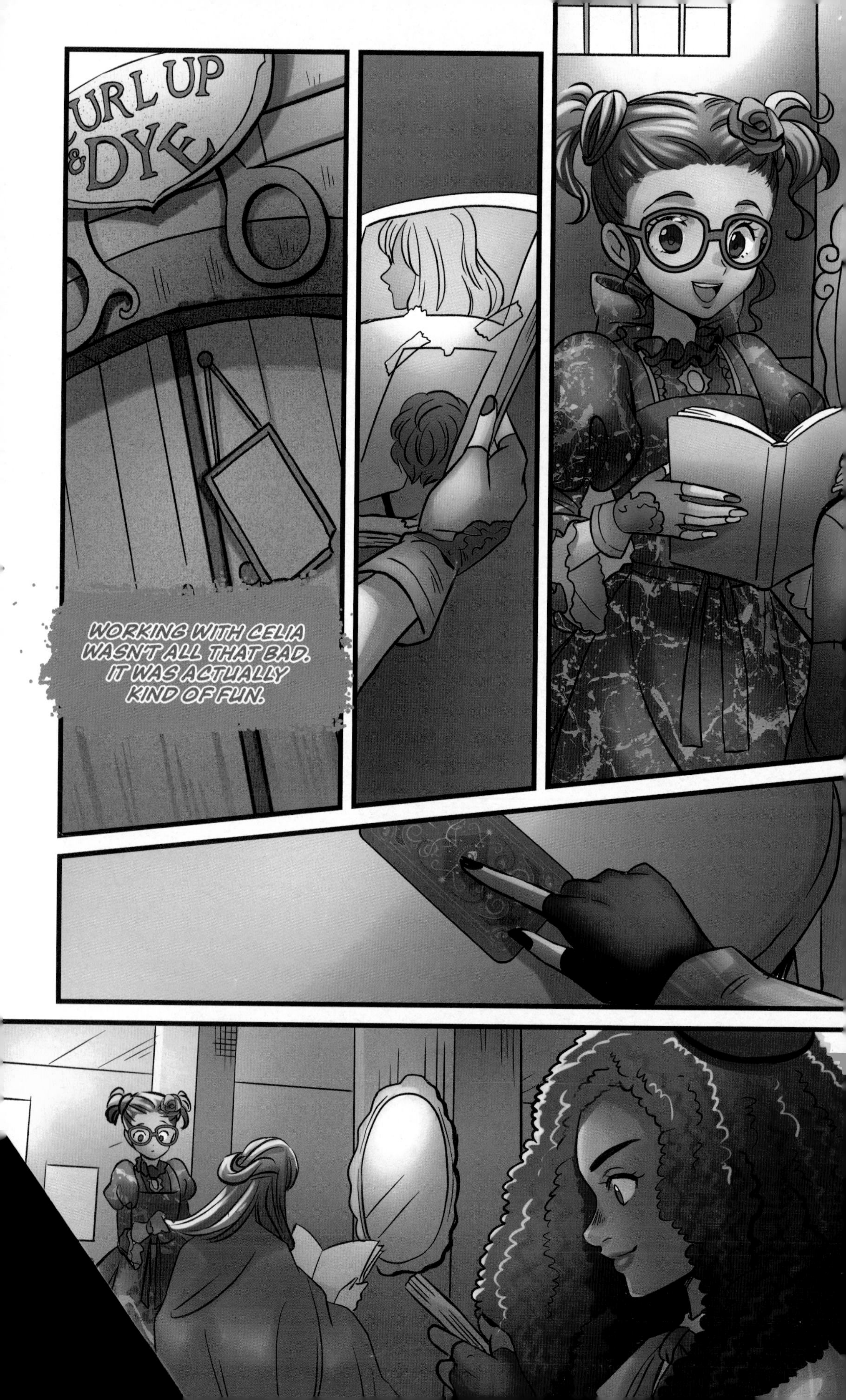
CURL UP & DYE
WORKING WITH CELIA WASN'T ALL THAT BAD. IT WAS ACTUALLY KIND OF FUN.

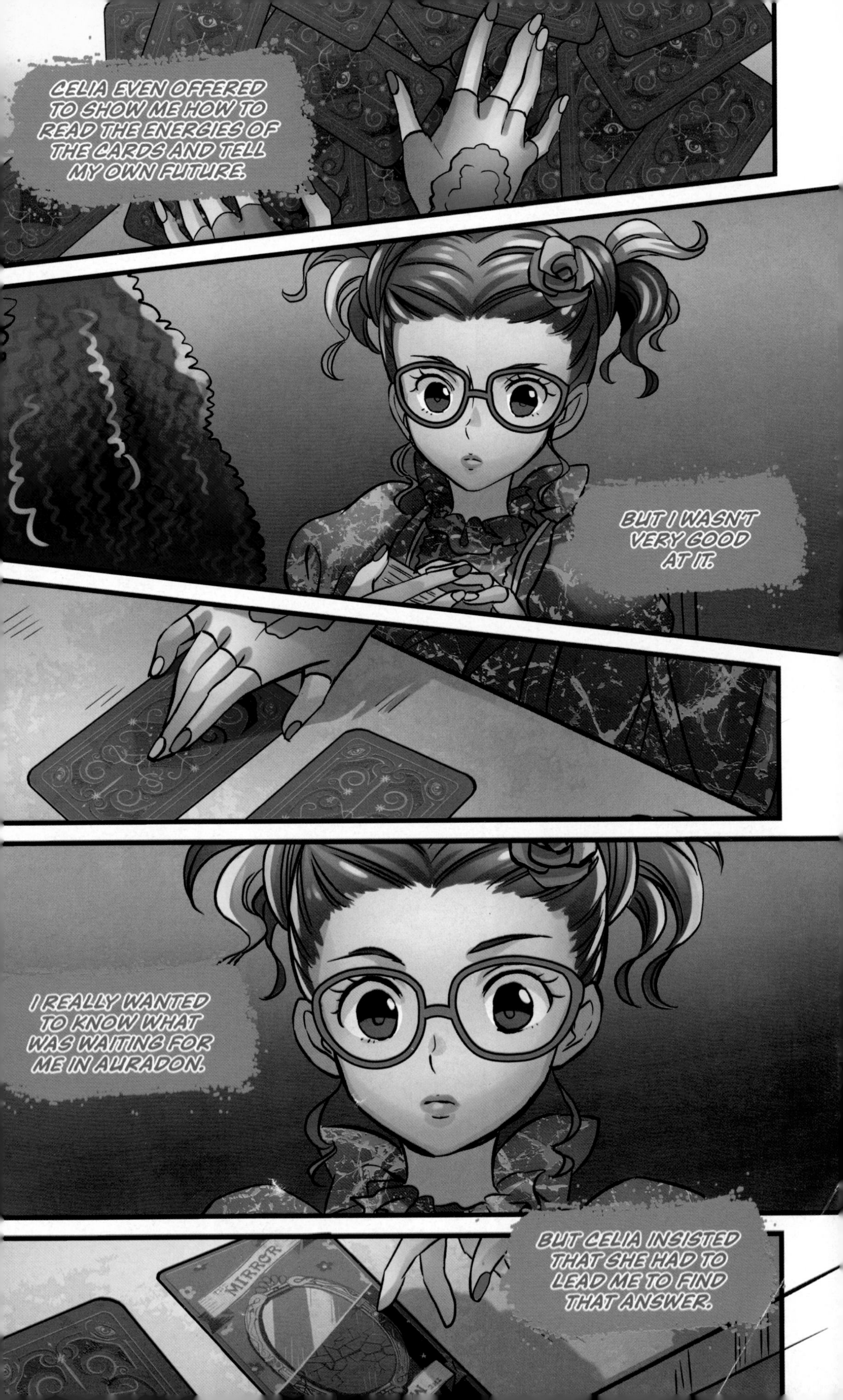
CELIA EVEN OFFERED TO SHOW ME HOW TO READ THE ENERGIES OF THE CARDS AND TELL MY OWN FUTURE.
BUT I WASN'T VERY GOOD AT IT.
I REALLY WANTED TO KNOW WHAT WAS WAITING FOR ME IN AURADON.
MIRROR
BUT CELIA INSISTED THAT SHE HAD TO LEAD ME TO FIND THAT ANSWER.

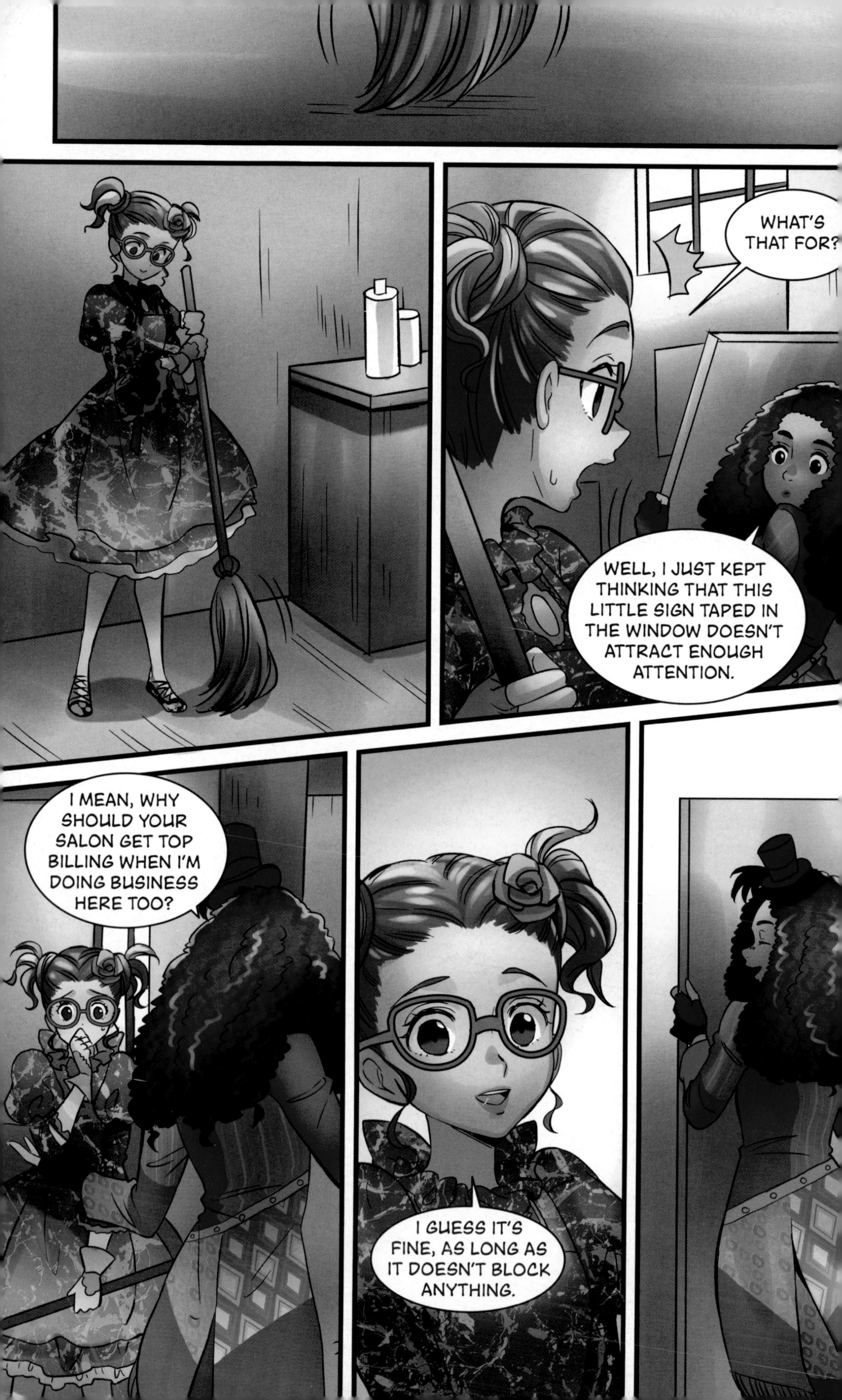
WHAT'S THAT FOR?
WELL, I JUST KEPT THINKING THAT THIS LITTLE SIGN TAPED IN THE WINDOW DOESN'T ATTRACT ENOUGH ATTENTION.
I MEAN, WHY SHOULD YOUR SALON GET TOP BILLING WHEN I'M DOING BUSINESS HERE TOO?
I GUESS IT'S FINE, AS LONG AS IT DOESN'T BLOCK ANYTHING.

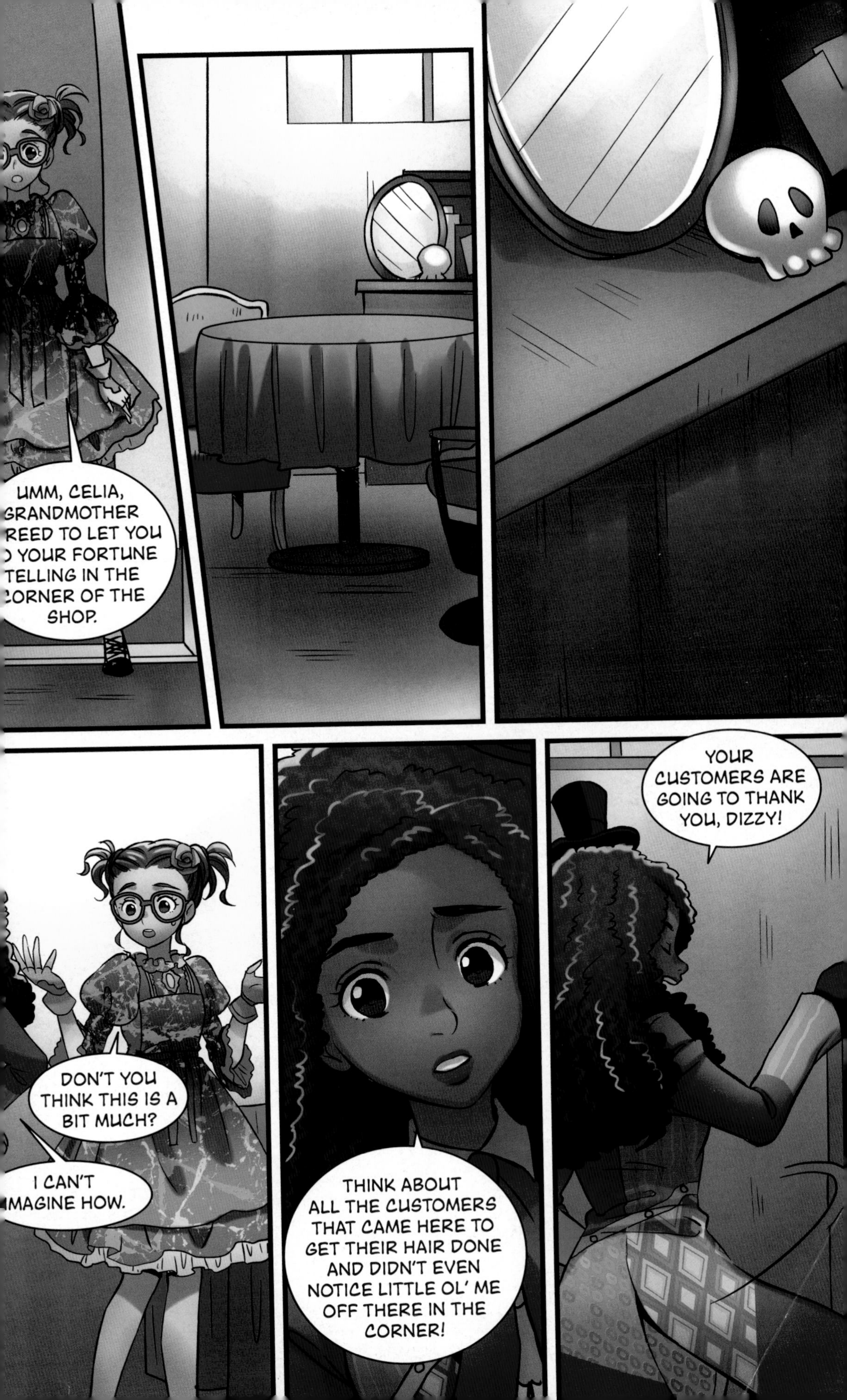
UMM, CELIA, GRANDMOTHER REED TO LET YOU YOUR FORTUNE TELLING IN THE CORNER OF THE SHOP.
DON'T YOU THINK THIS IS A BIT MUCH?
I CAN'T IMAGINE HOW.
THINK ABOUT ALL THE CUSTOMERS THAT CAME HERE TO GET THEIR HAIR DONE AND DIDN'T EVEN NOTICE LITTLE OL' ME OFF THERE IN THE CORNER!
YOUR CUSTOMERS ARE GOING TO THANK YOU, DIZZY!

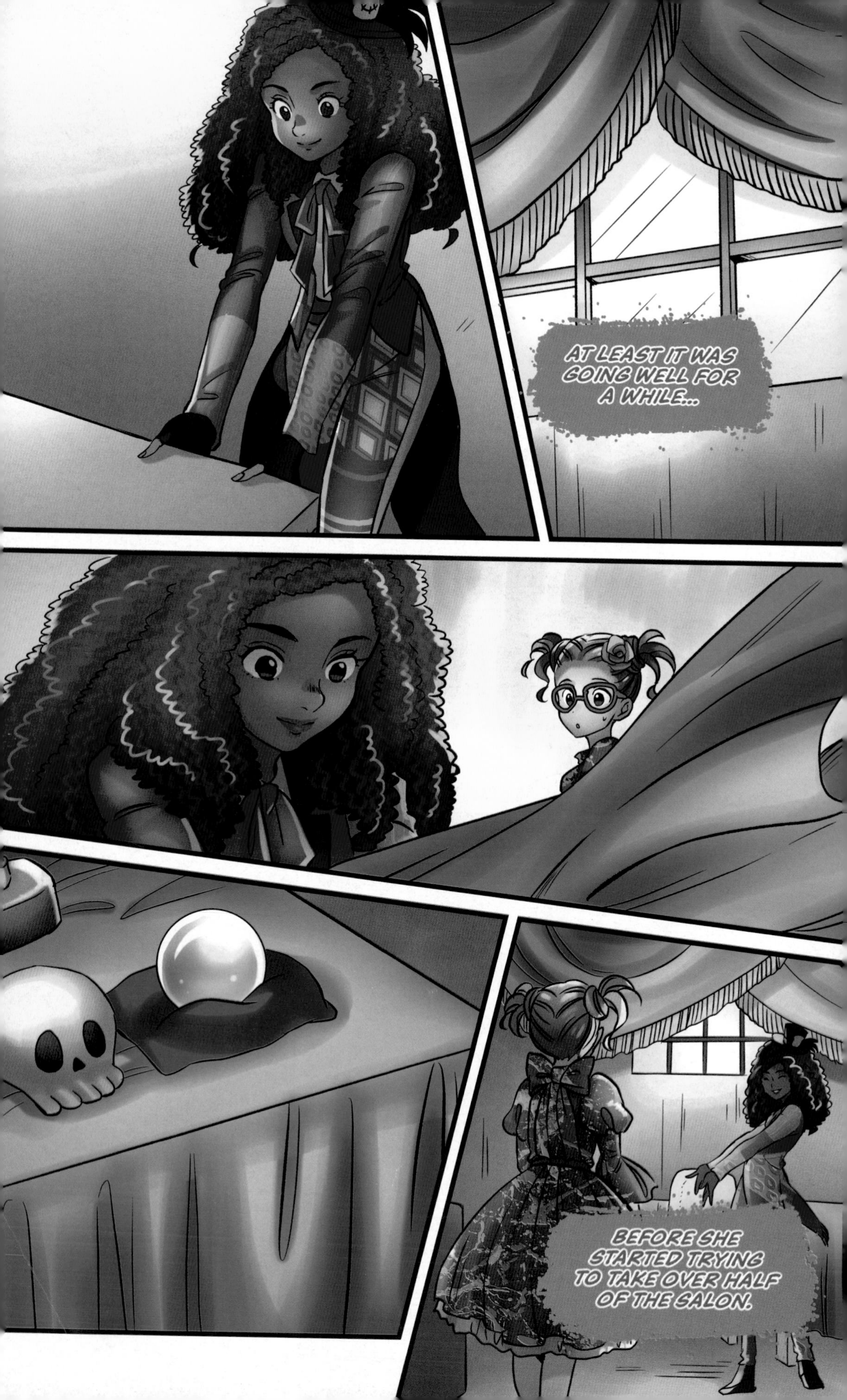
AT LEAST IT WAS GOING WELL FOR A WHILE...
BEFORE SHE STARTED TRYING TO TAKE OVER HALF OF THE SALON.

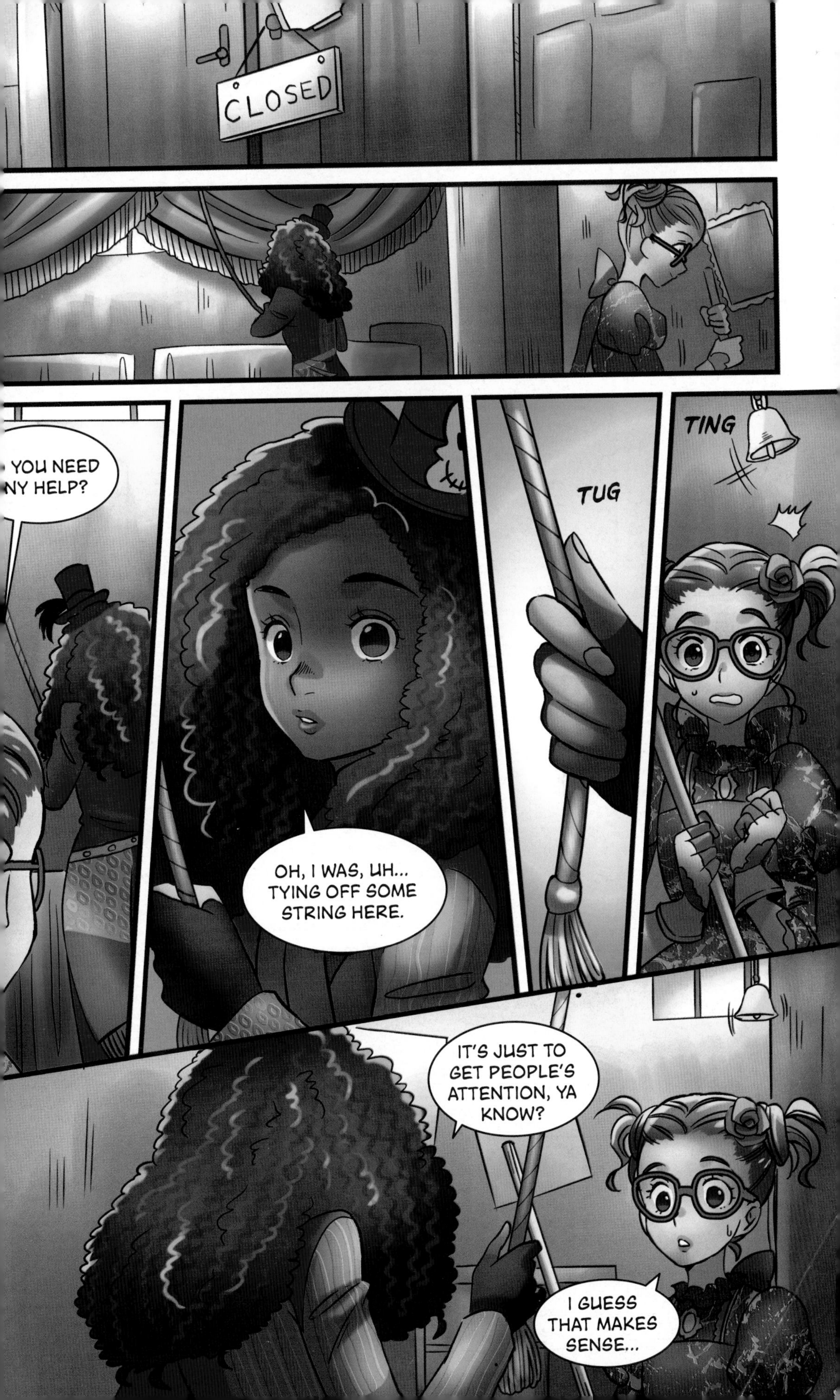
CLOSED
YOU NEED
NY HELP?
OH, I WAS, UH... TYING OFF SOME STRING HERE.
TUG
TING
IT'S JUST TO GET PEOPLE'S ATTENTION, YA KNOW?
I GUESS THAT MAKES SENSE...

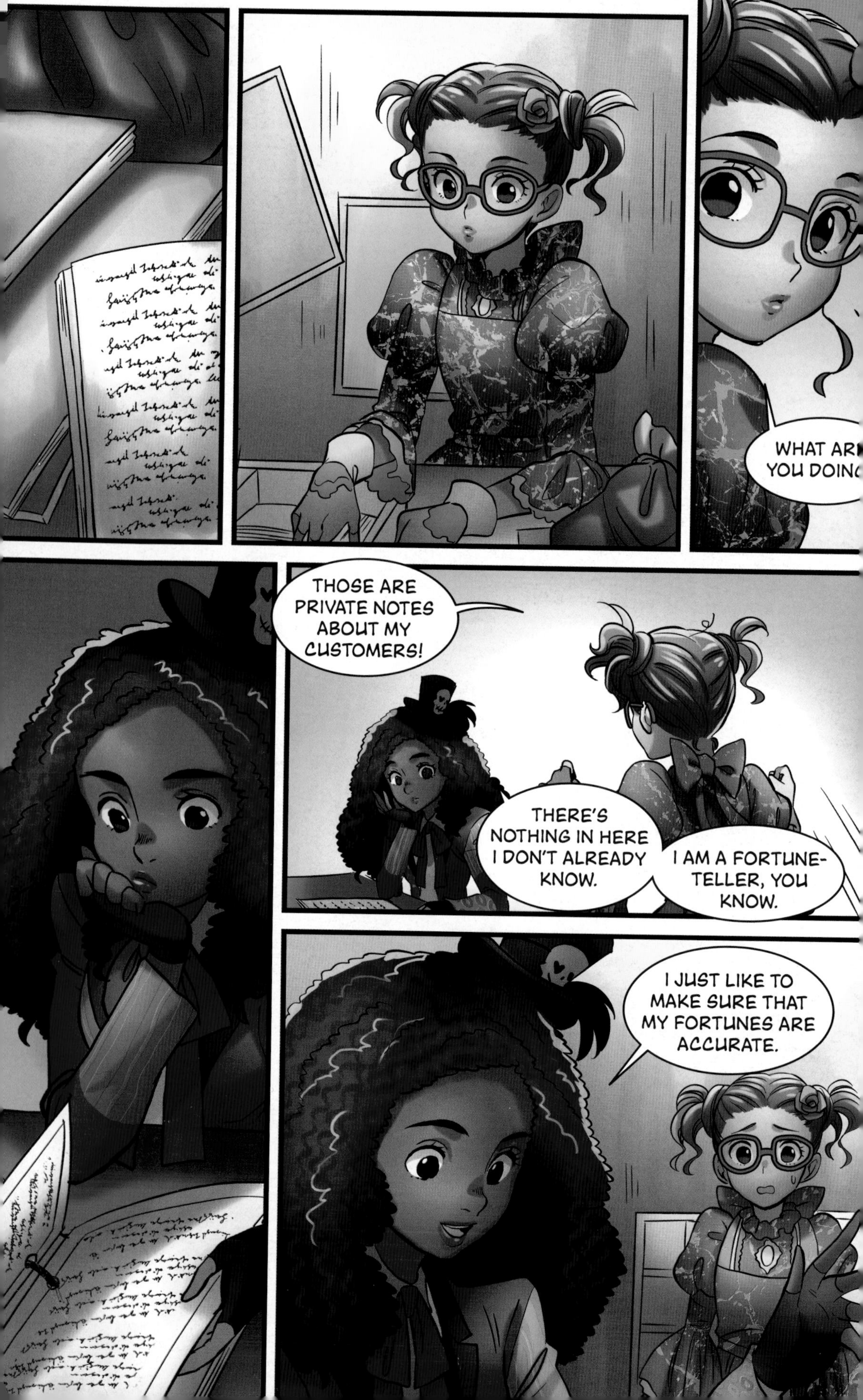
WHAT AR YOU DOIN
THOSE ARE PRIVATE NOTES ABOUT MY CUSTOMERS!
THERE'S NOTHING IN HERE I DON'T ALREADY KNOW.
I AM A FORTUNE-TELLER, YOU KNOW.
I JUST LIKE TO MAKE SURE THAT MY FORTUNES ARE ACCURATE.

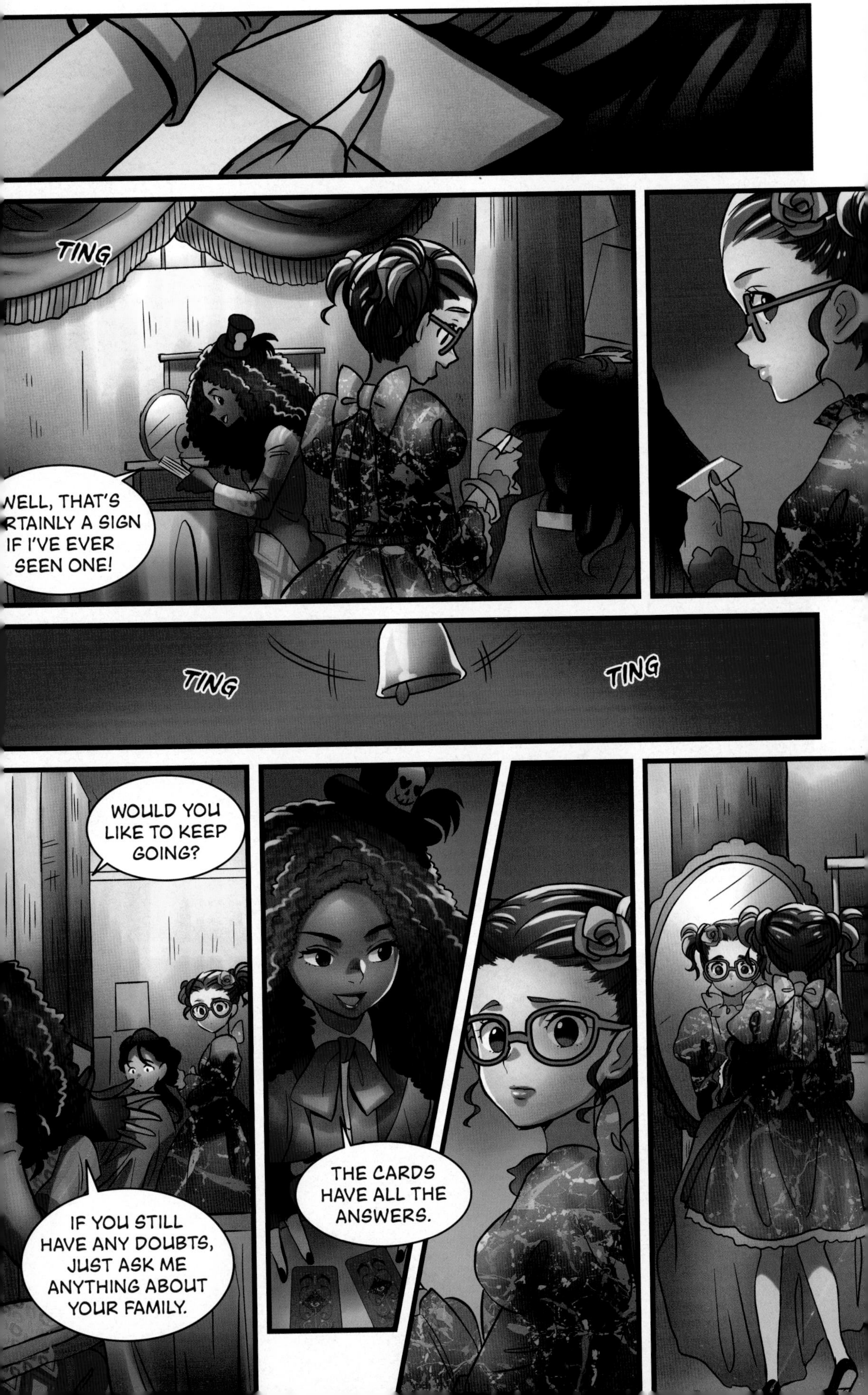
TING
WELL, THAT'S
RTAINLY A SIGN
IF I'VE EVER
SEEN ONE!
TING
TING
WOULD YOU LIKE TO KEEP GOING?
IF YOU STILL HAVE ANY DOUBTS, JUST ASK ME ANYTHING ABOUT YOUR FAMILY.
THE CARDS HAVE ALL THE ANSWERS.

WAS IT ALL JUST A HOAX?

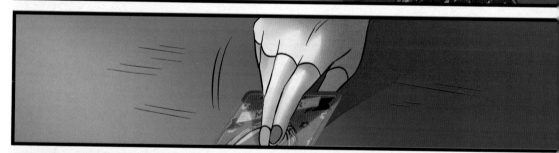

SHE SEEMED SO CONVINCING.

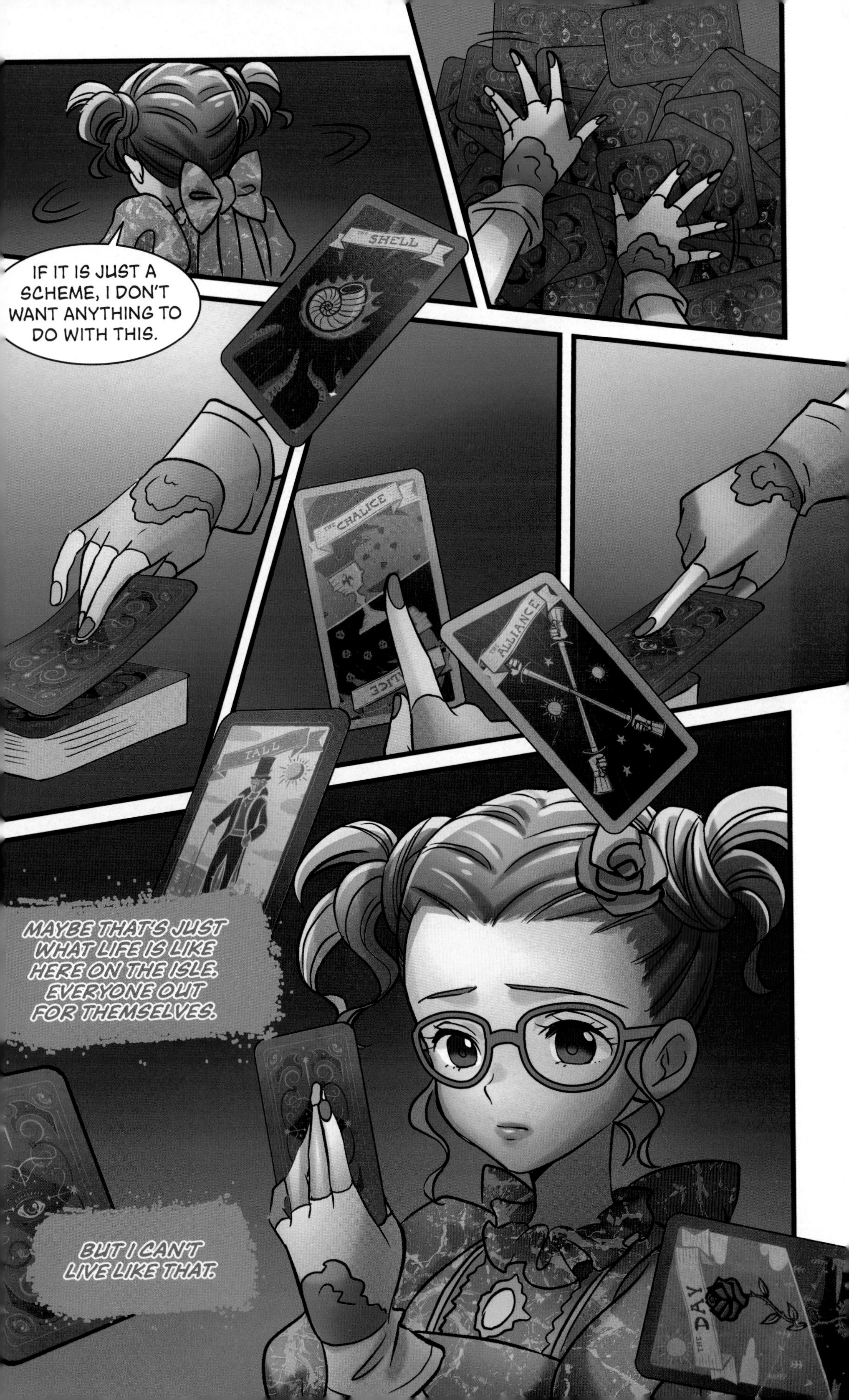

IF IT IS JUST A SCHEME, I DON'T WANT ANYTHING TO DO WITH THIS.
THE SHELL
THE CHALICE
THE ALLIANCE
TALL
MAYBE THAT'S JUST WHAT LIFE IS LIKE HERE ON THE ISLE. EVERYONE OUT FOR THEMSELVES.
BUT I CAN'T LIVE LIKE THAT.
THE DAY

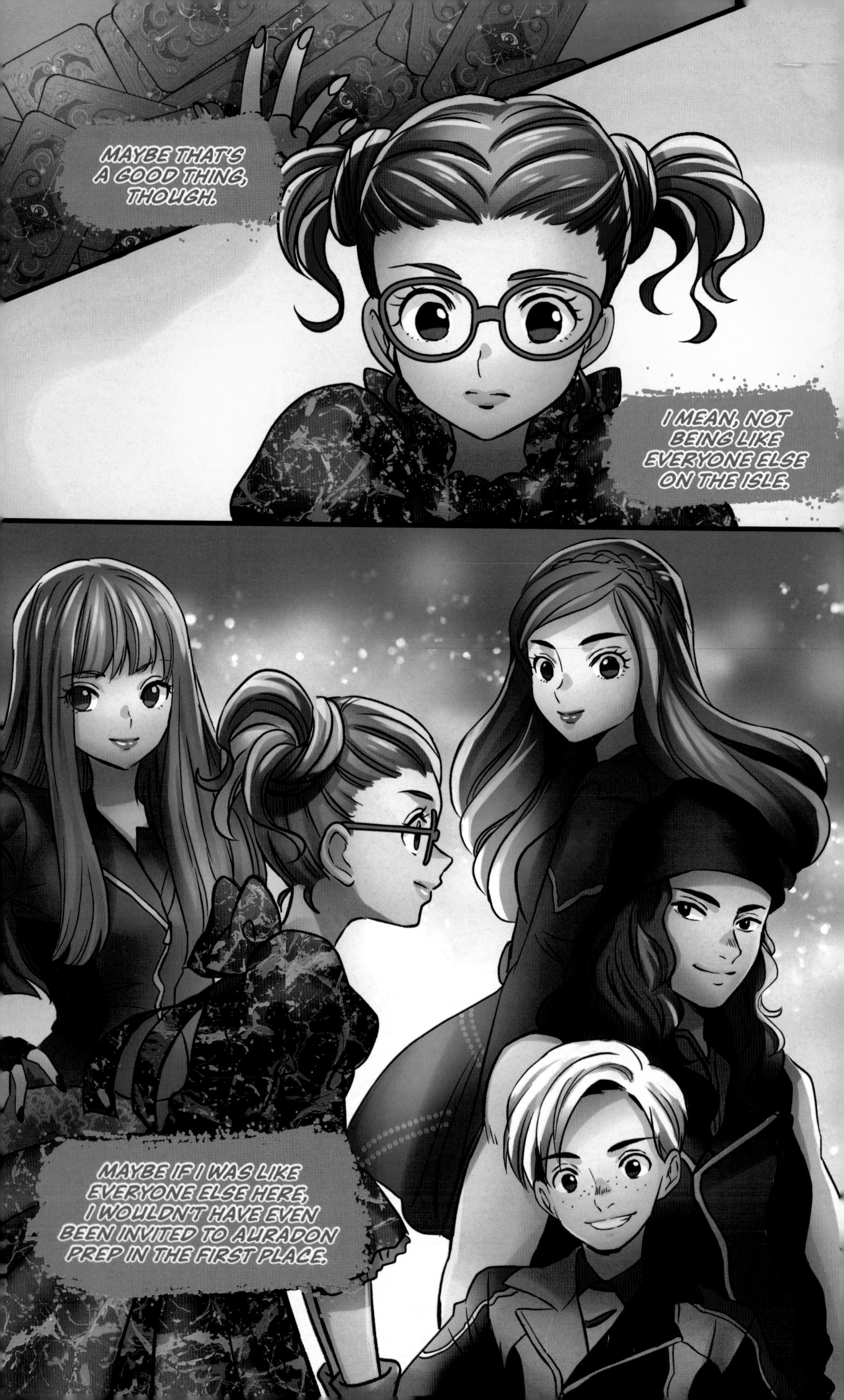
MAYBE THAT'S A GOOD THING, THOUGH.
I MEAN, NOT BEING LIKE EVERYONE ELSE ON THE ISLE.
MAYBE IF I WAS LIKE EVERYONE ELSE HERE, I WOULDN'T HAVE EVEN BEEN INVITED TO AURADON PREP IN THE FIRST PLACE.

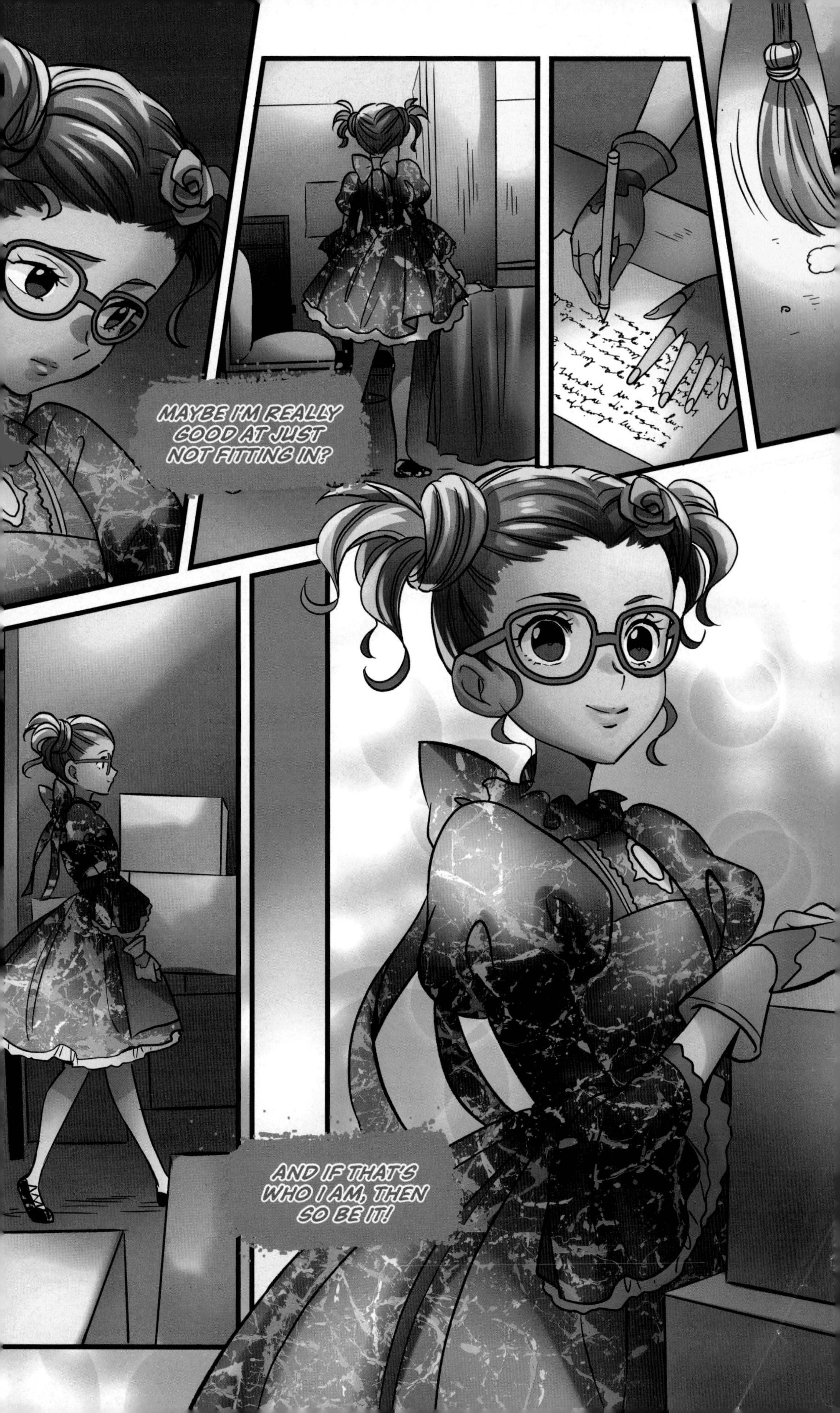
MAYBE I'M REALLY GOOD AT JUST NOT FITTING IN?
AND IF THAT'S WHO I AM, THEN SO BE IT!

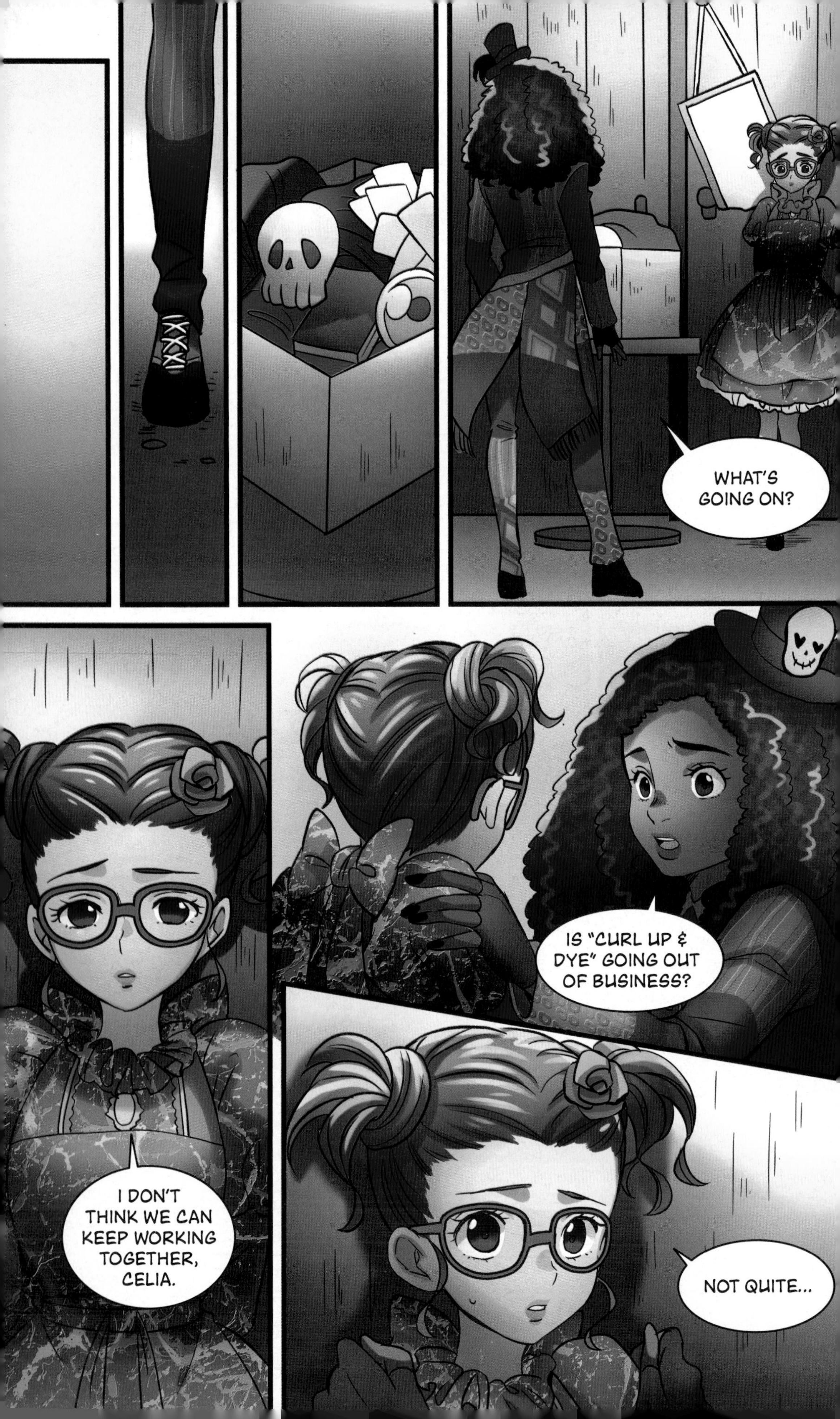
WHAT'S GOING ON?
IS "CURL UP & DYE" GOING OUT OF BUSINESS?
I DON'T THINK WE CAN KEEP WORKING TOGETHER, CELIA.
NOT QUITE...

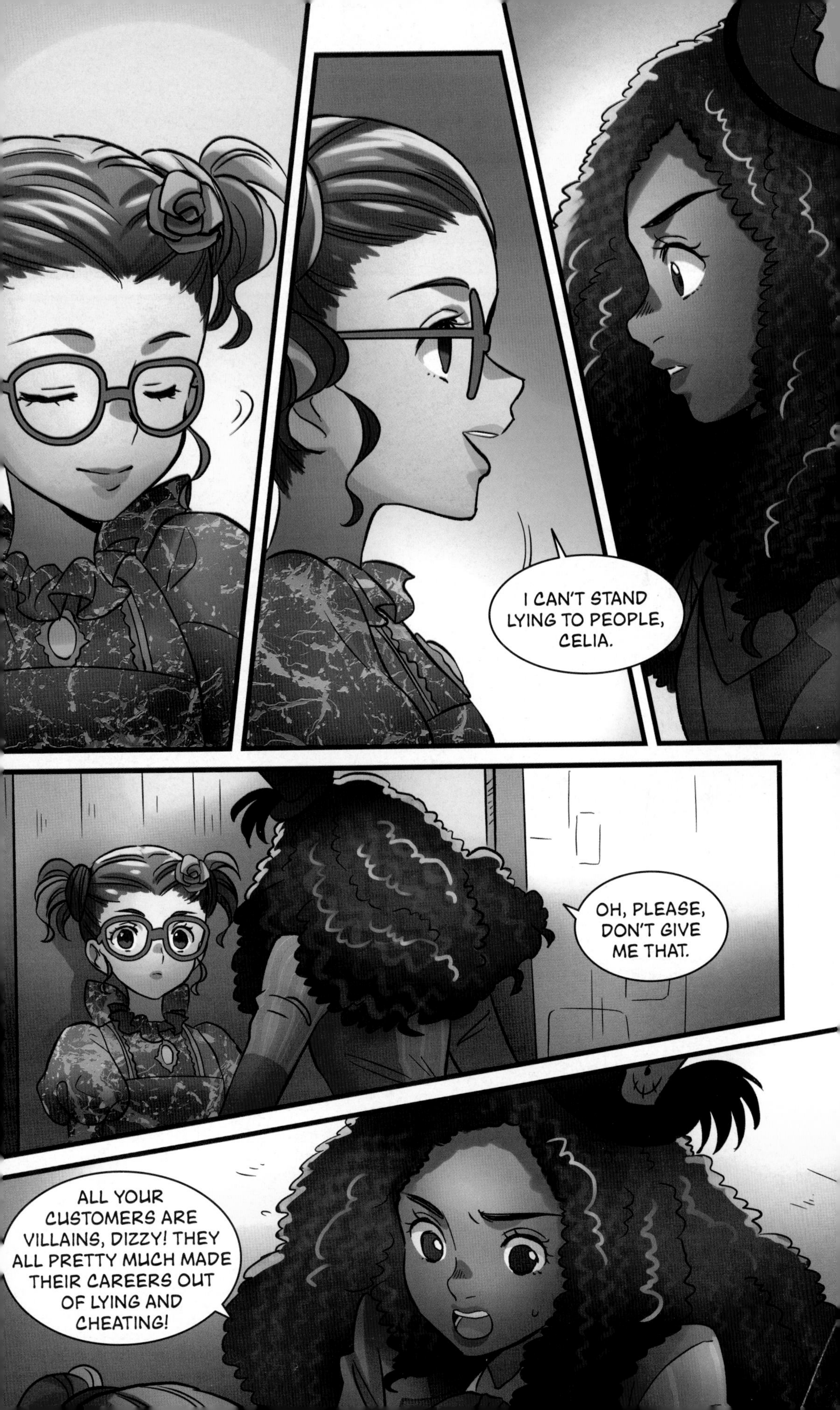
I CAN'T STAND LYING TO PEOPLE, CELIA.
OH, PLEASE, DON'T GIVE ME THAT.
ALL YOUR CUSTOMERS ARE VILLAINS, DIZZY! THEY ALL PRETTY MUCH MADE THEIR CAREERS OUT OF LYING AND CHEATING!

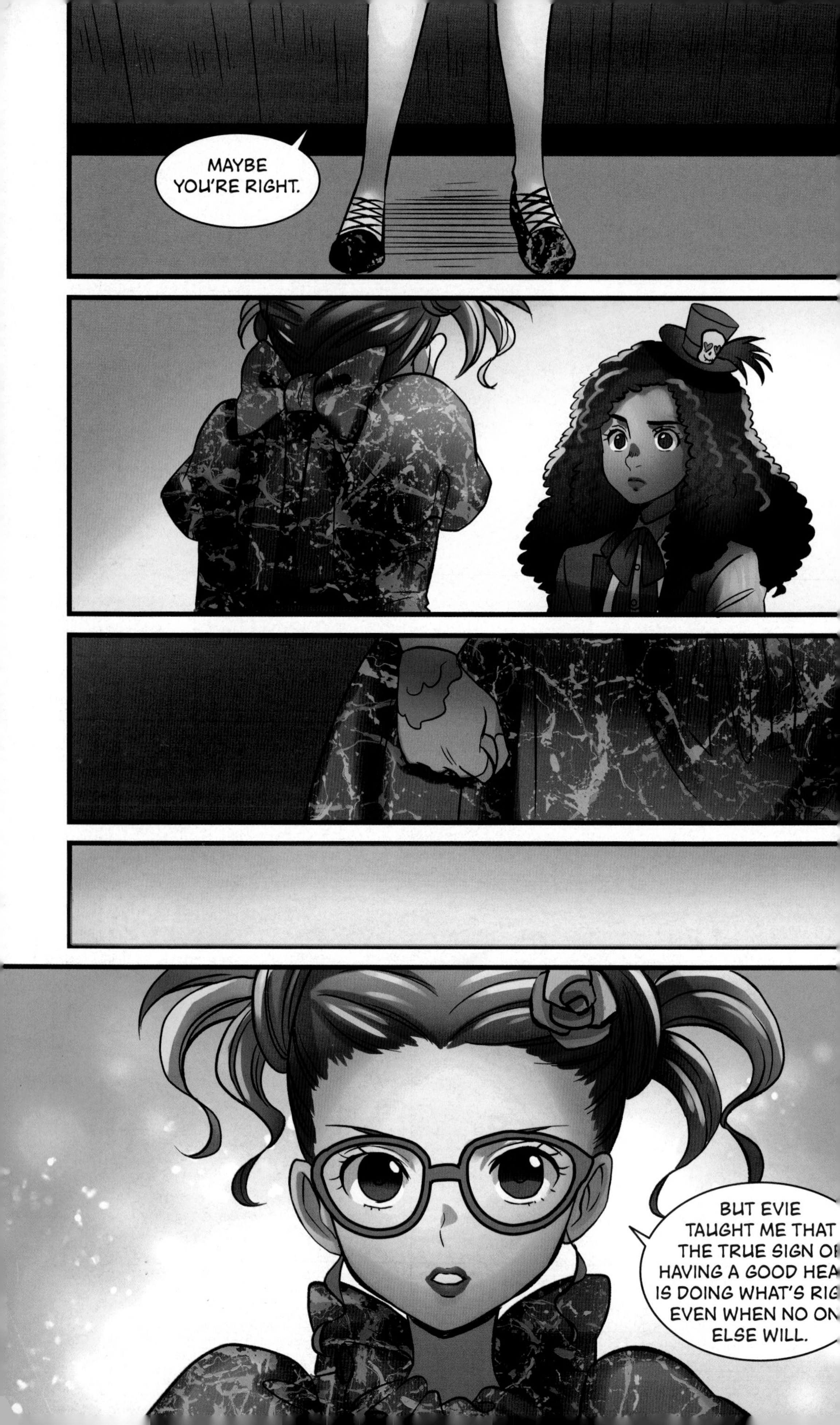
MAYBE YOU'RE RIGHT.
BUT EVIE TAUGHT ME THAT THE TRUE SIGN O HAVING A GOOD HEA IS DOING WHAT'S RIG EVEN WHEN NO ON ELSE WILL.

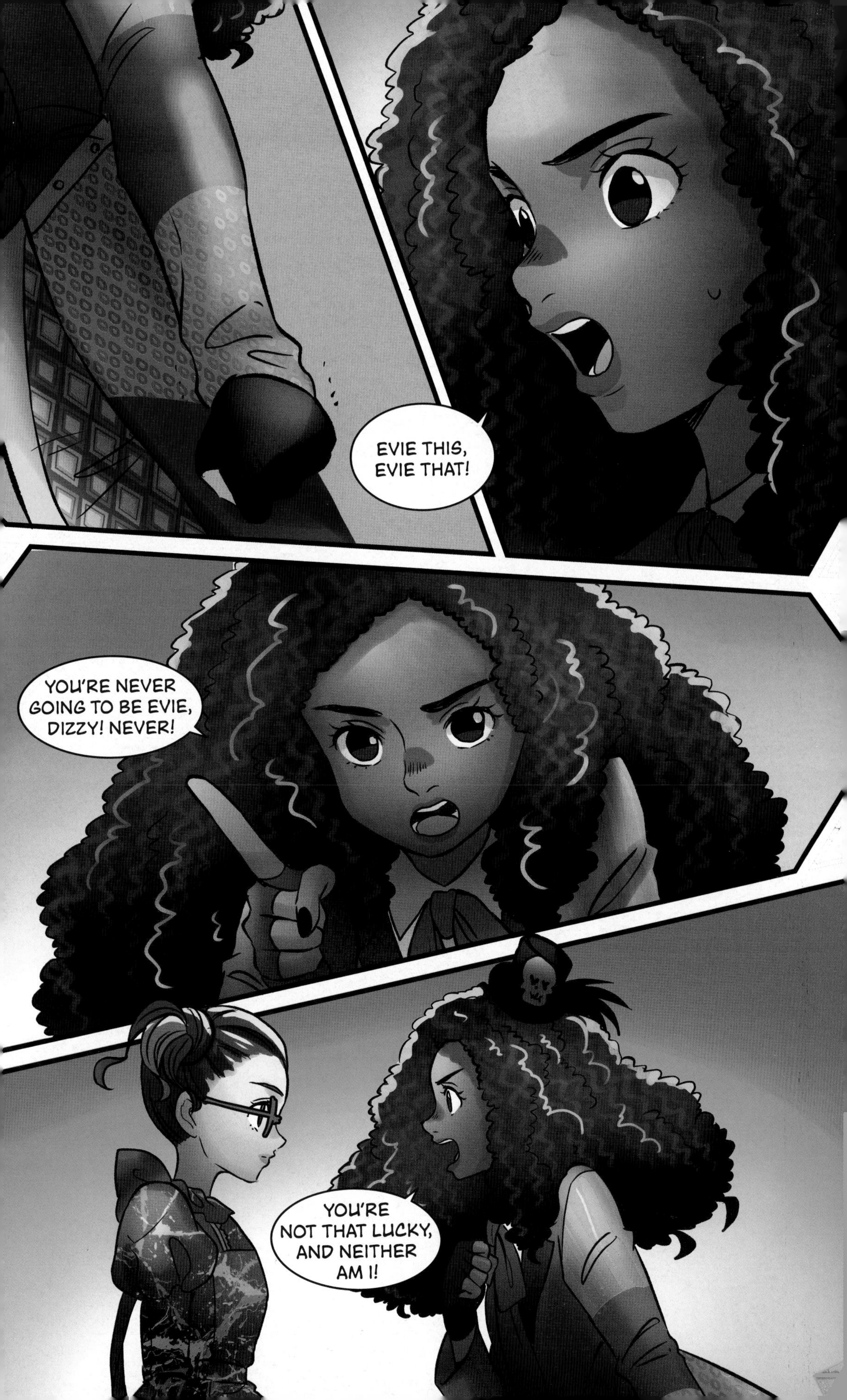
EVIE THIS, EVIE THAT!
YOU'RE NEVER GOING TO BE EVIE, DIZZY! NEVER!
YOU'RE NOT THAT LUCKY, AND NEITHER AM I!

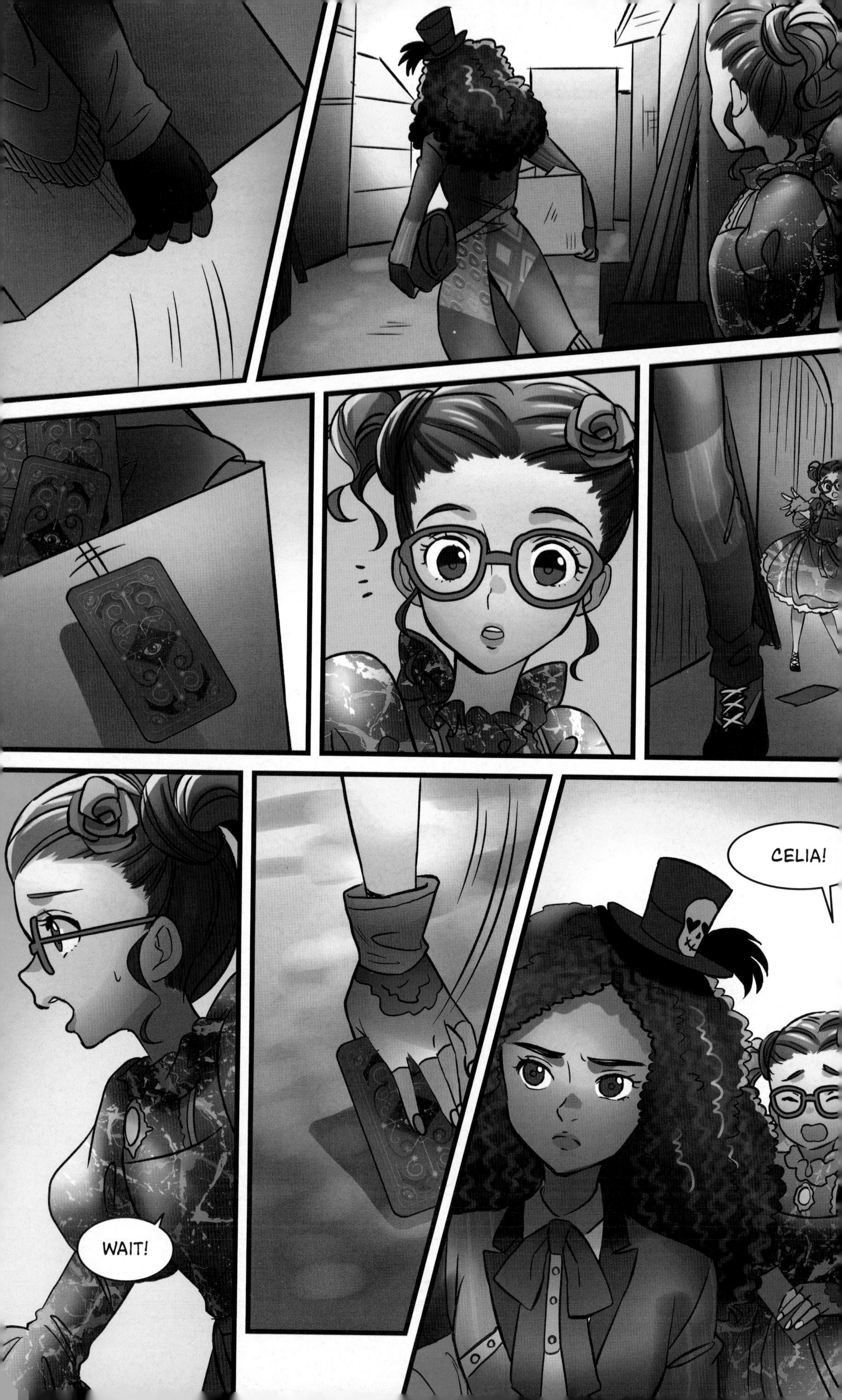
WAIT!
CELIA!

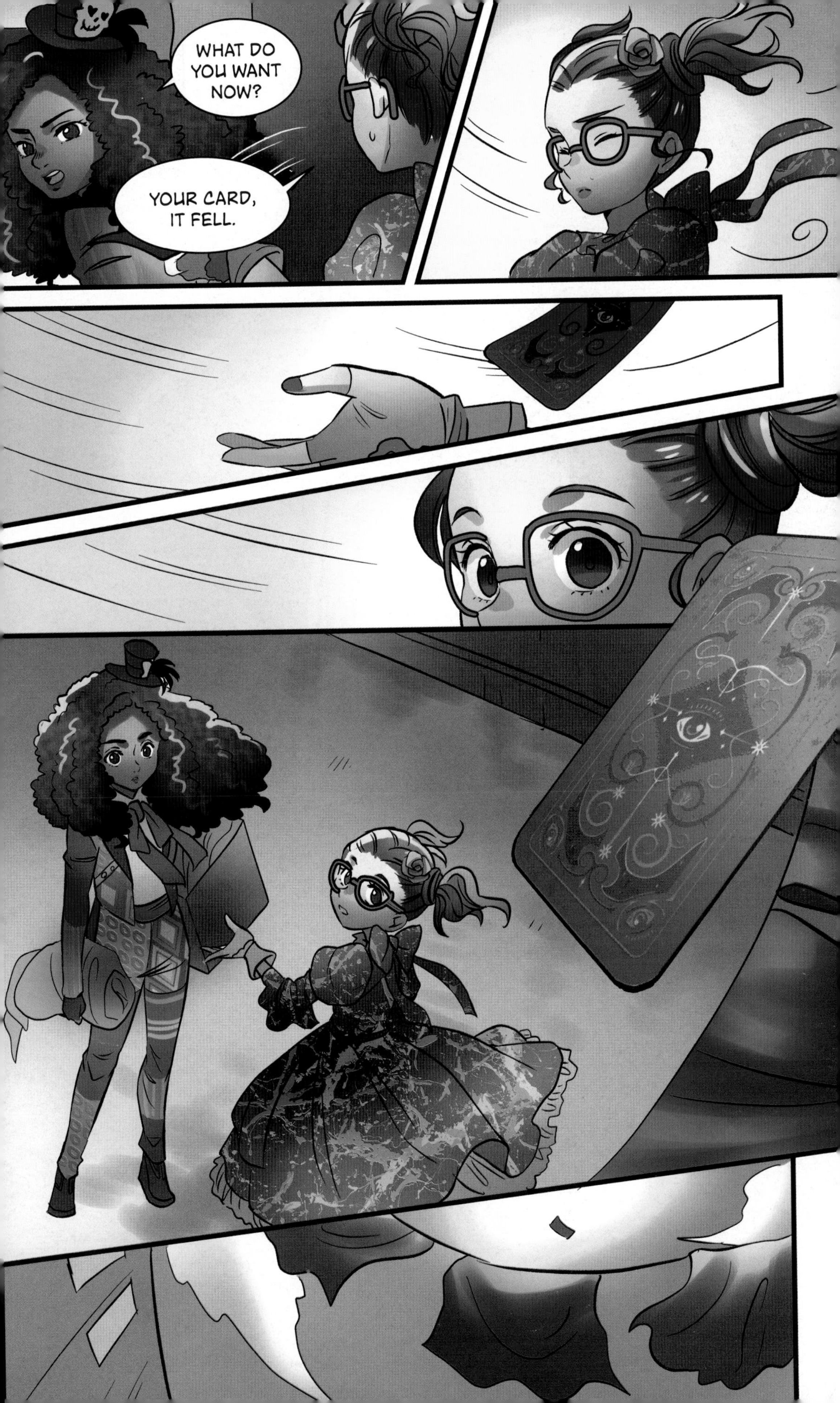
WHAT DO YOU WANT NOW?
YOUR CARD, IT FELL.

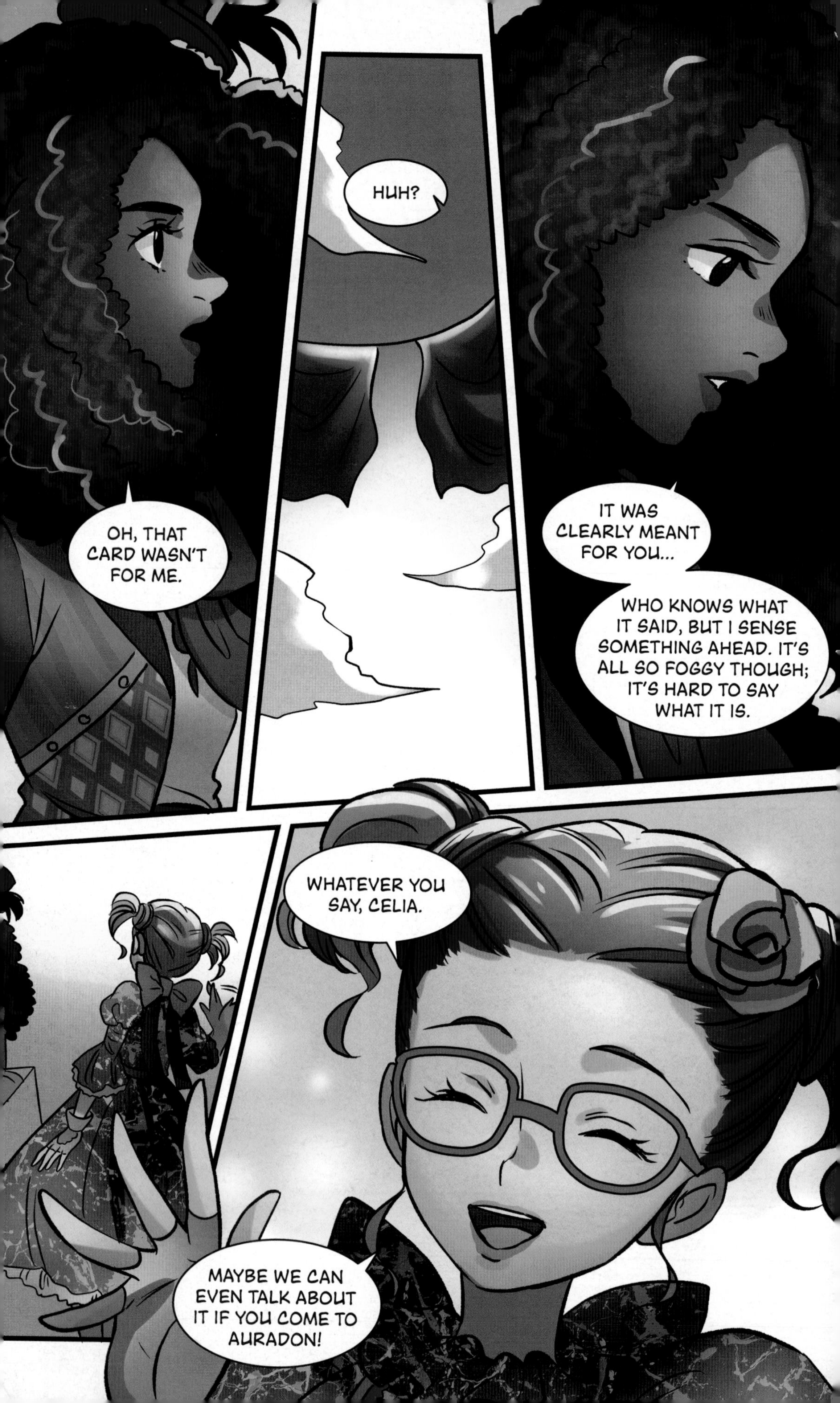
HUH?
OH, THAT CARD WASN'T FOR ME.
IT WAS CLEARLY MEANT FOR YOU...
WHO KNOWS WHAT IT SAID, BUT I SENSE SOMETHING AHEAD. IT'S ALL SO FOGGY THOUGH; IT'S HARD TO SAY WHAT IT IS.
WHATEVER YOU SAY, CELIA.
MAYBE WE CAN EVEN TALK ABOUT IT IF YOU COME TO AURADON!

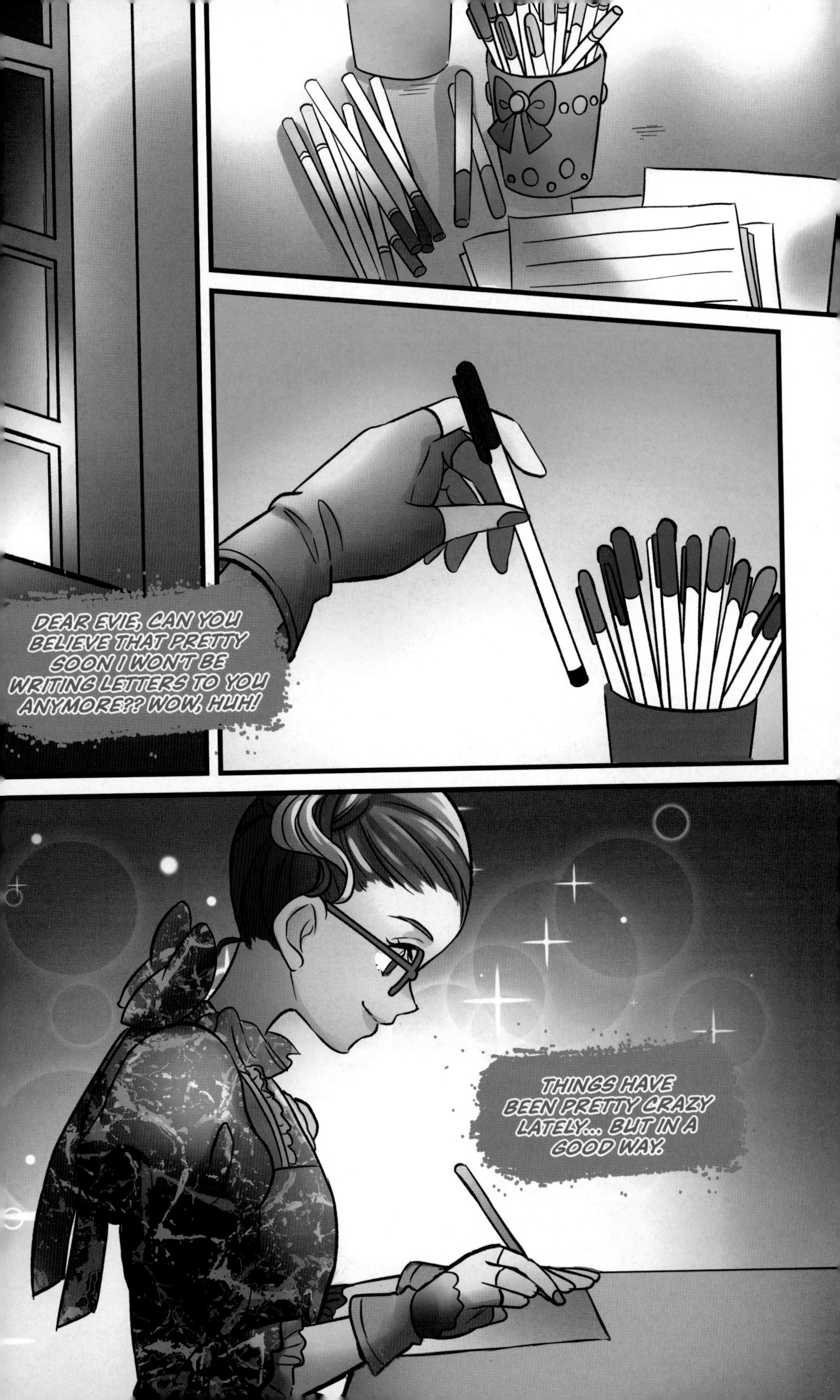
DEAR EVIE, CAN YOU BELIEVE THAT PRETTY SOON I WON'T BE WRITING LETTERS TO YOU ANYMORE?? WOW, HUH!
THINGS HAVE BEEN PRETTY CRAZY LATELY... BUT IN A GOOD WAY.

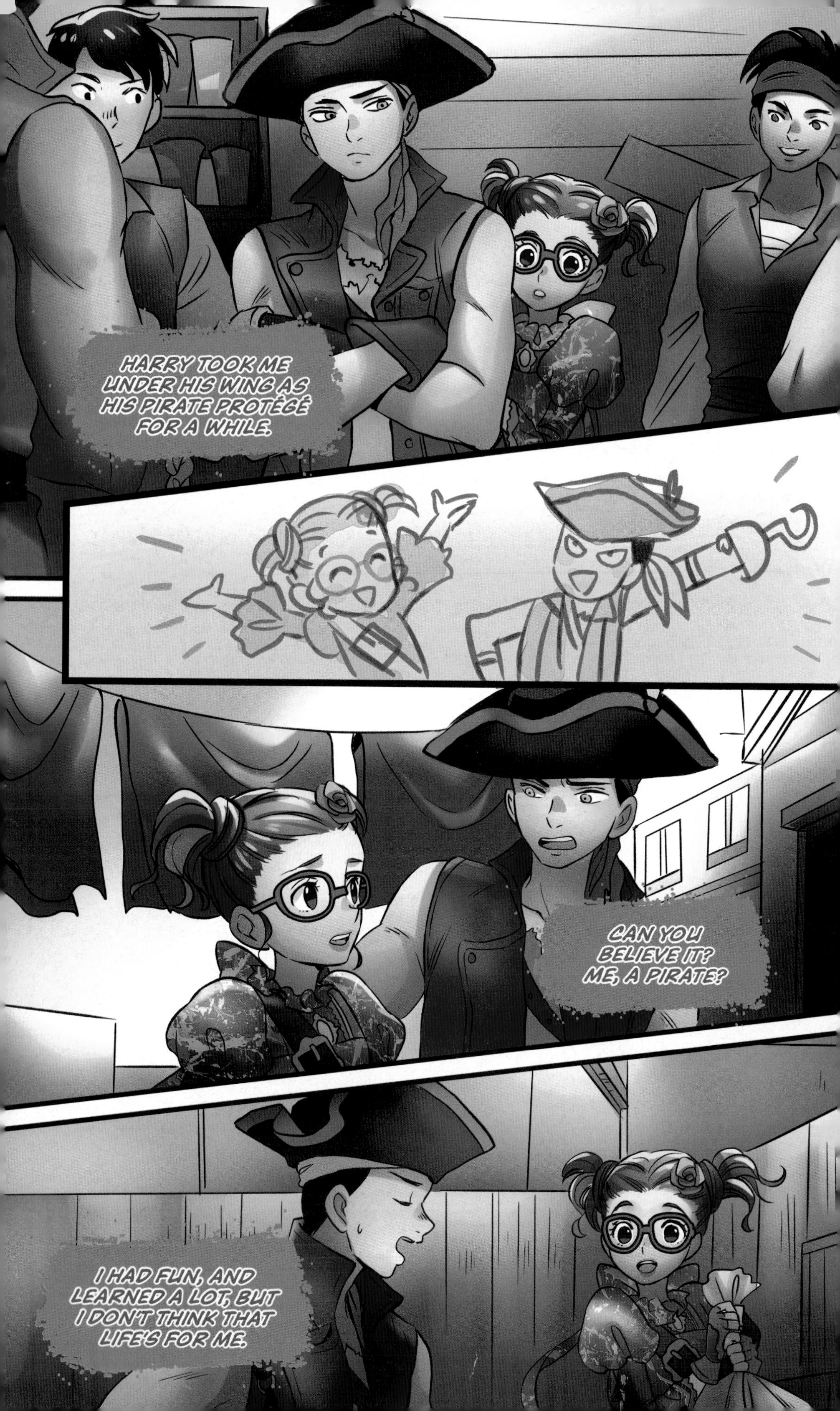
HARRY TOOK ME UNDER HIS WING AS HIS PIRATE PROTÉGÉ FOR A WHILE.
CAN YOU BELIEVE IT? ME, A PIRATE?
I HAD FUN, AND LEARNED A LOT, BUT I DON'T THINK THAT LIFE'S FOR ME.

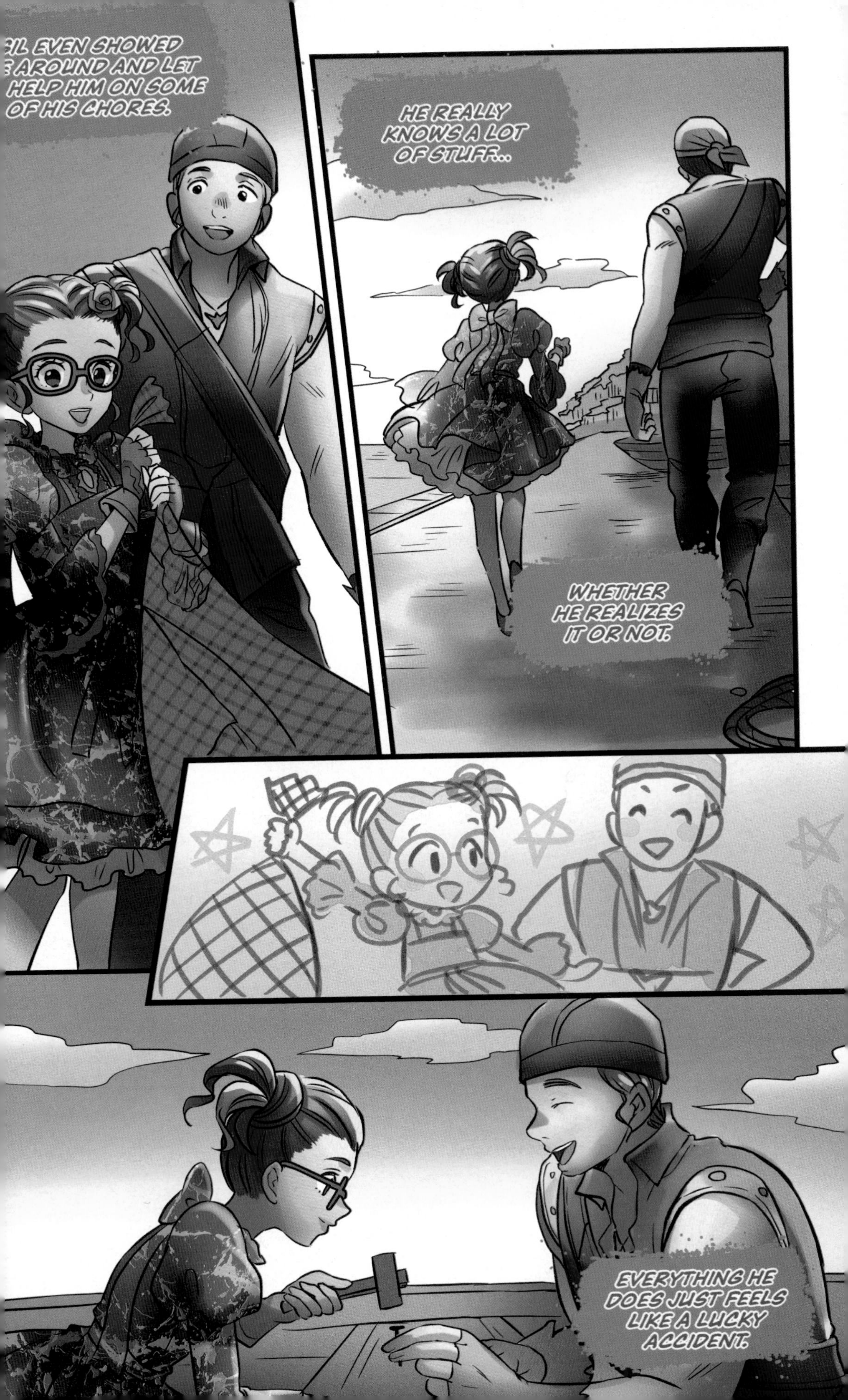
IL EVEN SHOWED E AROUND AND LET HELP HIM ON SOME OF HIS CHORES.
HE REALLY KNOWS A LOT OF STUFF...
WHETHER HE REALIZES IT OR NOT.
EVERYTHING HE DOES JUST FEELS LIKE A LUCKY ACCIDENT.

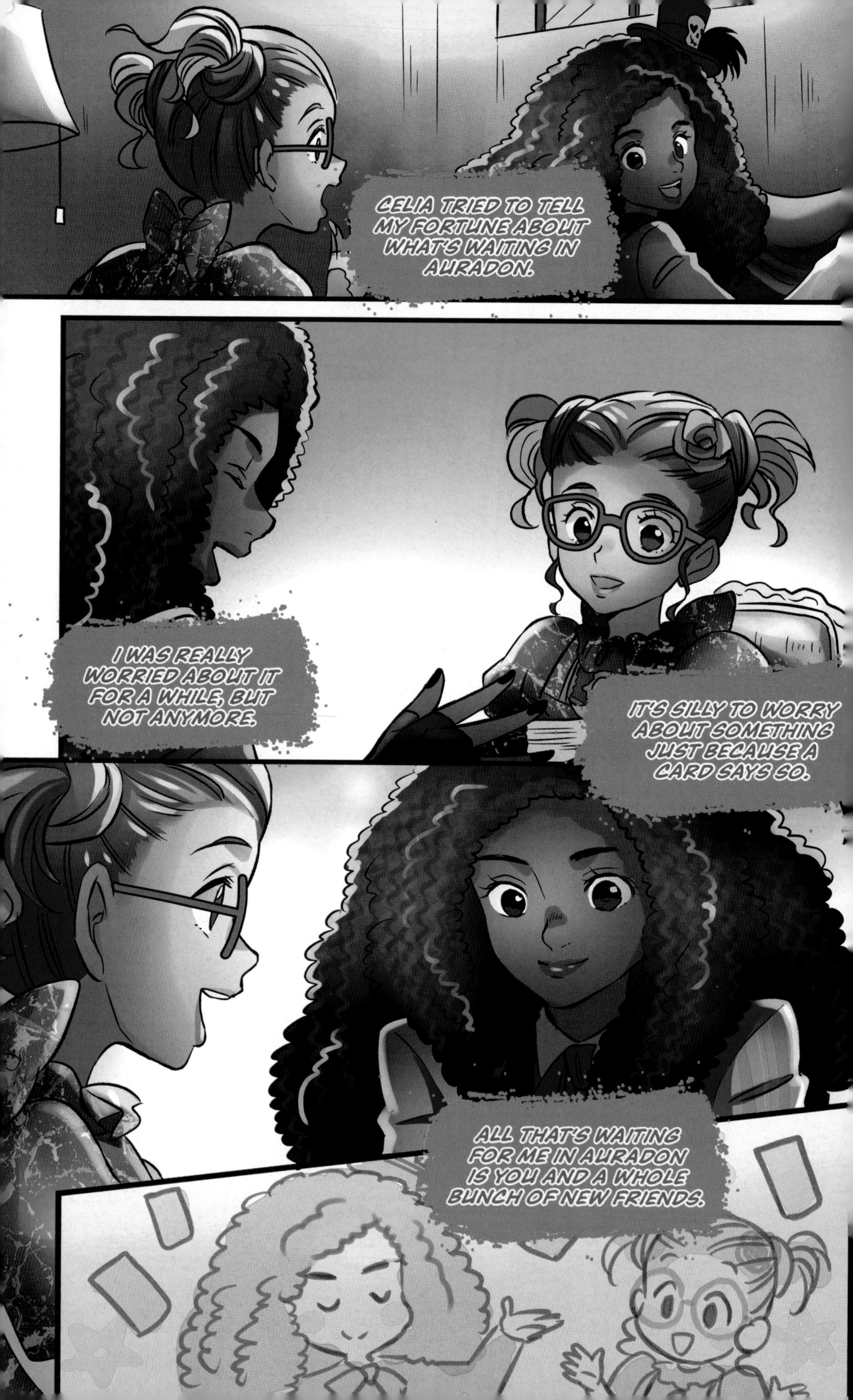
CELIA TRIED TO TELL MY FORTUNE ABOUT WHAT'S WAITING IN AURADON.
I WAS REALLY WORRIED ABOUT IT FOR A WHILE, BUT NOT ANYMORE.
IT'S SILLY TO WORRY ABOUT SOMETHING JUST BECAUSE A CARD SAYS SO.
ALL THAT'S WAITING FOR ME IN AURADON IS YOU AND A WHOLE BUNCH OF NEW FRIENDS.

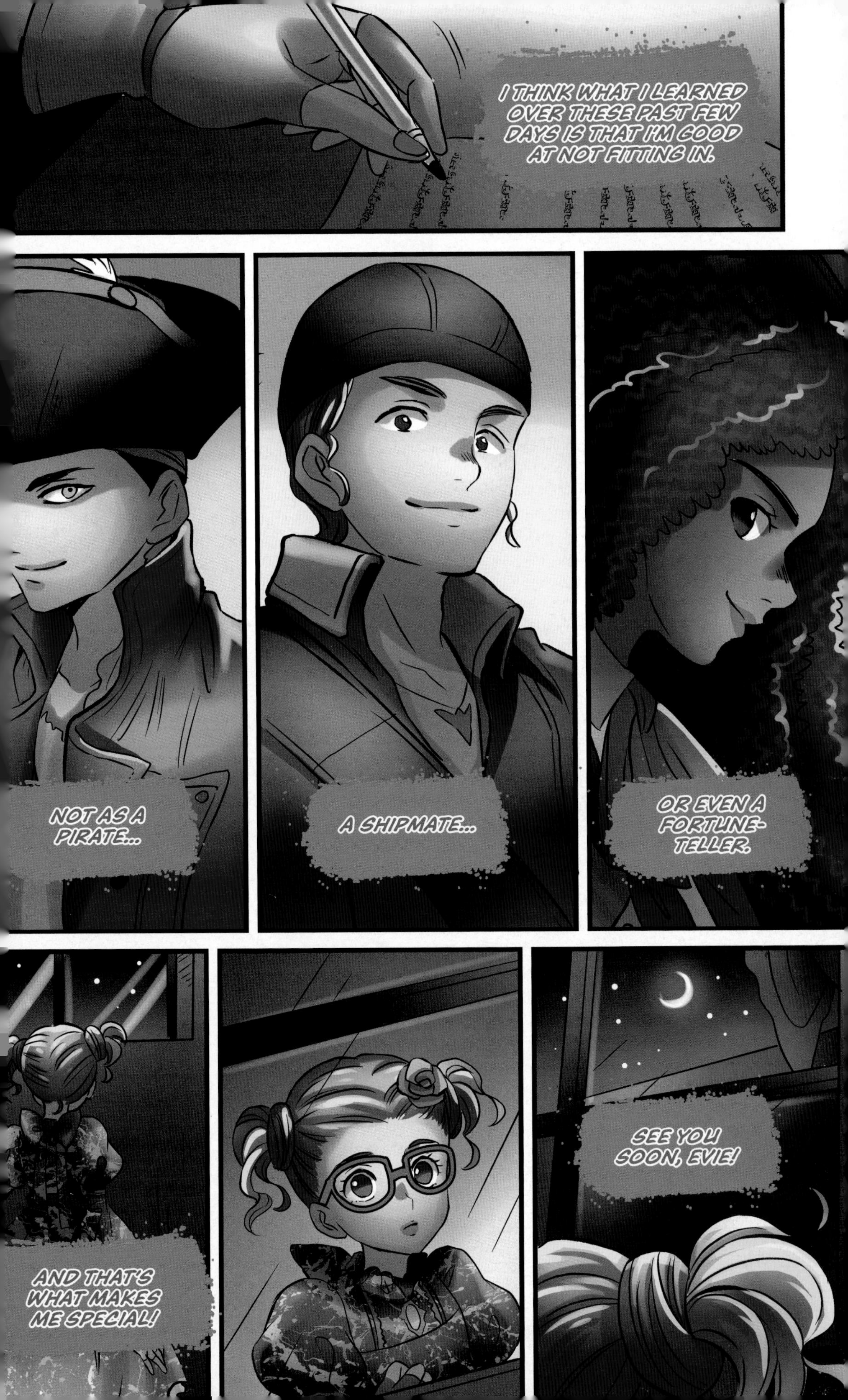
I THINK WHAT I LEARNED OVER THESE PAST FEW DAYS IS THAT I'M GOOD AT NOT FITTING IN.
NOT AS A PIRATE...
A SHIPMATE...
OR EVEN A FORTUNE-TELLER.
AND THAT'S WHAT MAKES ME SPECIAL!
SEE YOU SOON, EVIE!

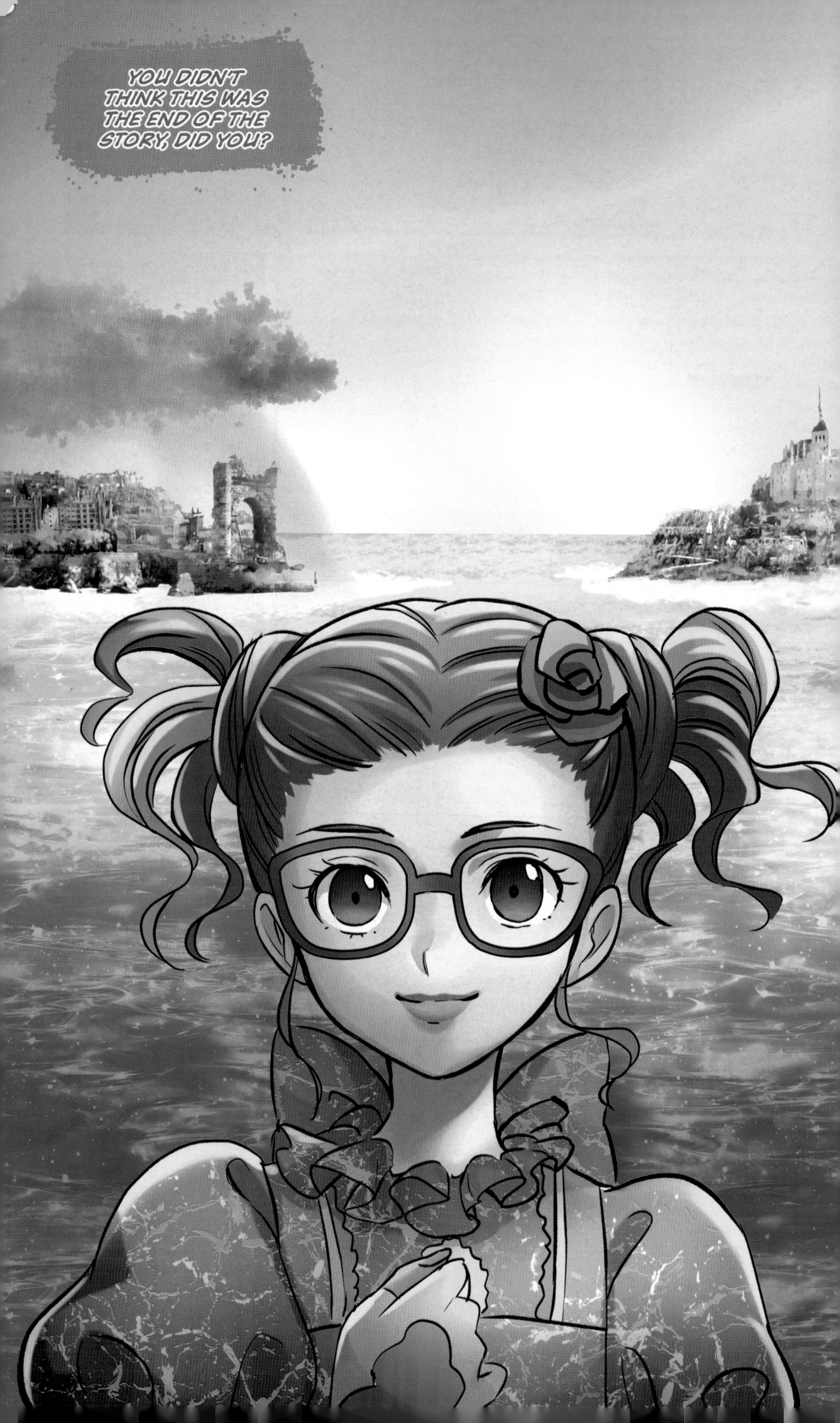
YOU DIDN'T THINK THIS WAS THE END OF THE STORY, DID YOU?

DIZZY'S NEW FORTUNE

BONUS ART

COVER SKETCHES

TAKE A PEEK AT SOME OF THE INITIAL COVER AND CHARACTER SKETCHES FOR *DIZZY'S NEW FORTUNE*!

Japanese artist Natsuki Minami worked on all of the art for the *Disney Descendants* manga series. Check out some early versions of her illustrations here and the step-by-step process leading up to the finished artwork seen in the book! Take a look at how the art changes between the storyboards and the final version.

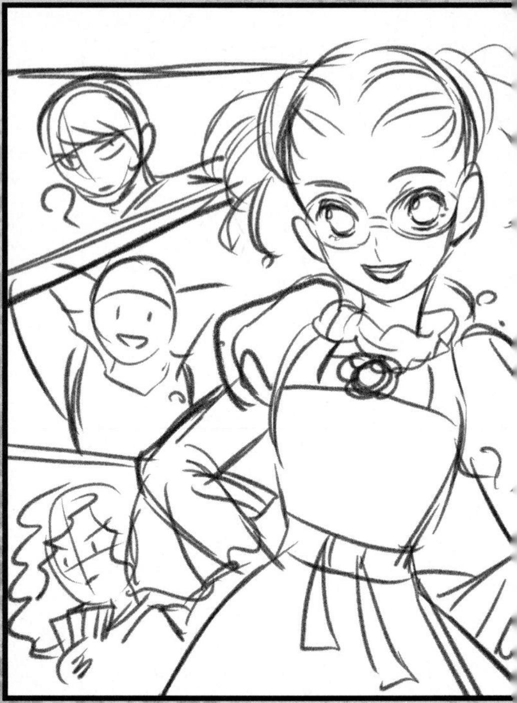

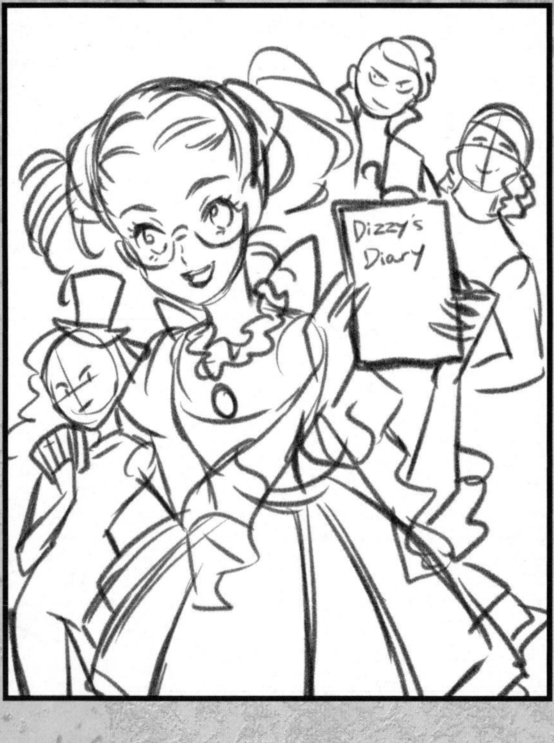
Dizzy's Diary

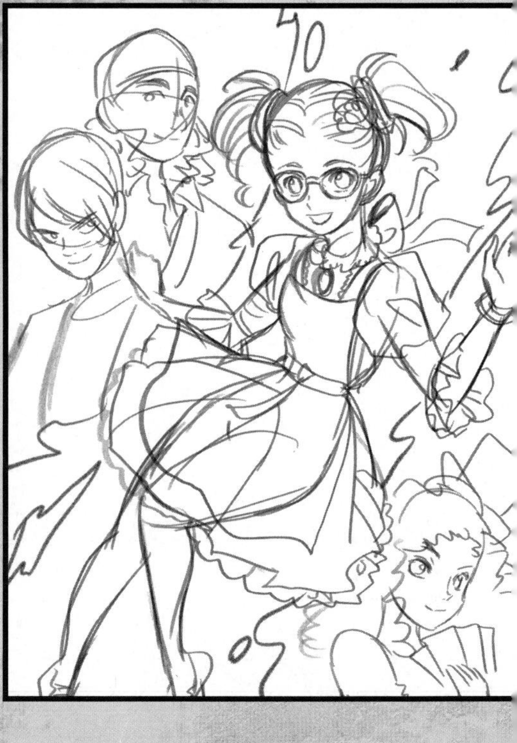

FINAL COVER ART

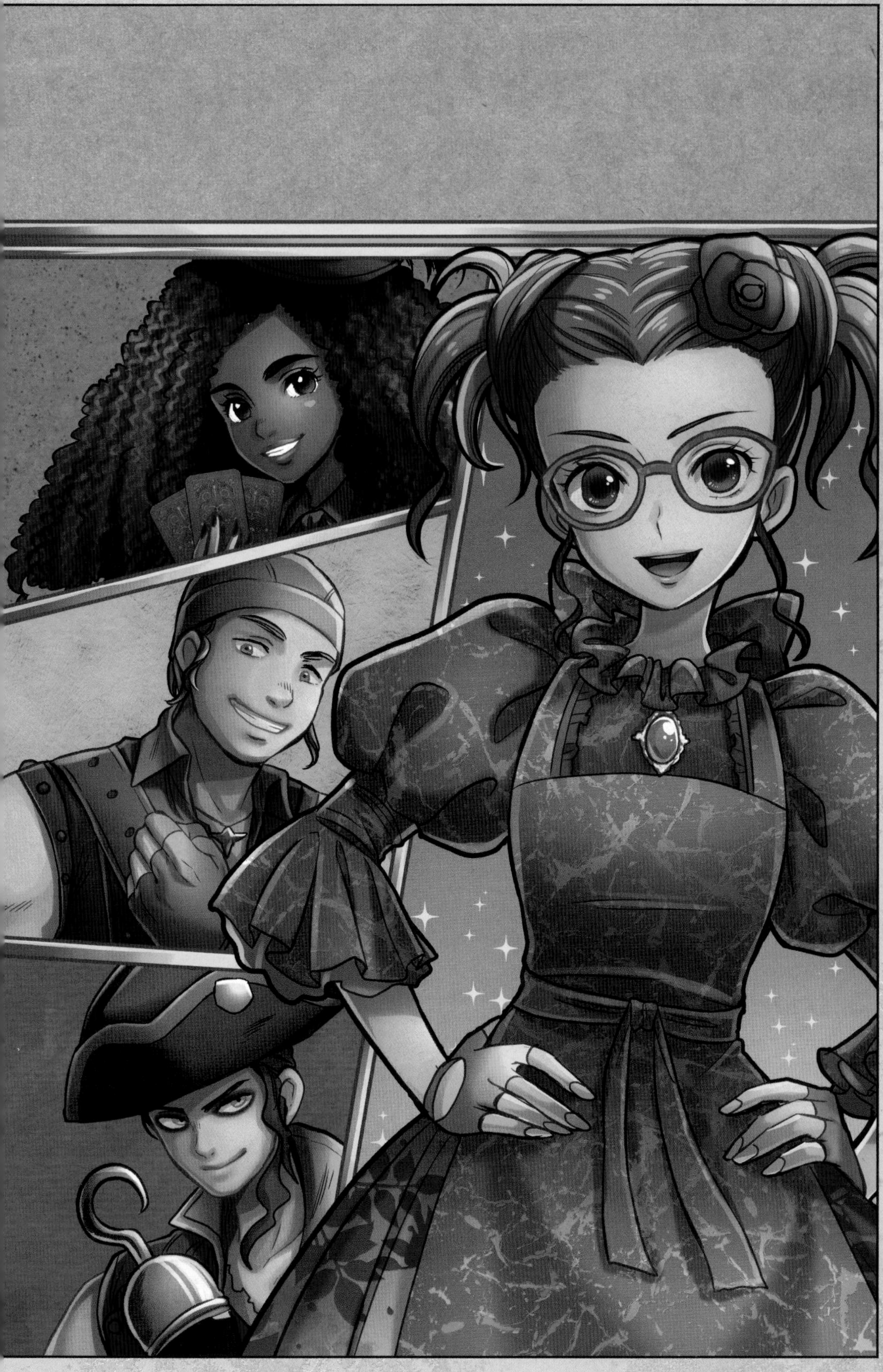

DIZZY

EARLY COLOR REFERENCE AND ART PROGRESSIONS

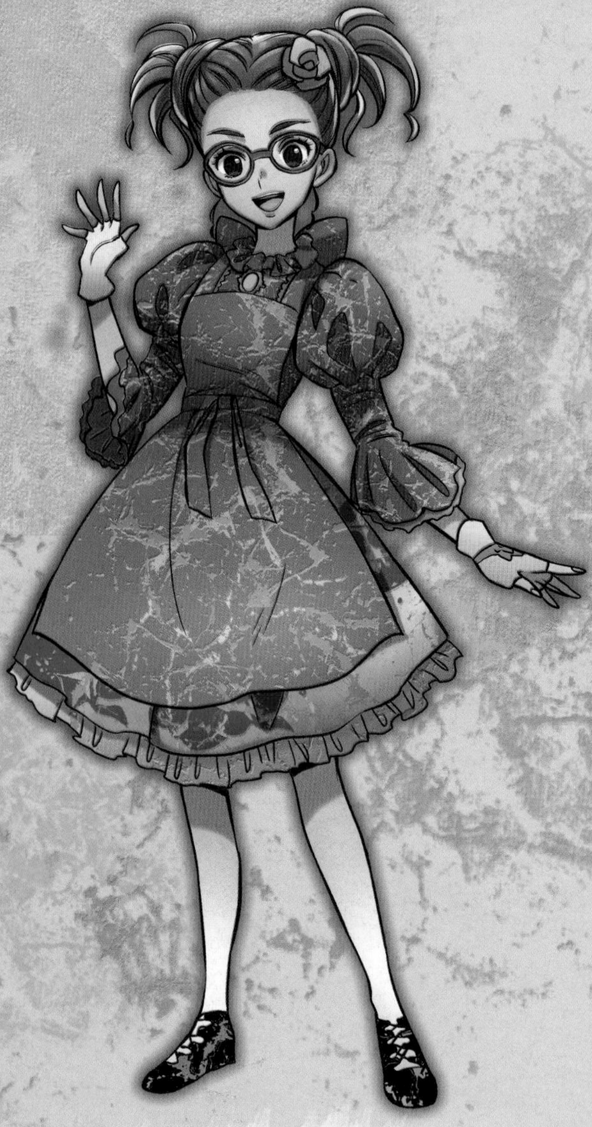

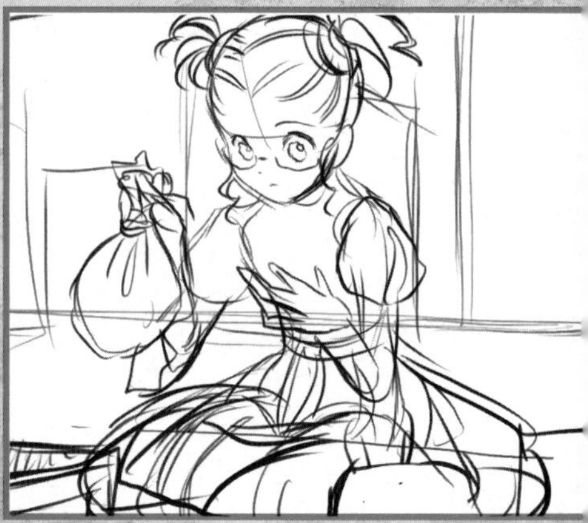

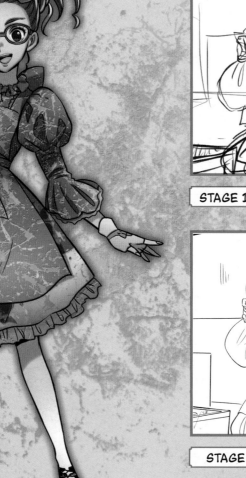

STAGE 1: STORYBOARDS

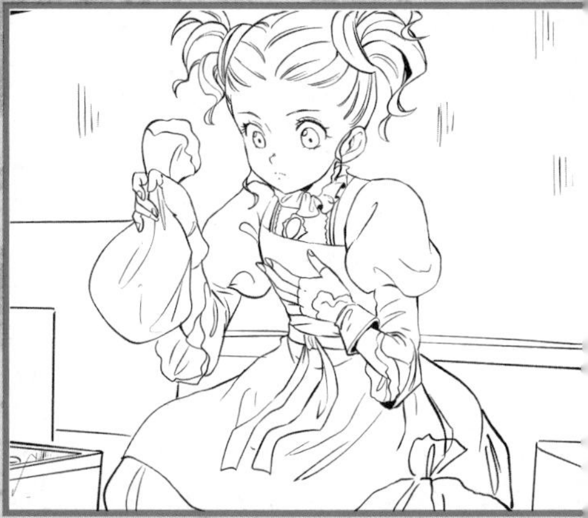

STAGE 2: INKS

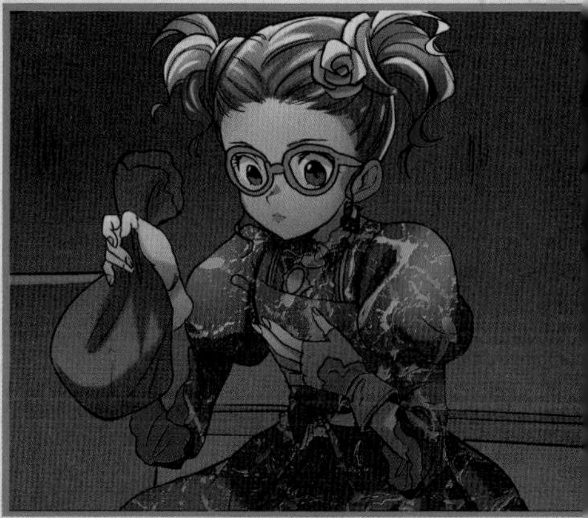

STAGE 3: COLORS

MORE ABOUT DIZZY

PERSONALITY
KIND, CREATIVE, EXCITABLE

STRENGTHS
HAIR STYLING AND ACCESSORIES DESIGNING

ITEM OF CHOICE
HAIR DYE

CELIA

EARLY COLOR REFERENCE AND ART PROGRESSIONS

STAGE 1: STORYBOARDS

STAGE 2: INKS

MORE ABOUT CELIA

PERSONALITY
CONFIDENT, CHARISMATIC, STEALTHY

STRENGTHS
FORTUNETELLING AND PERSUASION

ITEM OF CHOICE
DECK OF CARDS

STAGE 3: COLORS

HARRY

EARLY COLOR REFERENCE AND ART PROGRESSIONS

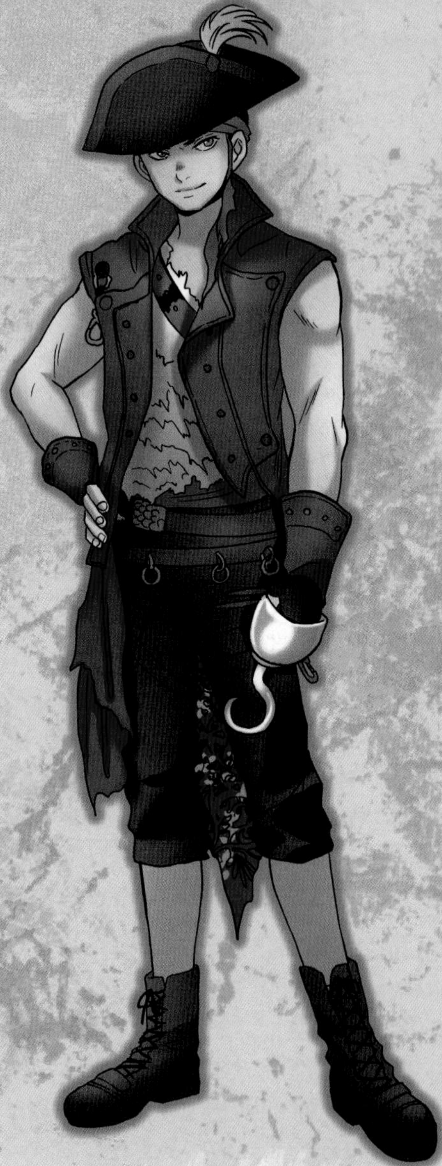

MORE ABOUT HARRY

PERSONALITY

UNPREDICTABLE, DANGEROUS, BOLD

STRENGTHS

LEADERSHIP AND FENCING

ITEM OF CHOICE

HOOK

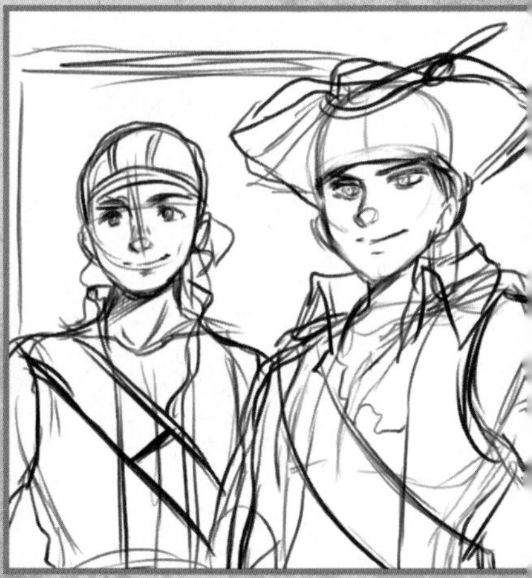

STAGE 1: STORYBOARDS

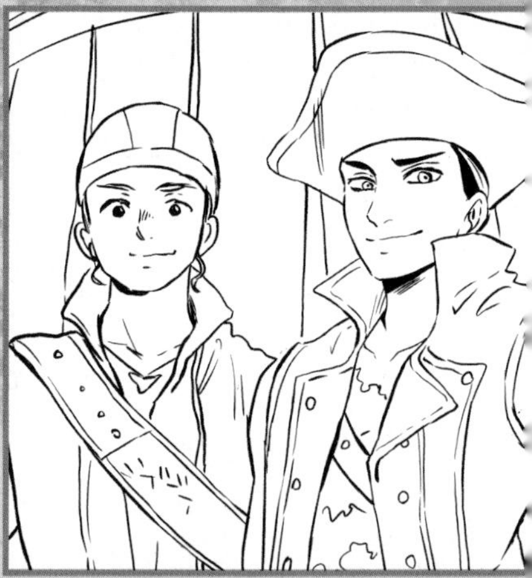

STAGE 2: INKS

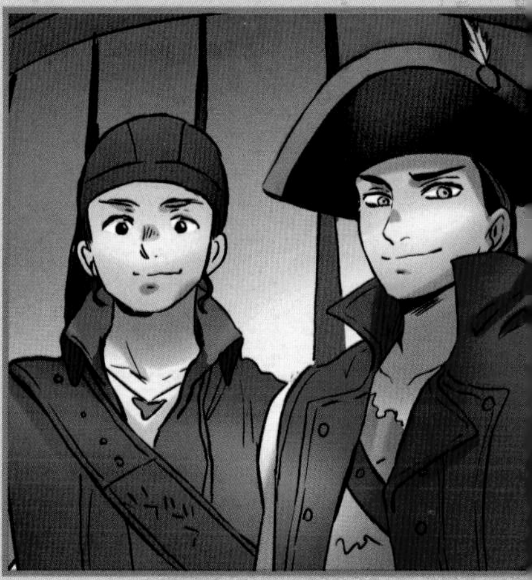

STAGE 3: COLORS

GIL

EARLY COLOR REFERENCE AND ART PROGRESSIONS

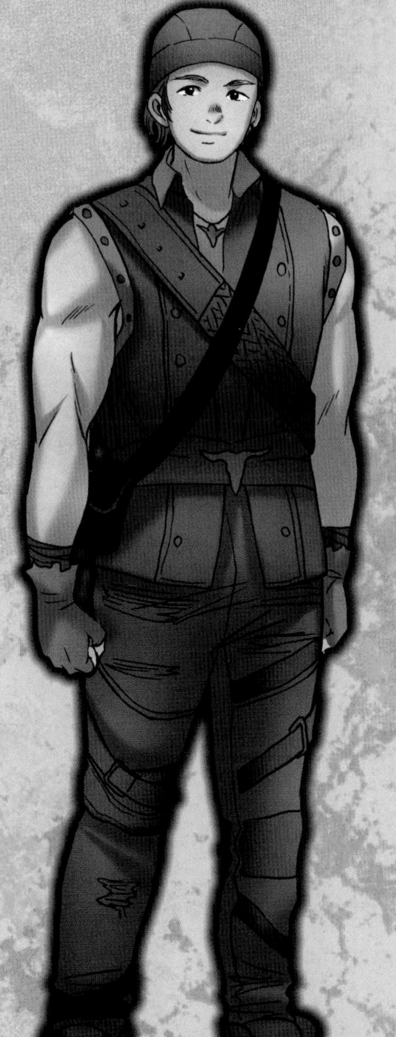

MORE ABOUT GIL

PERSONALITY
- ENERGETIC, EARNEST, CAREFREE

STRENGTHS
- SAILING AND ATHLETICISM

ITEM OF CHOICE
- SWORD

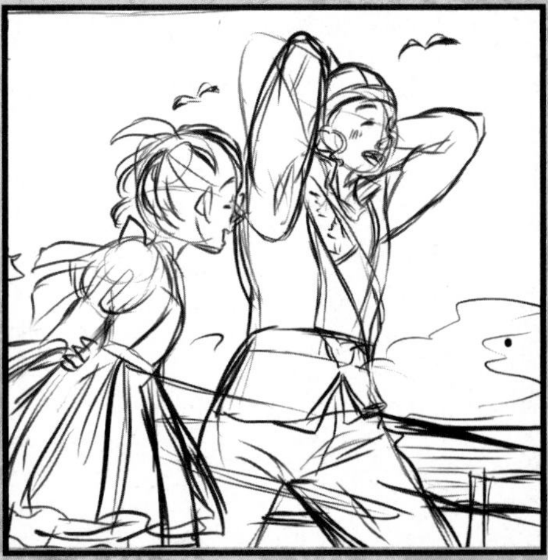

STAGE 1: STORYBOARDS

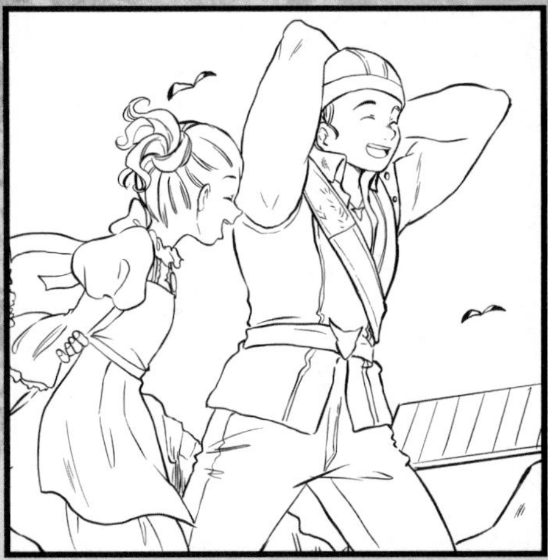

STAGE 2: INKS

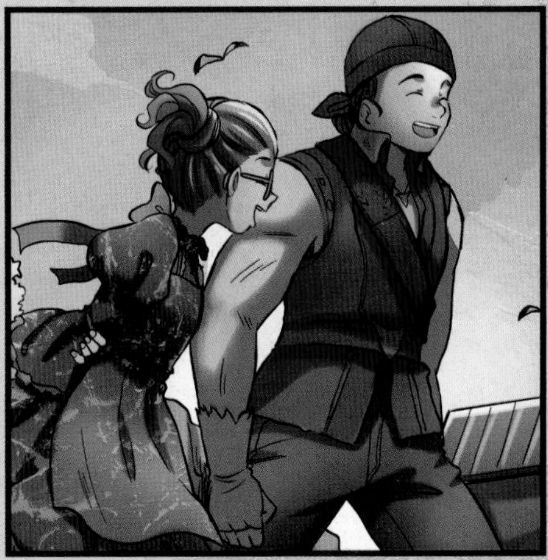

STAGE 3: COLORS

STEP-BY-STEP ART PROGRESSIONS

STAGE 1: STORYBOARDS

STAGE 2: INKS

STAGE 3: COLORS

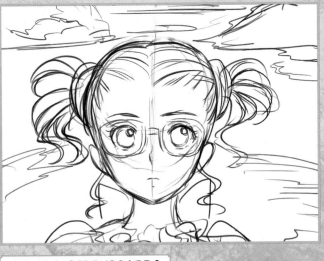

STAGE 1: STORYBOARDS

STAGE 2: INKS

STAGE 3: COLORS

DESCENDANTS

DISNEY
DESCENDANTS

TOKYOPOP

THE ROTTEN TO THE CORE TRILOGY
THE COMPLETE COLLECTION

Adapted By Jason Muell

Art By Natsuki Minami

DISNEY
MANGA 漫画

TOKYO POP

DISNEY DESCENDANTS

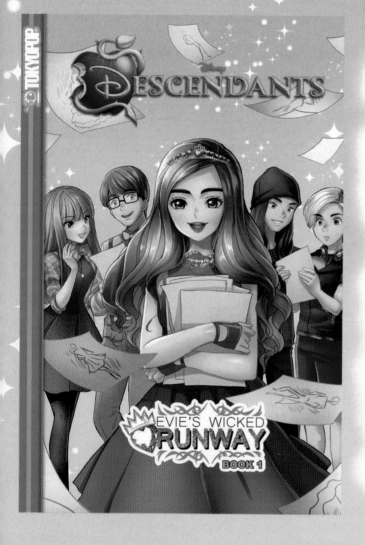

The Interscholastic Auradon Fashion Conte[st] is the biggest fashion eve[nt] of the year and students across Auradon are buzzi[ng] with anticipation. No one [is] more excited than Evie, t[he] villain kids' (VKs) reside[nt] fashionista and designer extraordinaire! The othe[r] VKs roll up their sleeves [to] help their friend, but wit[h] another Auradon studen[t] competing for the top pri[ze] alongside her, will Evie b[e] able to reach the top spot[?] And just how far are the other competitors prepare[d] to go to win first place?

TOKYO POP

Disney MANGA 漫画

EVIE'S WICKED RUNWAY

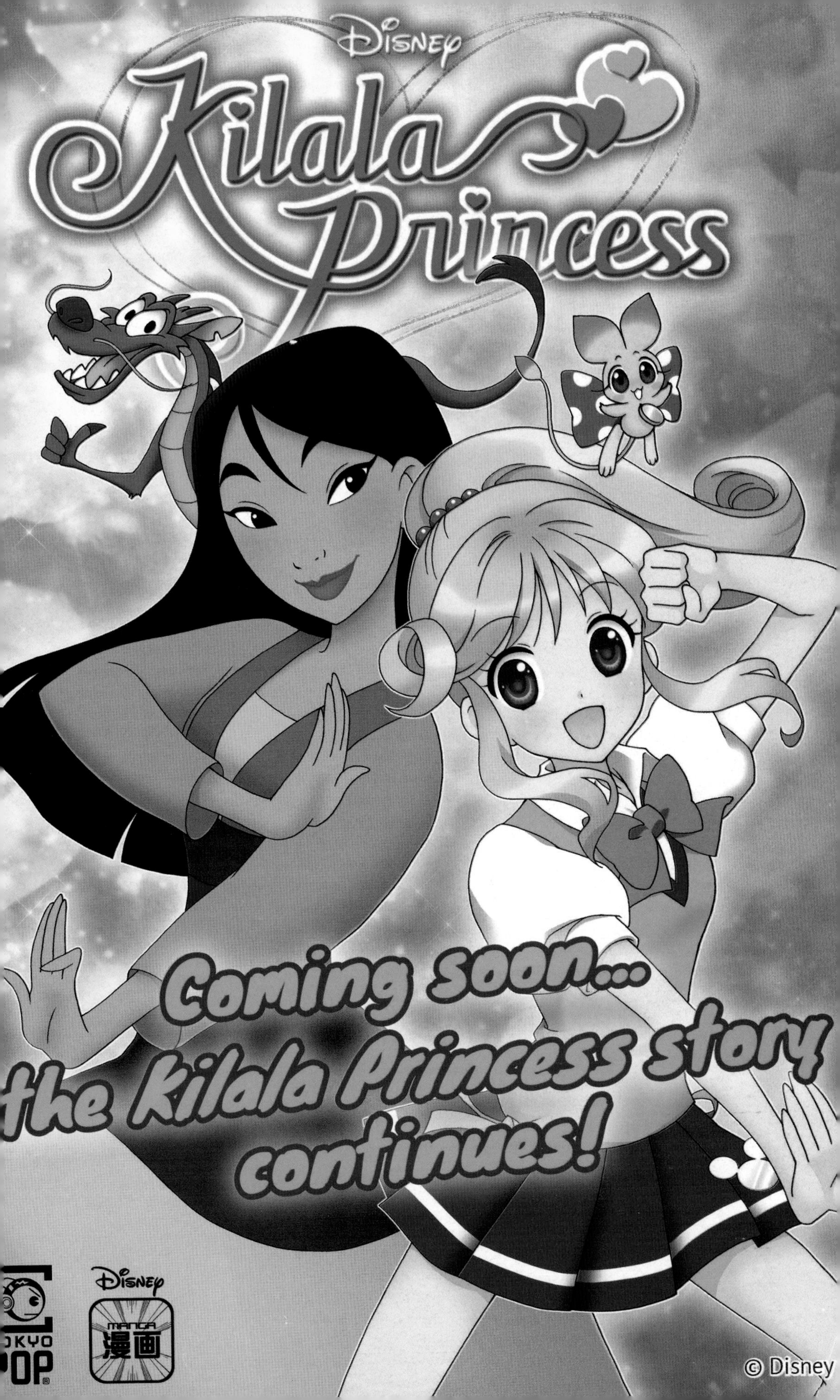
Disney
Kilala Princess
Coming soon...
the Kilala Princess story continues!
Disney
MANGA
漫画
© Disney

Add These Disney Manga to Your Collection Today!

SHOJO

- ☐ DISNEY BEAUTY AND THE BEAST
- ☐ DISNEY KILALA PRINCESS SERIES

FANTASY

- ☐ DISNEY DESCENDANTS SERIES
- ☐ DISNEY TANGLED
- ☐ DISNEY PRINCESS AND THE FROG
- ☐ DISNEY FAIRIES SERIES
- ☐ DISNEY MARIE: MIRIYA AND MAR

KAWAII

- ☐ DISNEY MAGICAL DANCE
- ☐ DISNEY STITCH! SERIES

PIXAR

- ☐ DISNEY • PIXAR TOY STORY
- ☐ DISNEY • PIXAR MONSTERS, INC.
- ☐ DISNEY • PIXAR WALL • E
- ☐ DISNEY • PIXAR FINDING NEMO

ADVENTURE

- ☐ DISNEY TIM BURTON'S THE NIGHTMARE BEFORE CHRISTMAS
- ☐ DISNEY ALICE IN WONDERLAND
- ☐ DISNEY PIRATES OF THE CARIBBEAN SERIES

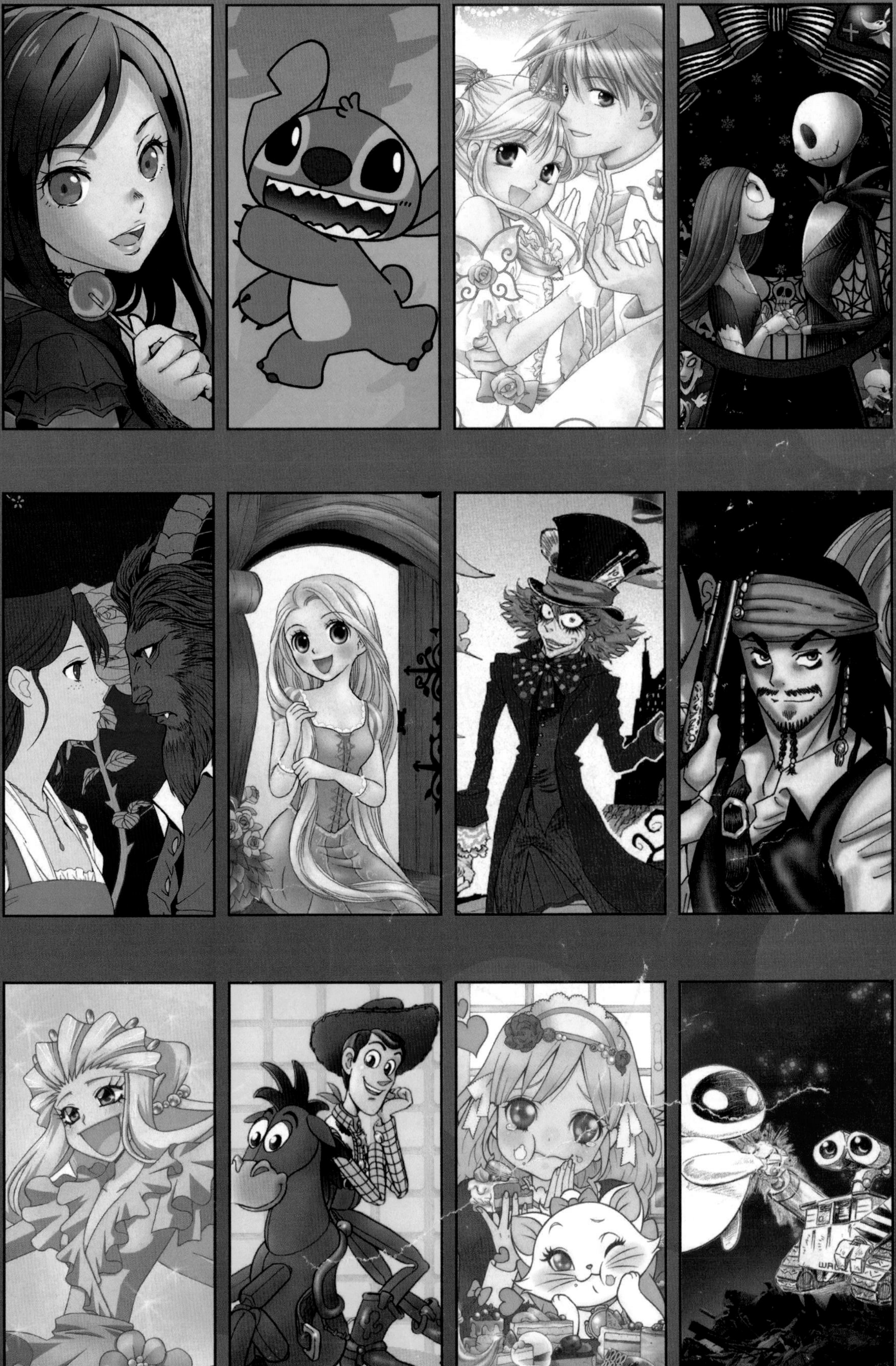

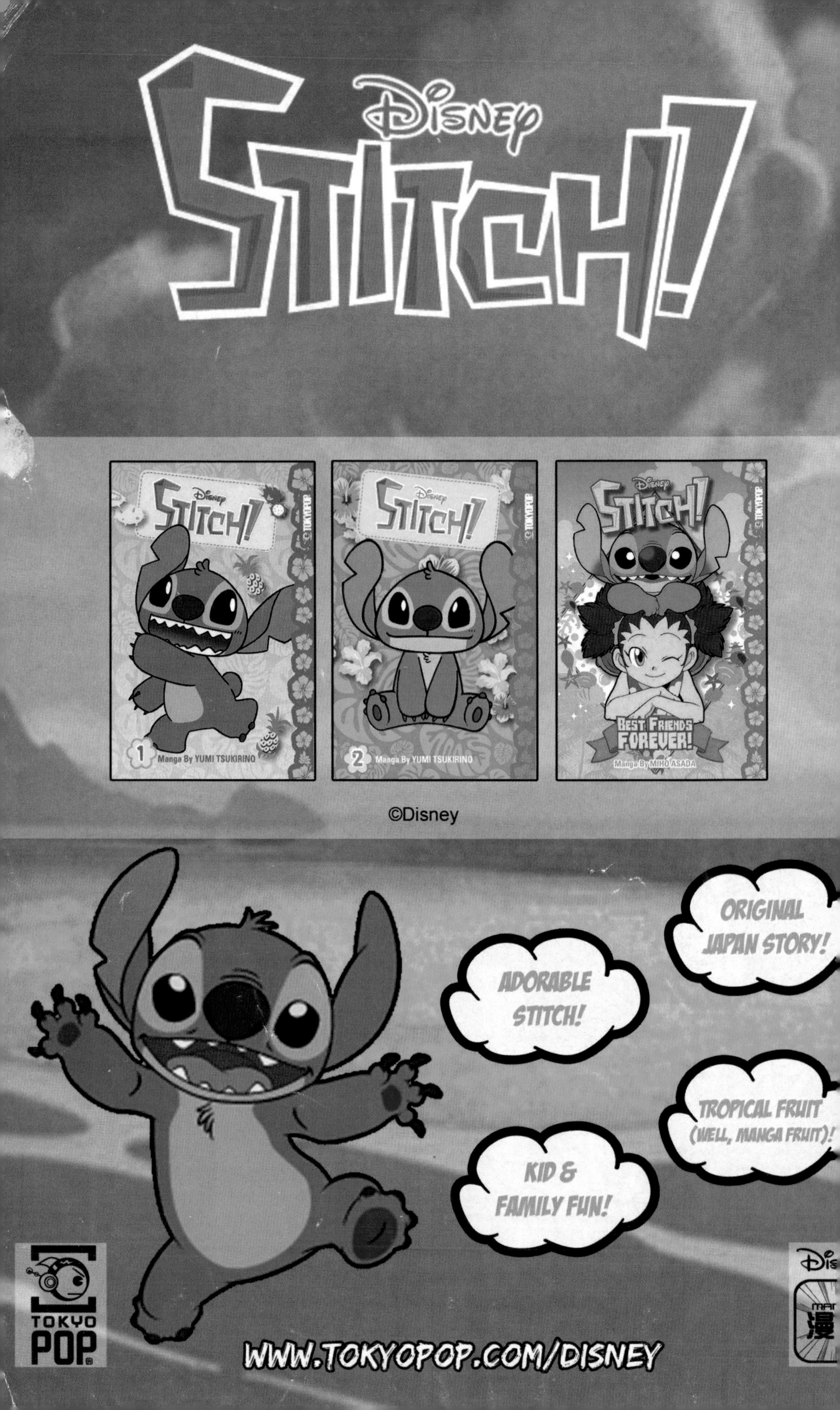
Disney
STITCH!
Disney STITCH!
1 Manga By YUMI TSUKIRINO
Disney STITCH!
2 Manga By YUMI TSUKIRINO
Disney STITCH!
BEST FRIENDS FOREVER!
Manga By MIHO ASADA
©Disney
ORIGINAL JAPAN STORY!
ADORABLE STITCH!
TROPICAL FRUIT (WELL, MANGA FRUIT)!
KID & FAMILY FUN!
TOKYO POP
WWW.TOKYOPOP.COM/DISNEY

GRIMMS
manga Tales

The Grimm's Tales
reimagined in manga!

Beautiful art by the talented
Kei Ishiyama!

Stories from Little Red Riding Hood
to Hansel and Gretel!

Disney Descendants: Dizzy's New Fortune
Story by : Jason Muell
Art by : Natsuki Minami
Based on the Disney Channel original movie series *Disney Descendants.*
Directed by : Kenny Ortega
Executive Produced by : Kenny Ortega and Wendy Japhet
Produced by : Tracey Jeffrey
Written by : Josann McGibbon & Sara Parriott

Publishing Associate - Janae Young
Marketing Associate - Kae Winters
Technology and Digital Media Assistant - Phillip Hong
Copy Editor - Sean Doyle
Editor - Janae Young
Graphic Designer - Phillip Hong
Retouching and Lettering - Vibrraant Publishing Studio
Editor-in-Chief & Publisher - Stu Levy

A 🐢 TOKYOPOP® Manga

TOKYOPOP and 🐢 are trademarks or registered trademarks of TOKYOPOP Inc.

TOKYOPOP Inc.
5200 W. Century Blvd. Suite 705
Los Angeles, 90045

E-mail: info@TOKYOPOP.com
Come visit us online at www.TOKYOPOP.com

f www.facebook.com/TOKYOPOP
🐦 www.twitter.com/TOKYOPOP
P www.pinterest.com/TOKYOPOP
📷 www.instagram.com/TOKYOPOP

978-1-4278-5840-5
First TOKYOPOP Printing: November 2019
10 9 8 7 6 5 4 3 2 1
Printed in CANADA